Flora N. Kightlinger

The Star Speaker

Flora N. Kightlinger

The Star Speaker

ISBN/EAN: 9783337410193

Printed in Europe, USA, Canada, Australia, Japan

Cover: Foto ©Andreas Hilbeck / pixelio.de

More available books at **www.hansebooks.com**

THE STAR SPEAKER

A Complete and Choice Collection

OF

THE BEST PRODUCTIONS BY THE BEST AUTHORS, WITH
AN EXHAUSTIVE TREATISE ON THE SUBJECT
OF VOCAL AND PHYSICAL CULTURE
AND GESTURING

BY

FLORA N. KIGHTLINGER

Fully Illustrated

STAR PUBLISHING COMPANY
JERSEY CITY
N. J.

PREFACE.

THE aim and scope of this work is to not only give our friends something to speak, but to teach them how to speak it.

There have been a number of excellent speakers placed on the market, from time to time, but never before has the subject of " How to Speak " been given with such exhaustive simplicity as we present it to our readers. Indeed, the subject of Vocal and Physical Culture and Gesturing, as heretofore given, have been very meager and wanting that clearness to make them easily understood by the young as well as the old.

Our idea has been to carry the student through a course of general instructions, with appropriate and numerous illustrations that will open an avenue of graceful, forcible and pleasing carriage and delivery for all occasions.

The selections for speaking have been chosen with very great care ; nothing that could in the slightest degree prove objectionable has been admitted. All the pieces are pure in language, lofty in sentiment, pithy, bright and sparkling. They cover the entire field of popular subjects with productions that at once entrance us and grow in favor as they become known and will never become common. Our selections are confidently offered to the public for its approval.

Our Juvenile Department gives the little ones appropriate selections for church, home and school entertainments. The perplexing question to " Mamma " of " something to speak " is admirably overcome in this department.

With this introduction we send forth " The Star Speaker " upon its mission with the earnest wish that its usefulness will equal the enthusiasm of its production.

MARYSVILLE, O., Oct. 15, 1892.

CONTENTS.

PHYSICAL CULTURE.

SELECTIONS.

LIST OF ILLUSTRATIONS.

General principles must be had from books. In conversation you never get a system.

Knowledge is of two kinds. We know a subject ourselves, or we know where we can find information upon it. When we enquire into any subject, the first thing we have to do is to know what books have treated of it.

Samuel Johnson.

THE STAR SPEAKER.

VOCAL CULTURE.

An exhaustive analysis of the subject is not attempted in the following pages; nor does the student need this; he only needs a few practical directions to aid him in getting the mastery over his voice and in acquiring a distinct conception of the various styles of composition by the aid of appropriate examples. Under each division are appended appropriate exercises for practice, and with them it is hoped these directions will be found sufficient for the purpose.

No book can supply the place of the living teacher. To the student nothing can make up for the want of judgment and taste; without these, he cannot hope to become an eloquent reader and speaker; with them, by attention to vocal culture, he will experience but little difficulty. Strength and smoothness of tone are too often regarded as the gift of nature. True, nature may favor many in this respect; but any one whose organs of speech are not defective may, by proper exercise and attention, acquire a deep, full, clear, resonant voice.

DIVISIONS.

QUALITY.

PURE TONE.

Pure Tone is free from any harsh, guttural, aspirated, nasal, or oral tone, and is made with a less expenditure of breath, and with less fatigue, than any other.

The essentials to purity of Tone are, deep breathing, control of the muscles of the throat regulating the vocal organs, and a free opening of the mouth.

A great cause of impurity of Tone is the expulsion of too much breath. To test its purity, in this respect, hold the back of the hand within an inch or two of the mouth while uttering the sound, and if a current of air from the mouth is perceptible by the hand, the tone is not pure.

Pure Tone is used in unimpassioned discourse; in the expression of light and agreeable emotions; and in sadness or grief when not mingled with solemnity.

Example.

Oh, young Lochinvar is come out of the west,—
Through all the wide border his steed was the best;
And save his good broadsword he weapon had none,—
He rode all unarmed, and he rode all alone.
So faithful in love, and so dauntless in war,
There never was knight like the young Lochinvar.

OROTUND QUALITY.

Orotund is a mode of intonation directly from the larynx, which gives fullness, clearness, and strength. It is the highest perfection of voice, and is used in solemn, pathetic, energetic, and vehement forms of expression. The Orotund usually admits of three degrees, designated, according to the intensity of the emotion: Effusive, or the language of solemnity and pathos; Expulsive, or the language of earnest declamation; Explosive, or the language of intense passion.

Orotund is used to express whatever is grand, vast, or sublime.

Examples.

1. O thou that rollest above, round as the shield of my fathers! whence are thy beams, O Sun! thy everlasting light?

2. I would call upon all the true sons of New England to co-operate with the laws of man and the justice of Heaven.

3. Rise, like a cloud of incense from the earth!
    Thou kingly spirit, throned among the hills,
    Thou dread ambassador from earth to heaven,
    Great hierarch! tell thou the silent sky,
    And tell the stars, and tell yon rising sun,
    Earth, with her thousand voices, praises God.

ASPIRATED QUALITY.

Aspirated Quality is not purity of tone, but consists in an excessive expulsion of breath in uttering sounds, making the sounds partly vocal and partly aspirate.   It is used in intense fear.

Examples.

1.—While thronged the citizens, with terror dumb,
    Or whispering with white lips—"The foe! they come! they
        come!"—*Byron.*

2. How ill this taper burns!
    Ha! who comes here?
    Cold drops of sweat hang on my trembling flesh,
    My blood grows chilly, and I freeze with horror!

3. Have mercy, Heaven! Ha! soft,
            'Tis but a dream.
    But then so terrible, it shakes my soul.

GUTTURAL QUALITY.

Guttural Quality also is opposed to purity of tone, and consists of a mode of utterance which seems to come through an obstructed throat.   It is the language of hatred, contempt, and loathing.

Example.

Thou slave! thou wretch! thou coward!
Thou little valiant, great in villainy!
Thou ever strong upon the stronger side!
Thou fortune's champion, thou dost never fight

But when her humorous ladyship is by
To teach thee safety!   Thou art perjured, too,
And sooth'st up greatness!   What a fool art thou,
A ramping fool, to brag, and stamp, and sweat,
Upon my party!   Thou cold-blooded slave,
Hast thou not spoke like thunder on my side!
Been sworn my soldier! bidding me depend
Upon thy stars, thy fortune, and thy strength?
And dost thou now fall over to my foes?
Thou wear a lion's hide?   Doff it for shame,
And hang a calf-skin on those recreant limbs.

Shakespeare.

NASAL QUALITY.

In this Quality, the voice sounds as if it came through
the nose.   It is caused by an imperfect opening of the
mouth and nasal passages.   It is never employed in correct
delivery, and may be avoided if the mouth and throat are
kept well open, by relaxing the muscles of the throat and
lower jaw.   We find an excellent example of this in Dr.
Holmes's poem, " The One Horse Shay."

Example.

But the deacon swore (as deacons do,
With an " I dew vum," or an " I tell yeou"),
He would build one shay to beat the taown,
'N' the keounty, 'n' all the kentry raoun;
It should be so built that it couldn' break daoun:
" Fur," said the deacon, " 'tis mighty plain
That the weakes' place mus' stan' the strain;
'N' the way to fix it, uz I maintain,
Is only jest
To make that place uz strong uz the rest."

FORCE.

Force, in vocal culture, has reference both to the loud-
ness of sound and the intensity of utterance.   The degrees
of it are—Subdued, Moderate, and Loud.

The voice should be exercised upon the vowels in all degrees of Force, from the gentlest to the most vehement. The hint is here repeated that the loudest tones must be made in such a manner as not to rasp the throat. So far from producing any unpleasant sensation, the right kind of practice will have a pleasant and exhilarating effect.

Seek to make the sounds always smooth and musical; and never lose sight of the fact that what is wanted in every-day use of the voice, in the school-room or elsewhere, is a pleasant and natural intonation. The practice of loud and sustained tones is an excellent means of improving the voice, but is to be the exception, not the rule, in ordinary reading. Yet the softest tone must be elastic and full of life, not dull and leaden.

The degree of Force required in reading a given passage depends upon the space to be filled by the reader's voice or the distance it must reach; upon the number of persons presumed to be addressed, and upon the emotion expressed.

Subdued Force is employed in the expression of pathos and solemnity, and is usually accompanied by Effusive Orotund Quality.

Examples.

1. Flow, softly flow, by lawn and lea,
     A rivulet, then a river;
   No more by thee my steps shall be,
     Forever and forever.

2. Oh hark! Oh hear! how thin and clear,
     And thinner, clearer, farther going;
   Oh sweet and far, from cliff and scar,
     The horns of Elf-land faintly blowing.

3. Tread lightly, comrades!—we have laid
     His dark locks on his brow—
   Like life—save deeper light and shade—
     We'll not disturb them now.

MODERATE FORCE.

Moderate Force is used in unimpassioned narrative, descriptive, and didactic composition.

Example.

When I look upon the tombs of the great, every emotion of envy dies in me; when I read the epitaphs of the beautiful, every inordinate desire goes out; when I meet with the grief of parents upon a tombstone, my heart melts with compassion; when I see the tomb of the parents themselves, I consider the vanity of grieving for those whom we must quickly follow. When I see kings lying by those who deposed them, when I consider rival wits placed side by side, or the holy men that divided the world with their contests and disputes, I reflect with sorrow and astonishment on the little competitions, factions, and debates of mankind. When I read the several dates of the tombs of some that died yesterday, and some six hundred years ago, I consider that great day when we shall all of us be cotemporaries, and make our appearance together.—*Addison.*

LOUD FORCE.

It is employed in the expression of the intenser passions and emotions.

Examples.

1. Up DRÀWBRIDGE! GROOM! What, WARDER, HÒ!
    Let the PORTCÙLLIS FALL!

2. 　　　　　　　Ye guards of liberty,
    I'm with you once again.   I call to you
    With all my voice.

3. From every hill, by every sea,
    In shouts proclaim the great decree,
    "All chains are burst, all men are free!"
    　　Hurrah, hurrah, hurrah!

PITCH.

One of the commonest faults, in school **reading** and **in** the delivery of many public speakers, is **a dull monotony** of tone. This sameness is still more disagreeable to the ear when the voice is kept strained upon a high key. Not less unpleasant is an incessant repetition of the same cant or sing-song. Elocutionary rules will do little or nothing toward removing these faults. Faithful drill is needed, under the guidance of good taste and a correct musical ear. To this must be added an appreciation of the sentiment of the piece at the moment of utterance.

The ability to manage the voice, with reference to Pitch, depends upon the control of the larynx and lower jaw. If the muscles be relaxed and the throat enlarged, the Pitch will be low; and each degree of contraction will be marked by a higher degree of Pitch.

The best means of cultivating this, is to speak to persons at different distances—far or near, according as a high or low degree is desired. Exercise in sudden transitions in Pitch will also be found invaluable to a complete mastery of the subject.

The distinctions of Pitch are—Low, Middle, High.

Examples.

LOW.

1. But, whatever may be our fate, be assured that this declaration will stand. It may cost treasure, and it may cost blood; but it will stand, and it will richly compensate for both.

2. How beautiful is night!
A dewy freshness fills the silent air;
No mist obscures, nor cloud, nor speck, nor stain
Breaks the serene of heaven.

MIDDLE.

1. An old clock, that had stood for fifty years in a farmer's kitchen without giving its owner any cause of complaint, early one summer's morning, before the family was stirring, suddenly stopped.

2.   A blind man would know that one was a gentleman and the other a clown, by the tones of their voices.

3.   The very law which molds a tear,
     And bids it trickle from its source,
   That law preserves the earth a sphere,
     And guides the planets in their course.

HIGH.

1.   I come! I come!—ye have called me long;
   I come o'er the mountains with light and song!
   Ye may trace my step o'er the wakening earth,
   By the winds which tell of the violet's birth,
   By the primrose stars in the shadowy grass,
   By the green leaves opening as I pass.

2.   Stand! the ground's your own, my braves!
   Will ye give it up to slaves?
   Will ye look for greener graves?
     Hope ye mercy still?
   What's the mercy despots feel?
   Hear it—in that battle peal!
   Read it—on yon bristling steel!
     Ask it!—ye who will.

STRESS.

The manner in which Force is applied, in reading and speaking, is termed Stress. There are usually reckoned five divisions: Radical, Median, Vanishing, Compound, and Tremor.

RADICAL STRESS.

In Radical Stress, the force of the utterance falls on the first part of the sound, and vanishes more or less rapidly. The long vowels afford fine exercises in this.

For example, in uttering the following couplet with spirit, we naturally give the Radical Stress upon the word "up," and its explosive character will be plainly perceived:

   Up! comrades, up!—in Rokeby's halls
   Ne'er be it said our courage falls!

But when this stress falls on words beginning with consonants, the effect upon the ear is not so sharp and incisive.

The Radical Stress is used in abrupt and startling emotions, and in the expression of positive and decisive convictions.

This stress is not always used in a violent manner.

Examples.

1.   Arm, arm, and out!

2.   I have but one lamp by which my feet are guided; and that is the lamp of experience. I know of no way of judging of the future but by the past.

MEDIAN STRESS.

In Median Stress, the force is applied so as to swell out the middle of the sound. The long vowels afford exercises in this as well as in Radical Stress.

The proper application of the Median Stress is one of the most refined and delicate beauties of utterance. A due degree of it in ordinary conversation distinguishes the man of culture from the boor.

Examples.

1.   O precious hours! O golden prime,
And affluence of love and time!

2.   Had I not, by deeply pondering the precepts of philosophy, and the lessons of the historian and the poet, imbued my mind with an early and intimate conviction that nothing in life is worthy of strenuous pursuit but honor and renown, and that, for the attainment of these, the extremes of bodily torture, and all the terrors of exile and of death, ought to be regarded as trifles, never should I have engaged in such a series of deadly conflicts for your safety, nor have exposed myself to these daily machinations of the most profligate of mankind.

VANISHING STRESS.

Vanishing Stress is that in which the force of utterance is withheld until the vanish or close of the sound is reached, ending suddenly, with percussive force.

Example.

Fret till your proud heart breaks;
Go, show your slaves how choleric you are,
And make your bondmen tremble.

COMPOUND STRESS.

Compound Stress is that in which the voice touches forcibly on the initial and final parts of the sound, but passes lightly over the middle portion of it. It is generally used to express a complication of emotions, as of surprise, indignation, and anger.

Example.

Gone to be married! gone to swear a peace!
It is not so; thou hast misspoke, misheard;
Be well advised, tell o'er thy tale again.
It cannot be; thou dost but SAY, 'tis so.

TREMOR OR INTERMITTENT STRESS.

Tremor or Intermittent Stress consists of a tremulous iteration of sound, or a number of short impulses resembling a wave.

The voice trembles in the natural expression of feebleness, grief, old age; and in any excessive emotion of whatever nature. Skillfully and delicately used, the tremor gives extreme effect to many emotional passages; but the excess of it greatly mars the effect of delivery.

Examples.

1.   Oh! I have lost you all!
    Parents, and home, and friends.

2. Go, preach to the coward, thou death-telling seer!
   Or, if gory Culloden so dreadful appear,
   Draw, dotard, around thy old wavering sight,
   This mantle, to cover the phantoms of fright.

3. My mother, when I learned that thou wast dead,
   Say, wast thou conscious of the tears I shed?
   Hovered thy spirit o'er thy sorrowing son,
   Wretch even then, life's journey just begun?

QUANTITY OR MOVEMENT.

By Quantity, in reading or speaking, is meant the length of time occupied in uttering a syllable or word.

LONG QUANTITY.

The day is cold, and dark, and dreary;
It rains, and the wind is never weary;
The vine still clings to the moldering wall,
But at every gust the dead leaves fall.
   And the days are dark and dreary.

MEDIUM QUANTITY.

When I was but an infant, tossed
   Upon my mother's knee;
And oft I've looked in youthful pride,
   Upon that hallowed spot,
And though I've wandered far from it,
   It never was forgot.

SHORT QUANTITY.

Quick! man the life-boat!   See you bark,
   That drives before the blast!
There's a rock ahead, the fog is dark,
   And the storm comes thick and fast.
Can human power, in such an hour,
   Avert the doom that's o'er her?
Her main-mast's gone, but she still drives on
   To the fatal reef before her.
      The life-boat!   Man the life-boat!

Nothing will compensate for inappropriateness in the rate of uttering a given passage. As the stately march of the solemn procession and the light trip of the joyous child are indicative of the states of mind which prompt them, so the movement which is proper in reading depends upon the emotion intended to be expressed. If the reader should ask himself what would be his manner of walking while under the influence of any particular emotion, it would be a safe guide to his rate of utterance. Animated and playful moods would manifest themselves in a light and buoyant step, sometimes tripping and bounding along. On the contrary, deep emotions of solemnity and awe can exist only with very slow movements. Dignity requires in its expression not only slowness but regularity of movement. Violent passion gives rise to irregular and impulsive speech. To this end practice should be had in reading with great precipitation, without losing a single syllable. Extreme slowness of utterance is very impressive when rightly applied, and the pupil should spare no pains to acquire this grace.

BREATHING.

Much of the success in reading or speaking depends upon breathing, as no one can read or speak well who cannot breathe well.

The exercises under Vocal Culture which are to aid breathing, as designated there, should be faithfully practiced by any who feel a deficiency in this direction. In practicing the development of breathing, always prefer a standing position to a sitting position, and let the action bring forth a natural but deep breathing. Practice inflating and inhaling the lungs until this can be done quite rapidly. A good practice is to inhale deeply and give out the voice slowly in prolonged vowel sounds.

Is effected by the action of the palate, tongue, lips, and jaws. The action must be neat, easy, and prompt, that perfect articulation may be made. A full and elastic command of the muscles of the mouth is highly necessary for the most distinct utterances. The exercise, as illustrated in Fig. A, will be found very beneficial in acquiring proper articulation, and free and full command of the muscles of the mouth and face.

First. Pronounce the vowel $\bar{e}$, extending the lips as much as possible sidewise, and showing the tips of the teeth.

Second. Pronounce *ah*, dropping the jaw and opening the mouth to its widest extent.

Third. Pronounce *oo* (as in *cool*), contracting the lips,

GESTURE FOR BEGINNING RECITATION

PHYSICAL CULTURE.

In taking up the study of Oratory we thoroughly understand that *mind* and *body* are mutually dependent upon each other for the best and most satisfactory progress. One cannot be advanced at the expense of the other and pleasing and lasting results be obtained. The teacher or student who neglects all consideration of *Physical* or *Vocal* training while forcing to the utmost mental acquirements, is justly considered an enemy rather than a friend of the very ends desired. We must not secure the development of the one at the expense of the other, and if we do, evils that are indeed lamentable insidiously creep upon us as the result of this error.

The ancient Greeks paid the same attention to physical culture as to mental training. Their gymnasia were schools for the body and mind. The monuments in art, science, and language which have come down to us more than confirm the wisdom of their ancient method. And what a strange inconsistency on our part, that while we pay such tributes to their excellencies, we too often ignore the means by which those excellencies were attained. We praise and copy their statuary, but seem to forget that the models for these classical features were furnished as a result of their physical training.

We go back to them to-day as our great exemplars in oratory, but are we willing to go through the drill which made these men such consummate masters of their art? Since it is not our national custom as it was theirs to give so much attention to the gymnasium and make it a part of our school duties, it devolves upon the student and the teacher to assume extra duties, and see that the body and voice are trained symmetrically with the mind, and that the highest and most perfect degree of oratory be attained.

Physical culture will first claim our attention, and naturally we ask, What practical results can reasonably be looked for by a system of physical exercises? We answer, Just that degree of improvement with which we *judiciously* apply ourselves to the task. It is not sufficient that the pupil is taking physical exercises. He must positively be gaining something and making improvement with each exercise taken. He must learn to distinguish between essential and non-essential exercises, and to know that the thorough and persevering practice of a few wisely directed movements is much more beneficent than a random and irregular practice of a large number of vague exercises. It is not enough that he be simply taking physical exercises, but each exercise chosen must have a definite aim and a practical value. He must know the main points to be kept in view, and each exercise that does not promote one or more of these ends should at once be discarded as comparatively useless. He will note the points to be kept in view, which will aid him very much in his training.

SYMMETRY OF FORM.

Nothing can add more to our grace as a speaker or aid us as much in a proper and forcible delivery in public speaking, as this one thing—a symmetrical form. Then our aim should always be to aid nature in a perfect and free development.

Teachers and parents cannot perform a higher service for their pupils and children than by leading them to see that a beneficent Creator has formed them according to His own idea, and that any willful distortion of the body is a sin as well as folly. This they should impress not only by precept but by example. Under this head we will note the following errors to guard against:

Sitting Position. Fig. 1.

Poise forward and back. Fig. 2.

SLENDER WAISTS.

Slender waists, especially in women, is one of the most common evils to overcome under this head. This error neither adds health nor beauty, but impairs both, and only an ignorant mind or perverted taste would ever regard it with favor.

ONE-SIDEDNESS,

or an unequal development of the two sides of the body, is another not uncommon fault, ofttimes brought about by habit, sometimes by the duties we have to perform being of such a nature as to task one side of our body more than the other. This can be overcome by being guarded, and the moment we find that one side is being developed or favored to the detriment of the other, we should so shift our work as to equalize the strain, making it come alternately on one side or the other, if it cannot be made to bear equally on each side at the same time.

HOLLOW CHEST,

which involves the pitching forward of the head and shoulders, ofttimes crooking the collar bone, causing the head to droop, and the shoulders to become round.

This can be easily overcome by making a practice every morning, possibly two or three times through the day, of throwing the shoulders back, taking three or four good long breaths, filling the lungs to their utmost, letting them relax slowly as the air passes out. Always walk or sit with head up and shoulders well thrown back.

PROPER POSITION AND CARRIAGE OF THE BODY.

This is a most important duty to be observed to augment and maintain the best results in physical training. Care should be taken that in sitting, standing, or walking, no exercise should be taken which in the least requires awkward or unnatural position or movements. Always walk or sit with the head up and the shoulders well thrown back.

HEALTH.

This is equally important as symmetry of the body in our obtaining perfection in oratory. A familiarity and proper attention to the hygienic laws there must be, or we cannot expect the development of those other forms which are essential to our success in public speaking. Proper habits of dress, diet, sleep, and cleanliness are as essential to our physical development as any course of exercises that may be gone through with.

If we possess that "pearl of great price," good bodily health, two very important functions to public speaking are attained.

FIRST, RIGHT HABITS OF BREATHING.

Our lungs should be trained to a full, free, and vigorous action. If our breathing is imperfect, all the functions of the body and mind are impeded. Any form of dress or costume which constrains or bears upon the lungs should be avoided. We should make a practice of deep breathing, avoiding, as it were, a breathing from the surface. In public speaking as well as in singing, some of the finest points and effects are brought about by the ability of the speaker having such full and perfect control of his lungs.

A good voice is the other function coming from health.

We all know how important it is that we should have complete command of our vocal organs, that our delivery may be smooth and impressive. The one greatest fault with the student is the unnatural, half-screaming tone which is often pursued in their recitations. A natural, easy, musical quality of voice which marks the refined person, should be cultivated in the school, play-ground, and at home. If a louder tone must be assumed, still make that tone pleasant, not harsh. By keeping in view these main points, and a careful and painstaking study of the following exercises, much good can be derived. We do not claim that we can make you orators, but you can add grace and force to your productions, and at least gain a degree of proficiency which will show that you are giving the subject proper attention. It would be impossible for us to prescribe any inflexible course of instruction or training, one that would not in a measure tax the ingenuity of the individual to adapt it most beneficially to his or her case. Nevertheless, an outline can be given which will serve as a guide to those wishing to follow physical training and acquire its benefits.

EXERCISES.

SITTING POSITION—(Figure 1.)

In taking up exercises for physical training the first requisite is a good sitting position. This is secured by training the pupils to sit (not lean) well back in their seats squarely in the position, with the shoulders back and the head erect. Let the lower part of the spine only rest against the back of the chair, with the feet squarely on the floor at an angle to each other of about fifty degrees. This will naturally bend the knees at a right angle, and let the feet be so placed as to throw the knees six to eight inches apart. Let the head be erect and not inclined either to the right or left. The eyes straight to the front, and the body raised to its full height, with the shoulders thrown squarely back, and thus bring the ear, shoulder, and hip in a vertical line. Let the hands fall easily in the lap, close to the body, the little fingers downward, bringing the palms together. In order to obtain a correct position it is not necessary that there should be rigidity, but properly follow these directions, being natural with it all. The two

Fig. 3.
Head turn right and left.

Fig. 4.
Head bend forward

Fig. 5.
Head bend back.

Fig 6.
Head bend right and left.

great faults to be avoided are the slipping forward and leaning the shoulder-blades against the upper part of the back of the seat.

This error tends to cause a curvature of the spine, and should be strenuously avoided. The other most common fault is a contraction of the chest, giving the body a drooping position, which should not be.

Let the lungs be full and the chest well thrown out. This position should be frequently practiced individually, remaining in it only a short time. It is the proper position to be assumed as a class or individual in taking the following exercises.

It is a good practice to sit occasionally in an easy, unconstrained manner, still being careful to preserve the essentials of the correct position. One will thus acquire the habit of keeping the shoulders in the proper position, with the head erect, even when bending forward over the desk or leaning easily back in the seat.

Care should be taken that one does not sit in a seat too small, which makes the movements cramped and unnatural, and pupils in a school should never be allowed to sit with one foot under them, as spinal difficulties have been brought about by this habit. Neither should the little ones be placed in seats where their feet do not touch the floor, as they never can assume a correct position unless the feet can be placed squarely on the floor.

POISING—(Figure 2.)

The exercise of poising forward and back (Figure 2) tends to give one command of the body and develop graceful and natural movement and attitude in sitting. This exercise can be followed nicely by counting in exact time of four to each movement, which is indeed the only way in which good class results can be obtained.

First. Keeping correct position, of body erect, shoulders

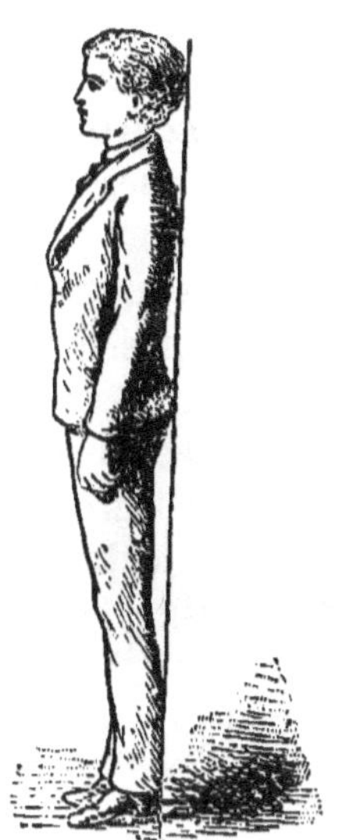

Fig. 7.

Standing Position.

Fig. 8.

well thrown back, and chin in position, inclining slowly forward from the perpendicular till touching the desk in front.

Second. Remain so for a moment, then by counting steadily return to the perpendicular or sitting position.

Third. Let the same movement be gone through with in a backward poise, steadily throwing the body back as far as the back of the seat will admit. Be careful not to get the chin too elevated and the neck bent, but maintain naturally, without stiffness, the sitting position.

Fourth. Remaining thus for a moment, return to correct position as before.

HEAD MOVEMENT—Turning right and left—(Figure 3.)

The following head movements will give a graceful and natural control of the head, which will be of incalculable value in bringing out the best results of gesturing that later on will be taken up. In fact it is folly for one to expect the best results in gesturing unless close attention and most diligent practice be given these preparatory steps. Although some good can be obtained without this drill by plunging at once into gesturing, the difference in improvement will be so greatly in favor of those following these physical exercises that those neglecting primary treatment must feel in comparison that their efforts have been almost useless and their time lost. These head movements are taken in the sitting position.

First. From the correct sitting position let the head be gradually turned to the right until the right eye comes in a straight line with the front of the shoulder.

Second. This exercise is best controlled by giving two counts to the turning of the head and letting the head remain in position during the third and fourth count; then return to front position as in the poising exercise.

Third. Turn the head to the left until the left eye is in a line with the left shoulder.

Fourth. Return to position, counting as before.

BENDING FORWARD AND BACKWARD—(Figures 4 and 5.)

First. In these head movements care should be taken that the head only from the base of the neck is moved, while the other part of the body remains in the correct sitting position. Following Figure 4, let the chin move gently and gradually (do not let it fall or come down with a jerk) until the face forms an angle of forty-five degrees with the trunk, or until the chin very nearly touches the chest.

Second. Remain in position while second and third count is being made, raise the head slowly, not by jerks, to the vertical position, taking care that you do not throw it too far back.

Third. Move the chin gently upward, the head backward, until the same angle as was obtained by the forward movement is reached, then as in movement second, gradually.

Fourth. Bring the head back to the proper position. In making these movements care must be taken that in bringing the head back to position you do not infringe upon the position of the opposite movement.

BENDING RIGHT AND LEFT—(Figure 6.)

First. Let the head gradually be bent directly downward and to the right at, as near as can be judged, an angle of forty-five degrees with the trunk, which will be just half-way between the correct sitting position and the level of the shoulders.

Second. Let the head be gradually and gently raised to proper position.

Third. Bend the head to the left until the same position is reached as in the movement to the right.

Fourth. Return to the position the same as in movement second.

In practicing these head movements, while some masters indulge in a quick movement as well as a moderate one, it is rather to be discouraged, as the results are not so beneficial, and one is apt to make the movement too quick, in which case a possible · serious accident or unpleasant strain may be occasioned. An ordinary and steady movement is the one to be preferred.

STANDING POSITION.

This position is of vital importance to the public speaker, and indeed it should be mastered by all, as nothing adds as much grace to any one as a correct, easy, and natural position while on the feet. No pains should be spared to get this position exactly, and the main points should be observed whenever standing, either reading, reciting, or in conversation, in order to establish as a habit an erect and dignified carriage of the body.

THE MILITARY POSITION—(Figures 7 and 8)

is the basis used in gaining this. Place the heels in a line firmly together, with the toes turned out at an angle of about sixty degrees. Let the body be square to the front, eyes looking straight forward, the knees straight, with the chest expanded and advanced, but without straining. Let the arms hang easily at the side, bringing each shoulder to equal height. Let the form be raised to the full height, with head erect, not drooping in either direction, chin slightly drawn in, and the whole body poised slightly forward, so that the weight bears mainly on the ball of the foot, bringing the whole figure into such a position that

Fig. 9

Speaker's Position.

Fig. 10

the ear, hip, knee, and ankle are in a line. The most frequent error in the standing position is a hollowing of the back, caused by throwing the head and shoulders too far back. Be sure that they are in a line, as before directed, and this will be avoided, and avoid drooping the head. Another serious fault is the throwing out of the hips, which interferes seriously with a graceful carriage of the body. This is also occasioned by a very zealous desire to "stand straight," by throwing the shoulders too far back, thus bending the upper part of the body, which causes this error. If the lower limbs are first placed in proper position and then the shoulders brought in line with them, this fault is easily obviated. From this position is assumed all the various changes in speaking and gesturing. As we have before cautioned, let each one master it thoroughly, and the acquiring of proper gesturing will follow much more easily and successfully by those who have given strict attention to attaining a correct standing position.

SPEAKER'S POSITION.

From the correct standing position both the correct position for speaking and reading (Figures 9 and 10) are assumed, with a slight change.

The speaker's position (Figure 9) is assumed by throwing the weight of the body firmly on the left foot and advancing the right foot about three or four inches, raising it slightly on the floor, with the knees slightly bent. This position is gracefully reversed by recovering correct standing position, care being taken that the foot does not slide on the floor, but lifted and placed back, and the weight thrown on the right foot with the left advanced, observing same directions as before. The speaker's position should be observed whenever standing to read, converse, or recite. By observing these rules, in a short time it will become a fixed habit, which of course does away with the slouchy

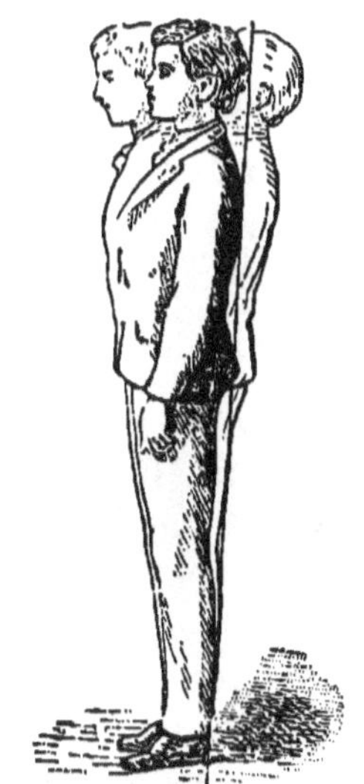

Fig. 11.

Poise forward and backward.

Fig. 12.

Rise on the Toes.

manner of standing on one foot, or the habit of giving the body the swaying movement from foot to foot, which is too common a fault with our young people.

READER'S POSITION—(Figure 10.)

This is the same as the speaker's position: with the right hand holding the book flatly open, with the thumb and little finger used to keep the book open and leaves down, the other three fingers beneath the book as a support. Let the elbow be advanced a few inches, with the forearm at an angle of about forty-five degrees, to secure perfect vision without bending the neck or body. A rest and change can be given in this the same as standing position, by also changing the book from the right to the left hand. These directions in holding the book should be observed in reading aloud in a sitting position as well as standing.

EXERCISES—Forward and Backward Poising—(Figure 11.)

First. Carry the weight of the body as far back as possible without lifting the heels or bending the spine. The ankle joints are alone brought into play in this movement. All the other joints of the body remain inflexible. By count return steadily to position.

Second. Carry the weight of the body as far back as possible. Let the weight be mainly on the heels, still without lifting the toes, with the rest of the body in the same position as on the forward movement. Return steadily to position.

RISING MOVEMENT—(Figure 12.)

From the standing position let the body be raised gently by lifting the heels and throwing the weight on the toes. This is accomplished by an extension of the instep. Let the position of the body remain as in the correct standing position, and give elevation to the body as much as possible, with the knees extended. The trunk and head by being kept in a straight line with the lower limbs are gradually thrown forward during the rising position without the body losing its balance.

Return gently and slowly to position after remaining standing through two counts. This same exercise may be practiced with benefit by rising on one foot at a time. This gives strength to the lower limbs, and a better general command of the body.

The forward and backward bending of the body as in Figures 13 and 14 should be practiced with care and gone through gently. They have the tendency to strengthen the muscles of the waist and back, and to give impulse to the digestive organs. Let the body be bent slowly forward, the feet remaining firmly fixed to the floor, bending only the hip joint. Let the arm fall naturally as the trunk goes forward as far as possible. Remain in this position a moment, and return slowly, taking care that during the entire movement the head with reference to the trunk is kept in a proper position, and as you rise let the hands gradually return in proper place. At the discretion of one taking this exercise the hands may be placed in position as in Figure 14. The backward movement is obtained in the same way, letting only the hip joint come into play.

BODY BENDED RIGHT AND LEFT—(Figure 15.)

The bending of the body as in Figure 15 should be made first slowly to the right, and let both feet remain firmly in position, and keep the knees straight; only the body from the hips up is brought into action in this exercise. Let the hands fall gently to the side, and bend far enough over until the hand touches the outside of the knee, returning to position. Repeat this exercise, bending the body to the left; with a short interval this may be practiced two or three times in succession with benefit, taking care that all the movements are made gently and without forcing the body.

WALKING—(Figure 16.)

In walking, the main points of the standing position must be observed: the body erect, head raised, eyes looking straight forward, with chest active as in Figure 16, arms falling easily and allowed a gentle natural swing. Let the step be quick in time and length, approaching as near as possible the military march, but avoid any rigidity or stamping. All the muscles of the body must be in a state of easy elastic tension. All lassitude, bending, carelessness, falling of the head, dangling of the limbs, bending of the trunk, and loose, irregular gazing should be avoided.

In a quick ordinary step the heel of the advanced foot strikes the ground first; in a very slow long step the outside toe strikes the ground first. The quick ordinary step is far preferable, and should be most practiced.

BODY TURNED RIGHT AND LEFT—(Figure 17.)

Assume the correct standing position as in Figure 7, then turn the trunk to the right; keep the legs straight and close together, with the feet firm; the head must not turn back except in unison with the body; let the arms and hands remain in the same relative position to the body as at the beginning of the movement. This movement is extended until an angle of about forty-five degrees is attained from the correct standing position, or until the eyes are looking directly from the right side, as in Figure 17. Returning to position, the left movement is practiced in the same way.

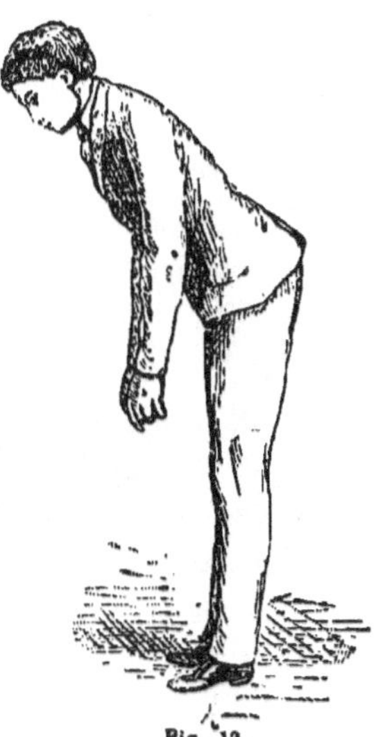

Fig. 13.
Body bend forward.

Fig. 14
Body bend back.

BENDING THE KNEES—(Figure 18.)

From the correct standing position take the position of
rising on the toes as in Figure 12, then slowly bend the
knees, allowing the body to descend perpendicularly until
you sit upon the knees as outlined in Figure 18. Let the
knees be slowly brought back to place and the body raised
upward, still maintaining the perpendicular position. This
is rather a severe exercise, and ought not to be repeated at
the commencement, but as the pupil grows accustomed to
it; later, as in the other exercises, it can be judiciously
taken with benefit two and three times in succession if
desired, and if found more congenial it can be practiced
with the arm crossed behind the back.

ARM AND CHEST EXPANSION MOVEMENTS.

So far the exercises have been to bring into play all
parts of the body except the arms. We now take up arm
movement, which is a most important one as to the graceful development of those limbs which play so important
a part in proper gesturing; also these exercises constitute
a most healthful chest development, as illustrated in Figure 20.

We first consider the movement as illustrated in Figure
20. Placing the hands on the chest, with the four fingers
just below the collar bone, with the forearms horizontal,
taking a deep breath through the nostrils and holding
the breath, strike on the chest rapid, light blows with
the flat of the fingers, and let the wrist be slack; give
out the breath through the nostrils, drop the arms to a
natural position at the side. This can be repeated several times after practice, and the blows are gradually in-
creased in force, but should never be rigid or jarring.
This is excellent chest exercise, combined with slight arm
movement.

Fig. 16.
Body turn right and left.

Fig 16
Walking.

FRONT ARM MOVEMENT AND CHEST EXPANSION—(Fig. 21.)

In these movements either position 8 or 10 can be used for the feet or lower limbs. In chest expansion exercise let the elbow be sharply bent and brought close to the side with clinched fist as in Figure 21; taking a deep inspiration and holding the breath, extend the arms to full length; relaxing the muscles, open the fists, with the palm of the hand outward, as in dotted line; remain thus for two counts and expand the chest as much as possible, bringing the arms quickly back to first position, expelling the breath through the nostrils. This movement can, after taking two or three inspirations, be practiced three or four times in succession.

CROSSED ARM MOVEMENT.

Let the arms be swinging loosely at the side as the right arm is shown in Figure 22; bring both arms into position as shown in left arm, and then by a quick movement, letting the joints of the arms be loose, strike the right hand on the left breast and the left on the right breast, striking with the palm of the hand a quick, elastic blow. Drop arms to the side again. This exercise can be repeated three or four times in succession. By a count of one for position as shown by the right hand; two, arms assume the position of the left arm; three, striking the chest; four, bringing into first position.

BENT ARM MOVEMENT—(Figure 23.)

Position as in Figure 23; with the forearms vertical, palms outward, tightly clinch the fist and bring the arms around, turning the palms in until they almost touch; assuming a position as in dotted line, with the hands brought two inches in front of the chin, bring the arms back to position, clinching the fist during the return

Fig. 17.
Bodyturn right and left.

Bend the Knees.
Fig. 18.

movement, and from the first position the exercise can be repeated, when the arms are dropped to the side for rest.

EXTENSION MOVEMENT—(Figures 24 and 25.)

Let the arms be extended horizontally, with the finger-tips touching, forming a graceful curve from the body, as in position *a*; then raise the arms to an angle of about forty-five degrees, as in position *b*, still keeping the finger-tips together, taking position *c*, and finally carry the arms as far back as possible, as in position *d*. In bending the arms, throw them out to the fullest possible extent, as in position *e*; then gradually dropping the arms while thrown still back as far as grace will permit, or until they are a little back of a horizontal line and in position *f*, bring them gradually to the front until they are about horizontal from the sides, as in position *g*, then drop to the sides as in position *h*. This exercise can be practiced making a rest at each position, or by a continuous movement, counting from one to eight. It is a severe movement, and should not be repeated until the pupil has become accustomed to it; then it can be gone through with several times as judgment would dictate.

BENT ARM MOVEMENT.

Place the tips of the fingers lightly on the shoulders as in Figure 26, bringing the elbows forward in front of the body. Lift the elbows as far as possible, as shown in the position of the dotted line, which will bring the palm of the hand directly over the shoulder; still continuing the forward and upward circular movement, bring the arms back into the forward position. Much benefit can be derived by expanding the chest to the fullest possible extent until the dotted line position is reached, then, as the arms are brought forward and down into position, let the breath

Fig. 20.
Arm Movements.

Fig. 21.
Chest Expansion.

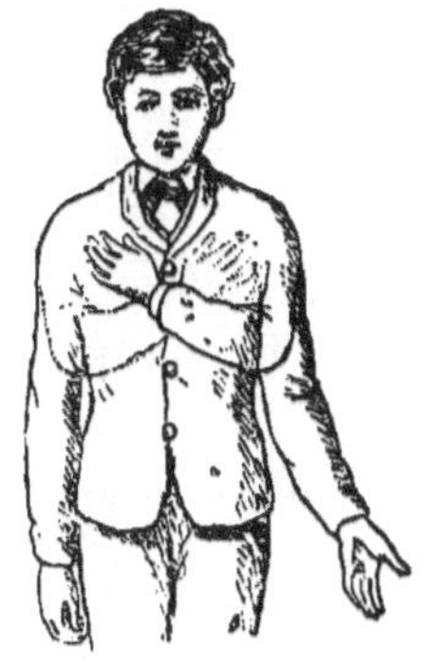

Fig. 22.

Fig. 23.
Bent Arm Movements.

be slowly exhaled through the nostrils. This is not only an excellent movement for the command of perfect movements of the arms, but is most beneficial in expanding the chest and developing the breathing capacity. It has been said that "the amount of work a person can do is not so much dependent on muscle as on the breathing capacity," and further, "The amount of oxygen received into the system is determined in a great measure by the capacity of the chest and the degree of the mobility of its wall."

UNEQUAL BREATHING—(Figure 30.)

Placing the palm of the left hand against the side in a position close to the arm-pit, as shown in Figure 30, and bringing the right arm directly over the head, tends to contract the left side, giving freer vent to the breathing of the right side. Practice with the deep breath three or four times, returning by count three, four, the arms to position at the side. Take by count one, two, the same position, rehearsing the position of the arms, and practice with three or four inspirations as before. This will be found very beneficial to the full development of the respiratory organs.

It is not considered best to dwell too long on any one exercise before taking up the succeeding one; let the student be made reasonably proficient in one and then proceed to the next, and as often as is judged expedient add a new movement, going through all the preceding ones that have been studied with each exercise. After the entire set of movements have been learned they can be practiced at discretion and will.

To aid either in class or individual exercise, we give fully outlined the order of procedure in assuming the standing position Figure 9; also the exercise of rising on the toes as shown in Figure 12, and the extension arm movement as shown in Figures 24 and 25.

Extension Movement, Fig. 24.

Fig. 27.
Unequal Breathing.

Fig. 26.
Movement bent Arms.

Extension Movement.
Fig. 25.

STANDING POSITION—(Figure 9.)

Prepare to stand !   Stand !   Position !

RISING ON THE TOES—(Figure 12.)

Rise ! one, two, (rise gradually,) three, four.   (Remain fixed during third and fourth counts.)   One, two, (descend to position,) three, four.   (Repeat.)   *Rest!*

EXTENSION MOVEMENTS—(Figures 24 and 25.)

One !   (Arms extended horizontally, middle fingers touching.) *Two !* (Arms elevated 45°.)   *Three !* (Arms over the head.) *Four!* (Arms as far back as possible, fingers still touching.) *One !* (Arms extended straight sidewise, raised 45°.)   *Two !* (Arms horizontal and back.)   *Three !* (Descend 45°.)   *Four !* (To place.) (Repeat.)   *Rest !*

GESTURING.

Gesturing embraces the various postures and motions of the body, as the head, shoulders and trunk, arms, hands and fingers, and the lower limbs and feet. It is the language of nature. The deaf-mute communicates by visible signs, and the infant knows a smile from a frown long before words have any meaning.

The advantage of a natural, graceful, and effective delivery is so important as to be considered by many paramount to the sentiments and language of a public speaker; hence, he who merely addresses the ear and not the eye lacks that great essential of a perfect orator.

In order to persuade men and move them to action, it is obviously better to address the eye and ear than the ear alone; if this is so, then it should be a study that this duty may be performed in the best manner possible. If, by a mere motion of the hand, we appeal, challenge, warn, threaten, and scorn, then let us be eager to study that which will enable us to perform these important duties in the most graceful and convincing manner.

As far back as history gives us any knowledge those who have attained a prominence as orators have made gesturing as deep a study as the language and sentiment that they utter; indeed, so great has been the achievement of oratorical art, so marked the success of those who have thoroughly cultivated it as contrasted with. others of equal or even superior talents in other respects but deficient in this, that many have been led to attach more importance to delivery than composition. The public speaker who neglects this part of an orator's education certainly suffers great loss.

The degree of perfection to which the art of gesturing was carried by the ancients is shown from the challenge of Cicero by Roscius, the latter contending that he could express the same idea in a greater variety of ways by his gestures than the former could by the use of words.

The incessant labors of Demosthenes, of Æschines, of Hortensius, of Isocrates, and of Gracchus show that these men agreed with Cicero and Roscius in the belief that to be an orator something more is needed than to *be born*.

If it belongs to Nature to furnish the world with ready-made orators, why does she not do it? Nature will perform her part, but obviously it is no more her province to provide finished orators than finished scholars or artists. We find the bestowment of natural gifts, but also see the necessity of cultivation, which brings about a degree of attainment proportionate to the industry and perseverance of the recipients. Cicero says: "It is of little consequence that you prepare what is to be spoken unless you are able to deliver your speech with freedom and grace." Nor is even that sufficient unless what is spoken be delivered by the voice, by the countenance, and by the gesture in such a manner as to give it a higher relish. Hamlet's instruction to the players ("Speak the speech, I pray you, as I pronounced it to you, trippingly on the tongue," etc.), guarding them against extravagance on the one hand and tameness on the other, is as serviceable to the orator as the actor.

Quintilian also says: "If delivery can produce such an effect as to excite anger, tears, and solicitudes in speech we know to be fictitious and vain, how much more powerful must it be when we are persuaded in reality! Nay, I venture to pronounce that even an indifferent oration, recommended by the force of action, would have more effect than the best destitute of this enforcement."

The acknowledged ability of Lord Chesterfield to judge in such matters will give weight to the following quotation from him: "If you would either please in a private company or persuade in a public assembly, air, looks,

JOY.

gestures, and proper graces are fully as necessary as the matter itself."

The success of Cicero, like that of Demosthenes, was close application to the study of rules and persevering practice in the art of gesturing. Æschines, a celebrated Athenian orator and rival of Demosthenes, excelled in extemporaneous oratory, of which he was called the inventor; yet Æschines paid such attention to gesture and its cultivation that he founded a school at Rhodes which became celebrated throughout the world. Hortensius, a personal friend of Cicero, although not possessed of the highest order of talent, in other respects was, on account of the grace of his delivery, accounted the rival of Cicero.

William Pitt, the distinguished parliamentarian, a man of overpowering eloquence, acquired this power of forcible speech by a severe course of training at Oxford, where he was as much noted for his skill as for his talent. The eloquence of Fox was of the highest type, and he was pronounced by many the most Demosthenean speaker since Demosthenes; yet his force as a public speaker has ever been acknowledged as due to his marvelous gesturing, acquired only by close application.

Lord Erskine, acknowledged to be the greatest of English advocates, is a striking example of the success attending the study of oratory; although his eminence was suddenly achieved, it was nevertheless the result of previous preparation. A remarkable instance of native genius combined with self-culture is found in the extraordinary history of Patrick Henry; with little aid from the schools, he rose head and shoulders above his contemporaries, and aroused three millions of people to the cry of " Liberty or Death ! " According to his own account, he was first inspired to oratory by the masterly delivery of the Rev. Samuel Davies, the great orator of the Presbyterian Church. This was followed by a close study of all the expressions and gestures that daily came before him, and

FEAR.

he became such a master of the art as to command and inspire all who heard him.

Henry Clay's great oratorical power he attributed himself to the fact that he made it a daily practice of reading and speaking the contents of some historical or scientific book. Not content with reading and storing his mind with the knowledge, he must put into expression and gesture what he read before he was satisfied. Daniel Webster, Edward Everett, Wendell Phillips, John B. Gough, and many other noted American orators owe their influence as public speakers as much to their manner of delivery and holding their hearers as to the subject-matter of their discourse.

We might follow up the argument with example after example, but enough has been said to convince the most skeptical that we must agree with Daniel Webster that eloquence, which is the culmination of oratory, is "logic on fire." Further, quoting from Webster, we conclude by saying that true eloquence, no matter what the subject-matter is, must be brought out by the dauntless spirit "speaking on the tongue, beaming from the eye, told by the wave of the hand and the motion of the arm, urging the whole man onward, right onward, to his object."

But since these conditions can be met, the student has no occasion to despair. The following illustrations and instructions in gesturing must be in a measure varied and supplemented to directly suit the occasion. The idea is not to lay down a direct line to come up to, but a general instruction that will open an avenue of graceful, forcible, and pleasing delivery for all occasions.

POSITION.

In taking up the study of gesturing, the first thing to be considered is the proper handling of the feet. It has been said, and truthfully, that "graceful position precedes

SORROW.

graceful action." The facility of movement is essential to both; hence the public speaker should stand erect and firm, but great care should be taken that it is an easy, natural firmness, and not in the least rigid. Let the weight of the body rest mainly upon one foot, so that the other may be readily used in changing the position as occasion may require. The supporting limb should be straight, while the knee of the other should be slightly bent. The feet should be placed three or four inches apart, with the toes turned outward, making an angle of about ninety degrees in an advanced position and seventy in a retired position. The space between the feet can be widened and the angles varied to suit the purpose of the speaker, but the position described is generally the one taken in the opening of an address, and the one most used through a discourse.

The positions suited to the ordinary purpose of public speaking, and from which all other positions by practice are acquired and derived, may be discriminated as follows:

First Position. Right foot advanced, the left supporting the weight of the body.

Second Position. Right foot advanced, supporting the body.

Third Position. Left foot advanced, right supporting the weight of the body.

Fourth Position. Left foot advanced, supporting the body.

Figures 1 and 2 represent first and second positions. The principal weight of the body rests upon the foot that is deeply shaded; the other foot, lightly shaded, rests lightly upon the floor. The change from the first to the second position is made by stepping forward with the right foot about half its length, throwing the principal weight upon it, which will naturally incline the body in an opposite direction from Figure 1, allowing only that part of the left foot which is shaded in Figure *b* to rest lightly on the floor.

Fig. 1.

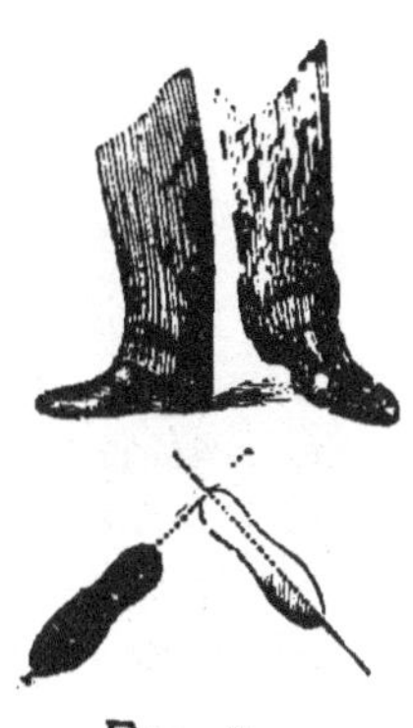

Fig. 2.

The third and fourth positions are simply a reverse of the positions just described.

In changing the positions of the feet the motions are to be made with the utmost simplicity. The speaker must advance, retire, or change almost imperceptibly, and it is to be particularly observed that the changes should not be too frequent, as this is apt to give an idea of anxiety or instability. The true time of movement is in exact coincidence with emphasis. The voice and bodily frame are thus kept in simultaneous action with the mind. Do not misunderstand that every address must be accompanied by change and motion of the body. The idea is not to set a public speaker in motion. Many of us no doubt are like the awkward youth whose father sent him to the dancing-master that he might learn to stand still, and we may need to study the subject that our actions may be abridged and made proper.

POSITION OF THE HANDS.

SUPINE POSITION—(Figure 3.)

We will next consider the position and use of the hands as giving particular emphasis to certain lines of thought and gesturing. The hand can be made to express a good deal. A careful study of its different positions should be made that its power may not be misused.

First we have, as in Figure 3, the supine position, or the one generally used in opening or closing an address. In this position the hands should be well opened, presenting the palm of the hand, slightly sloping from the thumb, to the audience, and the forefinger should be straight but not rigid, with the other fingers gracefully relaxed. The hand in this position is used in many full-arm gestures; in fact, the supine position of the hands is more used on the stage than any other in public speaking, and possesses great power of expression. It is employed in an emphatic

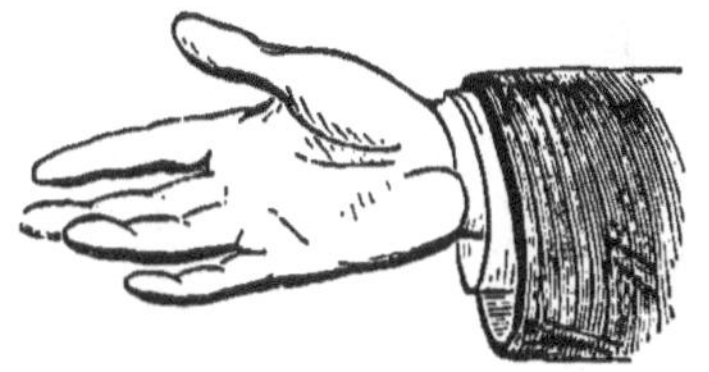

Fig. 3.

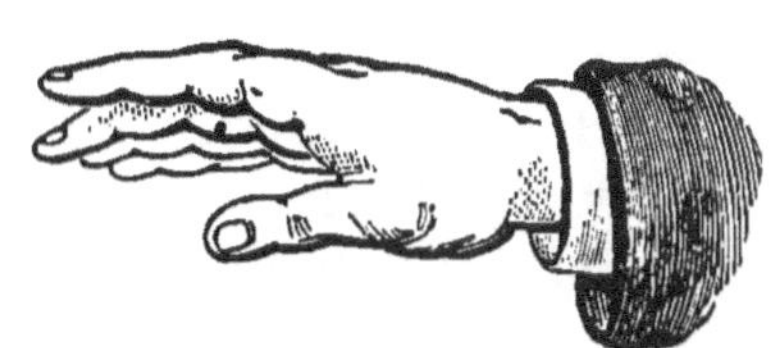

Fig. 4.

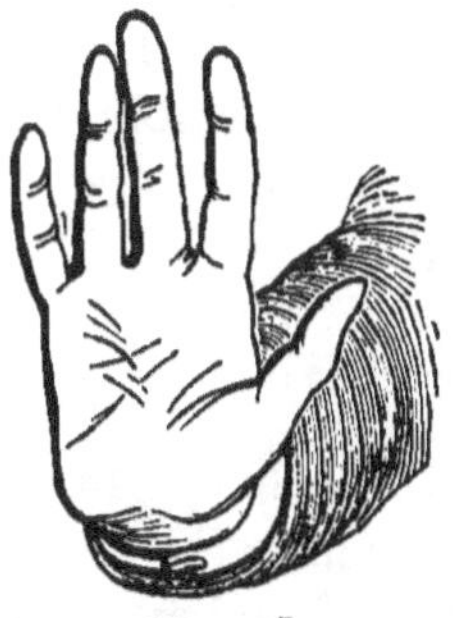

Fig. 5

Fig. 6.

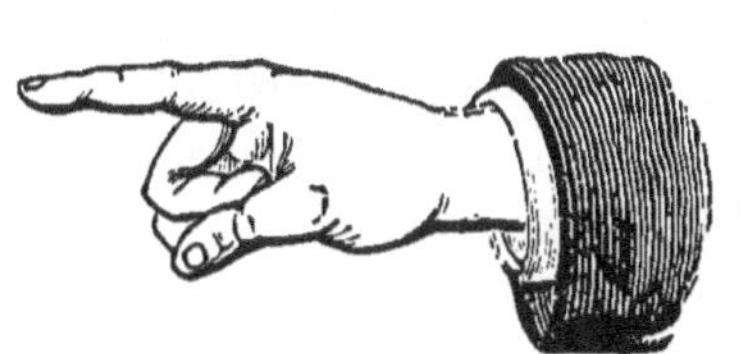

Fig. 7.

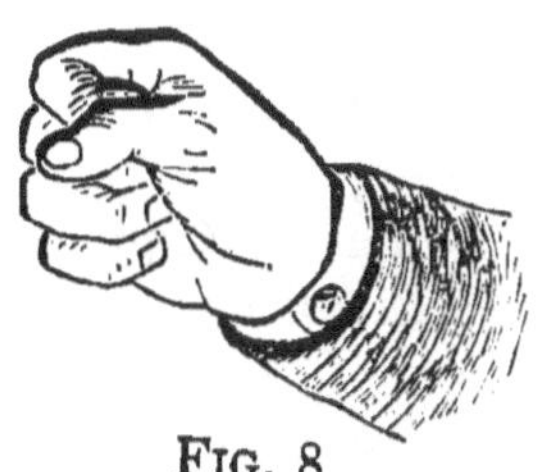

Fig. 8

assertion, in resolve, forcible demand, in submission, and other expressions that the student must intuitively know are derived from these and like character.

THE PRONE POSITION—(Figure 4.)

Next to the supine position comes the prone position of the hands, as shown in Figure 4. Note very carefully the exact position from which the prone presents the hands to the audience, with the palm of the thumb turned in and the greater part of the palms of the fingers presented to the audience, the forefinger slightly straighter than the rest, with an easy relaxed position in the whole hand. This position is used in repression, compulsion, aversion, command, suppression, and superposition.

HANDS VERTICAL—(Figure 5.)

As suggested in other positions of the hand, make a close study of this, that the exact force which the position gives may be brought out. The vertical hand is used in repulsion, removal, or aversion.

The vertical hand raised above the head is often used in . sacred deprecation.

THE INDEX FINGER—(Figures 6 and 7.)

The use of the index finger as shown in Figures 6 and 7 (either position can be used at the choice of the student) is expressive of forcible discrimination, particular designation, or emphatic reference. It is also used in reproach, scorn, or contempt, in which case Figure 7 is most preferable. In caution, warning, or threatening, the index finger is also very expressive.

CLINCHED HAND—(Figure 8.)

The clinched hand is used for extreme or special emphasis, anger, or defiance. It is also very expressive of

FIG. 9.

FIG. 10.

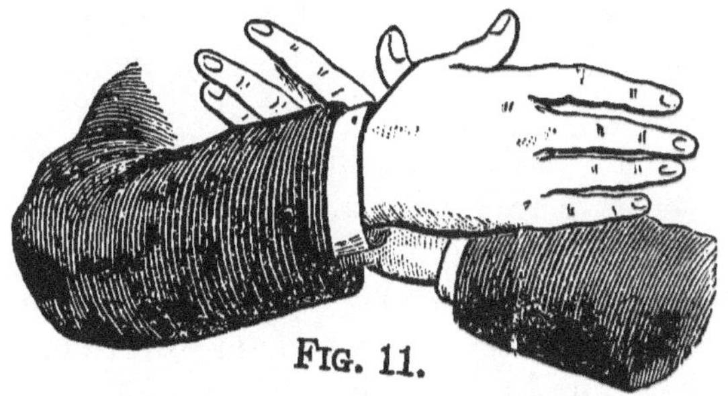

FIG. 11.

seizing, grasping. The most emphatic emphasis is made with the clinched hand, which is often used forcibly on the speaker's table with good effect, although care should be taken in this, that it is not overdone.

HANDS APPLIED—(Figure 9.)

Hands applied or brought squarely together, as shown in Figure 9, is most used in expressing adoration. This position should be very rarely used except in adoration, supplement, or imploring.

HANDS CLASPED—(Figure 10.)

The clasping of the hands, as shown in Figure 10, is used in supplication, earnest entreaty, and distress.

HANDS CROSSED—(Figure 11.)

This position is used in immolation or veneration, and is accompanied with a submissive bow of the head and dropping of the eye.

It must be remembered in using these positions of the hands that they are used with all the different positions that the arms may take, and we do not pretend to give, by any means, the full scope to which these positions may be used; but our idea is to give a general direction, which the student may find by his ingenuity can be used in any combination of gesturing.

Having given an outline for the use of the feet and hands, we now introduce the student to the different positions of gesturing. With each of these cuts we give a short description and appropriate example for their use. These, we are sure, carefully studied, will suggest an appropriate style of action in every case that may arise, and enable the student to bring out the finer shades of expression for every occasion.

ANGER.

It must not be assumed that the positions given are to be strictly maintained in exemplifying the particular kind of gesture they represent; in many instances the arms can be elevated or brought to the front where in the figure they may be in a lowered position; or raised to good effect in many instances where the figure may show them in a lowered position. We wish to convey the idea that while these are correct positions for the expressions they represent, they can with judgment and skill be used in a wider scope with grand effect.

RELIGIOUS DEVOTION.

ADORATION.

DESCRIPTION OF FIGURE.

The right foot moderately advanced; the attitude gracefully easy; the right arm bent at the elbow, the thumb being on a level with the shoulder; the hand open, the palm outward; the left arm hanging down perpendicular with and a short distance from the side, the hand nearly open, the palm down; the head slightly thrown back; the eyes upturned.

Examples.

1.　The sword of Washington! The staff of Franklin! Oh, sir, what associations are linked in adamant with these names! Washington, whose sword was never drawn but in the cause of his country, and never sheathed when wielded in his country's cause!

What other two men, whose lives belong to the eighteenth century of Christendom, have left a deeper impression of themselves upon the age in which they lived, and upon all after time?

2.　Oh, with what pride I used
　　To walk these hills, and look up to my God,
　　And bless him that the land was free.　'Twas free—
　　From end to end, from cliff to lake, 'twas free!
　　Free as our torrents are that leap our rocks
　　And plow our valleys, without asking leave!
　　Or as our peaks that wear their caps of snow
　　In very presence of the regal sun!

3.　And had he not high honor?—
　　　The hill-side for his pall;
　　To lie in state while angels wait,
　　　With stars for tapers tall;
　　And the dark rock-pines, like tossing plumes
　　　Over his bier to wave;
　　And God's own hand, in that lonely land,
　　　To lay him in the grave.

ADORATION.

ADMIRATION.

DESCRIPTION OF FIGURE.

The right foot very slightly advanced; the left knee
bent a little so as to bring the figure into an easy, agreeable posture; the form quite erect; the shoulders well
back; the right arm stretched out on a level with the
breast; the hand open, and the index finger pointed at
the object spoken of (or to); the left arm close to the hip,
but from the hip slightly extended from the body; the
hand expanded and palm down. Such an attitude and
expression would well befit these lines:

> 1.   Ah! there it stands, the same old house!
>   And there that ancient tree,
>   Where I first trod in boyish pride,
>   And laughed in happy glee.
>   But it is changed; the fence is gone
>   Which girded it around;
>   And here and there the fragments lie
>   Scattered upon the ground.

2.   Look abroad over this country; mark her extent, her
wealth, her fertility, her boundless resources, the great energies
which every day she develops, and which she seems already bending for that fatal race—tempting, yet always fatal to republics—
the race for physical greatness and aggrandizement. Behold, too,
that continuous and mighty tide of population, native and foreign,
which is forever rushing through this great valley toward the setting sun; sweeping away the wilderness before it like the grass
before the mower; waking up industry and civilization in its progress; studding the solitary rivers of the West with marts and
cities; dotting its boundless prairies with human habitations;
penetrating every green nook and vale; climbing every fertile
ridge; and still gathering and pouring onward, to form new States
in those vast and yet unpeopled solitudes, where the Oregon rolls
his majestic flood and "hears no sound save his own dashing."

ADMIRATION.

APPEAL.

DESCRIPTION OF FIGURE.

Right foot a little in advance; left knee very slightly bent; shoulders thrown back somewhat; face a little turned; eyes lifted heavenward; right arm extended; hand open, and a little above the level of the forehead; left arm extended almost horizontally, so as to bring the wrist just below the belt; the hand open, palm upward.

Examples.

1.   Ah! Brakenbury, I have done these things
That now give evidence against my soul
For Edward's sake; and see how he requites me!
O God! if my deep prayers can not appease thee,
But thou wilt be avenged on my misdeeds,
Yet execute thy wrath on me alone:
Oh, spare my guiltless wife, and my poor children!
I prithee, Brakenbury, stay by me;
My soul is heavy, and I fain would sleep.

2.   My tall and tawny king, come back!
Come swift, O sweet! why falter so?
Come, come! What thing has crossed your track?
I kneel to all the gods I know.
Oh, come, my manly Idaho!
Great Spirit, what is this I dread?
Why, there is blood! the wave is red!
That wrinkled chief, outstripped in race,
Dives down, and hiding from thy face,
Strikes underneath! He rises now!
Now plucks my hero's berry bough,
And lifts aloft his red fox head,
And signals he has won for me.
Hist, softly! Let him come and see.
Oh, come, my white-crowned hero, come!
Oh, come, and I will be your bride,
Despite yon chieftain's craft and might.

APPEAL.

COURAGE.

DESCRIPTION OF FIGURE.

The left foot a little in advance; the figure somewhat thrown back, so that the breast is well advanced; the arms fully extended; hands open; the right hand on a level with the forehead; the left on a level with the lower part of thigh; the right palm partly turned upward, the left partly down.

Examples.

1.   If ye are beasts, then stand here, like fat oxen, waiting for the butcher's knife. If ye are men—follow me! Strike down you guard, gain the mountain passes, and there do bloody work, as did your sires at old Thermopylæ! Is Sparta dead? Is the old Grecian spirit frozen in your veins, that you do crouch and cower like a belabored hound beneath his master's lash? Oh, comrades! warriors! Thracians!—if we must fight, let us fight for ourselves! If we must slaughter, let us slaughter our oppressors! If we must die, let it be under the clear sky, by the bright waters, in noble, honorable battle!

2.   An hour passed on;—the Turk awoke;
        That bright dream was his last:
     He woke to hear his sentries shriek,
        "To arms! they come! the Greek! the Greek!"
     He woke—to die 'midst flame, and smoke,
     And shout, and groan, and saber stroke,
        And death-shots, falling thick and fast
     As lightnings from the mountain cloud:
     And heard, with voice as trumpet loud,
        Bozzaris cheer his band:
     "Strike! till the last armed foe expires;
     Strike! for your altars and your fires;
     Strike! for the green graves of your sires,
        God, and your native land!"

COURAGE.

CAUTION.

DESCRIPTION OF FIGURE.

The right foot about an inch in advance; the legs close together; the form at ease; the right arm bent so that the back of the open fingers touch the lips; the left arm at the side, but slightly extended partly forward, partly sideways; the hand open, the palm downward.

Examples.

1.   Have patience, gentle friends; I must not read it:
It is not meet you know how Cæsar loved you.
You are not wood, you are not stones, but men;
And, being men, hearing the will of Cæsar,
It will inflame you, it will make you mad.
'Tis good you know not that you are his heirs;
For, if you should, oh, what would come of it!

2.   The king stood still
     Till the last echo died: then throwing off
     The sackcloth from his brow, and laying back
     The pall from the still features of his child,
     He bowed his head upon him, and broke forth
     In the resistless eloquence of woe.

3.   There was a sound of revelry by night,
     And Belgium's capital had gathered there
     Her beauty and her chivalry; and bright
     The lamps shone o'er fair women and brave men!
     A thousand hearts beat happily; and when
     Music arose with its voluptuous swell,
     Soft eyes looked love to eyes which spake again,
     And all went merry as a marriage-bell.
     But hush! hark! a deep sound strikes like a rising knell.
     Did ye not hear it? No, 'twas but the wind,
     Or the car rattling o'er the stony street.
     On with the dance, let joy be unconfined.
     No sleep till morn, when youth and pleasure meet
     To chase the glowing hours with flying feet.

CAUTION.

CURSING.

DESCRIPTION OF FIGURE.

The feet slightly separated, the right foot very little in advance; the right arm extended straight from the body, in the direction of the person or thing addressed; the hand almost open, fingers slightly contracted; the left arm stiffly at the side, some distance from the person, palm of open hand to the front; shoulders well back; head erect; lips wearing a fierce expression; eyes glancing malignantly.

Examples.

1. It is this accursed American war that has led us, step by step, into all our present misfortunes and national disgraces. What was the cause of our wasting forty millions of money, and sixty thousand lives? The American war! What was it that produced the French rescript and a French war? The American war! What was it that produced the Spanish manifesto and a Spanish war? The American war! What was it that armed forty-two thousand men in Ireland with the arguments carried on the points of forty thousand bayonets? The American war! For what are are we about to incur an additional debt of twelve or fourteen millions? This accursed, cruel, diabolical American war!

2.   Begone, thou insolent!
Why dost thou stand and gaze upon me thus?
Aye! watch the features well that threaten thee
With fraud and danger! In the wilderness
They shall avenge me—in the hour of want
Rise on thy view, and make thee feel
How innocent I am.

3.   Back to thy punishment,
False fugitive! and to thy speed add wings;
Lest with a whip of scorpions I pursue
Thy lingering, or, with one stroke of this dart
Strange horror seize thee, and pangs unfelt before!

CURSING.

DISLIKE.

DESCRIPTION OF FIGURE.

The right foot somewhat advanced; the left knee a little bent; the right arm almost falling straight, but a little advanced toward the middle of the figure; the left hand a little extended from the side; the hands almost open, the palms downward; the head a little drooped forward; the face turned toward the right shoulder. This position and expression indicates dislike or loathing. Such an appearance would be that of Othello, when he exclaims:

> "What committed?
> Committed!—Oh, thou public commoner!
> I should make very forges of my cheeks,
> That would to cinders burn up modesty,
> Did I but speak thy deeds."

Examples.

1.   Oh, I have passed a miserable night,
So full of ugly sights, of ghastly dreams,
That, as I am a Christian, faithful man,
I would not spend another such a night,
Though 'twere to buy a world of happy days,
So full of dismal terror was the time!
Methought that I had broken from the tower,
And was embarked to cross to Burgundy,
And in my company my brother Gloster,
Who from my cabin tempted me to walk
Upon the hatches. Thence we looked toward England.

2. Ay, down to the dust with them, slaves as they are!
From this hour let the blood in their dastardly veins,
That shrunk at the first touch of Liberty's war,
Be wasted for tyrants, or stagnate in chains.
Oh, shame! that in such a proud moment of life,
Worth the history of ages, when, had you but hurled
One bolt at your bloody invader, that strife
Between freemen and tyrants had spread through
the world.

DISLIKE..

DISDAIN.

DESCRIPTION OF FIGURE.

The weight of the body resting on the right foot; the left foot merely touching the toe to the ground; the right arm extended at full length, straight from the shoulder; the hand open, palm down; the left arm a little from the side; the hand extended; the palm down; the body proudly erect; the face turned to the right; the eyes following the pointing of the extended right hand. This position and gesture is indicative of pride and conscious self-superiority, as when Coriolanus, turning on the Roman rabble, exclaims:

> "Ye common cry of curs, whose breath I hate,
> As reek o' the rotten fens; whose love I prize
> As the dead carcasses of unburied men
> That do pollute the air!
>
>   I banish you!"

Example.

"BANISHED˅ from *Rome*˅?" What's *banished*ˆ, but set FREE
From daily contact of the things I *loathe*ˆ?
"Tried and convicted *traitor*˅?" Who˅ says this?
Who'll *prove*˅ it, at his *peril*ˆ, on *my* head?
*Banished*ˆ! I *thank*ˆ you for it. It breaks my chain.
I held some slack *allegiance* till *this*˅ hour;
But *now*ˆ my sword's my OWNˆ. Smile on, my lords;
I SCORNˆ to count what *feelings*˅, withered *hopes*˅,
Strong *provocations*˅, bitter, burning WRONGSˆ,
I have within my heart's hot cells shut up,
To *leave*ˆ you in your *lazy dignities*ˆ.
But here I stand and *scoff*ˆ you: here I fling
*Hatred*ˆ and full DEFIANCE˅ in your face.
Your consul's *merciful*ˆ! For this all *thanks*ˆ!

DISDAIN.

GRIEF.

DESCRIPTION OF FIGURE.

The right foot slightly advanced; the body fairly poised upon both feet; the left arm dropped close to the side; the right arm advanced a little to the front; both hands open; the right hand, the palm downward; the head slightly leaning forward; the eyes directed downward, with lids drooping.

Examples.

1.   How are the mighty fallen!—Saul and Jonathan were lovely and pleasant in their lives; and in their death they were not divided; they were swifter than eagles, they were stronger than lions.   Ye daughters of Israel, weep over Saul, who clothed you in scarlet, with other delights; who put on ornaments of gold upon your apparel!—How are the mighty fallen in the midst of the battle! O Jonathan! thou wast slain in thy high places! How are the mighty fallen, and the weapons of war perished!

2.   My life is cold, and dark, and dreary;
It rains, and the wind is never weary;
My thoughts still cling to the moldering past,
But the hopes of youth fall thick in the blast,
    And the days are dark and dreary.

3.   I loved him then—he loved me, too.   My heart
Still finds its fondness kindle if he smile;
The memory of our loves will ne'er depart;
And though he often sting me with a dart,
Venomed and barbed, and waste upon the vile
Caresses which his babe and mine should share,—
Though he should spurn me,—I will calmly bear
His madness; and should sickness come and lay
Its paralyzing hand upon him, then
I would with kindness all my wrongs repay,
Until the penitent should weep and say,
How injured and how faithful I have been!

GRIER

HATE.

DESCRIPTION OF FIGURE.

The right foot advanced so that its heel just precedes
the left foot; the body slightly bent back; the face turned
to the sky, the gaze directed upward, with a fierce expression; the eyes full of baleful light; the right arm held
straight up; the fingers very little curved; the left arm
extended from the person; the hand open, palm up.

Examples.

1. "Be that word our sign of parting, bird or fiend," I
        shrieked, upstarting;
    "Get thee back into the tempest and the night's Plutonian
        shore!
      Leave no black plume as a token of that lie thy soul hath
        spoken!
      Leave my loneliness unbroken! quit the bust above my
        door!
      Take thy beak from out my heart, and take thy form from
        off my door!"
            Quoth the raven, "Nevermore!"

2. I've scared you in the city; I've scalped you on the plain;
    Go, count your chosen where they fell beneath my leaden
        rain!
    I scorn your proffered treaty; the pale-face I defy;
    Revenge is stamped upon my spear, and blood my battle-
        cry!

3. And, "This to me!" he said;
    "An 'twere not for thy hoary beard,
    Such hand as Marmion's had not spared
    To cleave the Douglas' head!
    And, Douglas, more I tell thee here,
    E'en in thy pitch of pride,
    Here, in thy hold, thy vassals near,
    I tell thee, thou'rt defied!

HATE.

MODESTY.

DESCRIPTION OF FIGURE.

The right foot set fairly on the ground; the left heel a little lifted; the right arm at full length, but a few inches from the side; the hand open, the back of the hand in front; the left arm close to the body to the elbow; the forearm a little extended from the body, but tending downward; the hand open; the palm downward. This attitude and gesture will express modesty and respect for the persons addressed.

Examples.

1. Night, sable goddess! from her ebon throne,
    In rayless majesty, now stretches forth
    Her leaden scepter o'er a slumbering world.
    Silence how dead! and darkness how profound!
    Nor eye, nor listening ear an object finds.
    Creation sleeps.   'Tis as the general pulse
    Of life stood still, and Nature made a pause;
    An awful pause! prophetic of her end.
    And let her prophecy be soon fulfilled:
    Fate! drop the curtain; I can lose no more.

2.   Father, Thy hand
    Hath reared these venerable columns.   Thou
    Didst weave this verdant roof.   Thou didst look down
    Upon the naked earth, and forthwith rose
    All these fair ranks of trees.   They in Thy sun
    Budded, and shook their green leaves in Thy breeze,
    And shot toward heaven.   The century-living crow,
    Whose birth was in their tops, grew old and died
    Among their branches; till, at last, they stood.

3. Come, Antony, and young Octavius—come!
    Revenge yourselves alone on Cassius,
    For Cassius is aweary of the world.

MODESTY.

INVOCATION

DESCRIPTION OF FIGURE.

Heels well together; form erect; arms fully extended; the right hand above a level with the face; the left arm so that the hand is below the waist; the head turned sideways as though admiring the elevated objects looked at.

Examples.

1. May the Great Ruler of nations grant that the signal blessings with which He has favored ours may not, by the madness of party or by personal ambition, be disregarded and lost; and may His wise providence bring those who have produced this crisis to see the folly, before they feel the misery, of civil strife, and inspire a returning veneration for that Union which, if we may dare to penetrate His designs, He has chosen as the only means of attaining the high destinies to which we may reasonably aspire.

2.   Hail, holy light! offspring of heaven, first-born,
Or of the Eternal co-eternal beam.
May I express thee unblamed? since God is light,
And never but in unapproached light
Dwelt from eternity; dwelt then in thee.
Bright effluence of bright essence increate.
Or hear'st thou rather pure ethereal stream
Whose fountain who shall tell? Before the sun,
Before the heavens thou wert, and at the voice
Of God, as with a mantle didst invest
The rising world of waters dark and deep,
Won from the void and formless infinite.

3.   O Land! O Land!
For all the broken-hearted
The mildest herald by our fate allotted
Beckons, and with inverted torch doth stand
To lead us with a gentle hand
      To the land of the great departed—
      Into the Silent Land!

INVOCATION.

PATRIOTISM.

DESCRIPTION OF FIGURE.

The right foot a slight space in advance; the form elevated to full height; the right arm extended, and the hand just raised to a level with the eyes; the left arm extended, so that the wrist is on a level with the waist; the hand open, the palm horizontal with the body. Such an attitude would be suitable while delivering Scott's lines:

Examples.

1. Breathes there the man with soul so dead,
Who never to himself hath said,
This is my own, my native land!
Whose heart hath ne'er within him burned,
As home his footsteps he hath turned,
From wandering on a foreign strand!
If such there breathe, go, mark him well,
For him no minstrel raptures swell.

2. Thou, too, sail on, O Ship of State!
Sail on, O Union, strong and great!
Humanity, with all its fears,
With all its hopes of future years,
Is hanging breathless on thy fate!
We know what Master laid thy keel,
What workmen wrought thy ribs of steel,
Who made each mast, and sail, and rope,
What anvils rang, what hammers beat,
In what a forge and what a heat,
Were shaped the anchors of thy hope.

3. "Not one State shall be struck from this nation by treason." The fulfillment is at hand. Lifted to the air to-day it proclaims that after four years of war, "Not a State is blotted out." Hail to the flag of our fathers, and our flag! Glory to the banner that has gone through four years black with the tempests of war, to pilot the nation back to peace without dismemberment! And glory be to God, who above all hosts and banners hath ordained victory and shall ordain peace!

PATRIOTISM.

REGRET.

DESCRIPTION OF FIGURE.

The right foot forward; the legs well together; the right arm nearly perpendicular with the body; the hand about one foot from the thigh; the hand nearly open; the thumb and fingers pointing down; the left arm close to the body to the elbow, then slightly extending outward; the head turned a little backward, over the right shoulder, and very slightly inclined forward; the eyes gazing on the distance. This figure would aptly show regret at losing some loved object or country. Thus when Adam leaves Eden, he says:

> "Must I thus leave thee, Paradise? thus leave
> Thee, native soil! these happy walks and shades,
> Fit haunt of gods? where I had hoped to spend,
> Quiet, tho' sad, the respite of that day
> That must be mortal to us both.
>   . . . Thee, lastly, nuptial bower,
> From thee, how shall I part?"

Example.

Oh! that I could return once more to peace and innocence! —that I were once more an infant!—that I were born a beggar! the meanest kind! a peasant of the field! I would toil till the sweat of blood dropped from my brow, to purchase the luxury of one sound sleep—the rapture of a single tear! There *was* a time when I could weep with ease. Oh, days of bliss! Oh, mansion of my fathers! Scenes of my infant years, enjoyed by fond enthusiasm! Will you no more return?—no more exhale your sweets, to cool this burning bosom? Oh, *never, never* shall they return! No more refresh this bosom with the breath of peace! They are gone!—gone forever!

REGRET.

RESOLUTION.

DESCRIPTION OF FIGURE.

The heels well together; the form straight; the left arm nearly perpendicular with the body, and about nine inches from it; the right arm, as far as the elbow close to the body, from the elbow rather extended out; the palms of both hands turned down; the head held firmly but not boastingly erect. This position and manner would indicate firmness, as when Daniel Webster stoutly planted himself on the platform in old Faneuil Hall, and exclaimed:

"I take no step backward!"

Examples.

1.   Rise, fathers, rise! 'tis Rome demands your help;
Rise and revenge her slaughtered citizens,
Or share their fate! The slain of half her Senate
Enrich the fields of Thessaly, while we
Sit here, deliberating in cold debates,
If we should sacrifice our lives to honor,
Or wear them out in servitude and chains.
Rouse up, for shame! Our brothers of Pharsalia
Point at their wounds, and cry aloud, "To battle!"

2.   Rouse ye, Romans! rouse ye, slaves!
Have ye brave sons? Look, in the next fierce brawl,
To see them die. Have ye fair daughters? Look
To see them live, torn from your arms, distained,
Dishonored; and, if ye dare call for justice,
Be answered by the lash.

3. With malice toward none, with charity for all, with firmness in the right, as God gives us to see the right, let us strive on to finish the work we are in, to bind up the nation's wounds, to care for him who shall have borne the battle, and for his widow and his orphans—to do all which may achieve and cherish a just and lasting peace among ourselves and with all nations.

RESOLUTION.

LISTENING.

OUR FAVORITE SELECTIONS

IN

POEMS AND PROSE

FOR

READING AND SPEAKING.

111

THE CREEDS OF THE BELLS.

How sweet the chime of the Sabbath bells!
Each one its creed in music tells,
In tones that float upon the air
As soft as song, as pure as prayer;
And I will put in simple rhyme
The language of the golden chime;
My happy heart with rapture swells
Responsive to the bells, sweet bells!

"In deeds of love excel! excel!"
Chimed out from ivied towers a bell;
"This is the church not built on sands,
Emblem of one not built with hands;
Its forms and sacred rites revere;
Come worship here! Come worship here!
In rituals and faith excel!"
Chimed out the Episcopalian bell.

"Oh, heed the ancient landmarks well!"
In solemn tones exclaimed a bell.
"No progress made by mortal man
Can change the just, eternal plan;
With God there can be nothing new;
Ignore the false, embrace the true,
While all is well! is well! is well!"
Pealed out the good old Dutch church bell.

"Ye purifying waters, swell!"
In mellow tones rang out a bell;
"Though faith alone in Christ can save,
Man must be plunged beneath the wave,
To show the world unfaltering faith
In what the Sacred Scriptures saith:
Oh, swell! ye rising waters, swell!"
Pealed out the clear-toned Baptist bell.

"Not faith alone, but works as well,
Must test the soul!" said a soft bell;
"Come here and cast aside your load,
And work your way along the road,
With faith in God, and faith in man,
And hope in Christ where hope began;
Do well! do well! do well! do well!"
Rang out the Unitarian bell.

"Farewell! farewell! base world, forever!"
In touching tones exclaimed a bell.
"Life is a boon to mortals given
To fit the soul for bliss in heaven;
Do not invoke the avenging rod,
Come here and learn the way to God!
Say to the world, Farewell! farewell!"
Pealed forth the Presbyterian bell.

"To all the truth we tell! we tell!"
Shouted in ecstasies a bell;
"Come, all ye weary wanderers, see!
Our Lord has made salvation free!
Repent, believe, have faith, and then
Be saved, and praise the Lord, Amen!
Salvation's free, we tell! we tell!"
Shouted the Methodistic bell.

"In after life there is no hell!"
In raptures rang a cheerful bell;
"Look up to heaven this holy day,
Where angels wait to lead the way;
There are no fires, no fiends to blight
The future life; be just and right.
No hell! no hell! no hell! no hell!"
Rang out the Universalist bell.

"The Pilgrim Fathers heeded well
My cheerful voice," pealed forth a bell;

"No fetters here to clog the soul;
No abitrary creeds control
The free heart and progressive mind,
That leave the dusty path behind.
Speed well! speed well! speed well! speed well!"
Pealed forth the Independent bell.

"No pope, no pope, to doom to hell!"
The Protestant rang out a bell;
"Great Luther left his fiery zeal
Within the hearts that truly feel
That loyalty to God will be
The fealty that makes men free.
No images where incense fell!"
Rang out old Martin Luther's bell.

"All hail, ye saints in heaven that dwell
Close by the cross!" exclaimed a bell;
"Lean o'er the battlements of bliss,
And deign to bless a world like this;
Let mortals kneel before this shrine—
Adore the water and the wine!
All hail, ye saints, the chorus swell!"
Chimed in the Roman Catholic bell.

"Ye workers who have toiled so well
To save the race!" said a sweet bell;
"With pledge, and badge, and banner, come,
Each brave heart beating like a drum;
Be royal men of noble deeds,
For *love* is holier than creeds;
Drink from the well, the well, the well!"
In rapture rang the Temperance bell.

JOAN OF ARC COSTUME

CABIN PHILOSOPHY.

Jes' turn de back log ober, dar—an' pull your stools up nigher,
An' watch dat 'possum cookin' in de skillet by de fire:
Lemme spread my legs out on de bricks to make my feelin's flow,
An' I'll grin' you out a fac' or two, to take befo' you go.

Now, in dese busy wukin' days, dey's changed de Scripter fashions,
An' you needn't look to mirakuls to furnish you wid rations:
Now, when you's wantin' loaves o' bread, you got to go an' fetch 'em,
An' ef you's wantin' fishes, you mus' dig your wums an' ketch 'em.
For you kin put it down as sartin dat de time is long gone by,
When sassages an' taters use to rain fum out de sky!

Ef you think about it keerfully, and put it to the tes',
You'll diskiver dat de safes' plan is gin'ully de bes';
Ef you stumble on a hornets'-nes' an' make de critters scatter,
You need't stan' dar like a fool an' argerfy de matter;
An' when de yaller fever comes an' settles all aroun',
'Tis better dan de karanteen to shuffle out of town.

Dar's heap o' dreadful music in de very fines' fiddle;
A ripe an' mellow apple may be rotten in de middle;
De wises' lookin' trabeler may be de bigges' fool;
Dar's a lot o' solid kickin' in de humbles' kind o' mule;
De preacher ain't de holies' dat w'ars de meekes' look,
An' does de loudes' bangin' on de kiver of de Book!

De people pays deir bigges' bills in buyin' lots an' lan's;
Dey scatter all deir picayunes aroun' de peanut stan's;
De twenties an' de fifties goes in payin' orf deir rents,
But Heben an' de organ-grinder gits de copper cents.
I nebber likes de cullud man dat thinks too much o' eaten;
Dat frolics froo de wukin' days, and snoozes at de meetin';
Dat jines de Temp'rance 'Ciety, an' keeps a gettin' tight,
An' pulls his water-millions in de middle ob de night!

Dese milerterry nigger chaps, with muskets in deir han's,
Perradin' froo de city to de music ob de ban's,
Had better drop deir guns an' go to marchin' wid deir hoes
An' git an honest libbin' as dey chop de cotton rows,
Or de State may put 'em arter while to drillin' in de ditches,
Wid more'n a single stripe a-runnin' across deir breeches.
Well, you think dat doin' nuffin' 'tall is mighty sof' an' nice,
But it busted up de renters in de lubly paradise!
You see, dey bofe was human bein's, jes' like me an' you,
An' dey couldn't reggerlate deiselves wid not a thing to do;
Wid plenty wuk befo' 'em, an' a cotton crop to make,
Dey'd nebber thought o' loafin' 'roun' an chattin' wid de snake.

OLD FAMILIAR FACES.

CHARLES LAMB.

I HAVE had playmates, I have had companions,
In my days of childhood, in my joyful school days,
All, all are gone, the old familiar faces.

I have been laughing, I have been carousing,
Drinking late, sitting late, with my bosom cronies,
All, all are gone, the old familiar faces.

I loved a love once, fairest among women;
Closed are her doors on me, I must not see her—
All, all are gone, the old familiar faces.

I have a friend, a kinder friend has no man;
Like an ingrate, I left my friend abruptly;
Left him, to muse on the old familiar faces.

Ghost-like I paced round the haunts of my childhood;
Earth seem'd a desert I was bound to traverse,
Seeking to find the old familiar faces.

Friend of my bosom, thou more than a brother,
Why wert thou not born in my father's dwelling?
So might we talk of the old familiar faces—

How some they have died, and some they have left me,
And some are taken from me: all are departed;
All, all are gone, the old familiar faces.

HUNCHBACK JIM.

WHEN all things seem quite against me, and I deem my life a
    curse;
When, for fancied wrongs or real, thoughts of discontent I nurse;
Then I turn with softer feelings to a memory far and dim,
And again, through mist and shadow, stands before me Hunch-
    back Jim.

Pale and ghostly, weak and ailing, never feeling free from pain,
Oh! how bitter were his sufferings, yet who heard him e'er com-
    plain?
Though his sorrows grew around him, he was meek and patient
    still,
Ever gentle in his troubles and resigned to Heaven's will.

I could understand his trials, for he was my friend and mate,
And we worked for years together, coming early, going late;
And he often would, whilst toiling, pause in pain to gasp for
    breath,
Whilst his hands grew hot and fevered, and his face as pale as
    death.

And when I turned round to hold him, and to cool his burning
    brow,
"Thank you, Jack," he'd smile and murmur, "thank you, Jack,
    I'm better now;"
And while he still was speaking, he would stagger, fall, and faint—
Oh! what agony of suffering—yet not one word of complaint.

He went working on in sickness, when he should have been in
  bed,
But he had a feeble mother who looked up to him for bread,
And so on and on with patience, looking forward to the day
Which should make an end to sorrow with the broken mould of
  clay.

Fate condemned him to a city, far from pleasant grove and rill;
But he nursed, with mother's worship, flowers on his window-sill;
And he held each morn communion, in a language strangely
  sweet,
With the little birds that fluttered, picking crumbs upon the
  street.

He had never known the music of a wife's soft loving tone,
Nor the clasp of baby-fingers he could fondly call his own;
But the children all around us used to gladly run to him,
For they knew the loving-kindness of poor childless Hunchback
  Jim.

But at length there came the morning when I missed him at his
  place;
On the bench his tools lay listless, mourning for the wonted face;
Shadowed by a dark foreboding, drearily the daylight passed,
Till uneasy, fearing, doubting, I could go to him at last.

There he lay—his cheek grown hollow—on his narrow little bed,
And my footsteps broke the stillness with a solemn ghostly
  tread:
Yet he sweetly smiled upon me, and he tried to rise and speak,
But his tongue could give no utterance, and he fell back faint and
  weak.

Through the night the lamp burnt dimly, flick'ring with the throes
  of death,
And I sat and grieved, and watched him, in the dull smoke of my
  breath;
When his voice the silence startled: "It's a smiling land," he said,
"And she's coming! Yes, she's coming! Jack, it's Freedom—
  she's ahead!"

Sure, no purer life did Heaven ever summon unto rest;
Patience, faith, and sweet contentment dwelt within that gentle
    breast;
Soaring happy with the angels, do I love to think of him,
And I always feel the better for my thoughts of Hunchback Jim.

GOING AWAY.

THOMAS FROST.

So you've come here to ask me for Susie—don't stand there
    a-hangin' your head;
Leave the shame for them chaps as goes courtin' and ne'er has a
    penny to wed.
You've an eye on the duties of life, John; you're earnest, God-
    fearin' and true,
And I can't say as Susie's been foolish in givin' her heart up to
    you.

Since harvest I've knowd what was comin'; I'm gray, but my eye-
    sight is fair,
And I've seen quite a bit of your actin', at times when you least
    was aware;
I have seen how she'd blush at your footstep, like her mother at
    mine, long ago,
When the whole world of hope lay afore me—my world, that's
    now buried in snow.

And I'd made up my mind, John, to tell you, as I've no objections
    to bring,
For the Book says it's nat'ral for children to leave the old home
    and to cling
To the new ties as crops up around 'em—it's a draught we must
    all swaller down;
So I wish you good luck. Yes, I'm hoarse, boy; caught cold driv-
    ing in from the town.

Shut the door—bring that cheer to the chimley—the storm's pretty
    heavy to-night;
I was thinkin' just now of a Christmas when the snow lay as heavy
    and white
On the fields and the pond and the bushes—over all 'cept one sol-
    it'ry spot
Where the sexton had worked since the daylight—our family burial
    plot.

'Twas a poor kind of Christmas for me, boy, I came from the
    church-yard that day
With a heart just as dead as that dear one we'd left 'neath the
    cover of clay;
And I hoped and I prayed that the Master would soon break my
    life's heavy chain,
And open the gateway of heaven, and give me my loved one again.

That evenin' we sat, me and Susie, and whispered of her we had lost,
While the firelight got lower and lower, and the snow on the
    winders was tossed,
And the wind, that seemed full of our trouble, moaned over the
    desolate farm,
Until—well, worn out with my sorrow—I dropped off, her head
    on my arm.

When I woke it was daylight and clearin', and Susie was singin'
    so gay
The song of the "Old Oaken Bucket," that mother would hum all
    the day;
The kitchen was cozy and tidy—the teapot a puffin' like mad;
The shells all peeled off o' my eggs, too—an old-fashioned way
    mother had.

And, bless her, she wore mother's apron; to this day, though, she
    ha'n't no idea
That I saw her a-usin' that apron to wipe off a poor little tear.
As she stood in the light of that winder every line of her face and
    her hair
Was a joy of the past acted over—'twas her mother, not Susie,
    stood there!

Her mother, when I was like you, John, the wide world around
    me in bloom,
Then I knew that while I had been sleepin' her soul had come
    into this room
With a message from God to our Susie—a plan to relieve all my pain ;
For my heart could not break with its sorrow while I lived my
    life over again.

She has growed more and more like her mother, in face and in
    voice and in ways,
A sweet bit o' gladness and sunshine from out of my happiest days.
I have watched her like misers their treasure ; but to His holy will
    I must bow,
And—bless me, what's this ? I am faint, John—I've not felt my
    loss until now !

So you've come here to ask me for Susie ; well, boy, you're God-
    fearin' and true,
And I can't say she's been over hasty in givin' her heart up to you.
It is hard, but the Book says it's nat'ral, so I'll try to live selfish-
    ness down ;
Dear me ; why, how hoarse I'm gettin'—caught cold drivin' in
    from the town !

THE SNOW STORM.

RALPH WALDO EMERSON.

Announced by all the trumpets of the sky,
Arrives the snow ; and, driving o'er the fields,
Seems nowhere to alight ; the whited air
Hides hills and woods, the river, and the heaven,
And veils the farm-house at the garden's end.
The sled and traveller stopped, the courier's feet
Delayed, all friends shut out, the housemates sit
Around the radiant fire-place, inclosed
In a tumultuous privacy of storm.
    Come, see the north wind's masonry !
Out of an unseen quarry, evermore
Furnished with tile, the fierce artificer
Curves his white bastions with projected roof

Round every windward stake, or tree, or door;
Speeding, the myriad-handed, his wild work
So fanciful, so savage; naught cares he
For number or proportion.   Mockingly,
On coop or kennel he hangs Parian wreaths;
A swan-like form invests the hidded thorn;
Fills up the farmer's lane from wall to wall,
Maugre the farmer's sighs; and at the gate
A tapering turret o'ertops the work.
And when his hours are numbered, and the world
Is all his own, retiring as he were not,
Leaves, when the sun appears, astonished Art
To mimic in slow structures, stone by stone,
Built in an age, the mad wind's night-work,
The frolic architecture of the snow.

THE SNOW.

Oh, the snow, the beautiful snow,
Filling the sky and earth below;
Over the house-tops, over the street,
Over the heads of the people you meet;
Dancing, flirting, skimming along;
Beautiful snow! it cannot do wrong,
Flying to kiss a fair lady's cheek,
Clinging to lips in a frolicsome freak,
Beautiful snow from the heaven above,
Pure as an angel, gentle as love!

Oh, the snow, the beautiful snow,
How the flakes gather and laugh as they go
Whirling about in the maddening fun,
It plays in its glee with every one.
Chasing, laughing, hurrying by;
It lights on the face, and it sparkles the eye.
And the dogs, with a bark and a bound,
Snap at the crystals that eddy around:
The town is alive, and its heart in a glow,
To welcome the coming of beautiful snow.

How wildly the crowd goes swaying along,
Hailing each other with humor and song!
How the gay sledges, like meteors, pass by,
Bright for the moment, then lost to the eye—
Ringing, swinging, dashing they go,
Over the crust of the beautiful snow;
Snow so pure when it falls from the sky,
To be trampled in mud by the crowd rushing by,
To be trampled and tracked by the thousands of feet,
Till it blends with the filth in the horrible street.

Once I was pure as the snow—but I fell!
Fell, like the snow-flakes, from heaven to hell;
Fell, to be trampled as filth in the street;
Fell, to be scoffed, to be spit on and beat,
Pleading, cursing, dreading to die,
Selling my soul to whoever would buy,
Dealing in shame for a morsel of bread,
Hating the living, and fearing the dead;
Merciful God! have I fallen so low?
And yet I was once like the beautiful snow!

Once I was fair as the beautiful snow,
With an eye like a crystal, a heart like its glow;
Once I was loved for my innocent grace,
Flattered and sought for the charms of my face!
Father, mother, sisters, all,
God and myself, I've lost by my fall;
The veriest wretch that goes shivering by,
Will make a wide swoop lest I wander too nigh;
For all that is on, or above me, I know,
There is nothing that's pure as the beautiful snow.

How strange it should be that this beautiful snow
Should fall on a sinner with nowhere to go!
How strange it should be, when the night comes again,
If the snow and the ice struck my desperate brain,
Fainting, freezing, dying alone,
Too wicked for prayer, too weak for a moan

To be heard in the streets of the crazy town,
Gone mad in the joy of the snow coming down;
To be, and so die, in my terrible woe,
With a bed and a shroud of the beautiful snow.

YOUR HOUSE.

BE true to yourself at the start, young man,
  Be true to yourself and God;
Ere you build your house mark well the spot,
Test well the ground, and build you not
  On the sand or the shaking sod.

Dig, dig the foundation deep, young man,
  Plant firmly the outer wall;
Let the props be strong, and the roof be high,
Like an open turret toward the sky,
  Through which heavenly dews may fall.

Let this be the room of the soul, young man,
  When shadows shall herald care,
A chamber with never a roof or thatch
To hinder the light, or door or latch
  To shut in the spirit's prayer.

Build slow and sure; 'tis for life, young man—
  A life that outlives the breath;
For who shall gainsay the Holy Word?
"Their works do follow them," saith the Lord,
  "Therein there is no death."

Build deep, and high, and broad, young man,
  As the needful case demands;
Let your title-deeds be clear and bright,
Till you enter your claim to the Lord of Light,
  For the "House not made with hands."

LITTLE BO-PEEP.

UNFINISHED STILL.

A BABY'S boot and a skein of wool
    Faded, and soiled and soft;
Odd things, you say, and no doubt you're right,
Round a seaman's neck this stormy night,
    Up in the yards aloft.

Most like it's folly; but, mate, look here:
    When first I went to sea,
A woman stood on the far-off strand,
With a wedding-ring on the small, soft hand,
    Which clung so close to me.

My wife—God bless her! The day before,
    She sat beside my foot;
And the sunlight kissed her yellow hair,
And the dainty fingers, deft and fair,
    Knitted a baby's boot.

The voyage was over; I came ashore;
    What, think you, found I there?
A grave the daisies had sprinkled white,
A cottage empty and dark as night,
    And this beside the chair.

The little boot, 'twas unfinished still;
    The tangled skein lay near;
But the knitter had gone away to rest,
With the babe asleep on her quiet breast,
    Down in the church-yard drear.

FAREWELL.

FAREWELL!—but whenever you welcome the hour
That awakens the night-song of mirth in your bower,
Then think of the friend who once welcomed it too.
And forgot his own griefs to be happy with you.

His griefs may return, not a hope may remain
Of the few that have brightened his pathway of pain;
But he ne'er will forget the short vision that threw
Its enchantment around him, while lingering with you.

And still on that evening, when pleasure fills up
To the highest top sparkle each heart and each cup,
Where'er my path lies, be it gloomy or bright,
My soul, happy friends, shall be with you that night;
Shall join in your revels, your sports, and your wiles,
And return to me beaming all o'er with your smiles—
Too blest, if he tells me that, 'mid the gay cheer,
Some kind voice had murmured, "I wish he were here!"

Let Fate do her worst; there are relics of joy,
Bright dreams of the past which she cannot destroy;
Which come in the night-time of sorrow and care,
And bring back the features that joy used to wear.
Long, long be my heart with such memories filled!
Like the vase, in which roses have once been distilled—
You may break, you may shatter the vase if you will,
But the scent of the roses will hang round it still.

MERCY TO ANIMALS.

I would not reckon on my list of friends,
(Though graced with polished manners and fine sense,
Yet wanting sensibility,) the man
Who needlessly sets his foot upon a worm.
An inadvertent step may crush the snail
That crawls at evening in the public path;
But he that has humanity, forewarned,
Will tread aside, and let the reptile live.

The creeping vermin, loathsome to the sight,
And charged perhaps with venom, that intrudes,
A visitor unwelcome, into scenes
Sacred to neatness and repose, the alcove,

The chamber, or refectory, may die;
A necessary act incurs no blame.
Not so when, held within their proper bounds,
And guiltless of offence, they range the air,
Or take their pastime in the spacious field.
There they are privileged; and he that hunts
Or harms them there is guilty of a wrong,
Disturbs the economy of Nature's realm,
Who, when she formed, designed them an abode.

The sum is this: If man's convenience, health,
Or safety interfere, his rights and claims
Are paramount, and must extinguish theirs.
Else they are all—the meanest things that are—
As free to live, and to enjoy that life,
As God was free to form them at the first,
Who in his sovereign wisdom, made them all.
Ye, therefore, who love mercy, teach your sons
To love it too.

CREATION.

THE spacious firmament on high,
With all the blue ethereal sky
And spangled heavens, a shining frame,
Their great Original proclaim.
The unwearied sun from day to day
Does his Creator's power display,
And publishes to every land
The works of an Almighty Hand.

Soon as the evening shades prevail,
The moon takes up the wondrous tale,
And nightly to the listening earth
Repeats the story of her birth:
Whilst all the stars that round her burn,
And all the planets in their turn,
Confirm the tidings as they roll,
And spread the truth from pole to pole.

What, though in solemn silence all
Move round this dark terrestrial ball?
What, though nor real voice nor sound
Amid their radiant orbs be found?
In Reason's ear they all rejoice,
And utter forth a glorious voice;
Forever singing, as they shine,
" The Hand that made us is Divine."

A STRAY SUNBEAM.

My story is a simple one, its moral I don't know;
'Tis not a tale of incidents that happened long ago,
But a simple little story, put into simple rhyme,
That is a temperance lesson just suited to this time.
My hero was a wayward boy, big-hearted, full of fun,
Of brightest brain and intellect, a widow's only son;
For his father was a soldier, who fell in our late strife,
And left the widow with this babe to fight her way through
    life.
Oh, how she fairly worshipped him and lived for him alone,
And waited fondly for the day her darling would be grown,
And be her strong protector through her declining years;
Yes, she worshipped him and watched him, filled alike with hopes
    and fears;
For no father lived to govern the strong and wayward child,
And as he grew up older, he also grew more wild,
Till with drinking, gambling, everything that makes a downward
    start,
He made her life a torture and broke her loving heart.
One night, with boon companions, his brain was all afire,
When a message from a minister came speeding o'er the wire.
He took it without thinking—he read it and was dumb;
'Twas short, but oh, how awful: " Your mother's dying.   Come!"
How quickly sped he homeward, how crazed at every wait,
Till he reached that mother's bedside.   Alas! he came too late.
For the gentle voice was stilled, and, folded on her breast
Were the patient, loving hands that oft had laid her boy to rest,

And the lips that kissed the clustering curls from off his boyhood's
    brow
Were pale, and cold, and lifeless; no words of love came now,
And the heart that he had tortured, which every throb made
    sore,
Was touched by death's cold, icy hand, to beat for him no more.
He sank beside that bedside and smote his half-crazed brain,
And cried: "Come back, my mother!" Too late—he cried in vain;
And his kisses brought no love-light from the eyes that death had
    sealed.
Then with choking sobs of anguish down by her side he kneeled,
And from his heart that just before had known no thought of care,
There went up to his Maker this simple earnest prayer:
"O God, look down in pity upon a humbled one;
Forgive, O God, forgive me, for what my deeds have done;
And give, oh give, to aid me, thine arm, O Mighty One,
And let my mother's spirit watch o'er her wayward son."
And did He hear that prayer? Ah, yes. A newer life began.
The headstrong, reckless youth was changed into a noble man,
Whose deeds were all of kindness, of honor, and of love,
Protected by that spirit that hovered up above,
The spirit of his mother, whom death had claimed before,
And who waited, patient waited, for him at heaven's door.
And liquor did not touch the lips that fervent did appeal,
When by that mother's corpse her son a suppliant did kneel.
A year was gone, he stood beside the grave of that loved one,
And twilight came and darkling clouds shut out the setting sun;
And he murmured "Mother, darling, I'm standing by thy grave;
Thy spirit, ever near me, has made me strong and brave.
Be near me, angel mother, protect me by thy love,
And guide me ever onward, until we meet above."
He stopped, and lo, from through the gloom that marked the clos-
    ing day
There came a little sunbeam, a little silvery ray,
And it lingered there a moment with a soft caressing air
Upon the broad white forehead, 'neath the clustering curls of
    hair.
Oh, do the souls of loved ones watch? They do. Deny not this;
That little straying sunbeam was his angel mother's kiss.

BUSTIN' THE TEMPERANCE MAN.

HOARSELY demanding " Gimme a drink!"
  He sidled up to the bar,
And he handled his glass with the air of one
  Who had often before "been thar."
And a terrible glance shot out of his eyes,
  And over his hearers ran,
As he muttered, "I'm hangin' around the town
  Fer to bust that temp'rance man!

"I've heerd he's a-comin' with singin' and sich,
  And prayin' and heaps of talk;
And allows he'll make all fellers what drink
  Toe square to the temp'rance chalk.
I reckon"—and he pulled out a knife
  That was two feet long or more,
And he handled his pistols familiarly,
  While the crowd made a break for the door.

The good man came, and his voice was kind,
  And his ways were meek and mild;
"But I'm goin' to bust him," the roarer said—
  "Jess wait till he gits me riled."
Then he playfully felt of his pistol belt,
  And took up his place on the stage,
And waited in wrath for the temperance man
  To further excite his rage.

But the orator didn't; he wasn't that sort,
  For he talked right straight to the heart,
And somehow or other the roarer felt
  The trembling tear-drops start.
And he thought of the wife who had loved him well,
  And the children that climbed his knee,
And he said, as the terrible pictures were drawn,
  "He's got it kerrect—that's me!"

Then his thoughts went back to the years gone by,
  When his mother had kissed his brow,
As she tearfully told of the evils of drink,
  And he made her a solemn vow,
That he never should touch the poisonous cup
  Which had ruined so many before;
And the tears fell fast as he lowly said:
  "He's ketchin' me more and more!"

He loosened his hold on his pistols and knife,
  And covered his streaming eyes;
And though it was homely, his prayer went up—
  Straight up to the starlit skies.
Then he signed his name to the temperance pledge,
  And holding it high, said he,
"I came here to bust that temp'rance chap,
  But I reckon he's busted me."

THE PRICE OF A DRINK.

Five cents a glass, does any one think
That that is really the price of a drink?
Five cents a glass, some one might say,
"Why! that isn't very much to pay."
The price of a drink, let him decide
Who has lost his courage and his pride,
And who lies a grovelling heap of clay,
Not far removed from a beast to-day.
The price of a drink? let that one tell
Who sleeps to-night in a murderer's cell.
Honor and virtue, love and truth,
All the glory of pride and youth.
Hope of manhood, the wealth of fame,
High ambition the noble aim;
These are the treasures thrown away
As the price of a drink from day to day.

"Five cents a glass!" How Satan laughed,
As o'er the bar the young man chaffed;
And before the morning the victim lay
With his life-blood ebbing swiftly away;
And that was the price that he paid, alas,
For the pleasure of taking a social glass.
The price of a drink, if you want to know
What some are willing to pay for it, go
To that wretched hovel over there,
With its dingy window, and broken stair,
Where poverty dwells with its hungry brood,
Wild-eyed as demons for lack of food,
Where innocent ones are thus accursed,
To pay the price for another's thirst.
Five cents a glass, oh! if that were all,
The sacrifice would indeed be small;
But the money's worth is the least amount
You pay; whoever will keep an account
Will learn of the terrible waste and blight
That follows that ruinous appetite.
Five cents a glass, does any one think
That that is really the price of a drink?

LADY CLARE.

It was the time when lilies blow,
   And clouds are highest up in air,
Lord Ronald brought a lily-white doe
   To give his cousin, Lady Clare.

I trow they did not part in scorn;
   Lovers long betrothed were they;
They two will wed the morrow morn;
   God's blessing on the day!

"He does not love me for my birth,
   Nor for my lands so broad and fair;

He loves me for my own true worth,
   And that is well," said Lady Clare.

In there came old Alice the nurse,
   Said, "Who was this that went from thee?"
"It was my cousin," said Lady Clare;
   "To-morrow he weds with me."

"Oh, God be thanked!" said Alice the nurse,
   "That all comes round so just and fair:
Lord Ronald is heir of all your lands,
   And you are not the Lady Clare."

"Are ye out of your mind, my nurse, my nurse?"
   Said Lady Clare, "that ye speak so wild?"
"As God's above," said Alice the nurse,
   "I speak the truth; you are my child.

"The old Earl's daughter died at my breast;
   I speak the truth, as I live by bread!
I buried her like my own sweet child,
   And put my child in her stead."

"Falsely, falsely have ye done,
   Oh, mother," she said, "if this be true,
To keep the best man under the sun
   So many years from his due."

"Nay now, my child," said Alice the nurse,
   "But keep the secret for your life,
And all you have will be Lord Ronald's,
   When you are man and wife."

"If I'm a beggar born," she said,
   "I will speak out, for I dare not lie.
Pull off, pull off the brooch of gold,
   And fling the diamond necklace by."

"Nay now, my child," said Alice the nurse,
   "But keep the secret all ye can."
She said, "Not so; but I will know
   If there be any faith in man."

"Nay now, what faith?" said Alice the nurse;
  "The man will cleave unto his right."
"And he shall have it," the lady replied,
  "Tho' I should die to-night."

"Yet give one kiss to your mother dear!
  Alas, my child! I sinned for thee."
"Oh mother, mother, mother," she said,
  "So strange it seems to me.

"Yet here's a kiss for my mother dear,
  My mother dear, if this be so;
And lay your hand upon my head,
  And bless me, mother, ere I go."

She clad herself in a russet gown,
  She was no longer Lady Clare;
She went by dale, and she went by down,
  With a single rose in her hair.

The lily-white doe Lord Ronald had bought
  Leapt up from where she lay,
Dropt her head in the maiden's hand,
  And followed her all the way.

Down stept Lord Ronald from his tower:
  "O Lady Clare, you shame your worth!
Why come you drest like a village maid,
  That are the flower of the earth?"

"If I come drest like a village maid,
  I am but as my fortunes are;
I am a beggar born," she said,
  "And not the Lady Clare."

"Play me no tricks," said Lord Ronald,
  "For I am yours in word and in deed;
Play me no tricks," said Lord Ronald,
  "Your riddle is hard to read."

Oh, and proudly stood she up!
  Her heart within her did not fail;

She looked into Lord Ronald's eyes,
　And told him all her nurse's tale.

He laughed a laugh of merry scorn;
　He turned, and kissed her where she stood.
"If you are not the heiress born,
　And I," said he, "the next in blood,

"If you are not the heiress born,
　And I," said he, "the lawful heir,
We two will wed to-morrow morn,
　And you shall still be Lady Clare."

MARRIED FOR LOVE.

"Yes, Jack Brown was a splendid fellow,
　But married for love, you know;
I remember the girl very well—
　Sweet little Kitty Duffau.
Pretty, and loving, and good,
　And bright as a fairy elf,
I was very much tempted indeed
　To marry Kitty myself.

"But her friends were all of them poor,
　And Kitty had not a cent;
And I knew I should never be
　With 'love in a cottage' content.
So Jack was the lucky wooer,
　Or unlucky—anyway
You can see how shabby his coat,
　And his hair is turning gray.

"But I'm told he thinks himself rich
　With Kitty and homely joys;
A cot far away out of town,
　Full of noisy girls and boys.

Poor Jack! I'm sorry, and all that,
  But of course he very well knew
That fellows who marry for love
  Must drink of the liquor they brew."

And the handsome Augustus smiled,
  His coat was in perfect style,
And women still spoke of his grace,
  And gave him their sweetest smile.
But he thought that night of Jack Brown,
  And said, "I'm growing old;
I think I must really marry
  Some beautiful girl with gold."

Years passed, and the bachelor grew
  Tiresome, and stupid, and old;
He had not been able to find
  The beautiful girl with gold.
Alone with his fancies he dwelt,
  Alone in the crowded town,
Till one day he suddenly met
  The friend of his youth, Jack Brown.

"Why, Gus!" "Why, Jack!" What a meeting!
  Jack was so happy and gay;
The bachelor sighed for content,
  As he followed his friend away
To the cot far out of town,
  Set deep in its orchard trees,
Scented with lilies and roses,
  Cooled with the ocean breeze.

"Why, Jack, what a beautiful place!
  What did it cost?" "Oh, it *grew.*
There were only three rooms at first,
  Then soon the three were too few,
So we added a room now and then;
  And oft in the evening hours,
Kitty, the children and I
  Planted the trees and flowers.

"And they grew as the children grew
   (Jack, Harry, and Grace and Belle)."
"And where are the youngsters now?"
   "All happy and doing well.
Jack went to Spain for our house,—
   His road is level and clear,—
And Harry's a lawyer in town,
   Making three thousand a year.

"And Grace and Belle are well married,—
   They married for love, as is best;
But often our birdies come back
   To visit the dear home nest.
So my sweet wife Kitty and I
   From labor and care may cease;
We have enough, and age can bring
   Nothing but love and peace."

But over and over again
   The bachelor thought that night,
"Home, and wife, and children!
   Jack Brown was, after all, right.
Oh! if in the days of my youth
   I had honestly loved and wed!
For now when I'm old there's no one cares
   Whether I'm living or dead."

THANKSGIVING.

AMID the groanings of the dying year
A sudden stillness falls upon the air,
As if time held his breath and paused in sad and silent
     contemplation;
Nature is wrapped in solitude, as in a pall,
Hushed is the song of merry woodland birds;
The rills but faintly murmur as they flow,
The forest trees have dropped their crown
Of scarlet, gold and russet brown,

And now they stand, like sentinels unplumed,
To see their sire, the year, entombed;
The sere and withered leaves unrustled lie—
No passing breeze to voice their mourning sigh
For the bright, transient glow that fled
When fell from heaven the fatal autumn frosts;
The barren earth is ready for the robe
That hides alike her beauty and decay.
Ere winter comes to break this perfect calm
With the wild storms that mark his cruel sway,
The earth and sea and air await man's voice
To lead their song of love and gratitude.
Raise high the anthem, oh! ye hills, and you,
Ye mountain-tops, reply with joyous shouts,
As from the temples reared by human hands
Now mouldered back to common dust,
By holy prayer and praise so consecrate,
That sunbeams fallen aslant upon the floor
Seem golden pathways leading to the skies,
Ascends this hymn of loving thankfulness:
"Praise God, who blest and brought us to this hour.
Praise Him that plenty crowns our Harvest Home,
Praise Him that by the fulness of His love
Grim death hath walked with conscious steps and slow
Amid the accustomed haunts of men,
Praise Him that His kind hand hath kept all plagues,
And wasting sickness, and distress of war
From this our well-beloved and happy land."
The circling echoes die upon the air,
All heads are bowed, and words of benediction fall
From Him whose trembling hands the bread of life
Hath broke, since these, who now in manly grace
Before Him stand, laughed in their childish glee,
As, dripping with the consecrated flood,
He laid His hand in blessing on their heads,
With kindly words and parting clasp, each turns
From friend and neighbor on this day of days.
For sire and dame have called the children home
To the dear spot that gave them birth,

Around one hearth, the hearts whose warm life-stream
Forth from the self-same fountain glowed;
Within the ruddy glow from cheerful fire
Which gleams out on the frosty air, and tells
Of joys and comforts bounteous and rich,
Prepared to crown this glad Thanksgiving Day.
Here baskets heaped with luscious fruits, and there
The sparkling cider brims the generous cup
Within the hearth-nook, stored by grandma's care;
The nuts for little ones to crack, as round
The ring flies joke, and song, and merry tale,
And spicy odors rise and mingle with
The genial warmth that glows and thrills
Each life-drop in its course to run more swift,
The welcome summons comes, " Partake," and soon
Each guest is placed beside the generous feast.
The gray-haired sire sits in the place where he
The honor of his house maintained when two
Made all the household band, though years have fled,
And many winters turned his locks to snow,
He still presides with courteous ease and grace.
And she who crowns his life with joy, and shares
Alike his blessings and his cares, as they
The rugged path of life together walk,
Smiles on the scene, as if no hour of grief
Had marred her girlish dream of wedded bliss;
"All, all are here, who hold each other dear."
Where other eyes behold an empty space,
To her the place is filled with unseen guests,
Whose presence brings such peace and rest
As falls upon the souls of those who look
Up to the golden throne, where He who reigns
In love and wisdom perfect guides and solves
The chaos and the doubts of this, our world,
And in His own divinely chosen hour
Will turn our sorrow into joy,
And fill our mouths with songs of praise.

THANKS.

THANKS in old age—thanks ere I go,
For health, the midday sun, the impalpable air—for life, mere life,
For precious ever-lingering memories (of you, my mother dear—
      you, father—you, brothers, sisters, friends),
For all my days—not those of peace alone—the days of war the
      same,
For gentle words, caresses, gifts from foreign lands,
For shelter, wine and meat—for sweet appreciation,
(You distant, dim unknown—or young or old—countless, unspeci-
      fied, readers belov'd,
We never met, and ne'er shall meet—and yet our souls embrace,
      long, close and long;)
For beings, groups, love, deeds, words, books—for colors, forms,
For all the brave strong men—devoted, hardy men—who've for-
      ward sprung in freedom's help, all years, all lands,
For braver, stronger, more devoted men—(a special laurel ere I go,
      to life's war's chosen ones,
The cannoneers of song and thought—the great artillerists—the
      foremost leaders, captains of the soul:)
As soldier from an ended war return'd—As traveller out of
      myriads, to the long procession retrospective,
Thanks—joyful thanks!—a soldier's, traveller's thanks.

ALONE.

I MISS you, my darling, my darling,
    The embers burn low on the hearth;
And still is the stir of the household,
    And hushed is the voice of its mirth;
The rain plashes fast on the terrace,
    The wind past the lattices moan,
The midnight chimes out from the minster,
    And I am alone.

I want you, my darling, my darling;
  I am tired with care and with fret;
I would nestle in silence beside you,
  And all but your presence forget,
In the hush of the happiness given
  To those who through trusting have grown
To the fulness of love in contentment;
  But I am alone.

I call you, my darling, my darling!
  My voice echoes back on the heart;
I stretch my arms to you in longing,
  And, lo! they fall empty apart;
I whisper the sweet words you taught me,
  The words that we only have known,
Till the blank of the dumb air is bitter,
  For I am alone.

I need you, my darling, my darling!
  With its yearning my very heart aches;
The load that divides us weighs harder;
  I shrink from the jar that it makes.
Old sorrows rise up to beset me;
  Old doubts make my spirit their own,
Oh, come through the darkness and save me,
  For I am alone.

THE OLD ARM CHAIR.

I LOVE it! I love it! and who shall dare
To chide me for loving that old arm chair?
I've treasured it long as a sainted prize,
I've bedewed it with tears and embalmed it with sighs,
'Tis bound by a thousand bands to my heart
Not a tie will break, not a link will start.
Would you know the spell? A mother sat there!
And a sacred thing is that old arm chair.

In childhood's hour I lingered near
That hallowed seat with a listening ear,
To the gentle words that mother would give,
To fit me to die, and teach me to live.
She told me shame would never betide,
With truth for my creed and God for my guide;
She taught me to lisp my earliest prayer,
As I knelt beside that old arm chair.

I sat and I watched her many a day
When her eye grew dim, and her locks were gray,
And I almost worshipped her when she smiled
And turned from her Bible to bless her child:
Years rolled on, but the last one sped,
My idol was shattered, my earth-star fled!
I felt how much the heart can bear,
When I saw her die in that old arm chair.

'Tis past! 'tis past! but I gaze on it now
With quivering lip and throbbing brow;
'Twas there she nursed me, 'twas there she died,
And memory still flows with the lava tide.
Say it is folly, and deem me weak,
As the scalding drops start down my cheek;
But I love it! I love it! and cannot tear
My soul from my mother's old arm chair!

WE ARE NOT ALWAYS GLAD WHEN WE SMILE.

J. W. RILEY.

We are not always glad when we smile,
　For the heart in a tempest of pain
May live in the guise of a laugh in the eyes,
　As the rainbow may live in the rain;
And the stormless night of our woe
　May hang out a radiant star,
Whose light in the sky of distress is a lie
　As black as the thunder clouds are.

We are not always glad when we smile,
  For the world is so fickle and gay,
That our doubts and our fears, and our griefs and our
      tears,
  Are laughingly hidden away;
And the touch of a frivolous hand
  May oftener wound than caress,
And the kisses that drip from the reveller's lip
  May oftener blister than bless.

We are not always glad when we smile,
  But the conscience is quick to record
That the sorrow and the sin we are holding within
  Is pain in the sight of the Lord;
Yet ever—O ever till pride
  And pretence shall cease to revile,
The inner recess of the heart must confess
  We are not always glad when we smile.

OLD TIMES.

WILLIAM G. EGGLESTON.

How I wish I had lived when creation
  Knew nothing of sin nor of woe,
When each man was in life's highest station,
  And no one was above nor below;
When the world had a roseate glow
  And customs and fashions were new—
Then the earth was an Eden— But no;
  Old times were too good to be true.

In old times no foreign migration
  Turned political cakes into dough;
No man had a wife's poor relation
  To take in pecuniary tow;

Then every man hoed his own row,
  And life had a leaf-tinted hue,
For each mortal was happy— But no;
  Old times were too good to be true.

Time was when a nightly libation
  To Bacchus and Pan was "the go,"
When the cerebral exacerbation
  Was yet undiscovered, although
Men surely should reap what they sow.
  Then a pauper a princess could woo,
And live with her parents— But no;
  Old times were too good to be true.

In old times some slight deviation
  From the right didn't lay a man low,
And a sinner's eternal salvation
  Could be bought for a chapel or so.
Then men didn't go to and fro,
  Telling other folks what they should do;
Each minded his business— But no;
  Old times were too good to be true.

ENVOI.

The worry, the sad tribulation
Of the present is past computation.
Once the question was " What do you know?"
But now 'tis " How much do you owe?"
Shall we rub out? Begin all anew?—
Old times were too good to be true.

AIN'T HE CUTE?

ARRAYED in snow-white pants and vest
  And other raiment fair to view,
  I stood before my sweetheart Sue,—
The charming creature I love best.
"Tell me, and does my costume suit?"
  I asked that apple of my eye,
  And then the charmer made reply—
"Oh, yes, you do look awful cute!"

Although I frequently had heard
  My sweetheart vent her pleasure so,
  I must confess I did not know
The meaning of that favorite word.

But presently at window side
  We stood, and watched the passing throng,
  And soon a donkey passed along,
With ears like sails extending wide.
And gazing at the doleful brute
  My sweetheart gave a merry cry,—
  I quote her language with a sigh,—
"O Charlie, ain't he awful cute?"

OUR OWN.

IF I had known in the morning
  How wearily all the day
    The words unkind
    Would trouble my mind
  I said when you went away;
I had been more careful, darling,
  Nor given you needless pain;
    But we vex "our own"
    With look and tone
  We may never take back again.

For though in the quiet evening
  You may give us the kiss of peace,
    Yet it might be
    That never for me
The pain of the heart should cease.
How many go forth in the morning
  That never come home at night!
    And hearts have broken
    For harsh words spoken
That sorrow can ne'er set right;

We have careful thoughts for the stranger,
  And smiles for the sometime guest;
    But oft for "our own"
    The bitter tone,
Though we love "our own" the best.
Ah! lips with the curve impatient!
  Ah! brow with that look of scorn!
    'Twere a cruel fate
    Were the night too late
To undo the work of the morn.

IN ANSWER.

ROSE HARTWICK THORPE.

"Madam, we miss the train at B——,"
  "But can't you make it, sir?" she gasped.
"Impossible; it leaves at three,
  And we are due a quarter past."
"Is there no way? Oh, tell me then,
  Are you a Christian?" "I am not."
"And are there none among the men
  Who run the train?" "No—I forgot—
I think this fellow over here,
  Oiling the engine, claims to be."
She threw upon the engineer
  A fair face white with agony.

"Are you a Christian?"   "Yes, I am."
  "Then, O sir, won't you pray with me,
All the long way, that God will stay,
  That God will hold the train at B——?"
"'Twill do no good, it's due at three
  And"——"Yes, but God *can* hold the train;
My dying child is calling me,
  And I *must* see her face again.
Oh, *won't you* pray?"   "I will," a nod
  Emphatic, as he takes his place.
When Christians grasp the arm of God
They grasp the power that rules the rod.

Out from the station swept the train,
  On time, swept on past wood and lea;
The engineer, with cheeks aflame,
  Prayed, "O Lord, hold the train at B——,"
Then flung the throttle wide, and like
  Some giant monster of the plain,
With panting sides and mighty strides,
  Past hill and valley swept the train.

A half, a minute, two are gained;
  Along those burnished lines of steel,
His glances leap, each nerve is strained,
  And still he prays with fervent zeal.
Heart, hand and brain, with one accord,
  Work while his pray'r ascends to Heaven,
"Just hold the train eight minutes, Lord,
  And I'll make up the other seven."

With rush and roar through meadow lands,
  Past cottage homes, and green hillsides,
The panting thing obeys his hands,
  And speeds along with giant strides.

They say an accident delayed
  The train a little while; but He
Who listened while his children prayed,
  In answer, held the train at B——.

THE FISHING PARTY.

Wunst we went a-fishing—me
An' my Pa an' Ma—all three,
When there was a picnic, way
Out to Hanch's woods, one day.

An' there was a crick out there,
Where the fishes is, an' where
Little boys 't ain't big and strong
Better have their folks along.

My Pa he jist fished an' fished!
An' my Ma she said she wished
Me an' her was home; an' Pa
Said he wished so wors'n Ma.

Pa said if you talk, er say
Anythin', er sneeze, er play,
Hain' no fish, alive er dead,
Everlgo' to bite, he said.

Purt' nigh dark in town when we
Got back home; and Ma, says she,
Now she'll have a fish fer shore!—
An' she buyed one at the store.

Nen, at supper, Pa he won't
Eat no fish, an' says he don't
Like 'em. An' he pounded me
When I choked!—Ma, didn't he?

FAMILY FINANCIERING.

"They tell me you work for a dollar a day;
How is it you clothe your six boys on such pay?"

"I know you will think it conceited and queer,
But I do it because I'm a good financier."

"There's Pete, John, Jim, and Joe, and William and Ned.
A half dozen boys to be clothed up and fed.

"And I buy for them all good, plain victuals to eat;
But clothing—I only buy clothing for Pete.

"When Pete's clothes are too small for him to get on,
My wife makes 'em over and gives 'em to John.

"When for John, who is ten, they have grown out of date,
She just makes 'em over for Jim, who is eight.

"When for Jim they've become too ragged to fix,
She just makes 'em over for Joe, who is six.

"And when little Joseph can wear 'em no more,
She just makes 'em over for Bill, who is four.

"And when for young Bill they no longer will do,
She just makes 'em over for Ned, who is two.

"So you see if I get enough clothing for Pete,
The family is furnished with clothing complete."

"But when Ned has got through with the clothing, and when
He has thrown it aside—what do you do with it then?

"Why, once more we go round the circle complete,
And begin to use it for patches for Pete."

BLUE AND GRAY.

MARIETTA LILLY SLAIGHT.

On a lovely morn in April,
   In the year of Sixty-one,
A startled cry ran through the land—
   Hostilities begun!
On Sumter's brow, the Stars and Stripes,

The nation's pride and boast,
Had fallen! and a brother's blood
  Been shed by rebel host.
It rolled o'er hill and valley!
  It echoed from each crag!
Till three hundred thousand freemen
  Went forth to save their flag!
Full many a woman's heart grew sad,
  And sank in deep dismay,
When she saw her loved ones going
  To the battles far away;
For well they knew that some brave hearts.
  So loyal, and so true,
Would soon be stilled forever,
  'Neath their shrouds of Union blue.
'Twas *duty* called, and they obeyed—
  They knew their cause was just,
So they yielded up their dear ones,
  For in Heaven they put their trust.
Ah! not alone were they in suffering,
  They, who struggled with the foe;
For the hearts they left behind them
  Bore a fearful weight of woe.
In many a lowly cottage,
  In many a grander home,
Fond hearts grew weary watching
  For the one who ne'er would come.
Not only at the hearthstone
  Where the soldier boy so true,
Went out for country's honor,
  Great things to dare and do—
But other, anxious, loving hearts,
  As they kneeled down to pray,
Remembered at the throne of grace,
  Their gallant Boys in Gray.
Till, from one common brotherhood,
  North, East, and South, and West,
The prayer arose,—" Eternal King,
  Do what Thou deemest best."

And the God of Battles stretched His hand
　To stay the tide of blood,
For a mighty wrong, which He'd condemned,
　Had perished in that flood.
The strife is o'er, the victory ours,
　And the Stars and Stripes again
O'er North and South triumphant wave,
　Cleansed of this blot—this stain.
No solid North, no solid South,
　Let sectional strivings cease,
Our brothers' blood was freely spilled,
　Let it be a bond of peace.
In many a quiet church-yard,
　On many a battle-ground,
Through our re-united country,
　These sleepers pale, are found.
Question not, ye that stand above them,
　On which side did they fight;
Enough to know they perished
　For what they deemed was right.
They're brothers now, God willed it so,
　And in the last great day,
He will not ask them if, on earth,
　They wore the " Blue or Gray."

THE SLEEPING SENTINEL.

FRANCIS DE HAES JANVIER.

[The incidents woven into the following beautiful verses relate to William
Scott, a young soldier from Vermont, who, while on duty as a sentinel at
night, fell asleep, and, having been condemned to die, was pardoned by the
President.　They form a brief record of his life at home and in the field, and
of his glorious death in defence of the Union.]

'Twas in the sultry summer-time, as war's red records show,
When patriot armies rose to meet, a fratricidal foe;
When from the North, and East, and West, like the upheaving sea,
Swept forth Columbia's sons, to make our country truly free.

Within a prison's dismal walls, where shadows veiled decay,
In fetters, on a heap of straw, a youthful soldier lay;
Heart-broken, hopeless, and forlorn, with short and feverish breath,
He waited but th' appointed hour to die a culprit's death.

Yet, but a few brief weeks before, untroubled with a care,
He roamed at will, and freely drew his native mountain air—
Where sparkling streams leap mossy rocks, from many a wood-
      land font,
And waving elms and grassy slopes give beauty to Vermont;—

Where, dwelling in a humble cot, a tiller of the soil,
Encircled by a mother's love, he shared a father's toil—
Till, borne upon the wailing winds, his suffering country's cry
Fired his young heart with fervent zeal, for her to live or die.

Then left he all:—a few fond tears, by firmness half concealed,
A blessing, and a parting prayer, and he was in the field—
The field of strife, whose dews are blood, whose breezes war's hot
      breath,
Whose fruits are garnered in the grave, whose husbandman is Death!

Without a murmur he endured a service new and hard;
But, wearied with a toilsome march, it chanced one night, on
      guard,
He sank, exhausted, at his post, and the gray morning found
His prostrate form—a sentinel asleep upon the ground!

So, in the silence of the night, aweary on the sod,
Sank the disciples, watching near the suffering Son of God;
Yet Jesus, with compassion moved, beheld their heavy eyes,
And, though betrayed to ruthless foes, forgiving, bade them rise!

But God is love—and finite minds can faintly comprehend
How gentle Mercy, in His rule, may with stern Justice blend;
And this poor soldier, seized and bound, found none to justify,
While war's inexorable law decreed that he must die.

———

'Twas night.—In a secluded room, with measured tread and slow,
A statesman of commanding mien paced gravely to and fro.

Oppressed, he pondered on a land by civil discord rent;
On brothers armed in deadly strife:—it was the President!

The woes of thirty millions filled his burdened heart with grief;
Embattled hosts, on land and sea, acknowledged him their chief;
And yet, amid the din of war, he heard the plaintive cry
Of that poor soldier, as he lay in prison, doomed to die!

———

'Twas morning.—On a tented field, and through the heated haze,
Flashed back, from lines of burnished arms, the sun's effulgent
    blaze;
While, from a sombre prison-house, seen slowly to emerge,
A sad procession, o'er the sward, moved to a muffled dirge.

And in the midst, with faltering step, and pale and anxious face,
In manacles, between two guards, a soldier had his place.
A youth—led out to die;—and yet it was not death, but shame,
That smote his gallant heart with dread, and shook his manly
    frame!

Still on, before the marshalled ranks, the train pursued its way
Up to the designated spot, whereon a coffin lay—
His coffin! And, with reeling brain, despairing, desolate—
He took his station by its side, abandoned to his fate!

Then came across his wavering sight strange pictures in the air:
He saw his distant mountain home; he saw his parents there;
He saw them bowed with hopeless grief, through fast declining
    years;
He saw a nameless grave; and then, the vision closed—in tears!

Yet once again. In double file, advancing, then, he saw
Twelve comrades, sternly set apart to execute the law—
But saw no more:—his senses swam—deep darkness settled
    round—
And, shuddering, he awaited now the fatal volley's sound!

Then suddenly was heard the noise of steeds and wheels ap-
    proach,—
And, rolling through a cloud of dust, appeared a stately coach.

On, past the guards, and through the field, its rapid course was
    bent,
Till, halting, 'mid the lines was seen the nation's President!

He came to save that stricken soul, now waking from despair;
And from a thousand voices rose a shout which rent the air!
The pardoned soldier understood the tones of jubilee,
And, bounding from his fetters, blessed the hand that made him
    free!

—————

'Twas Spring.—Within a verdant vale, where Warwick's crystal
    tide
Reflected o'er its peaceful breast, fair fields on either side:
Where birds and flowers combine to cheer a sylvan solitude,
Two threatening armies, face to face, in fierce defiance stood!

Two threatening armies!　One invoked by injured Liberty—
Which bore above its patriot ranks the symbol of the Free;
And one, a rebel horde, beneath a flaunting flag of bars,
A fragment, torn by traitorous hands from Freedom's Stripes and
    Stars!

A sudden burst of smoke and flame, from many a thundering gun,
Proclaimed, along the echoing hills, the conflict had begun;
While shot and shell athwart the stream with fiendish fury sped,
To strew among the living lines the dying and the dead!

Then, louder than the roaring storm, pealed forth the stern com-
    mand,
"Charge! soldiers, charge!" and, at the word, with shouts, a fear-
    less band,
Two hundred heroes from Vermont, rushed onward, through the
    flood,
And upward, o'er the rising ground, they marked their way in
    blood!

The smitten foe before them fled, in terror from his post—
While, unsustained, two hundred stood, to battle with a host!
Then, turning, as the rallying ranks, with murderous fire replied,
They bore the fallen o'er the field, and through the purple tide!

The fallen!   And the first who fell in that unequal strife
Was he whom Mercy sped to save when Justice claimed his life—
The pardoned soldier!   And, while yet the conflict raged around—
While yet his life-blood ebbed away through every gaping wound—

While yet his voice grew tremulous, and death bedimmed his eye—
He called his comrades to attest he had not feared to die!
And, in his last expiring breath, a prayer to Heaven was sent,
That God, with His unfailing grace, would bless our President!

WHISPERIN' BILL.

So you're takin' the census, mister?   There's three of us livin' still,
My wife, an' I, an' our only son, that folks call Whisperin' Bill;
But Bill couldn't tell ye his name, sir, an' so it's hardly worth givin',
For ye see a bullet killed his mind, an' left his body livin'.

Set down for a minute, mister; ye see Bill was only fifteen
At the time o' the war, an' as likely a boy as ever this world has
    seen;
An' what with the news of battles lost, the speeches an' all the
    noise,
I guess every farm in the neighborhood lost a part of its crop o'
    boys.

'Twas harvest-time when Bill left home; every stalk in the fields o'
    rye
Seemed to stand tip-top to see him off an' wave him a fond good-
    bye;
His sweetheart was here with some other girls—the sassy little
    Miss!
An' pretendin' she wanted to whisper 'n his ear, she gave him a
    rousin' kiss.

Oh, he was a handsome feller. an' tender an' brave an' smart,
An' tho' he was bigger than I was, the boy had a woman's heart.
I couldn't control my feelin's. but I tried with all my might,
An' his mother an' me stood a-cryin' till Bill was out o' sight.

His mother she often 'told him when she knew he was goin' away,
That God would take care o' him, maybe, if he didn't forgit to
    pray;
An' on the bloodiest battle-fields, when bullets whizzed in the air,
An' Bill was a-fightin' desperit, he used to whisper a prayer.

Oh, his comrades has often told me that Bill never flinched a bit,
When every second a gap in the ranks told where a ball had hit.
An' one night when the field was covered with the awful harvest
    o' war,
They found my boy 'mongst the martyrs o' the cause he was
    fightin' for.

His fingers were clutched in the dewy grass—oh, no, sir, he wasn't
    dead,
But he lay sort of helpless an' crazy with a rifle-ball in his head;
An' if Bill had really died that night I'd give all I've got worth
    givin';
For ye see the bullet had killed his mind an' left his body livin'.

An officer wrote an' told us how the boy had been hurt in the
    fight,
But he said that the doctors reckoned they could bring him round
    all right,
An' then we heard from a neighbor, disabled at Malvern Hill,
That he thought in the course of a week or so he'd be comin' home
    with Bill.

We was that anxious t' see him we'd set up an' talk o' nights
Till the break o' day had dimmed the stars an' put out the north-
    ern lights;
We waited an' watched for a month or more, an' the Summer was
    nearly past,
When a letter came one day that said they'd started for home at
    last.

I'll never forgit the day Bill came—'twas harvest-time again—
An' the air-bloom over the yellow fields was sweet with the scent o'
    the grain;

The door-yard was full o' the neighbors, who had come to share
    our joy,
An' all of us sent up a mighty cheer at the sight o' that soldier boy.

An' all of a sudden somebody said: "My God! don't the boy know
    his mother?"
An' Bill stood a-whisperin', fearful like, an' starin' from one to
    another:
"Don't be afraid, Bill," said he to himself, as he stood in his coat
    o' blue,
"Why, God'll take care o' you, Bill; God'll take care o' you."

He seemed to be loadin' an' firin' a gun, an' to act like a man who
    hears
The awful roar o' the battle-field a-soundin' in his ears;
I saw that the bullet had touched his brain an' somehow made it
    blind,
With the picture o' war before his eyes an' the fear o' death in his
    mind.

I grasped his hand, an' says I to Bill, "Don't ye remember me?
I'm yer father—don't ye know me? How frightened ye seem to
    be!"
But the boy kep' a-whisperin' to himself, as if 'twas all he knew,
"God'll take care o' you, Bill; God'll take care o' you."

He's never known us since that day, nor his sweetheart, an' never
    will:
Father an' mother an' sweetheart are all the same to Bill.
An' many's the time his mother sets up the whole night through,
An' smooths his head, and says: "Yes, Bill, God'll take care o'
    you."

Unfortunit? Yes, but we can't complain. It's a livin' death more
    sad
When the body clings to a life o' shame an' the soul has gone to
    the bad;
An' Bill is out o' the reach o' harm an' danger of every kind.
We only take care of his body, but God takes care of his mind.

PAT'S CONFEDERATE PIG.

When the war broke out Pat was first to enlist;
He'd fight wid shillaly or fight wid his fist.

Now Patrick was fresh from the ould, ould, sod,
And carried a gun as he'd carry a hod.

He'd soon learn to shoot it, he said, without doubt,
If they'd put in the load phile he'd watch it come out.

But when he had shot it he said he had ruther
Be pricked wid the one end than kicked wid the other!

His rations of whisky he'd drink at one swig,
And never mark time but he'd end wid a jig.

They went to the front.   Pat thought it was hard,
The very first night to be put upon guard.

Yet he paced back and forth, out in the night air,
Rehearsing his "Halt" and "Who goes there?"

"I'm to shoot at the rebels, and aim at the heart—
But how is a stranger to tell 'em apart?

"I'm to know Mr. Rebel, the officers say,
By the clothes he has on, supposed to be gray!

"Is a gintleman judged by the cut of his clothes,
As a toper is tould by the tint of his nose?

"But how can I tell if he come in the dark?
Must I judge of the tree by feelin' the bark?

"I'll be sure of his wardrobe, bedad, ere I shoot!
To be the right man he must wear the wrong suit!

"Oi think I'll surround him, the first thing I say;
Then axe him this question: Your coat, is it gray?

"But I swear by the phiskey that's in my canteen
"I'll not throuble him if he's wearin' the green!"

'Tis late in the night—all the camp is asleep—
When Pat hears a noise that makes his flesh creep!

Something crawls through the brush!   Pat halooes out "Halt!"
And "Who goes there?   If ye're deaf, it's yer fault!"

All he hears is: r-r-ruff!   r-r-ruff! that sounds like a grunt—
"He's a rough, sure!" says Pat, "for his language is blunt!

"March here and surrender me Reb, or ye die!
Come! oud wid yer business!   I'll bet yer a spy——"

U-g-h-w-e-e!   U-g-h-w-e-e!   "Holy murther!   Phat language is that?
'Tis some foreign tongue, I'll be blowed!" muttered Pat.

"An officer, sure—but betwixt you and me,
Is the whole army wid ye?"   U-g-h-w-e-e!   U-g-h-w-e-e!   U-g-h-w-e-e!
       U-g-h-w-e-e!

"We?   We?" muttered Pat.   "Surely that's Frinch for yes!
I'll captur an army!   Hold aisy, I guess.

"I'd bether have help—so I'll call up the crowd.
The rebels are on us!" he cries out aloud.

"The rebels are on us!"   Out rush the whole corps,
Surrounding the woods, which they quickly search o'er—

They sweep through the brush on a double-quick jog,
But all they can find is a dirty white hog!

They cursed till they laughed and laughed till they cried,
For rousing the army next day Pat was tried.

"Court-martialed!" said Pat.   "My offinse is not big!
Phy not try the army for rousin' the pig?

"But, since I've no lawyer to fix up me case
Wid fiction I'll give the truth in its place.

"He came in the night wid a lie in his mouth,
Just loike a Confederate, straight from the South!

"I axed him this question, fur I couldn't see,
Are you, sir, a spy!   Then he answered—We! We!

"As I am a soldier, I ne'er dance a jig,
But he was a rebel disguised as a pig!

" I've brought into court, to confirm phat Oi say,
These bristles, that prove he was wearin' the 'gray!'

" 'Twas all that was left me, I'm sad to relate,
Fur the rest of the pig, sirs, you officers ate!

" I'll spake out me moind—sire I'll die but it's true—
There's many a pig here that's wearin' the 'blue!'"

THE GRAND ARMY BUTTON.

How dear to my heart are the comrades I cherish,
  Who stood by my side in the battle's dark hour;
Who offered their lives that the land should not perish
  The nation our fathers had left us for dower;
Who stayed not to question the right to defend her,
  The mother who bore them, when enemies pres'd,
But, foremost in battle, scorned coward surrender,
  And earned there the signet that shines on their breast—
The little bronze button, the veteran's button,
  The Grand Army button that shines on their breast!

'Tis the token of deeds of true patriot daring;
  'Tis the pledge of high courage in battle's affray;
There earned they the right to the honor of wearing
  The symbol whose glory grows brighter each day.
No jewelled insignia, with diamonds entwining,
  No cross of the Legion, by princes possess'd,
Can ennoble the bosom on which it is shining
  Like the little bronze button they wear on their breast—
The eloquent button, the deed-telling button,
  The Grand Army button that shines on their breast.

Wherever I see one, 'mid plainness or splendor,
  In the garments of wealth or of poverty dres'd,
I know that the heart of a soldier is under
  If the little bronze button but shines on the breast.

So in life will I cherish, all honors exceeding,
    And when, the march past, they shall lay me to rest,
Like a soldier I'll slumber, earth's tumult unheeding,
    And the little bronze button shall sleep on my breast—
The Grand Army button, the heart cherished button,
    The battle won button shall sleep on my breast.

MOTHER'S FOOL.

"'Tis plain to me," said the farmer's wife,
"These boys will make their marks in life.
They never were made to handle a hoe,
And at once to college they ought to go.
Yes, John and Henry,—'tis clear to me,—
Great men in this world are sure to be;
But Tom, he's little above a fool.
So John and Henry must go to school."

"Now, really wife," quoth Farmer Brown,
As he set his mug of cider down,
"Tom does more work in a day, for me,
Than both of his brothers do in three.
Book learnin' will never plant beans or corn,
Nor hoe potatoes—sure as you're born—
Nor mend a rood of broken fence;
For my part give me common sense."

But his wife the roost was bound to rule,
And so "the boys" were sent to school;
While Tom, of course, was left behind,
For his mother said he had no mind.

Five years at school the students spent,
Then each one into business went.
John learned to play the flute and fiddle,
And parted his hair (of course) in the middle;

Though his brother looked rather higher than he,
And hung out his shingle,—"H. Brown, M. D."
Meanwhile at home, their brother Tom
Had taken a "notion" into his head;
Though he said not a word, but trimmed his trees,
And hoed his corn and sowed his peas.
But somehow, either "by hook or crook,"
He managed to read full many a book.

Well, the war broke out, and "Captain Tom"
To battle a hundred soldiers led;
And when the rebel flag went down,
Came marching home as "*General* Brown."
But he went to work on the farm again,
Planted his corn and sowed his grain,
Repaired the house and broken fence;
And people said he had common sense.

Now, common sense was rather rare,
And the state house needed a portion there.
So our "family dunce" moved into town,
And people called him "Governor Brown";
And his brothers, that went to the city school,
Came home to live with mother's fool.

NOBODY'S CHILD.

[The following poem was written by Miss Phila H. Case, and originally appeared in the *Schoolday Magazine*, in March, 1867. It has been noticed and copied and sung and spoken almost everywhere, even finding its way into more than one English publication, and has really become a little "nobody's child," so far as its authorship and due credit are concerned.

Two years ago the poem was set to music and published, in St. Louis, ascribed to "E. D." Later it appeared in books of selections under the name of "Phila H. Child," but has very often appeared without credit whatever.]

ALONE in the dreary, pitiless street,
With my torn old dress, and bare, cold feet,
All day I have wandered to and fro,
Hungry and shivering, and nowhere to go;

The night's coming on in darkness and dread,
And the chill sleet beating upon my bare head.
Oh! why does the wind blow upon me so wild?
Is it because I am nobody's child?

Just over the way there's a flood of light,
And warmth and beauty, and all things bright; .
Beautiful children, in robes so fair,
Are carolling songs in their rapture there.
I wonder if they, in their blissful glee,
Would pity a poor little beggar like me,
Wandering alone in the merciless street,
Naked and shivering, and nothing to eat?

Oh! what shall I do when the night comes down,
In its terrible blackness all over the town?
Shall I lay me down 'neath the angry sky,
On the cold, hard pavement, alone to die,
When the beautiful children their prayers have said,
And their mammas have tucked them up snugly in bed?
For no dear mother on *me* ever smiled,—
Why is it, I wonder, I'm nobody's child?

No father, no mother, no sister, not one
In all the world loves me, e'en the little dogs run
When I wander too near them; 'tis wondrous to see,
How everything shrinks from a beggar like me!
Perhaps 'tis a dream; but sometimes, when I lie
Gazing far up in the dark blue sky,
Watching for hours, some large, bright star,
I fancy the beautiful gates are ajar,

And a host of white-robed nameless things,
Come fluttering o'er me on gilded wings;
A hand that is strangely soft and fair
Caresses gently my tangled hair,
And a voice like the carol of some wild bird—
The sweetest voice that was ever heard—
Calls me many a dear, pet name,
Till my heart and spirit are all aflame.

They tell me of such unbounded love,
And bid me come up to their home above;
And then with such pitiful, sad surprise,
They look at me with their sweet, tender eyes,
And it seems to me, out of the dreary night,
I am going up to that world of light;
And away from the hunger and storm so wild,
I am sure I shall then be somebody's child.

'OSTLER JOE.

I STOOD at eve, as the sun went down, by a grave where a woman
lies,
Who lured men's souls to the shores of sin with the light of her
wanton eyes,
Who sang the song that the siren sang on the treacherous Lurely
height,
Whose face was as fair as a summer day, and whose heart was
black as night.

Yet a blossom I fain would pluck to-day from the garden above
her dust;
Not the languorous lily of soulless sin nor the blood-red rose of
lust,
But a sweet white blossom of holy love that grew in the one green
spot
In the arid desert of Phyrne's life, where all was parched and hot.

* * * * * * *

In the summer when the meadows were aglow with blue and
red,
Joe, the 'ostler of the Magpie, and fair Annie Smith were wed.
Plump was Annie, plump and pretty, with a cheek as white as
snow;
He was anything but handsome, was the Magpie's 'ostler, Joe.

But he won the winsome lassie. They'd a cottage and a cow,
And her matronhood sat lightly on the village beauty's brow.

Sped the months and came a baby—such a blue-eyed baby boy !
Joe was working in the stables when they told him of his joy.

He was rubbing down the horses, and gave them then and there,
All a special feed of clover just in honor of the heir ;
It had been his great ambition, and he told the horses so,
That the Fates might send a baby who might bear the name of
      Joe.

Little Joe the child was christened, and like babies, grew apace ;
He'd his mother's eyes of azure and his father's honest face.
Swift the happy years went over, years of blue and cloudless sky ;
Love was lord of that small cottage, and the tempests passed them
      by.

Passed them by for years, then swiftly burst in fury o'er their home ;
Down the lane by Annie's cottage chanced a gentleman to roam ;
Thrice he came and saw her sitting by the window with her child,
And he nodded to the baby, and the baby laughed and smiled.

So at last it grew to know him—little Joe was nearly four ;
He would call the pretty " gemplun " as he passed the open door,
And one day he ran and caught him, and in child's play pulled
      him in,
And the baby Joe had prayed for brought about the mother's sin.

'Twas the same old wretched story that for ages bards have sung ;
'Twas a woman weak and wanton and a villain's tempting tongue ;
'Twas a picture deftly painted for a silly creature's eyes
Of the Babylonian wonders and the joy that in them lies.

Annie listened and was tempted ; she was tempted and she fell,
As the angels fell from Heaven to the blackest depths of Hell ;
She was promised wealth and splendor and a life of guilty sloth,
Yellow gold for child and husband—and the woman left them
      both.

Home one eve came Joe the 'ostler with a cheery cry of " Wife,"
Finding that which blurred forever all the story of his life.
She had left a silly letter—through the cruel scrawl he spelt ;
Then he sought the lonely bedroom, joined his horny hands and
      knelt.

"Now, O Lord, O God, forgive her, for she ain't to blame!" he
    cried,
"For I owt t'a seen her trouble, and 'a gone away and died.
Why, a wench like her—God bless her!—'twasn't likely as her'd
    rest,
With that bonny head forever on a 'ostler's ragged vest.

"It was kind in her to bear me all this long and happy time,
So for my sake please forgive her, though you count her deed a
    crime;
If so be I don't pray proper, Lord, forgive me, for you see
I can talk all right to 'osses, but I'm nervous like with Thee."

Ne'er a line came to the cottage from the woman who had flown,
Joe, the baby, died that winter, and the man was left alone;
Ne'er a bitter word he uttered, but in silence kissed the rod,
Saving what he told his horses; saving what he told his God.

Far away in mighty London rose the woman into fame,
For her beauty won men's homage, and she prospered in her shame;
Quick from lord to lord she flitted, higher still each prize she won,
And her rival paled beside her as the stars beside the sun.

Next she made the stage her market, and she dragged art's temple
    down
To the level of a show-place for the outcasts of the town.
And the kisses she had given to poor 'Ostler Joe for naught
With their gold and costly jewels rich and titled lovers bought.

Went the years by with flying footsteps while her star was at its
    height,
Then the darkness came on swiftly, and the gloaming turned to
    night.
Shattered strength and faded beauty tore the laurels from her
    brow;
Of the thousands who had worshipped never one came near her
    now

Broken down in health and fortune, men forgot her very name,
Till the news that she was dying woke the echoes of her fame,
And the papers in their gossip mentioned how an "actress" lay
Sick to death in humble lodgings, growing weaker every day.

One there was who read the story in a far-off country place,
And that night the dying woman woke and looked upon his face.
Once again the strong arms clasped her that had clasped her long
    ago,
And the wearied head lay pillowed on the breast of 'Ostler Joe.

All the past had been forgotten, all the sorrow and the shame;
He had found her sick and lonely, and his wife he now could claim;
Since the grand folks who had known her one and all had slunk
    away,
·He could clasp his long lost darling and no man would say him nay.

In his arms death found her lying, in his arms her spirit fled;
And his tears came down in torrents as he knelt beside her dead.
Never once his love had faltered through her base, unhallowed life:
And the stone above her ashes bears the honored name of wife.

    *   *   *   *   *   *   *

That's the blossom I fain would pluck to-day from the garden above
    her dust;
Not the languorous lily of soulless sin nor the blood-red rose of lust:
But a sweet white blossom of holy love that grew in one green spot
In the arid desert of Phyrne's life, where all was parched and hot.

NEW YEAR'S EVE.

Good old days—dear old days
    When my heart beat high and bold—
When the things of earth seemed full of mirth
    And the future a haze of gold!
Oh, merry was I that winter night,
    And gleeful our little one's din,
And tender the grace of my darling's face
    As we watched the New Year in.
But a voice—a spectre's, that mocked at love—
    Came out of the yonder hall;
"Tick-tock, tick-tock!" 'twas the solemn clock
    That ruefully croaked to all.

Yet what knew we of the griefs to be
  In the year we longed to greet?
Love—love was the theme of the sweet, sweet dream
  I fancied might never fleet!
But the spectre stood in that yonder gloom, .
  And these were the words it spake:
"Tick-tock, tick-tock!"—and they seemed to mock
  A heart about to break.

'Tis New Year's eve, and again I watch
  In the old familiar place,
And I'm thinking again of that old time when
  I looked on a dear one's face.
Never a little one hugs my knee,
  And I hear no gleeful shout—
I am sitting alone by the old hearth-stone,
  Watching the old year out.
But I welcome the voice in yonder gloom
  That solemnly calls to me:
"Tick-tock, tick-tock!"—for so the clock
  Tells of a life to be;
"Tick-tock, tick-tock!"—'tis so the clock
  Tells of eternity.

CHRISTMAS-NIGHT IN THE QUARTERS.

IRWIN RUSSELL.

WHEN merry Christmas-day is done,
And Christmas-night is just begun;
While clouds in slow procession drift
To wish the moon-man "Christmas gift,"
Yet linger overhead, to know
What causes all the stir below;
At Uncle Johnny Booker's ball
The darkeys hold high carnival.

From all the country-side they throng,
With laughter, shouts, and scraps of song—
Their whole deportment plainly showing
That to THE FROLIC they are going.
Some take the path with shoes in hand,
To traverse muddy bottom-land;
Aristocrats their steeds bestride—
.Four on a mule, behold them ride!
And ten great oxen draw apace
The wagon from "de oder place,"
With forty guests, whose conversation
Betokens glad anticipation.
Not so with him who drives: old Jim
Is sagely solemn, hard, and grim,
And frolics have no joys for him.
He seldom speaks, but to condemn—
Or utter some wise apothegm—
Or else, some crabbed thought pursuing,
Talk to his team, as now he's doing:

> Come up heah, Star!   Yee-bawee!
>   You alluz is a-laggin'—
> Mus' be you think I's dead,
>   And dis de huss you's draggin'—
> You's mos' too lazy to draw yo' bref,
>   Let 'lone drawin' de waggin.
>
> Dis team—quit bel'rin, sah!
>   De ladies don't submit 'at—
> Dis team—you ol' fool ox,
>   You heah me tell you quit 'at?
> Dis team's—des like de 'Nited States;
>   *Dat's* what I's tryin' to git at!
>
> De people rides behind
>   De pollytishners haulin'—
> Sh'u'd be a well-bruk ox,
>   To foller dat ar callin'—
> An' sometimes nuffin won't do dem steers,
>   But what dey mus' be stallin'!

Woo bahgh!   Buck-kannon!   Yes, sah,
  Sometimes dey will be stickin';
An' den, fus thing dey knows,
  Dey takes a rale good lickin'—
De folks gits down; an' den watch out
  For hommerin' an' kickin'.

Dey blows upon dey hands,
  Den flings 'em wid de nails up,
Jumps up an' cracks dey heels,
  An' pruzntly dey sails up,
An' makes dem oxen hump deysef,
  By twistin' all dey tails up!

In this our age of printer's ink,
'Tis books that show us how to think—
The rule reversed, and set at naught,
That held that books were born of thought;
We form our minds by pedant's rules;
And all we know, is from the schools;
And when we work, or when we play,
We do it in an ordered way—
And Nature's self pronounce a ban on,
Whene'er she dares transgress a canon.
Untrammelled thus, the simple race is,
That "works the craps" on cotton-places!
Original in act and thought,
Because unlearned and untaught,
Observe them at their Christmas party.
How unrestrained their mirth—how hearty!
How many things they say and do,
That never would occur to you!
See Brudder Brown—whose saving grace
Would sanctify a quarter-race—
Out on the crowded floor advance,
To "beg a blessin' on dis dance."

O Mahsr! let dis gath'rin fin' a blessin' in yo' sight!
Don't jedge us hard for what we does—you know its Chrismus
  night;

An' all de balunce ob de year, we does as right's we kin—
Ef dancin's wrong—oh, Mahsr! let de time excuse de sin!

We labors in de vineya'd—workin' hard, an' workin' true—
Now, shorely you won't notus, ef we eats a grape or two,
An' takes a leetle holiday—a leetle restin'-spell—
Bekase, nex' week, we'll start in fresh, an' labor twicet as well.

Remember, Mahsr—min' dis, now—de sinfulness ob sin
Is 'pendin' 'pon de sperrit what we goes an' does it in;
An' in a righchis frame ob min' we's gwine to dance an' sing;
A-feelin' like King David, when he cut de pigeon-wing.

It seems to me—indeed it do—I mebbe mout be wrong—
That people raly *ought* to dance, when Chrismus comes along;
Dey dance bekase dey's happy—like de birds hops in de trees;
De pine-top fiddle soundin' to de blowin' ob de breeze.

We has no ark to dance afore, like Isrul's prophet king;
We has no harp to soun' de chords, to holp us out to sing;
But 'cordin' to de gif's we has we does de bes' we knows—
An' folks don't 'spise de vi'let-flow'r bekase it aint de rose.

You bless us. please sah, eben ef we's doin' wrong to-night;
Kase den we'll need de blessin' more'n ef we's doin' right;
An' let de blessin' stay wid us, untell we comes to die,
An' goes to keep our Chrismus wid dem sheriffs in de sky!

Yes, tell dem preshis anjuls we's a-gwine to jine 'em soon;
Our voices we's a-trainin' for to sing de glory tune;
We's ready when you wants us, an' it aint no matter when—
O Mahsr! call yo' chillen soon, an' take 'em home!   Amen.

> The rev'rend man is scarcely through,
> When all the noise begins anew,
> And with such force assaults the ears,
> That through the din one hardly hears
> Old Fiddling Josey "sound his A"—
> Correct the pitch—begin to play—
> Stop, satisfied—then, with the bow,
> Rap out the signal dancers know:

Git yo' pardners fust kwattilion!
 Stomp yo' feet, an' raise 'em high;
Tune is: "Oh! dat water-million!
 Gwine to git to home bime-bye."
S'lute yo' pardners!—scrape perlitely—
 Don't be bumpin' gin de res'—
Balance all!—now, step out rightly,
 Alluz dance yo' lebbel bes'.
Fo'wa'd foah!—whoop up niggers!
 Back ag'in!—don't be so slow—
Swing cornahs!—min' de figgers;
 When I hollers, den yo' go.
Top ladies cross ober!
 Hol' on, till I takes a dram—
Gemmen solo!—yes I's sober—
 Kaint say how de fiddle am—
Hands around!—hol' up yo' faces,
 Don't be lookin' at yo' feet!
Swing yo' pardners to yo' places!
 Dat's de way—dat's hard to beat.
Sides fo'w'd!—when you's ready—
 Make a bow as low's you kin!
Swing acrost wid opp'site lady!
 Now we'll let you swap agin:
Ladies change!—shet up dat talkin';
 Do yo' talkin' arter while—
Right an' lef'!—don' want no walkin'—
 Make yo' steps, an' show yo' style!

And so the "set" proceeds—its length
Determined by the dancers' strength;
And all agree to yield the palm
For grace and skill, to "Georgy Sam,"
Who stamps so hard, and leaps so high,
"Des watch him!" is the wond'ring cry—
De nigger mus' be, for a fac',
Own cousin to a jumpin'-jack."
On, on, the restless fiddle sounds—
Still chorused by the curs and hounds—

Dance after dance succeeding fast,
Till SUPPER is announced at last.
That scene—but why attempt to show it?
The most inventive modern poet,
In fine new words whose hope and trust is
Could form no phrase to do it justice!
When supper ends—that is not soon—
The fiddle strikes the same old tune;
The dancers pound the floor again,
With all they have of might and main;
Old gossips, *almost* turning pale,
Attend Aunt Cassy's gruesome tale
Of conjurors, and ghosts, and devils,
That in the smoke-house hold their revels
Each drowsy baby droops his head,
Yet scorns the very thought of bed:—
So wears the night; and wears so fast,
All wonder when they find it passed,
And hear the signal sound, to go,
From what few cocks are left to crow.
Then, one and all you hear them shout:
"Hi!   Booker! fotch de banjo out,
An' gib us *one* song 'fore we goes—
One ob de berry bes' you knows!"
Responding to the welcome call,
He takes the banjo from the wall,
And tunes the strings with skill and care—
Then strikes them with a master's air;
And tells, in melody and rhyme,
This legend of the olden time:

Go way, fiddle!—folks is tired o' hearin' you a-squawkin'.
Keep silence fur yo' betters—don't you heah de banjo talkin'?
About de 'possum's tail, she's gwine to lecter—ladies, listen!—
About de ha'r what isn't dar, an' why de ha'r is missin':

"Dar's gwine to be a oberflow," said Noah, lookin' solemn—
For Noah tuk the "Herald," an' he read de ribber column—
An' so he sot his hands to work a-cl'arin' timber patches,
An' 'lowed he's gwine to build a boat to beat de steamah "Natchez."

Ol' Noah kep' a-nailin', an' a-chippin', an' a-sawin';
An' all de wicked neighbors kep' a-laughin' an' a-pshawin';
But Noah didn't min' 'em—knowin' whut wuz gwine to happen;
An' forty days an' forty nights de rain it kep' a-drappin'.

Now, Noah had done cotched a lot ob ebry sort o' beas'es—
Ob all de shows a-trabbelin', it beat 'em all to pieces!
He had a Morgan colt, an' sebral head o' Jarsey cattle—
An' druv 'em 'board de Ark as soon's he heered de thunder rattle.

Den sech anoder fall ob rain!—it come so awful hebby,
De ribber riz immejitly, an' busted troo de lebbee;
De people all wuz drownded out—'cep' Noah an' de critters,
An' men he'd hired to work de boat—an' one to mix de bitters.

De Ark she kep' a-sailin', an' a-sailin', *an'* a-sailin';
De lion got his dander up, an' like to bruk de palin'—
De sarpints hissed—de painters yelled—tell, what wid all de fussin',
You c'u'dn't hardly heah de mate a-bossin' 'roun' an' cussin.'

Now, Ham, de only nigger whut wuz runnin' on de packet,
Got lonesome in de barber-shop, an' c'u'dn't stan' de racket;
An' so, for to amuse he-se'f, he steamed some wood an' bent it,
An' soon he had a banjo made—de fust dat wuz invented.

He wet de ledder, stretched it on; made bridge an' screws, an'
          apron;
An' fitted in a proper neck—'twuz berry long an' tap'rin';
He tuk some tin, an' twisted him a thimble for to ring it;
An' den de moighty question riz: how wuz he gwine to string it?

De 'possum had as fine a tail as dis dat I's a-singin';
De ha'rs so long, an' thick, an' strong,—des fit for banjo stringin';
Dat nigger shaved 'em off as short as wash-day-dinner graces;
An' sorted ub 'em by de size, from little E's to basses.

He strung her, tuned her, struck a jig,—twuz "Nebber min' de
          wedder"—
She soun' like forty-lebben bands a playin' all togedder;
Some went to pattin'; some to dancin'; Noah called de figgers,
An' Ham he sot an' knocked de tune, de happiest ob niggers.

Now, sence dat time—it's mighty strange—dere's not de slightes'
    showin'
Ob any ha'r at all upon de 'possum's tail a-growin';
An' curi's, too,—dat nigger's ways: his people nebber los' 'em—
For whar you finds de nigger—dar's de banjo an' de 'possum!

      The night is spent; and as the day
      Throws up the first faint flash of gray,
      The guests pursue their homeward way;
      And through the field beyond the gin,
      Just as the stars are going in,
      See Santa Claus departing—grieving—
      His own dear Land of Cotton leaving.
      His work is done—he fain would rest,
      Where people know and love him best—
      He pauses—listens—looks about—
      But go he must; his pass is out;
      So, coughing down the rising tears,
      He climbs the fence and disappears.
      And thus observes a colored youth—
      (The common sentiment, in sooth);
      "Oh! what a blessin' tw'u'd ha' been,
      Ef Santy had been born a twin!
      We'd hab two Chrismuses a yeah—
      Or p'r'aps *one* brudder'd *settle* heah!"

ANNIE'S AND WILLIE'S PRAYER.

'Twas the eve before Christmas; "Good-night" had been said,
And Annie and Willie had crept into bed;
There were tears on their pillows, and tears in their eyes,
And each little bosom was heavy with sighs,
For to-night their stern father's command had been given
That they must retire precisely at seven
Instead of eight; for they troubled him more
With questions unheard of than ever before.

He told them he thought this delusion a sin,
No such a thing as "Santa Claus" ever had been,
And he hoped, after this, he should never more hear
How he scrambled down chimneys with presents each year.
And this is the reason why two little heads
So restlessly tossed on their soft, downy beds.

Eight, nine, and the clock in the steeple tolled ten—
Not a word had been spoken by either till then;
When Willie's sad face from the blanket did peep,
And whispered, "Dear Annie, is you fast asleep?"
"Why no, brother Willie," a sweet voice replies,
"I've tried in vain, but I can't shut my eyes;
For somehow it makes me so sorry because
Dear papa had said there is no 'Santa Claus;'
Now *we* know there is, and it can't be denied,
For he came every year before mamma died;
But then I've been thinking that she used to pray,
And God would hear everything mamma would say,
And perhaps she asked Him to send Santa Claus here
With his sacks full of presents he brought every year."
"Well, why tan't we p'ay dest as mamma did then,
And ask Him to send him with presents aden?"
"I've been thinking so, too," and without a word more
Four bare little feet bounded out on the floor,
And four little knees the soft carpet pressed,
And two tiny hands were clasped close to each breast.

"Now, Willie, you know we must firmly believe
That the presents we ask for we're sure to receive,
You must wait just as still till I say amen,
And by that you will know that your turn has come then.—
Dear Jesus, look down on my brother and me,
And grant us the favor we're asking of Thee:
I want a nice book full of pictures, a ring,
A writing desk, too, that shuts with a spring.
Bless papa, dear Jesus, and cause him to see
That Santa Claus loves us as much even as he;
Don't let him get fretful and angry again
At dear brother Willie and Annie, amen!"

" Please, Desus, 'et Santa Taus tome down to-night,
And bring us some presents before it is 'ight.
I want he sould dive me a bright little box,
Full of at'obats, some other nice blocks,
And a bag full of tandy, a book, and a toy,
Amen, and then, Desus, I'll be a dood boy."
Their prayers being ended, they raised up their heads,
And with hearts light and cheerful again sought their beds;
They were soon lost in slumber—both peaceful and deep,
And with fairies in dream-land were roaming in sleep.

Eight, nine, and the little French clock had struck ten
Ere the father had thought of his children again;
He seems now to hear Annie's half-smothered sighs,
And to see the big tears standing in Willie's blue eyes.
"I was harsh with my darlings," he mentally said,
"And should not have sent them so early to bed;
But when I was troubled—my feelings found vent,
For bank stock to-day has gone down ten per cent.
   But of course they've forgot their troubles ere this,
But then I denied them the thrice-asked-for kiss;
But just to make sure I'll steal up to their door,
For I never spoke harsh to my darlings before."

So saying, he softly ascended the stairs.
And arriving at their door heard both of their prayers.
His Annie's "bless papa" draws forth the big tears,
And Willie's grave promise falls sweet on his ears.
"Strange, strange, I've forgotten," said he, with a sigh,
"How I longed when a child to have Christmas draw nigh.
I'll atone for my harshness," he inwardly said,
"By answering their prayers, ere I sleep in my bed."

Then he turned to the stairs and softly went down,
Threw off velvet slippers and silk dressing-gown,
Donned hat, coat, and boots, and was out in the street—
A millionaire facing the cold winter sleet:
He first went to a wonderful "Santa Claus" store
(He knew it, for he'd passed it the day before),
And there he found *crowds* on the same errand as he,
Making purchase of presents, with glad heart and free,

Nor stopped he until he had bought everything
From a box full of candy to a tiny gold ring.
Indeed, he kept adding so much to his store
That the various presents outnumbered a score!
Then homeward he turned with his holiday load,
And with Aunt Mary's aid in the nursery 'twas stowed.
Miss Dolly was seated beneath a pine tree,
By the side of a table spread out for a tea;
A writing desk then in the centre was laid,
And on it a ring for which Annie had prayed;
Four acrobats painted in yellow and red
Stood with a block house on a beautiful sled;
There were balls, dogs and horses, books pleasing to see,
And birds of all colors were perched in the tree;
While Santa Claus, laughing, stood up in the top,
As if getting ready for more presents to drop;
And as the fond father the picture surveyed
He thought for his trouble he had amply been paid.
And he said to himself as he brushed off a tear,
"I'm happier to-night than I have been for a year.
I've enjoyed more true pleasure than ever before.
What care I if bank stock falls ten per cent. more?
Hereafter I'll make it a rule, I believe,
To have Santa Claus visit us each Christmas eve."

So thinking, he gently extinguished the light,
And tripped down-stairs to retire for the night.
As soon as the beams of the bright morning sun
Put the darkness to flight and the stars one by one,
Four little blue eyes out of sleep opened wide,
And at the same moment the presents espied.
Then out of their beds they sprang with a bound,
And the very gifts prayed for were all of them found;
They laughed and they cried in their innocent glee,
And shouted for papa to come quick and see
What presents old Santa Claus had brought in the night
(Just the things they had wanted) and left before light.

"And now," said Annie, in a voice soft and low,
"You'll believe there's a Santa Claus, papa, I know;"

While dear little Willie climbed up on his knee,
Determined no secret between them should be;
And told, in soft whispers, how Annie had said,
That their dear blessed mamma, so long ago dead,
Used to kneel down and pray by the side of her chair,
And that God, up in heaven, had answered her prayer!
"Then we dot up and prayed dust as well as we tould,
And Dod answered our prayers; now wasn't He dood?"
"I should say that He was if He sent you all these,
And knew just what presents my children would please.
(Well, well, let him think so, the dear little elf,
'Twould be cruel to tell him I did it myself.")

Blind father! who caused your stern heart to relent?
And the hasty word spoken so soon to repent?
'Twas the Being who bade you steal softly up-stairs,
And made you his agent to answer their prayers.

THE PIED PIPER OF HAMELIN.

HAMELIN town's in Brunswick,
      By famous Hanover city;
   The river Weser, deep and wide,
   Washes its wall on the southern side;
   A pleasanter spot you never spied;
      But, when begins my ditty,
   Almost five hundred years ago,
   To see the townsfolk suffer so
      From vermin was a pity.

Rats!
They fought the dogs, and killed the cats,
      And bit the babies in the cradles,
   And ate the cheeses out of the vats,
      And licked the soup from the cook's own ladles,
   Split open the kegs of salted sprats,
   Made nests inside men's Sunday hats,
   And even spoiled the women's chats,

By drowning their speaking
With shrieking and squeaking
In fifty different sharps and flats.
At last the people in a body
To the Town Hall came flocking:
"'Tis clear," cried they, "our Mayor's a noddy;
And as for our Corporation—shocking
To think we buy gowns lined with ermine
For dolts that can't or won't determine
What's best to rid us of our vermin!
You hope, because you're old and obese,
To find in the furry civic robe ease?
Rouse up, sirs! Give your brains a racking
To find the remedy we're lacking,
Or, sure as fate, we'll send you packing!"
At this the Mayor and Corporation
Quaked with a mighty consternation.
An hour they sat in council,
At length the Mayor broke silence,
"O for a trap, a trap, a trap!"
Just as he said this, what should hap
At the chamber door but a gentle tap!
"Bless us," cried the Mayor, "what's that?
Only a scraping of shoes on the mat?
Anything like the sound of a rat
Makes my heart go pit-a-pat!
Come in!"—the Mayor cried, looking bigger:
And in did come the strangest figure,
His queer long coat from heel to head
Was half of yellow and half of red:
And he himself was tall and thin,
With sharp blue eyes, each like a pin,
He advanced to the Council-table:
And, "Please your honors," said he, "I'm able,
By means of a secret charm, to draw
All creatures living beneath the sun,
That creep, or swim, or fly, or run."
(And his fingers, they noticed, were ever straying,
As if impatient to be playing

Upon this pipe, as low it dangled
Over his vesture so old-fangled.)
"If I can rid your town of rats,
   Will you give me a thousand guilders?"
"One? fifty thousand!"—was the exclamation
Of the astonished Mayor and Corporation.

   Into the street the Piper stept,
To blow the pipe his lips he wrinkled,
And green and blue his sharp eyes twinkled,
And ere three shrill notes the pipe uttered,
You heard as if an army muttered;
   And out of the house the rats came tumbling.
Great rats, small rats, lean rats, brawny rats,
Brown rats, black rats, gray rats, tawny rats,
Brothers, sisters, husbands, wives—
Followed the Piper for their lives.

   Until they came to the river Weser,
Wherein all plunged and perished
   —Save one, who, stout as Julius Cæsar,
Swam across, and lived to carry
To Rat-land home his commentary,
Which was: "At the first shrill notes of the pipe,
I heard a sound as of scraping tripe,
And a moving away of pickle-tub-boards,
And a leaving ajar of conserve cupboards,
And it seemed as if a voice
   (Sweeter far than by harp or by psaltery
Is breathed) called out: 'O rats, rejoice!

   The world is grown to one vast drysaltery!'"
You should have heard the Hamelin people
Ringing the bells till they rocked the steeple.
"Go," cried the Mayor, "and get long poles!
Poke out the nests and block up the holes!

   Consult with carpenters and builders,
And leave in our town not even a trace
Of the rats!"—when suddenly up the face
Of the Piper perked in the market-place,
   With a "First, if you please, my thousand guild-
      ers!"

A thousand guilders!   The Mayor looked blue;
So did the Corporation too.
To pay this sum to a wandering fellow
With a gipsy coat of red and yellow!
"Besides," quoth the Mayor, with a knowing wink,
"Our business was done at the river's brink;
But, as for the guilders, what we spoke
Of them, as you very well know, was in joke.
Besides, our losses have made us thrifty;
A thousand guilders!   Come, take fifty!"
The Piper's face fell, and he cried:
"No trifling!   I can't wait: beside,
    With you, don't think I'll bate a stiver!
And folks who put me in a passion
May find me pipe to another fashion."
"How?" cried the Mayor, "d'ye think I'll brook
Being worse treated than a cook?
You threaten us, fellow?   Do your worst;
Blow your pipe there till you burst."
    Once more he stept into the street:
And to his lips again
Laid his long pipe of smooth straight cane
And ere he blew three notes (such sweet
    Soft notes as yet musician's cunning
Never gave the enraptured air),
There was a rustling, that seemed like a bustling
Of merry crowds justling, at pitching and hustling,
Small feet were pattering, wooden shoes clattering,
Little hands clapping, and little tongues chattering,
And, like fowls in a farm-yard when barley is scatter-
        ing,
    Out came the children running.
The Mayor was dumb, and the Council stood
As if they were changed into blocks of wood,
And could only follow with the eye
That joyous crowd at the Piper's back.
As the Piper turned from the High Street
To where the Weser rolled its waters
Right in the way of their sons and daughters!

However he turned from south to west,
And to Koppelberg Hill his steps addressed,
"He never can cross that mighty top!
And we shall see our children stop!"
When lo! as they reached the mountain's side,
A wondrous portal opened wide,
As if a cavern were suddenly hollowed;
And the Piper advanced and the children followed,
And when all were in to the very last,
The door in the mountain-side shut fast.
　　Did I say all? No! one was lame,
And could not dance the whole of the way;
　　And in after-years, if you would blame
His sadness, he was used to say:
"It's dull in our town since my playmates left;
I can't forget that I'm bereft
Of all the pleasant sights they see,
Which the Piper also promised me:
For he led us, he said, to a joyous land,
Joining the town, and just at hand.
　　My lame foot would be speedily cured,
The music stopped, and I stood still,
And found myself outside the hill."
The Mayor sent east, west, north, and south,
To offer the Piper by word of mouth,
　　Wherever it was men's lot to find him,
Silver and gold to his heart's content,
If he'd only return the way he went,
　　And bring the children all behind him.
But when they saw 'twas a lost endeavor,
And Piper and dancers were gone forever,
　　They wrote the story on a column,
And on the great church window painted
The same, to make the world acquainted
How their children were stolen away,
And there it stands to this very day.
And I must not omit to say
That in Transylvania there's a tribe
Of alien people that ascribe

The outlandish ways and dress,
On which their neighbors lay such stress,
To their fathers and mothers having risen
Out of some subterraneous prison,
Into which they were trepanned
Long time ago in a mighty band
Out of Hamelin town in Brunswick land,
But how or why they don't understand.
So, Willy, let you and me be wipers
Of scores out with all men—especially pipers:
And, whether they pipe us free from rats or from mice,
If we've promised them aught, let us keep our promise

NO SECTS IN HEAVEN.

Talking of sects till late one eve,
Of the various doctrines the saints believe,
That night I stood, in a troubled dream,
By the side of a darkly flowing stream.

And a "Churchman" down to the river came;
When I heard a strange voice call his name:
"Good father, stop; when you cross this tide,
You must leave your robes on the other side."

But the aged father did not mind,
And his long gown floated out behind,
As down to the stream his way he took,
His pale hands clasping a gilt-edged book.

"I'm bound for heaven; and when I'm there,
Shall want my Book of Common Prayer;
And, though I put on a starry crown,
I should feel quite lost without my gown."

Then he fixed his eyes on the shining track,
But his gown was heavy and held him back;

And the poor old father tried in vain
A single step in the flood to gain.

I saw him again on the other side,
But his silk gown floated on the tide;
And no one asked, in that blissful spot,
Whether he belonged to the "church" or not.

Then down to the river a Quaker strayed;
His dress of a sober hue was made:
"My coat and hat must all be gray—
I cannot go any other way."

Then he buttoned his coat straight up to his chin,
And staidly, solemnly waded in,
And his broad-brimmed hat he pulled down tight,
Over his forehead so cold and white.

But a strong wind carried away his hat,
A moment he silently sighed over that;
And then, as he gazed to the farther shore,
The coat slipped off, and was seen no more.

As he entered heaven his suit of gray
Went quietly sailing, away, away;
And none of the angels questioned him
About the width of his beaver's brim.

Next came Dr. Watts, with a bundle of psalms
Tied nicely up in his aged arms,
And hymns as many, a very wise thing,
That the people in heaven "all 'round" might sing.

But I thought that he heaved an anxious sigh,
As he saw that the river ran broad and high;
And looked rather surprised as one by one
The psalms and hymns in the wave went down.

And after him, with his MSS.,
Came Wesley, the pattern of godliness;
But he cried, "Dear me! what shall I do?
The water has soaked them through and through."

And there on the river far and wide,
Away they went down the swollen tide;
And the saint, astonished, passed through alone,
Without his manuscripts, up to the throne.

Then, gravely walking, two saints by name
Down to the stream together came;
But as they stopped at the river's brink,
I saw one saint from the other shrink.

"Sprinkled or plunged? may I ask you, friend,
How you attained to life's great end?"
"Thus, with a few drops on my brow."
"But *I* have been dipped as you see me now.

"And I really think it will hardly do,
As I'm 'close communion,' to cross with you.
You're bound, I know, to the realms of bliss,
But you must go that way, and I'll go this."

Then straightway plunging with all his might,
Away to the left—his friend to the right,
Apart they went from this world of sin,
But at last together they entered in.

And now, when the river was rolling on,
A Presbyterian church went down;
Of women there seemed an innumerable throng,
But the men I could count as they passed along.

And concerning the road they never could agree,
The *old* or the *new* way, which it could be,
Nor never a moment stopped to think
That both would lead to the river's brink.

And a sound of murmuring, long and loud,
Came ever up from the moving crowd;
"You're in the old way, and I'm in the new;
That is the false, and this is the true"—
Or "I'm in the old way, and you're in the new;
That is the false, and *this* is the true."

But the *brethren* only seemed to speak:
Modest the sisters walked and meek,
And if ever one of them chanced to say
What trouble she met on the way,
How she longed to pass to the other side,
Nor feared to cross over the swelling tide,

A voice arose from the brethren then,
"Let no one speak but the holy men;
For have ye not heard the words of Paul,
'Oh, let the women keep silence all?'"

I watched them long in my curious dream,
Till they stood by the borders of the stream;
Then, just as I thought, the two ways met;
But all the brethren were talking yet,
And would talk on till the heaving tide
Carried them over side by side—
Side by side, for the way was one;
The toilsome journey of life was done;
And all who in Christ the Saviour died,
Came out alike on the other side.

No forms, or crosses, or books had they,
No gowns of silk or suits of gray;
No creeds to guide them, or MSS.;
For all had put on Christ's righteousness.

PAPA'S LETTER.

I was sitting in my study,
    Writing letters, when I heard,
"Please, dear mamma, Mary told me
    Mamma mustn't be 'isturbed;

"But I's tired of the kitty,
    Want some ozzer fing to do!
Witing letters, is 'ou, mamma?
    Tan't I wite a letter, too?"

"Not now, darling, mamma's busy;
  Run and play with kitty, now."
"No, no, mamma, me wite letter—
  Tan if 'ou will show me how."

I would paint my darling's portrait
  As his sweet eyes searched my face—
Hair of gold and eyes of azure,
  Form of childish, witching grace.

But the eager face was clouded,
  As I slowly shook my head,
Till I said, "I'll make a letter
  Of you, darling boy, instead."

So I parted back the tresses
  From his forehead high and white,
And a stamp in sport I pasted
  'Mid its waves of golden light.

Then I said, "Now, little letter,
  Go away, and bear good news."
And I smiled as down the staircase
  Clattered loud the little shoes.

Leaving me, the darling hurried
  Down to Mary in his glee:
"Mamma's witing lots of letters;
  I's a letter, Mary—see?"

No one heard the little prattler
  As once more he climbed the stair,
Reached his little cap and tippet,
  Standing on the entry chair.

No one heard the front door open,
  No one saw the golden hair
As it floated o'er his shoulders
  In the crisp October air.

Down the street the baby hastened
  Till he reached the office door.

"I's a letter, Mr. Postman,
  Is there room for any more?

"'Cause dis letter's doin' to papa:
  Papa lives with God, 'ou know.
Mamma sent me for a letter;
  Does 'ou fink 'at I tan go?"

But the clerk in wonder answered,
  "Not to-day, my little man."
"Den I'll find anuzzer office,
  'Cause I must go if I tan."

Fain the clerk would have detained him,
  But the pleading face was gone,
And the little feet were hastening—
  By the busy crowd swept on.

Suddenly the crowd was parted,
  People fled to left and right
As a pair of maddened horses
  At the moment dashed in sight.

No one saw the baby figure—
  No one saw the golden hair,
Till a voice of frightened sweetness
  Rang out on the autumn air.

'Twas too late—a moment only
  Stood the beauteous vision there,
Then the little face lay lifeless,
  Covered o'er with golden hair.

Reverently they raised my darling,
  Brushed away the curls of gold,
Saw the stamp upon the forehead,
  Growing now so icy cold.

Not a mark the face disfigured,
  Showing where a hoof had trod;
But the little life was ended—
  "Papa's letter" was with God.

AN ORDER.

MRS. SARAH DE W. GAMWELL.

" You heard my order, painter,
  The very words I said:
All in your finest colors,
  Vermilion and Indian red!
And those wonderful combinations
  An artist only knows,
Like moonlight on the water,
  Like dewdrops on a rose.

" From the top to the bottom, painter,
  The very words I said!
And up from the sure foundations
  To the arches overhead;
Make them like things of beauty,
  Garnish and decorate all;
Each room, each frieze and ceiling,
  Each balustrade and hall.

" But there's one exception, painter,
  (I spoke of it before),
A little mark on a panel
  Behind a closet door!
Only a mark on a panel
  Behind a closet door,
And the pencilled words below it
  Are ' Mabel, aged four.'

" You have my order, painter,
  You know my secret, too!
No hand may touch that panel
  Till ' heaven and earth are new,'
And I go to meet my darling,
  Not lost, but gone before;
I shall know her when I see her,
  My ' Mabel, aged four.' "

MORTALITY.

[This was President Lincoln's favorite poem. He knew every word and line of it, and it is said that he often took great pleasure in his meditative moods in repeating the poem. The words in themselves are well worth any one's attention, but since having been the favorite poem of our martyred President it finds a warmer spot in all our hearts.]

OH, why should the spirit of mortal be proud?
Like a fast-flitting meteor, a fast-flying cloud,
A flash of the lightning, a break of the wave,
He passes from life to his rest in the grave.

The leaves of the oak and the willow shall fade,
Be scattered around and together be laid;
And the young and the old, and the low and the high,
Shall moulder to dust and together shall lie.

The child that a mother attended and loved,
The mother that infant's affection that proved,
The husband that mother and infant that blessed,
Each, all, are away to their dwelling of rest.

The maid on whose cheek, on whose brow, in whose eye,
Shone beauty and pleasure,—her triumphs are by;
And the memory of those that beloved her and praised,
Are alike from the minds of the living erased.

The hand of the king that the sceptre hath borne,
The brow of the priest that the mitre hath worn,
The eye of the sage, and the heart of the brave,
Are hidden and lost in the depths of the grave.

The peasant whose lot was to sow and to reap,
The herdsman who climbed with his goats to the steep,
The beggar that wandered in search of his bread,
Have faded away like the grass that we tread.

The saint that enjoyed the communion of Heaven,
The sinner that dared to remain unforgiven,

The wise and the foolish, the guilty and just,
Have quietly mingled their bones in the dust.

So the multitude goes, like the flower and the weed,
That wither away to let others succeed;
So the multitude comes, even those we behold,
To repeat every tale that hath often been told.

For we are the same that our fathers have been;
We see the same sights that our fathers have seen,—
We drink the same stream, and we feel the same sun,
And we run the same course that our fathers have run.

The thoughts we are thinking our fathers would think;
From the death we are shrinking from, they too would shrink;
To the life we are clinging to, they too would cling;
But it speeds from the earth like a bird on the wing.

They loved, but their story we cannot unfold;
They scorned, but the heart of the haughty is cold;
They grieved, but no wail from their slumbers may come;
They joyed, but the voice of their gladness is dumb.

They died,—ay! they died; and we things that are now,
Who walk on the turf that lies over their brow,
Who make in their dwellings a transient abode,
Meet the changes they met on their pilgrimage road.

Yea! hope and despondency, pleasure and pain,
Are mingled together like sunshine and rain;
And the smile and the tear and the song and the dirge
Still follow each other, like surge upon surge.

'Tis the wink of an eye, 'tis the draught of a breath,
From the blossom of health to the paleness of death,
From the gilded saloon to the bier and the shroud,—
Oh, why should the spirit of mortal be proud?

ONLY A BABY'S HAND.

"Big time to-night," the drummers said,
    As to supper they sat them down;
"To-morrow's Sunday, and now's our chance
    To illuminate the town."

"Good!" cries Bill Barnes, the jolliest—
    The favorite of all;
"Yes; let's forget our troubles now
    And hold high carnival."

The supper done, the mail arrives;
    Each man his letters scanning,
With fresh quotations—up or down—
    His busy brain is cramming.

But Bill—"why, what's come over him—
    Why turn so quick about?"
He says—just as his pards start forth,
    "I guess I won't go out."

His letter bore no written word,
    No prayer from vice to flee;
Only a tracing of a hand—
    A baby's hand—of three.

What a picture comes before his mind—
    What does his memory paint?
A baby at her mother's knee—
    His little white-robed saint.

What cares a man for ridicule
    Who wins a victory grand?
Bill slept in peace, his brow was smoothed
    By a shadowy little hand.

Naught like the weak things of the world
    The power of sin withstand;
No shield between man's soul and wrong
    Like a little baby hand.

PAUL REVERE'S RIDE.

LISTEN, my children, and you shall hear
Of the midnight ride of Paul Revere,
    On the eighteenth of April, in Seventy-five;
    Hardly a man is now alive
Who remembers that famous day and year.

He said to his friend, "If the British march
    By land or sea from the town to-night,
Hang a lantern aloft in the belfry-arch
    Of the North Church tower, as a signal light,—
One if by land, and two if by sea;
And I on the opposite shore will be,
Ready to ride and spread the alarm
Through every Middlesex village and farm,
For the country-folk to be up and to arm."

Meanwhile his friend, through alley and street,
    Wanders and watches with eager ears,
    Till in the silence around him he hears
        The muster of men at the barrack-door,
The sound of arms, and the tramp of feet,
    And the measured tread of the grenadiers
        Marching down to their boats on the shore.
Then he climbed to the tower of the church,
Up the wooden stairs, with stealthy tread,
To the belfry-chamber overhead.

Meanwhile, impatient to mount and ride,
Booted and spurred, with a heavy stride,
    On the opposite shore walked Paul Revere.
Now he patted his horse's side,
    Now gazed on the landscape far and near,
Then impetuous stamped the earth,
And turned and tightened his saddle-girth;
But mostly he watched with eager search
The belfry-tower of the old North Church,

As it rose above the graves on the hill,
Lonely, and spectral, and sombre, and still.

And lo! as he looks, on the belfry's height
A glimmer, and then a gleam of light!
  He springs to the saddle, the bridle he turns,
But lingers and gazes, till full on his sight
  A second lamp in the belfry burns!
A hurry of hoofs in a village street,
  A shape in the moonlight, a bulk in the dark,
  And beneath from the pebbles, in passing, a spark
Struck out by a steed that flies fearless and fleet,—
  That was all! And yet, through the gloom and the light,
  The fate of a nation was riding that night;
  And the spark struck out by that steed, in his flight,
Kindled the land into flame with its heat.

It was twelve by the village clock,
  When he crossed the bridge into Medford town.
It was one by the village clock,
  When he rode into Lexington.
He saw the gilded weathercock
  Swim in the moonlight as he passed,
And the meeting-house windows, blank and bare,
Gaze at him with a spectral glare,
  As if they already stood aghast
At the bloody work they would look upon.

You know the rest. In the books you have read
How the British regulars fired and fled,—
How the farmers gave them ball for ball,
From behind each fence and farmyard-wall,
Chasing the red-coats down the lane,
Then crossing the fields to emerge again
Under the trees at the turn of the road,
And only pausing to fire and load.

So through the night rode Paul Revere;
  And so through the night went his cry of alarm
  To every Middlesex village and farm,—
A cry of defiance, and not of fear,—

A voice in the darkness, a knock at the door,
And a word that shall echo for evermore!
For, borne on the night-wind of the Past,
Through all our history, to the last,
  In the hour of darkness and peril and need,
The people will waken and listen to hear
  The hurrying hoof-beat of that steed,
And the midnight message of Paul Revere.

ANNABEL LEE.

It was many and many a year ago,
  In a kingdom by the sea,
That a maiden lived whom you may know
  By the name of Annabel Lee;
And this maiden she lived with no other thought
  Than to love and be loved by me.

I was a child, and she was a child
  In this kingdom by the sea;
But we loved with a love that was more than love,
  I and my Annabel Lee,—
With a love that the winged seraphs of heaven
  Coveted her and me.

And this was the reason that long ago,
  In this kingdom by the sea,
That her high-born kinsman came,
  And bore her away from me,
To shut her up in a sepulchre,
  In this kingdom by the sea.

The angels, not so happy in heaven,
  Went envying her and me,
Yes! that was the reason (as all men know)
  In this kingdom by the sea,
That the wind came out of the cloud by night,
  Chilling and killing my Annabel Lee.

But our love it was stronger by far than the love
  Of those who were older than we,
  Of many far wiser than we;
And neither the angels in heaven above
  Nor the demons down under the sea,
Can ever dissever my soul from the soul
  Of the beautiful Annabel Lee.

For the moon never beams without bringing me dreams
  Of the beautiful Annabel Lee,
And the stars never rise but I feel the bright eyes
  Of the beautiful Annabel Lee.
And so, all the night-tide I lie down by the side
Of my darling, my darling, my life, and my bride,
  In her sepulchre there by the sea,
  In her tomb by the sounding sea.

LEADVILLE JIM.

He came to town one winter day;
He had walked from Leadville all the way;
He went to work in a lumber yard,
And wrote a letter that ran: "Dear Pard,
Stick to the claim, whatever you do,
And remember that Jim will see you through."
For, to quote his partner, "they owned a lead
Mid der shplendidest brospects, und nodings to ead."

When Sunday came he brushed his coat,
And tied a handkerchief round his throat,
Though his feet in hob-nailed shoes were shod,
He ventured to enter the house of God.

When, sharply scanning his ill-clad feet,
The usher gave him the rearmost seat.
  By chance the loveliest girl in town
Came late to the house of God that day,
And, scorning to make a vain display

Of her brand new, beautiful Sunday gown,
  Beside the threadbare man sat down.
When the organ pealed she turned to Jim,
And kindly offered her book to him.
Held half herself, and showed him the place,
And then, with genuine Christian grace,
She sang soprano, and he sang bass,
While up in the choir the basso growled,
The tenor, soprano, and alto howled,
And the banker's son looked back and scowled.

The preacher closed his sermon grand
With an invitation to "join the band."
Then quietly from his seat uprose
The miner, dressed in his threadbare clothes,
And over the carpeted floor walked down,
The aisle of the richest church in town.
In spite of the general shudder and frown,
He joined the church and went his way;
But he did not know he had walked that day
O'er the sensitive corns of pride, rough-shod;
For the miner was thinking just then of God.
A little lonely it seemed to him
  In the rearmost pew when Sunday came;
One deacon had dubbed him "Leadville Jim,"
  But the rest had forgotten quite his name.

And yet 'twas never more strange than true,
God sat with the man in the rearmost pew,
Strengthened his arm in the lumber yard,
And away in the mountains helped his "Pard."

But after awhile a letter came
Which ran: "Dear Yim—I haf sell our claim,
Und I send you a jeek for half der same.
A million, I dought, was a pooty good brice,
Und my *heart* said to sell, so I took its advice—
You know what I mean if you lofe a fraulein—
Good-bye. I am going to marry Katrine."

The hob-nailed shoes and rusty coat
Were laid aside, and another note
Came rippling out of the public throat,
The miner was now no longer "Jim,"
But the deacons "Brothered" and "Mistered" him;
Took their buggies and showed him round.
And, more than the fact of his wealth, they found
Through the papers which told the wondrous tale,
That the fellow had led his class at Yale.
Ah! the maidens admired his splendid shape,
Which the tailor had matched with careful tape;
But he married the loveliest girl in town,
The one who once by his side sat down,
When up in the choir the basso growled,
Then tenor, soprano, and alto howled,
And the banker's son looked back and scowled.

UNCLE NED'S DEFENCE.

My breddren and sisters, I rises for to splain
Dis matter what ye's talkin' 'bout; I hopes to make it plain.
I'm berry sorry dat de ting hab come before de church,
For when I splains it you will see dat it am nuffin' much.

My friends, your humble speakah, while trabblin' heah below,
Has nebber stopped to hoard up gold and silber for to show,
He's only stoppin' heah a spell; we all hab got to die,
And so I always tried to lay my treasure up on high.

Da's just one ting dat pesters me, and dat am dis, you see,
De rabens fed old Lijah, but de creturs won't feed me;
Da's got above dar business, and just go swoopin' 'round,
And nebber stop to look at me, awaitin' on de ground.

I waited mighty sartin like, my faith was powerful strong,
I reckoned dat dem pesky birds would surely come along;
But oh, my friendly hearers, my faith hes kotched a fall,
Dem aggravatin' fowls went by and never stopped at all.

De meal and flour was almost gone, de pork barrel gettin' low,
And so one day I 'cluded dat I had better go
To brudder Johnson's tater patch to borrer just a few.
'Twas evening 'fore I got a start—I had so much to do.

It happened dat de night was dark, but dat I didn't mind,
I knowed de way to dat dar patch—'twas easy nuff to find,
And den I didn't care to meet dat Johnson, for I knowed
Dat he would sass me 'bout de mess ob taters dat I owed.

I got de basket full at last, and tuck it on my back,
And den was goin' to tote it home, when somethin' went kerwhack,
I tot it was a cannon; but it just turned out to be
Dat Johnson's one-hoss pistol a-pointin' straight at me.

I tried to argufy wid him, I 'pologized a heap,
But he said dat stealin' taters was as mean as stealin' sheep;
Ob course I could not take dat dar, it had an ugly sound,
So de only ting for me to do was just to knock him down.

And now, my friendly hearers, de story all am told,
Ob course I pounded Johnson till he yelled for me to hold;
An' now I hopes you 'grees wid me, dat dis yer case and such
Am berry triflin' matters to fotch before de church.

THE MILKMAID.

A MILKMAID, who poised a full pail on her head,
Thus mused on her prospects in life, it is said:
"Let me see,—I should think that this milk will procure
One hundred good eggs, or fourscore, to be sure.

"Well then,—stop a bit,—it must not be forgotten,
Some of these may be broken, and some may be rotten;
But if twenty for accident should be detached,
It will leave me just sixty sound eggs to be hatched.

"Well, sixty sound eggs,—no, sound chickens, I mean:
Of these some may die,—we'll suppose seventeen,

Seventeen ! not so many,—say ten at the most,
Which will leave fifty chickens to boil or to roast.

"But then there's their barley; how much will they need?
Why, they take but one grain at a time when they feed,—
So that's a mere trifle; now, then, let us see,
At a fair market price how much money there'll be.

"Six shillings a pair—five—four—three-and-six,
To prevent all mistakes, that low price I will fix;
Now what will that make? fifty chickens, I said,—
Fifty times three-and-sixpence,—*I'll ask Brother Ned!*

"Oh, but stop,—three-and-sixpence a *pair* I must sell 'em !
Well, a pair is a couple,—now then let us tell 'em.
A couple in fifty will go (my poor brain !),
Why, just a score times, and five pair will remain.

"Twenty-five pair of fowls,—now how tiresome it is
That I can't reckon up so much money as this !
Well, there's no use in trying, so let's give a guess,—
'll say twenty pounds, *and it can be no less.*

"Twenty pounds, I am certain, will buy me a cow,
Thirty geese and two turkeys,—eight pigs and a sow;
Now if these turn out well, at the end of the year,
I shall fill both my pockets with guineas, 'tis clear. "

Forgetting her burden, when this she had said,
The maid superciliously tossed up her head;
When, alas for her prospects ! her milk-pail descended,
And so all her schemes for the future were ended.

This moral, I think, may be safely attached,—
" Reckon not on your chickens before they are hatched."

THAT GRUMBLING OLD WOMAN.

THERE was an old woman, and—what do you think?—
She lived upon nothing but victuals and drink!
But though victuals and drink were the chief of her diet,
Yet this grumbling old woman never was quiet.
—MOTHER GOOSE.

She had a nice cottage, a hen-house and barn,
And a sheep whose fine wool furnished blankets and yarn;
A cow that supplied her with butter and cheese,
A large flock of geese, and a hive full of bees.

Yet she grumbled and grumbled from morning till night,
For this foolish old woman thought nothing went right;
E'en the days of the week were all wrong, for on Sunday
She always declared that she wished it was Monday.

If cloudless and fair was the long summer day,
And the sun smiled down on the new-mown hay,
"There's a drought," she said, "as sure as you're born!
If it don't rain soon, it will ruin the corn!"

But when descended the gentle rain,
Blessing the bountiful fields of grain,
And bringing new life to flower and bud,
She said there was coming a second flood.

She never gave aught to the needy and poor;
The outcast and hungry she turned from her door.
"Shall I work," she said, with a wag of the head,
"To provide for the idle and lazy their bread?"

But the rich she regarded with envy and spite;
She said 'twas a shame—'twasn't decent nor right,—
That the haughty old squire, with his bow-legged son,
Should ride with two horses, while she rode with one.

And the crabbed old fellow,—to spite her, no doubt,—
Had built a new barn like a palace throughout,
With a cupola on it, as grand as you please,
And a rooster that whirled head and tail with the breeze.

"I wish, so I do," she said, cocking her eye,
"There'd come a great whirlwind, and blow it sky-high!"
And e'en as she spoke, a loud rushing was heard,
And the barn to its very foundations was stirred.

It stood the shock bravely, but—pitiful sight!—
The wind took the old woman up like a kite!
As she sailed up aloft over forest and hill,
Her tongue, so they say, it kept wagging on still.

And where she alighted, no mortal doth know,
Or whether she ever alighted below.

MORAL.

My moral, my dears, you will find if you try;
And if you don't find any, neither can I.

FAILED.

YES, I'm a ruined man, Kate—everything gone at last;
Nothing to show for the trouble and toil of the weary years that
    are past;
Houses and lands and money have taken wings and fled;
This very morning I signed away the roof from over my head.

I shouldn't care for myself, Kate; I'm used to the world's rough
    ways;
I've dug and delved and plodded along through all my manhood
    days;
But I think of you and the children, and it almost breaks my heart;
For I thought so surely to give my boys and girls a splendid start.

So many years on the ladder, I thought I was near the top—
Only a few days longer, and then I expected to stop,
And put the boys in my place, Kate, with an easier life ahead;
But now I must give the prospect up; that comforting dream is
    dead.

"I am worth more than my gold, eh?"   You're good to look at
    it so;
But a man isn't worth very much, Kate, when his hair is turning
    to snow.
My poor little girls, with their soft white hands, and their innocent
    eyes of blue.
Turned adrift in the heartless world—what can and what will they
    do?

"An honest failure?"   Indeed it was; dollar for dollar was paid;
Never a creditor suffered, whatever people have said.
Better are rags and a conscience clear than a palace and flush of
    shame.
One thing I shall leave to my children, Kate; and that is an hon-
    est name.

What's that?   "The boys are not troubled, they are ready now to
    begin
And gain us another fortune, and work through thick and thin?"
The noble fellows! already I feel I haven't so much to bear;
Their courage has lightened my heavy load of misery and despair.

"And the girls are so glad it was honest: they'd rather not dress
    so fine,
And think they did it with money that wasn't honestly mine?"
They're ready to show what they're made of—quick to earn and to
    save—
My blessed, good little daughters! so generous and so brave!

And you think we needn't fret, Kate, while we have each other left,
No matter of what possessions our lives may be bereft?
You are right.   With a quiet conscience, and a wife so good and
    true,
I'll put my hand to the plough again; and I know that we'll pull
    through.

PEGGING AWAY.

THERE was an old shoemaker, sturdy as steel,
  Of great wealth and repute in his day,
Who, if questioned his secret of luck to reveal,
  Would chirp like a bird on a spray,
"It isn't so much the vocation you're in,
  Or your liking for it," he would say,
"As it is that forever, through thick and through thin,
  You should keep up a-pegging away."

I have found it a maxim of value, whose truth
  Observation has proved in the main;
And which well might be vaunted a watchword by youth
  In the labor of hand and of brain;
For even if genius and talent are cast
  Into work with the strongest display,
You can never be sure of achievement at last
  Unless you keep pegging away.

There are shopmen who might into statesmen have grown,
  Politicians for handiwork made,
Some poets who better in workshops had shone,
  And mechanics best suited in trade;
But when once in the harness, however it fit,
  Buckle down to your work night and day,
Secure in the triumph of hand or of wit,
  If you only keep pegging away.

There are times in all tasks when the fiend Discontent
  Advises a pause or a change,
And, on field far away and irrelevant bent,
  The purpose is tempted to range;
Never heed, but in sound recreation restore
  Such traits as are slow to obey,
And then, more persistent and staunch than before,
  Keep pegging and pegging away.

Leave fitful endeavors for such as would cast
   Their spendthrift existence in vain.
For the secret of wealth in the present and past,
   And of fame and of honor, is plain;
It lies not in change, nor in sentiment nice,
   Nor in wayward exploit and display,
But just in the shoemaker's homely advice
   To keep pegging and pegging away.

CURFEW MUST NOT RING TO-NIGHT.

ENGLAND'S sun was slowly setting o'er the hills so far away,
Filling all the land with beauty at the close of one sad day;
And the last rays kissed the forehead of a man and maiden fair,
He with step so slow and weaken'd, she with sunny, floating
    hair;
He with sad, bowed head, and thoughtful, she with lips so cold and
    white,
Struggling to keep back the murmur, "Curfew must not ring to-
    night."
"Sexton," Bessie's white lips faltered, pointing to the prison old,
With its walls so dark and gloomy—walls so dark and damp and
    cold—
"I've a lover in that prison, doomed this very night to die
At the ringing of the Curfew, and no earthly help is nigh.
Cromwell will not come till sunset," and her face grew strangely
    white,
As she spoke in husky whispers, "Curfew must not ring to-night."
"Bessie," calmly spoke the sexton—every word pierced her young
    heart
Like a thousand gleaming arrows, like a deadly poisoned dart—
"Long, long years I've rung the Curfew from that gloomy,
    shadowed tower;
Every evening, just at sunset, it has told the twilight hour;
I have done my duty ever, tried to do it just and right,
Now I'm old, I will not miss it; girl, the Curfew rings to-night!"

Wild her eyes and pale her features, stern and white her thoughtful
    brow,
And within her heart's deep centre, Bessie made a solemn vow;
She had listened while the judges read, without a tear or sigh,
"At the ringing of the Curfew—Basil Underwood *must die.*"
And her breath came fast and faster, and her eyes grew large and
    bright—
One low murmur, scarcely spoken—"Curfew *must not* ring to-
    night!"
She with light step bounded forward, sprang within the old church
    door,
Left the old man coming slowly paths he'd trod so oft before;
Not one moment paused the maiden, but with cheek and brow
    aglow,
Staggered up the gloomy tower, where the bell swung to and fro;
Then she climbed the slimy ladder, dark, without one ray of light,
Upward still, her pale lips saying: "Curfew shall not ring to-night."
She has reached the topmost ladder, o'er her hangs the great dark
    bell,
And the awful gloom beneath her, like the pathway down to hell;
See, the ponderous tongue is swinging, 'tis the hour of Curfew
    now,
And the sight has chilled her bosom, stopped her breath and paled
    her brow.
Shall she let it ring? No, never! her eyes flash with sudden light,
As she springs and grasps it firmly—"Curfew shall not ring to-
    night!"
Out she swung, far out, the city seemed a tiny speck below;
There, 'twixt heaven and earth suspended, as the bell swung to and
    fro;
And the half-deaf sexton ringing (years he had not heard the bell),
And he thought the twilight Curfew rang young Basil's funeral
    knell;
Still the maiden clinging firmly, cheek and brow so pale and white,
Stilled her frightened heart's wild beating—"*Curfew shall not ring
    to-night.*"
It was o'er—the bell ceased swaying, and the maiden stepped once
    more
Firmly on the damp old ladder, where for hundred years before

Human foot had not been planted; and what she this night had
    done
Should be told in long years after—as the rays of setting sun
Light the sky with mellow beauty, aged sires with heads of white
Tell the children why the Curfew did not ring that one sad night.
O'er the distant hills came Cromwell; Bessie saw him, and her
    brow,
Lately white with sickening terror, glows with sudden beauty
    now;
At his foot she told her story, showed her hands all bruised and
    torn;
And her sweet young face so haggard, with a look so sad and worn,
Touched his heart with sudden pity—lit his eyes with misty light;
"Go, your lover lives!" cried Cromwell; "Curfew shall not ring
    to-night."

ELEGY WRITTEN IN A COUNTRY CHURCH-YARD.

THOMAS GRAY.

THE curfew tolls the knell of parting day,
    The lowing herd winds slowly o'er the lea,
The ploughman homeward plods his weary way,
    And leaves the world to darkness and to me.

Now fades the glimmering landscape on the sight,
    And all the air a solemn stillness holds,
Save where the beetle wheels his droning flight,
    And drowsy tinklings lull the distant folds;

Save that from yonder ivy-mantled tower,
    The moping owl does to the moon complain
Of such as, wandering near her secret bower,
    Molest her ancient solitary reign.

Beneath those rugged elms, that yew-tree's shade,
    Where heaves the turf in many a mouldering heap,
Each in his narrow cell for ever laid,
    The rude forefathers of the hamlet sleep.

The breezy call of incense-breathing morn,
  The swallow twittering from the straw-built shed,
The cock's shrill clarion, or the echoing horn,
  No more shall rouse them from their lowly bed.

For them no more the blazing hearth shall burn,
  Or busy housewife ply her evening care;
No children run to lisp their sire's return,
  Or climb his knees the envied kiss to share.

Oft did the harvest to their sickle yield,
  Their furrow oft the stubborn glebe has broke;
How jocund did they drive their team a-field!
  How bowed the woods beneath their sturdy stroke!

Let not Ambition mock their useful toil,
  Their homely joys, and destiny obscure;
Nor Grandeur hear with a disdainful smile
  The short and simple annals of the poor.

The boast of heraldry, the pomp of power,
  And all that beauty, all that wealth e'er gave,
Await alike the inevitable hour:—
  The paths of glory lead but to the grave.

Nor you, ye Proud, impute to these a fault,
  If Memory o'er their tomb no trophies raise,
Where through the long-drawn aisle and fretted vault
  The pealing anthem swells the note of praise.

Can storied urn or animated bust
  Back to its mansion call the fleeting breath?
Can Honor's voice provoke the silent dust,
  Or Flattery soothe the dull cold ear of Death?

Perhaps in this neglected spot is laid
  Some heart once pregnant with celestial fire;
Hands that the rod of empire might have swayed
  Or waked to ecstasy the living lyre:

But Knowledge to their eyes her ample page,
    Rich with the spoils of time, did ne'er unroll;
Chill Penury repressed their noble rage,
    And froze the genial current of the soul.

Full many a gem of purest ray serene,
    The dark unfathomed caves of ocean bear;
Full many a flower is born to blush unseen
    And waste its sweetness on the desert air.

Some village Hampden, that with dauntless breast
    The little tyrant of his fields withstood;
Some mute inglorious Milton here may rest,
    Some Cromwell guiltless of his country's blood.

The applause of listening senates to command,
    The threats of pain and ruin to despise,
To scatter plenty o'er a smiling land,
    And read their history in a nation's eyes.

Their lot forbade: nor circumscribed alone
    Their growing virtues, but their crimes confined;
Forbade to wade through slaughter to a throne,
    And shut the gates of mercy on mankind.

The struggling pangs of conscious truth to hide,
    To quench the blushes of ingenuous shame,
Or heap the shrine of Luxury and Pride
    With incense kindled at the Muse's flame.

Far from the madding crowd's ignoble strife,
    Their sober wishes never learned to stray;
Along the cool sequestered vale of life
    They kept the noiseless tenor of their way.

Yet even these bones from insult to protect,
    Some frail memorial still erected nigh
With uncouth rhymes and shapeless sculpture decked,
    Implores the passing tribute of a sigh.

Their name, their years, spelt by the unlettered Muse,
    The place of fame and elegy supply;

And many a holy text around she strews,
   That teach the rustic moralist to die.

For who, to dumb Forgetfulness a prey,
   This pleasing anxious being e'er resigned,
Left the warm precincts of the cheerful day,
   Nor cast one longing, lingering look behind?

On some fond breast the parting soul relies,
   Some pious drops the closing eye requires;
E'en from the tomb the voice of Nature cries,
   E'en in our ashes live their wonted fires.

For thee, who, mindful of the unhonored dead,
   Dost in these lines their artless tale relate;
If chance, by lonely Contemplation led,
   Some kindred spirit shall inquire thy fate;

Haply some hoary-headed swain may say;
   "Oft have we seen him at the peep of dawn
Brushing with hasty steps the dews away,
   To meet the sun upon the upland lawn.

"There at the foot of yonder nodding beech,
   That wreathes its old fantastic roots so high,
His listless length at noontide would he stretch,
   And pour upon the brook that babbles by.

"Hard by yon wood, now smiling as in scorn,
   Muttering his wayward fancies he would rove;
Now drooping, woeful, wan, like one forlorn,
   Or crazed with care, or crossed in hopeless love.

"One morn I missed him on the 'customed hill,
   Along the heath and near his favorite tree;
Another came; nor yet beside the rill,
   Nor up the lawn, nor at the wood was he;

"The next, with dirges due, in sad array,
   Slow through the churchway path we saw him borne;
Approach and read—for thou canst read—the lay
   Graved on the stone beneath yon aged thorn."

THE EPITAPH.

Here rests his head upon the lap of Earth,
  A Youth to Fortune and to Fame unknown;
Fair Science frowned not on his humble birth,
  And Melancholy marked him for her own.

Large was his bounty, and his soul sincere,
  Heaven did a recompense as largely send;
He gave to Misery all he had—a tear;
  He gained from Heaven—'twas all he wished—a friend.

No further seek his merits to disclose,
  Or draw his frailties from their dread abode—
There they alike in trembling hope repose—
  The bosom of his Father and his God.

THE BRAVEST OF BATTLES.

JOAQUIN MILLER.

The bravest battle that ever was fought,
  Shall I tell you where and when?
On the maps of the world you'll find it not;
  'Twas fought by the mothers of men.

Nay, not with cannon or battle shot,
  With sword or nobler pen;
Nay, not with eloquent word or thought
  From mouth of wonderful men.

But deep in a walled-up woman's heart—
  Of woman that would not yield,
But bravely, silently bore her part—
  Lo! there is the battle-field.

No marshalling troop, no bivouac song,
  No banner to gleam and wave!
But oh, these battles, they last so long—
  From babyhood to the grave.

FOUR SUNBEAMS.

FOUR little sunbeams came earthward one day,
Shining and dancing on their way,
  Resolved that their course should be blest,
"Let us try," they all whispered, "some kindness to do,
Not seek our own pleasure all the day through,
  Then meet in the eve in the west."

One sunbeam ran in a low cottage door,
And played "hide-and-seek" with a child on the floor,
  Till the baby laughed loud in his glee,
And chased in delight his strange playmate so bright,
The little hands grasping in vain for the light
  That ever before them would flee.

One crept to the couch where an invalid lay,
And brought him a dream of the sweet summer day,
  Its bird song, and beauty, and bloom,
Till pain was forgotten, and weary unrest,
And in fancy he roamed through the scenes he loved best,
  Far away from the dim darkened room.

One stole in the heart of a flower that was sad,
And loved and caressed her until she was glad,
  And lifted her white face again ;
For love brings content to the lowliest lot,
And finds something sweet in the dreariest spot,
  And lightens all labor and pain.

And one, where a little blind girl sat alone,
Not sharing the mirth of her playfellows, shone
  On hands that were folded and pale,
And kissed the poor eyes that had never known sight,
That never would gaze on the beautiful light
  Till the angels had lifted the veil.

At last when the shadows of evening were falling,
And the sun, their father, his children was calling,
  Four sunbeams passed into the west,

All said: " We have found in seeking the pleasure
Of others, we find to the full our own measure."
  Then softly they sank to their rest.

LET BY-GONES BE BY-GONES.

LET by-gones be by-gones.   If by-gones were clouded
  By aught that occasioned a pang of regret,
O, let them in darkest oblivion be shrouded;
  'Tis wise and 'tis kind to forgive and forget.

Let by-gones be by-gones, and good be extracted
  From ill over which it is folly to fret;
The wisest of mortals have foolishly acted—
  The kindest are those who forgive and forget.

Let by-gones be by-gones.   O, cherish no longer
  The thought that the sun of affection has set;
Eclipsed for a moment, its rays will be stronger,
  If you, like a Christian, forgive and forget.

Let by-gones be by-gones.   Your heart will be lighter
  When kindness of yours with reception has met;
The flame of your love will be purer and brighter,
  If, God-like, you strive to forgive and forget.

Let by-gones be by-gones.   O, purge out the leaven
  Of malice, and try an example to set
To others, who, craving the mercy of Heaven,
  Are sadly too slow to forgive and forget.

Let by-gones be by-gones.   Remember how deeply
  To Heaven's forbearance we all are in debt;
They value God's infinite goodness too cheaply
  Who heed not the precept, " Forgive and forget."

HIT THE NAIL ON THE HEAD.

THE world is no hive where the drone may repose,
  While others are gleaning its honey with care;
Nor will he succeed who is dealing his blows
  At random, and recklessly hits everywhere.
But choose well your purpose, then breast to the strife,
  And hold to it firmly, by rectitude led;
Give your heart to that duty, and strike for your life,
  And with every stroke, hit the nail on the head.

If Fate is against thee ne'er falter nor fret,
  'Twill not mend your fortunes, nor lighten your load;
Be earnest, still earnest, and you will forget
  You e'er had a burden to bear on the road.
And when at the close, what a pleasure to know,
  That you, never flinching, however life sped,
Gave your heart to your duty, your strength to each blow,
  And with every stroke, hit the nail on the head.

GUILTY OR NOT GUILTY.

SHE stood at the bar of justice,
  A creature wan and wild,
In form too small for a woman,
  In features too old for a child;
For a look so worn and pathetic
  Was stamped on her pale young face,
It seemed long years of suffering
  Must have left that silent trace.

"Your name," said the judge, as he eyed her
  With a kindly look, yet keen;
"Is Mary McGuire, if you please, sir."
  "And your age?" "I'm turned fifteen."

"Well, Mary,"—and then from a paper
   He slowly and gravely read,
"You are charged here—I'm sorry to say it—
   With stealing three loaves of bread.

"You look not like an offender,
   And I hope that you can show
The charge to be false. Now, tell me
   Are you guilty of this, or no?"
A passionate burst of weeping
   Was at first her sole reply,
But she dried her eyes in a moment
   And looked in the judge's eye.

"I will tell you just how it was, sir;
   My father and mother are dead,
And my little brother and sisters
   Were hungry, and asked me for bread.
At first I earned it for them
   By working hard all day,
But somehow times were bad, sir,
   And the work all fell away.

"I could get no more employment;
   The weather was bitter cold;
The young ones cried and shivered—
   Little Johnny's but four years old;
So, what was I to do, sir?
   I am guilty, but do not condemn,
I took—oh, was it stealing?—
   The bread to give to them."

Every man in the court-room—
   Graybeard and thoughtless youth—
Knew, as he looked upon her,
   That the prisoner told the truth.
Out of their pockets brought 'kerchiefs,
   Out from their eyes sprung tears,
And out from old faded wallets
   Treasures hoarded for years.

The judge's face was a study,
  The strangest you ever saw,
As he cleared his throat and murmured
  Something about the law;
For one so learned in such matters,
  So wise in dealing with men,
He seemed on a simple question
  Sorely puzzled just then.

But no one blamed him, or wondered,
  When at last these words they heard:
"The sentence of this young prisoner
  Is, for the present, deferred."
And no one blamed him, or wondered
  When he went to her and smiled,
And tenderly led from the court-room
  Himself, the "guilty" child.

THE STARLESS CROWN.

WEARIED and worn with earthly care, I yielded to repose,
And soon before my raptured sight a glorious vision rose.
I thought, while slumbering on my couch in midnight's solemn
    gloom,
I heard an angel's silvery voice, and radiance filled my room.
A gentle touch awakened me; a gentle whisper said,
"Arise, O sleeper, follow me!" and through the air we fled;
We left the earth so far away that like a speck it seemed,
And heavenly glory, calm and pure, across our pathway streamed.

Still on he went; my soul was wrapped in silent ecstasy;
I wondered what the end would be, what next would meet my eye.
I knew not how we journeyed through the pathless fields of light,
When suddenly a change was wrought, and I was clothed in white.
We stood before a city's walls, most glorious to behold;
We passed through streets of glittering pearl, o'er streets of purest
    gold.

It needed not the sun by day, nor silver moon by night;
The glory of the Lord was there, the Lamb Himself its light.

Bright angels paced the shining streets, sweet music filled the air,
And white-robed saints, with glittering crowns, from every clime
  were there;
And some that I had loved on earth stood with them round the
  throne.
"All worthy is the Lamb," they sang, "the glory His alone."
But, fairer far than all beside, I saw my Saviour's face,
And as I gazed, He smiled on me, with wondrous love and grace,
Slowly I bowed before His throne, o'erjoyed that I at last
Had gained the object of my hopes, that earth at length was past.

And then in solemn tones, He said, "Where is the diadem
That ought to sparkle on thy brow, adorned with many a gem?
I know thou hast believed on Me, and life, through Me, is thine,
But where are all those radiant stars that in thy crown should shine?
Yonder thou seest a glorious throng, and stars on every brow;
For every soul they led to Me, they wear a jewel now;
And such thy bright reward had been, if such had been thy deed,
If thou hadst sought some wandering feet in paths of peace to lead.

"I did not mean that thou should'st tread the way of life alone,
But that the clear and shining light which round thy footsteps shone
Should guide some other weary feet to My bright home of rest,
And thus in blessing those around, thou hadst thyself been blest."
The vision faded from my sight; the voice no longer spake;
A spell seemed brooding o'er my soul, which long I feared to break,
And when at last I gazed around, in morning's glimmering light,
My spirit fell, o'erwhelmed amid that vision's awful night.

I rose and wept with chastened joy that yet I dwelt below—
That yet another hour was mine, my faith by works to show,
That yet some sinner I might tell of Jesus' dying love,
And help to lead some weary soul to seek a home above.
And now while on the earth I stay, my motto this shall be,
"To live no longer to myself, but to Him who died for me."
And graven on my inmost soul this word of truth divine,
"They that turn many to the Lord, bright as the stars shall shine."

GOOD-NATURE.

HENRY WARD BEECHER.

Good-nature—what a blessing! Without it a man is like a wagon without springs, he has the full benefit of every stone and way-rut. Good-nature is the prime-minister of a good conscience. It tells of the genial spirit within, and good-nature never fails of a wholesome effect without.

Good-nature is not only the government of one's own spirit, but it goes far in its effects upon those of others. It manifests itself on every street; it humanizes man; it softens the friction of a business world. Good-nature is the harmonious act of conscience. Good-nature in practical affairs is better than any other; better than what men call justice; better than dignity; better than standing on one's rights, which is so often the narrowest and worst place to stand on one can find.

A man who knows how to hold on to his temper is the man who is respected by the community. And one who has a good nature, successfully travels about as does he who goes upon the principle—little of baggage, but plenty of money! A man who is armed with hopefulness, cheerfulness, and a genial spirit, is one who is going to be of practical and beneficent usefulness to his fellow-man. There are no things by which the troubles and difficulties of this life can be resisted better than with wit and humor. And let the happy person who possesses these—if he be brought into the folds of the Church—not allow conversion to deprive him of them. God has constituted these in man, and especially when they are so salient in meeting good-naturedly the trials of this world, they should be used. Happiness, at last, is dependent upon a soul that has holy communion with its Creator—"for in Him we have life eternal." Men also fail in happiness because they refuse to read the great lessons found in the great book of nature. Happiness is to be sought in the possession of true manhood rather than in its internal conditions.

LIBERTY.

ORVILLE DEWEY.

Liberty is a solemn thing—a welcome, a joyous, a glorious thing, if you please; but it is a solemn thing. A free people must be a thoughtful people. The subjects of a despot may be reckless and gay if they can. A free people must be serious; for it has to do the greatest thing that ever was done in the world—to govern itself.

That hour in *human life* is most serious, when it passes from parental control into free manhood: then must the man bind the righteous law upon himself more strongly than father or mother ever bound it upon him. And when a people leaves the leading-strings of prescriptive authority, and enters upon the ground of freedom, that ground must be fenced with law; it must be tilled with wisdom; it must be hallowed with prayer. The tribunal of justice, the free school, the holy church, must be built there to intrench, to defend, and to keep the sacred heritage.

Liberty, I repeat, is a solemn thing. The world, up to this time, has regarded it as a boon, not as a bond. And there is nothing, I seriously believe, in the present crisis of human affairs, there is no point in the great human welfare, on which men's ideas so much need to be cleared up, to be advanced, to be raised to a higher standard, as this grand and terrible responsibility of freedom.

In the universe there is no trust so awful as *moral freedom;* and all good civil freedom depends upon the use of that. But look at it. Around every human, every rational being is drawn a circle; the space within is cleared from obstruction, or at least from all coercion; it is sacred to the being who stands there; it is secured and consecrated to his own responsibility. May I say it? God Himself does not penetrate there with any absolute, any coercive power! He compels the winds and waves to obey Him; He compels animal instincts to obey Him, but He does not *compel man* to obey. That sphere He leaves free; He brings influences to bear upon it; but the last, final, solemn, infinite question between right and wrong, He leaves to man **himself.**

Ah! instead of madly delighting in his freedom, I could imagine a man to protest, to complain, to tremble, that such a tremendous prerogative is accorded to him. But it is accorded to him; and nothing but willing obedience can discharge that solemn trust; nothing but a heroism greater than that which fights battles, and pours out its blood on its country's altar—the heroism of self-renunciation and self-control.

Come that liberty! I invoke it with all the ardor of the poets and orators of freedom; with Spencer and Milton, with Hampden and Sidney, with Rienzi and Dante, with Hamilton and Washington, I invoke it. Come that liberty! come none that does not lead to that. Come the liberty that shall strike off every chain, not only of iron, but of iron law, of painful constriction, of fear, of enslaving passion, of mad self-will, the liberty of perfect truth and, love of holy faith and glad obedience!

CHRISTMAS.

WASHINGTON IRVING.

There is something in the very season of the year that gives a charm to the festivity of Christmas.

At other times we derive a great portion of our pleasures from the mere beauties of nature. Our feelings sally forth and dissipate themselves over the sunny landscape, and " we live abroad and everywhere." The song of the bird, the murmur of the stream, the breathing fragrance of spring, the soft voluptuousness of summer, the golden pomp of autumn, earth with its mantle of refreshing green, and heaven with its deep, delicious blue and its cloudy magnificence, all fill us with mute but exquisite delight. and we revel in the luxury of mere sensation.

But in the depth of winter, when nature lies despoiled of every charm, and wrapped in her shroud of sheeted snow, we turn for our gratifications to moral sources. The dreariness and desolation of the landscape, the short, gloomy days and darksome nights. while they circumscribe our wanderings, shut in our feelings also from rambling abroad. and make us more keenly disposed for the pleasure of the social circle. Our thoughts are more concentrated; our friendly sympathies more aroused. We feel more sensibly the charm of each other's society, and are brought more closely together by dependence on each other for enjoyment. Heart calleth unto heart, and we draw our pleasures from the deep wells of loving-kindness which lie in the quiet recesses of our bosoms; and which, when resorted to, furnish forth the pure element of domestic felicity.

The pitchy gloom without makes the heart dilate on entering the room filled with the glow and warmth of the evening fire. The ruddy blaze diffuses an artificial summer and sunshine through the room, and lights up each countenance in a kindlier welcome. Where does the honest face of hospitality expand into a broader and more cordial smile—where is the shy glance of love more sweetly eloquent than by the winter fireside? And as the hollow blast of wintry wind rushes through the hall, claps the distant door, whistles about the casement, and rumbles down the chimney, what can be more grateful than that feeling of sober and sheltered security with which we look around upon the comfortable chamber and the scene of domestic hilarity?

PURE WATER.

PAUL DENTON.

Paul Denton, a missionary in the early days of Texas, when the State was a Mexican province, collected a crowd at a barbecue where he promised there should be plenty to drink of the best of liquors. He did this that he might draw a crowd to preach to them. After the barbecue was over, one of the boldest asked, "Where is your liquor?"

The following was Denton's beautiful answer:

There—there is the liquor which God, the Eternal, brews for His children.

Not in the simmering still, over smoking fires, choked with poisonous gases, and surrounded with stench of sickening odors and rank corruption, doth your Father in heaven prepare that precious essence of life—pure cold water. But in the green shade and grassy dell, where the red deer wanders and the child loves to play, there God brews it; and down, low down, in the deepest valleys, where the fountains murmur and the rills sing; and high up on the mountain-tops, where the naked granite glitters like gold in the sun; where hurricanes howl music; where big waves roar the chorus, sweeping the march of God—there He brews it, that beverage of life, health-giving water.

And everywhere it is a thing of beauty; gleaming in a dew-drop; singing in the summer rain; shining in the ice-gem, till the trees seem turning to living jewels, spreading a golden veil over the setting sun, or white gauze round the midnight moon; sporting in the glacier; dancing in the hail-shower; folding bright snowy curtains softly above the wintry world, and weaving the many-colored iris, that seraph's zone of the sky, whose warp is the rain of earth, whose woof is the sunbeam of heaven, all checkered o'er with celestial flowers by the mystic hand of refrac-tion—still always beautiful: that blessed cold water. No poison bubbles on its brink; its foam brings not madness and murder; no blood stains its liquid glass; pale widows and starving orphans weep not burning tears in its clear depths; no drunkard's shriek-ing from the grave curses it in words of despair! Speak out, my friends, would you exchange it for the demon's drink—Alcohol?

SPIKE THAT GUN.

The great struggle for victory on the heights of Inkerman was decided by a young officer bravely carrying out an order to spike a gun that was sweeping down the troops with its shot and shell. The battery had to be approached with great care, or the attack-ing party would be swept away before the gun could be reached. The officer in command led his men under the cover of some rising ground, and then waited his opportunity to face the battery. At first a brother officer who accompanied the party said that it was perfect madness to attempt an attack, and the men began to feel that it was charging into the arms of death; but the officer who had received the order to spike that gun was determined to carry it out or die in the attempt; and, addressing his small party, said: "If no man will stand by me, I shall go alone. Who'll volunteer?" He went out from the shelter of the rising ground where he had halted his men and faced the battery. No sooner did the men see his brave determination to carry out his instructions than they rushed to the front, and, with a victorious shout, took the battery and spiked the gun. That brave deed turned the battle-scales to victory in favor of the British. The Russians lost all heart when the battery, which had done such deadly mischief to the troops all that fearful day, was silenced, and the gun spiked.

The conflict between good and evil is still raging. Year after year rolls on and the deadly strife continues. The ranks have been thinned, but new recruits rush in to fill the gaps. The insatiate battery of destruction belches forth its death-dealing missiles, thousands and tens of thousands are falling around us—who will volunteer to silence that battery? Who will spike that gun?

DON'T WORRY.

If you want a good appetite, don't worry. If you want a healthy body, don't worry. If you want things to go right in your homes or your business, don't worry. Women find a sea of trouble in their housekeeping. Some one says they often put as much worry and anxiety into a loaf of bread, a pie, or a cake, into the weekly washing and ironing, as should suffice for much weightier matters. This accounts largely for the angularity of American women. Nervousness, which may be called the reservoir of worrying—its fountain and source—is the bane of the American race. It is not confined to the women, by any means, but extends to the men as well. Even business men are sometimes afflicted, so we have heard, and so our advice not to yield to this habit will be most kindly received by all classes of readers. What good does fretting do? It only increases with indulgence, like anger, or appetite, or love, or any other human impulse. It deranges one's temper, excites unpleasant feelings toward everybody, and confuses the mind. It affects the whole person, unfits one for the proper completion of the work whose trifling interruption or disturbance started the fretful fit. Suppose these things go wrong to-day, the to-morrows are coming, in which to try again, and the thing is not worth clouding your own spirit and those around you, injuring yourself and them physically—for the mind affects the body —and for such a trifle. Strive to cultivate a spirit of patience, both for your own good and the good of those about you. You will never regret the step, for it will not only add to your own happiness, but the example of your conduct will affect those with whom you associate, and in whom you are interested. Suppose somebody makes a mistake, suppose you are crossed, or a trifling accident occurs; to fly into a fretful mood will not mend, but help to hinder the attainment of what you wish. Then, when a thing is beyond repair, waste no useless regrets over it, and do no idle fretting. Strive for that serenity of spirit that will enable you to make the best of all things. That means contentment in its best sense; and contentment is the only true happiness of life. A pleasant disposition and good work will make the whole surroundings ring with cheerfulness.

A LIFE SAVED.

DETROIT FREE PRESS.

He wanted legal advice, and when the lawyer told him to state his case, he began:

"About two years ago I was fool enough to fall in love."

"Certainly—I understand."

"And for a year past I have been engaged to her."

"Of course."

"A few months ago I found, upon analyzing my heart, that I did not love her as I should. My affections had grown cold."

"Certainly they had—go on."

"I saw her pug nose in its true shape, and I realized that her shoes were No. 6."

"Exactly, and you made up your mind to break off the match? That was perfectly proper."

"Yes, that was my object; but she threatens to sue me for a breach of promise."

"Certainly she does, and she'll do it, too. Has she any love-letters from you?"

"That's the hang of it. She tallies up 326."

"And do they breathe your life?"

"I should say they did; but I think I've got her tight. All them letters are written on wrapping-paper, and with pencil, and I've come to ask you if such writing as that will stand law?"

"Of course it will.   If you had written it with a slate and pencil she could hold you."

"Great hokey! but is that so?"

"It is."

"And she's got me fast?"

"She has."

"Well, that settles that matter, and I suppose I'll have to give in and marry her?"

"Unless—"

"Unless what?"

"You can buy her off."

"Egad! that's it—that's the idea, and you have saved my life! Buy her off—why didn't I think of it before? Say, where's the dollar store? I'll walk in on her with a set of jewelry, a flirtation fan, a card-case, and two bracelets, and she'll give me a quit-claim deed and throw in all the poetry I ever sent her to boot!"

AUNT JEMIMA'S COURTSHIP.

AS READ BY LOLA WOOD RUSK.

Waal, girls—if you must know—reckon I must tell ye. Waal, 'twas in the winter time, and father and I were sitting alone in the kitchen. We wur sitting thar sort o' quiet like, when father sez, sez he to me, "Jemima!" And I sez, sez I, "What, sir?" And he sez, sez he, "Wa'n't that a rap at the door?" and I sez, sez I, "No, sir." Bimeby, father sez to me again, sez he, "Are you sure?" And I sez, sez I, "No, sir." So I went to the door, and opened it, and sure enough there stood—a man. Waal, he came in and sat down by father, and father and he talked about almost everything you could think of; they talked about the farm, they talked about the crops, and they talked about poli*tics*, and they talked about all other ticks.

Bimeby, father sez to me, sez he, "Jemima!" And I sez, sez I, "What, sir?" And he sez. "Can't we have some cider?" And I sez, sez I, "I suppose so." So I went down cellar and brought up a pitcher of cider, and I handed some cider to father, and then I handed some to the man; and father he drinks, and the man he drinks, till they drink it all up. After a while father sez to me, sez he, "Jemima!" And I sez, sez I, "What, sir?" And he sez, sez he, "Ain't it most time for me to be thinking about going to bed?" And I sez, sez I, "Indeed, you are the best judge of that yourself, sir." "Waal," he sez, sez he, "Jemima, bring me my dressing-gown and slippers." And he put them on and arter a while he went to bed.

And there sat that man; and bimeby he began a-hitching his chair up toward mine—oh, my! I was all in a flutter. And then he sez, sez he, "Jemima?" And I sez, sez I, "What, sir?" And he sez, sez he, "Will you have me?" And I sez, sez I, "No, sir!" for I was 'most scared to death. Waal, there we sat, and arter a while, will you believe me, he began backing his chair closer and closer to mine, and sez he, "Jemima?" And I sez, sez I, "What, sir?" And he sez, sez he, "Will you have me?" And I sez, sez I, "No, sir!" Waal, by this time he had his arm around my waist, and I hadn't the heart to take it away, 'cause the tears was a-rollin' down his cheeks, and he sez, sez he, "Jemima?" And I sez, sez I, "What, sir?" And he sez, sez he, "For the third and last time, I sha'n't ask ye agin, will ye have me?" And I sez, sez I, "Yes, sir,"—fur I didn't know what else to say.

TAMING AN ALLIGATOR.

"Ye see that item in one of the papers 'bout tamin' young alligators, I reckon," said a countryman, capturing the city editor by the buttonhole, and drawing him into a doorway. "Ye know the paper said 'twas the fash'nable thing to do."

"I don't remember. Perhaps I did. What of it?" asked the city editor.

"I tried it," said the countryman. "A friend of mine brought me one down from New Orleans. and I'm a-trainin' that alligator for the children to play with."

"How does the experiment progress?"

"I don't know 'bout the experiment; the alligator's thrivin'. He was six weeks old when I got him. two months ago, and he's seven years old now. People in our parts say he's all the alligator I'll ever need."

"What does he do?" asked the city editor.

"Well it's here. When he came he was a sportive little un and just warbled 'round friendly. He was chiefly mouth, an' we used to feed him fur the fun of seein' him eat. Now we skin 'round when we see him comin' fur the fun of seein' him go hungry."

"Is he dangerous?"

"I haven't been close enough to see. He ate up my dog, and when I left this mornin' he was in the sty arguin' the question of pork as a diet with the pig. My wife thinks if the pig has any luck he'll find the cow we lost."

"Better get rid of him, hadn't you?" suggested the city editor.

"I don't know," replied the countryman. "We've got so much stored away in him now that it seems like givin' up most of our property, and besides, my oldest girl says she can't hear of havin' her leg go in among strangers."

"Did he bite her leg off?"

"Sure! Took it off short! Then there's the baby. We hate to part with the baby's grave, so we sorter try and keep the alligator along. My wife insists on keepin' him, 'cause she thinks she seen a couple of peddlers go in one day, pack and all, and she's got an idea the packs may come to the front again if we hold on. Besides, she seen that item about tame alligators bein' fash'nable, and she's a good deal on style."

"But do you call that alligator tamed?"

"Certainly. He comes right into the house same as any of us, and keeps himself. He's got that heel," and the countryman pointed to a mutilated foot. "There's my son's wife, too. She's part alligator now. He ate her up a week ago, and the boy hasn't got over his arm yet. The alligator got the arm too."

"Great Scott!" ejaculated the city editor.

"Oh, yes. It's lively down there. When he puts himself up, he's business. He is the lightningest alligator for a tame one y'ever saw. When we first got him, we used him fur a tack-hammer—drew nails with him; but now he's the head of the family, except payin' the rent. When there's any mysterious disappearance round our parts, the coroner comes and views the alligator. That ends it. When the baby was snatched, they held an inquest in a tree. The jury was all on one limb, and the alligator underneath, a-lookin' up. Bimeby the limb broke, and the jury disappeared in a row, just as they sat. We didn't wait fur any verdict. The coroner gave me a permit, and after the funeral we shied an empty coffin at the alligator. Then when the minister said, 'Dust to dust,' we all dusted. Do you remember whether that item said what a real tame alligator ought to feed on?"

"Don't recollect seeing it at all. Aren't you afraid he'll eat up some of your family?"

"Think he's liable to?" asked the countryman, with a curious expression of visage.

"Yes, indeed," replied the city editor. "Suppose he should swallow your mother-in-law?"

"Ah!" said the countryman, "he might get her, mightn't he? You think I'd better keep him then?" and the countryman leaned up against the door and gave himself up to reflection.

As he drew away and left, the city editor heard him say, "So he might; so he might."

BRACE UP.

"Brace up!" We like that slang phrase. We like it because there is lots of soul in it. You never knew a mean, stingy, snivel-souled man to walk up to an afflicted neighbor, slap him on the shoulder and tell him to brace up. It is a big-hearted, open-handed, whole-souled fellow that comes along when you are cast down and squares off in front of you and tells you: "That won't do, old fellow, brace up!" It is he that tells you a good story and makes you laugh in spite of yourself. He lifts the curtain that darkens your soul, and lets in the cheering sunlight. It is he that reminds you there never was a brilliant sunset without clouds. He may not tell you so in just such words, but he will make you "brace up" and see the silver lining for yourself.

Have you been engaged in risky speculation, and just when you expected to gather in your golden gains, stocks fell and you found yourself a bankrupt? Don't get discouraged, take to drink to drown your troubles, or commit any other rash act prompted by force of adverse circumstances; brace up! You have gained wisdom from experience, strength from the struggle, brace up and go ahead!

There is no tonic like this to restore the dormant energies, no course of gymnastics equal to it for strengthening nerve and muscle;—don't drug the system with patent nostrums, don't fool away time with dumb-bells, brace up! brace up! and health, strength, and enthusiasm will urge you on to still greater achievements and to ultimate success.

"Look up—not down! The mists that chill and blind thee
   Strive with pale wings to take a sunward flight;
Upward the green boughs reach; the face of nature,
   Watchful and glad, is lifted to the light.
The strength that saves comes never from the ground
But from the mountain-tops that shine around.

"Look forward, and not back! Each lost endeavor
   May be a step upon thy chosen path;
All that the past withheld, in larger measure,
   Somewhere, in willing trust, the future hath—
Near and more near the ideal stoops to meet
The steadfast coming of unfaltering feet."
   Brace up! Brace up!

THE TOLL-GATE OF LIFE.

We are all on our journey. The world through which we are passing is in some respects like a turnpike—all along where vice and folly have erected their toll-gates for the accommodation of those who choose to call as they go—and there are very few of all the hosts of travelers who do not occasionally stop a little at one or the other of them, and consequently pay more or less to the tax-gatherers. Pay more or less we say, because there is a great variety, as well in the amount as in the kind of toll exacted at these different stopping-places.

Pride and fashion take heavy tolls of the purse—many men have become beggars by paying at their gates—the ordinary rates they charge are heavy, and the road that way is none of the best.

Pleasure offers a very smooth, delightful road at the outset; she tempts the traveler with many fair promises, and wins thousands; but she takes—without mercy; like an artful robber, she allures till she gets her victim in her power, and then she strips him of wealth and money, and turns him off a miserable object, into the worst of our most rugged roads of life.

Intemperance plays the part of a sturdy villain. He is the very worst toll-gatherer on the road, for he not only gets from his customers their money and their health, but he robs them of their very brain. The men you meet on the road, ragged and ruined in fame and fortune, are generally his visitors.

And so we might go on enumerating many others who gather toll from the unwary. Accidents often happen, it is true, along the road, but those who do not get through at least tolerably well, have been stopping by the way at some of these places. The plain, common-sense men who travel straight forward, get through without much difficulty.

This being the state of things, it becomes every one at the outset, if he intends to make a comfortable journey, to take care what kind of company he keeps in with. We are all apt to do as companions do—stop where they stop, and pay toll where they pay. The chances are ten to one but our choice in this particular always decides our fate.

Be careful of your habits, these make men. And they require long and careful culture, ere they grow up to a second nature. Good habits we speak of. Bad habits are easily acquired—they are spontaneous weeds, that flourish rapidly and rankly without care or culture.

MRS. GREYLOCK TELLS ABOUT THE PLAY.

"Was the play good, my dear?" asked Mr. Greylock the other night, after his wife had come home from the theater, where she had been with some friends.

"Good!" cried little Mrs. Greylock, enthusiastically, "it was just grand, Mortimer! It was a lovely play, and the dresses! In the first act she wore one of the most bewilderingly beautiful things I ever saw in all my mortal life—a pale apple-green skirt, brocaded in the sweetest shade of pink, with a perfectly magnificent train of ——"

"Was her acting good?"

"——heavy silver brocade without a particle of trimming on it. But the waist was trimmed all over with something I couldn't make out, although I strained my eyes trying to all the time she was on the stage. It was an evening dress, and when she first came on she had on ——"

"But was she any good as an actress?"

"My dear, please don't interrupt—an opera cloak of soft pink plush, lined with apple-green satin, with the loveliest fringe, with seed pearls shining in it, and ——"

"But tell me about her acting."

"Then in the second act she wore the most magnificent bridal costume I ever laid my eyes on—a heavy, shining, ivory satin, with the most immense court train, and yards and yards of the loveliest Brussels lace. The whole front of the dress was one mass of tiny flounces of real lace, and down the sides there were cascades of the lace and pearl passementerie, while at the back ——"

"But the play, my dear, I ——"

"And the sleeves of the dress were of the lace, and they hung clear to the ground, away from the arm, you know. I never saw anything like it before; I can't begin to describe it to you, but it was perfectly ——"

"You need not describe any more of it, my dear; I'd rather hear about ——"

"Then in the next act she came on in the most exquisite thing —a lovely shade of rose-pink silk, made with a sweeping train over a petticoat of Turkish embroidery. Oh! that embroidery was too sweet! She wore with the dress a ——"

"Come, come, my dear, have done with her gowns, and ——"

"Yes, yes, I am done with the gowns; but I was going to tell you about her jewels. With the pink dress she wore a perfectly gorgeous diamond necklace, and in her ears she had ——"

"I don't care a continental what she had in her ears—don't care much whether she had any ears at all or not. Can she act? That's what I'd like to know."

"Act? Of course she can act. I never saw a woman more perfectly self-possessed than she was. She never sat down or rose awkwardly a single time, and I never saw any one manage a train more gracefully than she, and in the fourth act her train was so immense! It was one of the heaviest Lyons velvet, with a front of netted silk; she wore with it the heaviest girdle of jet I ever saw. Her arms were bare. She'd beautiful arms, too, and ——"

"At least, tell me what the play was."

"——diamonds on her wrists and on a velvet around her throat, and—oh, the play, did you ask?"

"Yes, what was the play?"

"Why, it was—it was—now, let me see—what was the play? Strange, I remember seeing it on the—run downstairs and get my muff, dear, and you'll find a program in it. I really don't remember just what the name of the play was."

GOOD OLD MOTHERS.

Somebody has said that "a mother's love is the only virtue that did not suffer by the fall of Adam." Whether Adam fell or not, it is quite clear that the unselfish love of a good mother is the crowning glory of the race. No matter how long and how sorely it may be tried, its arms are ever open to receive the returning prodigal. One faithful heart never loses its affection for the wanderer who has strayed from the fold. Adversity and sorrow may come with all their terrible force, but the motherly affection clings to its idol closely. We never see a good old mother sitting in the arm-chair that we do not think of the storms which have pelted into her cheerful face without souring it. Her smile is a solace, her presence a benediction. A man may stand more exertion of some kinds than a woman, but he is apt to lose much of his laughter, his cheerfulness, his gentleness, and his trust. Yet we rarely find a frail mother whose spirit has been worn threadbare and unlovely by trials that would have turned a dozen men into misanthropes and demons. A sweet old mother is common. A sweet old father is not so common. In exhaustless patience, hope, faith, and benevolence the mothers are sure to lead. Alas, that their worth too often is not fully known and properly appreciated until they pass beyond mortal reach! God bless the good old mothers!

AFTER TWENTY YEARS.

The coffin was a plain one—a poor, miserable pine coffin. One flower on the top; no lining of white satin for the pale brow; no smooth ribbons about the coarse shroud. The brown hair was laid decently back, but there was no primped cap with the tie beneath the chin. The sufferer of cruel poverty smiled in her sleep; she had found bread, rest, and health.

"I want to see my mother," sobbed a poor little child, as the undertaker screwed down the top.

"You cannot; get out of my way, boy; why does not some one take the brat?"

"Only let me see one minute!" cried the orphan, clutching the side of the charity box, as he gazed upon the coffin, agonized tears streaming down the cheeks on which the childish bloom ever lingered. Oh! it was painful to hear him cry the words: "Only once; let me see my mother, only once!"

Quickly and brutally the heartless monster struck the boy away, so that he reeled with the blow. For a moment the boy stood panting with grief and rage—his blue eyes distended, his lips sprang apart, fire glistened through his eyes as he raised his little arm with a most unchildish laugh, and screamed: "When I'm a man I'll be revenged for that!"

There was a coffin and a heap of earth between the mother and the poor forsaken child—a monument much stronger than granite, built in the boy's heart, the memory of the heartless deed.

. . . .

The court-house was crowded to suffocation.

"Does any one appear as this man's counsel?" asked the judge.

There was a silence when he had finished, until, with lips tightly pressed together, a look of strange intelligence blended with haughty reserve on his handsome features, a young man stepped forward with a firm tread and a kindly eye to plead for the friendless one. He was a stranger, but at the first sentence there was a silence. The splendor of his genius entranced—convinced.

The man who could not find a friend was acquitted.

"May God bless you, sir; I cannot!" he exclaimed.

"I want no thanks," replied the stranger.

"I—I—I—believe you are unknown to me."

"Sir, I will refresh your memory. Twenty years ago this day you struck a broken-hearted little boy away from his mother's coffin. I was that boy."

The man turned pale.

"Have you rescued me then to take my life?"

"No; I have a sweeter revenge. I have saved the life of a man whose brutal conduct has rankled in my breast for the last twenty years. Go, then, and remember the tears of a friendless child."

The man bowed his head in shame, and went from the presence of magnanimity—as grand to him as it was incomprehensible.

YOUNG MAN, BE PROVIDENT!

Save a part of your weekly earnings, even if it be no more than a quarter dollar, and put your savings monthly in a savings-bank.

Buy nothing till you can pay for it, and buy nothing that you do not need.

A young man who has grit enough to follow these rules will have taken the first step upward to success in business. He may be compelled to wear a coat a year longer, even if it be unfashionable; he may have to live in a smaller house than some of his young acquaintances; his wife may not sparkle with diamonds nor be resplendent in silk or satin, just yet; his children may not be dressed as dolls or popinjays; his table may be plain but wholesome, and the whizz of the beer or champagne cork may never be heard in his dwelling; he may have to get along without the earliest fruit or vegetables; he may have to abjure the club-room, the theater and the gambling hell, and reverence the Sabbath day and read and follow the precepts of the Bible instead, but he will be better off in every way for this self-discipline. Yes, he may do all these without detriment to his manhood, or health, or character. True, empty-headed folk may sneer at him and affect to pity him; but he will find that he has grown strong-hearted and brave enough to stand the laugh of the foolish. He has become an independent man. He never owes anybody, and so he is no man's slave. He has become master of himself, and a master of himself will become a leader among men, and prosperity will crown his every enterprise. Young man! life's discipline and life's success come from hard work and early self-denial; and hard-earned success is all the sweeter at the time when old years climb up on your shoulder and you need propping up.

THE SPOOPENDYKES.

THE OLD GENTLEMAN TAKES EXERCISE ON A BICYCLE.

"Now, my dear," said Mr. Spoopendyke, hurrying up to his wife's room, "if you'll come down in the yard I've got a pleasant surprise for you."

"What is it?" asked Mrs. Spoopendyke, "what have you got, a horse?"

"Guess again," grinned Mr. Spoopendyke. "It's something like a horse."

"I know! It's a new parlor carpet. That's what it is!"

"No, it isn't, either. I said it's something like a horse; that is, it goes when you make it. Guess again."

"Is it paint for the kitchen walls?" asked Mrs. Spoopendyke, innocently.

"No, it ain't, and it ain't a hogshead of stove blacking, nor a set of dining-room furniture, nor it ain't seven gross of stationary washtubs. Now, guess again."

"Then it must be some lace curtains for the sitting-room windows. Isn't that just splendid?" and Mrs. Spoopendyke patted her husband on both cheeks and danced up and down with delight.

"It's a bicycle, that's what it is!" growled Mr. Spoopendyke. "I bought it for exercise and I'm going to ride it. Come down and see me."

"Well, ain't I glad," ejaculated Mrs. Spoopendyke. "You ought to have more exercise; if there's exercise in anything, it's in a bicycle. Do let's see it!"

Mr. Spoopendyke conducted his wife to the yard and descanted at length on the merits of the machine.

"In a few weeks I'll be able to make a mile a minute," he said, as he steadied the apparatus against the clothes-post and prepared to mount. "Now you watch me go to the end of this path."

He got a foot into one treadle and went head first into a flower patch, the machine on top, with a prodigious crash.

"Hadn't you better tie it up to the post until you get on?" suggested Mrs. Spoopendyke.

"Leave me alone, will ye?" demanded Mr. Spoopendyke, struggling to an even keel. "I'm doing most of this myself. Now you hold on and keep your mouth shut. It takes a little practice, that's all."

Mr. Spoopendyke mounted again and scuttled along four or five feet and flopped over on the grass-plot.

"That's splendid!" commended his wife. "You've got the idea already. Let me hold it for you this time."

"If you've got any extra strength you hold your tongue, will ye?" growled Mr. Spoopendyke. "It don't want any holding. It ain't alive. Stand back and give me room, now."

The third trial Mr. Spoopendyke ambled to the end of the path and went down all in a heap among the flower-pots.

"That's just too lovely for anything!" proclaimed Mrs. Spoopendyke. "You made more'n a mile a minute, that time."

"Come and take it off!" roared Mr. Spoopendyke. "Help me up! Dod gast the bicycle!" and the worthy gentleman struggled and plunged around like a whale in shallow water.

Mrs. Spoopendyke assisted in righting him and brushed him off.

"I know where you make your mistake," said she. "The little wheel ought to go first, like a buggy. Try it that way going back."

"Maybe you can ride this bicycle better than I can," howled Mr. Spoopendyke. "You know all about wheels! What you need now is a lantern in your mouth and ten minutes behind time to be the City Hall clock! If you had a bucket of water and a handle you'd make a steam grindstone! Don't you see the big wheel has got to go first?"

"Yes, dear," murmured Mrs. Spoopendyke, "but I thought if you practiced with the little wheel at first, you wouldn't have so far to fall."

"Who fell?" demanded Mr. Spoopendyke. "Didn't you see me step off? I tripped, that's all. Now you just watch me go back."

Once more Mr. Spoopendyke started in, but the big wheel turned around and looked him in the face, and then began to stagger.

"Look out!" squealed Mrs. Spoopendyke.

Mr. Spoopendyke wrenched away and kicked and struggled, but it was of no avail. Down he came, and the bicycle was a hopeless wreck.

"What'd ye want to yell for!" he shrieked. "Couldn't ye keep your measly mouth shut? What'd ye think ye are, anyhow, a fog horn? Dod gast the measly bicycle!" and Mr. Spoopendyke hit it a kick that folded it up like a bolt of muslin.

"Never mind, my dear," consoled Mrs. Spoopendyke, "I'm afraid the exercise was too violent anyway, and I'm rather glad you broke it."

"I suppose so," snorted Mr. Spoopendyke. "There's sixty dollars gone."

"Don't worry, love. I'll go without the carpet and curtains, and the paint will do well enough in the kitchen. Let me rub you with arnica."

But Mr. Spoopendyke was too deeply grieved by his wife's conduct to accept any office at her hands, preferring to punish her by letting his wound smart rather than get well, and thereby relieve her of any anxiety she brought on herself by acting so outrageously under the circumstances.

A JUMPER FROM JUMPVILLE.

"Say!" he called as he walked across the street to a policeman yesterday at the circus grounds, "have you seen a slim little chap with a red mustache and a diamond pin?"

"I don't remember."

"Well, I want to hunt him up. If you'll help me find him I'll give you a yoke of two-year old steers."

"What's he done?"

"Say, I'm mad all over, but I can't help but—ha! ha! ha!— laugh at the way he gumfuzzled me half an hour ago. I'm a flat, I am! I'm rich pasture for cows! I'm turnips with a heap of green tops!"

"What's the story?"

"Well, I was over there under a wagon counting my money. I brought in fifteen dollars. I was a-wondering whether I'd better keep it in my hind pocket or pin it inside my vest, when the little chap comes creeping under and says: 'Pardner, there's a wicked crowd around here. Put that money in your boot.' Say!"

"Yes."

"Struck me as the sensiblest thing I could do. It was in bills, and I pulled off my right boot and chucked 'em in. Say! d'ye see anything green in that?"

"No."

"Well, I hadn't walked around long before a chap comes up and remarks that he has five dollars to bet to a quarter that he can outjump me. Say, d'ye know me?"

"No."

"Well, when I'm home I'm the tallest jumpist of Washtenaw County. I jump higher and farther than anything, animal or

human. I kiver more ground than a panther; I sail higher than
a jumpin' hoss. I'm open to even bets day or night, and I go out
and jump 'leven feet to astonish the children. When that 'ere
stranger offered sich odds I looked at his legs for a minute and
remarked that I was his huckleberry."

"I see."

"Say, up went the stakes, off cum my butes and I outjumped
him by three feet six."

"And what?"

"And when I looked around for my butes that infernal little
hornet with the sandy mustache had made off with the one the
cash was in. Say!"

"Yes."

"I live on Jumpin' Creek. I'm the creek myself. I'm called a
daisy when I'm home, and every time I trade hosses or shot-guns
or dogs I paralyze the other feller. I'm previous. I'm prussic
acid. I'm razors. Say!"

"Yes."

"If I kin lay hands on that little chap I'll make every bone crack.
But it was a good one on me. Eh? Ever see it beaten? Played
me for a fool and hit me the fust time. Say! If you see me—
ha! ha! ha!—laughing, don't think I'm tight: I'm mad. But
say! old Jumpin' Creek was too smart, wasn't he? Needed something to thin his blood, and he got it from a chap who didn't seem
to know putty from the band-wagon! Say! Ha! ha! ha!"

TEDDY O'ROURKE.

MALCOLM DOUGLAS.

Teddy O'Rourke's my chum, you see,
An' how it happened was, him an' me
Was down at the dock with the rest that day,
A-lookin' for somethin' to come our way,
Fur shines, I tell ye, was precious few,
An' we thought we could pick up a dime or two,
Along with some of the other chaps,
Luggin' a feller's valise, perhaps.

It was time the boat was a-gittin' in,
An' of all the crowd on the dock who'd been
Waitin' fur friends, none took our eye
Like two who was standin' just close by—
A lady, if ever was one, I guess,
You could tell as much by her way an' dress,
With a little girl who had 'bout the looks
Of them kids you see in the picture-books,
With her big blue eyes an' her hair like gold;
I s'pose she was four or five years old.
An' blest if she doesn't tell Ted and me
How her pa's on board an' how glad she'll be
When he is home with 'em both again;
An' Teddy he sees the boat just then.

Well, the boat swings into the slip at last,
An' while they're busy a-makin' fast,
With the passengers ready a'most to land,
The little girl loses her mother's hand,
When every one's crowdin' and pushin' hard,
An' blamed if she doesn't fall overboard!
I can't ezzactly tell how she does,
'Cause 'fore I knows it, why, there it was.
An' then there follers a great big splash
As Teddy goes after her in a flash!

Talk about swimmin', now, Ted kin swim!
Not one of the fellers I knows tops *him*.
Stay under the longest you ever see;
Dive about twict as high as me;
Go out so fur you'd be skairt clean through;
Why, they ain't a thing 'at he dassent do!
More like a duck, I guess you'd say
If you ever saw him in, some day—
An', though the tide is a-runnin' strong,
He strikes right out, an' it ain't so long
'Fore he's clingin' with her to the slippery spiles,
An' she's safe—an' he just looks up an' smiles!

Then they get the little girl up all right,
An' there's nothin' the matter with her 'cept fright,

While Teddy unhelped climbs up the beams
With the water a-runnin' from him in streams;
An' while he's shiverin', kind o', there,
The little girl's ma don't seem to care
At all fur the people a-standin' by,
But gives him a kiss an' begins to cry;
An' the little girl's pa ain't noways slow
In grabbin' his hand—an' he won't let go;
While everybody upon the pier
Just whoops her up in a bustin' cheer,
An' one of 'em yells out, after that,
"Come, chip in, all of you!   Here's the hat!"

An' didn't they?   Well, now, they just *did!*
Teddy was allers a lucky kid!
An', while around with the hat they goes,
Every one reaches down in his clo'es,
An' you'd laugh to see how the ol' plug fills
With dimes an' quarters an' halfs an' bills,
Till at last it's a-holdin' so much tin
Looks 's if the crown would just bust right in;

An' they takes the money 'at they have riz,
An' they goes to Teddy an' says it's his.
"What?" says Teddy.   "This ain't all mine!"
An' you oughter have seed his black eyes shine,
An' I feels so good 'at I gives him a shove,
Fur I knows just what he's a-thinkin' of—
It's about his mother, who's purty old,
An' that sister of his'n the doctor's told
If she only could go for a good long spell
Out in the country she might git well.
An' every one laughs 'cause he stares so hard,
While the little girl's pa takes out a card
That says where Teddy's to call next day,
An' they goes in a hack of their own away.

That's about all, 'cept Teddy O'Rourke
Has got a chance, and has gone to work
In the little girl's pa's big dry-goods store;
An' he ain't a-shinin' 'em up no more.

An' now he's a-goin' to free-school, nights,
An' he's learnin' so 'at he reads an' writes,
While I tells him to keep on peggin' away,
An' he'll be a big duck hisself, some day.
—An' me? Oh, Teddy'll look out fur me—
Teddy O'Rourke's my *chum*, you see!

JIM SHATTUCKS.

S. W. FOSS.

Oh! he'd hurl the dictionary promiscus through the air,
And he'd jab statistics inter ye from almost ev'rywhare.
        An' ol' Erastus Beebe
        Said he et a cyclopedy
Ev'ry mornin' 'ith his breakfast; an' I b'lieve he did, I swear.

An' in knowledge of the Scriptur he could lay the parson flat,
'Bout Melchizidek an' Moses, Jonah and Jehosophat,
        An' you couldn't fin' his ekil
        In Leviticus or Zekil;
He kep' all the law an' prophets packed away beneath his hat.

He'd kote Congressional reports jest like his A, B, C;
An' of all the laws and statoots he possessed a full idee,
        An' he'd argify on science
        'Ith all the intellectual giants,
An' he'd run 'em from their burrows, an' he'd chase 'em up a tree.

An' down to Peleg Perkins' store he useter sit an' talk.
One day w'en he wuz spoutin' in there comes an orkered gawk,
        An' he kinder sneaked an' sidled
        Like a hoss that isn't bridled,
An' Jim pitched into him an' tried to make him toe the chalk.

An' the gawk he looked so silly that we kinder pitied him,
An' Peleg Perkins whispered: "Kinder stroke him easy, Jim."
        Then the gawk he squirmed and wriggled
        'Til the gal clerk up an' giggled.
Then he waded in an' argered like a blessed seraphim!

He pelted Jim 'ith school-books till I tell ye it wuz rich,
An' he'd whelt him with the Bible as he'd beat it with a switch,
        In the history of Chiny,
        Timbuctoo, and North Carliny,
Theology and jollogy, geogerfy an' sich.

He'd·kote the President's message an' his inaugeral speech,
An' no crumbs in wisdom's pantry seemed to be beyond his
        reach;
        All his'try he would gabble on,
        Fr'm Boston back to Bab'lon;
W'en he shook the tree of knowledge every shake would drop
        a peach.

An' Jim he sorter wilted, an' then hung down his head,
An' he slowly shuffled from the store, but not a word he said,
        An' we all knew ol' Jim Shattucks
        Had met his Appomattox;
Nex' day his children foun' him in the upper corn-field, dead!

ELDER LAMB'S DONATION.

WILL CARLETON.

Good old Elder Lamb had labored for a thousand nights and
        days,
And had preached the blessed Bible in a multitude of ways;
Had received a message daily over Faith's celestial wire,
And had kept his little chapel full of flames of heavenly fire;
He had raised a num'rous family, straight and sturdy as he
        could,
And his boys were all considered as unnaturally good;
And his "slender sal'ry" kept him till went forth the proclama-
        tion,
"We will pay him up this season with a gen'rous, large donation."

So they brought him hay and barley, and some corn upon the ear,
Straw enough to bed his pony for forever and a year;
And they strewed him with potatoes of inconsequential size,
And some onions whose completeness drew the moisture from
        his eyes;

And some cider—more like water, in an inventory strict;
And some apples, pears, and peaches, that the autumn gales had
    picked;
And some strings of dried-up apples—mummies of the fruit cre-
    ation—
Came to swell the doleful census of old Elder Lamb's donation.

Also radishes and turnips pressed the pumpkins' cheerful cheek,
Likewise beans enough to furnish half of Boston for a week;
And some butter that was worthy to have Samson for a foe,
And some eggs whose inner nature held the legend, "Long
    ago!"
And some stove-wood, green and crooked, on his flower-beds
    was laid,
Fit to furnish fire departments with the most substantial aid.
All things unappreciated found this night their true vocation
In the Museum of Relics, known as Elder Lamb's donation.

There were biscuits whose material was their own secure de-
    fense;
There were sauces whose acuteness bore the sad pluperfect
    tense;
There were jellies undissected, there were mystery-laden pies;
There was bread that long had waited for the signal to arise;
There were cookies tasting clearly of the drear and musty past;
There were doughnuts that in justice 'mongst the metals might
    be classed;
There were chickens, geese, and turkeys that had long been on
    probation,
Now received in full connection at old Elder Lamb's donation.

Then they gave his wife a wrapper made for some one not so
    tall,
And they brought him twenty slippers, every pair of which was
    small;
And they covered him with sackcloth, as it were, in various bits,
And they clothed his helpless children in a wardrobe of misfits;
And they trimmed his house with "Welcome," and some bric-à-
    bracish trash,
And one absent-minded brother brought five dollars all in cash!

Which the good old pastor handled with a thrill of exultation,
Wishing that in filthy lucre might have come his whole donation !

Morning came at last in splendor; but the Elder, wrapped in
 gloom,
Knelt amid decaying produce and the ruins of his home;
And his piety had never till that morning been so bright,
For he prayed for those who brought him to that unexpected
 plight.
But some worldly thoughts intruded, for he wondered o'er and
 o'er,
If they'd buy that day at auction what they gave the night be-
 fore ?
And his fervent prayer concluded with the natural exclamation,
"Take me to Thyself in mercy, Lord, before my next donation."

ARCHIE'S MOTHER.

ROSE HARTWICK THORPE.

"Archie's wife ?   Yes, dear, but where's Archie ?
 My first kiss is waiting for him,
For since his good-by that sad morning,
 Past the years my tears have made dim,
No kiss has lain over his kisses,
 No love has come into my life.
But he—who has had his caresses ?
 I ask you this—you, his wife.

" He's not here to welcome his mother,
 What's wrong ?   Is my dear son ill ?
You came ?   Yes, dear, but remember,
 Archie's place none other can fill.
'Twas business detained him, I reckon.
 Well, well, I won't let it annoy :
No doubt he is climbing the ladder
 Of fame he dreamed of as a boy.

"You are a sweet girl.   I don't blame you
 For taking first place in his heart.

It has seemed to me—don't be offended,
    I'm his mother, and know every part
Of his nature, and somehow his letters
    Have been rather downcast of late,
He is writing so often for money,
    And hints at things sad to relate.

"I thought you were childish and giddy,
    Extravagant, too, I confess;
But I see no reason to chide you
    For extravagance in your dress.
Your pretty pink frock is quite tidy,
    Your collar as white as the snow;
But if you don't spend them for laces,
    Where is it the dollars all go?

"The carriage? Oh, well, never mind it,
    We'll walk if it isn't far;
I'm quite numb and weary with sitting
    So long in the dusty car.
Thanks, dear. Archie's arm would be stronger.
    To think I shall see him to-day,
My tall, handsome son! How is baby?
    Are his eyes blue like yours, or gray?

"Not overly strong? It's a mercy
    I came to you now; for I know
All about the needs of a baby,
    And the food that will make him grow.
My Archie was puny and sickly
    For years, the most of the time
I kept the breath of life in him,
    By doses of brandy and wine.

"Yes, brandy and wine are great blessings
    To mothers, in many a way;
Without them I couldn't have raised him
    To love us and bless us to-day.
And the little rogue learned to like them:
    Why, he'd take the bitterest pill
With only a swallow of porter
    To wash it down. Dear, are you ill?

You're not going to lose your baby:
  Just give me a plenty of time,
And he shall be strong and rosy.
  I'll cure him as I cured mine!
"'You'd rather he'd die!' Alice Dutton,
  I'm surprised, nay shocked, I confess.
Are you Christian or Pagan, I wonder,
  That you dare stand here and express
Such heathenish views! Will the Father
  Work miracles, think, for your son?
Will He take your sick boy and cure him,
  Till your part is faithfully done?

"'Tis a shame on your son to suggest it,
  A shame on your darling and mine!
Why, six generations of Duttons
  Have proved themselves stronger than wine,
Not once disgracing their manhood.
  Don't mention it, Alice, I pray;
Your boy is the last of the lineage—
  Do you think him less noble than they?

"Disgrace is unknown to a Dutton
  In all their ancestral line.
Do you fear that their blue blood is tarnished
  And weakened by mixture with thine?
Nay, child, your grave apprehensions
  Are shadowless as the wind:
Don't weep so, dear, Archie's mother
  Never meant to be unkind.

"You are like a fair, gentle daughter,
  Your face is so tender and sweet.
You are like—But where are we going?
  Why turn down that terrible street?
This house? Why, child, 'tis a hovel!
  See that drunken man stretched in the way!
Don't show me rum's wretchedness, Alice,
  I'm worn out with travel to-day.

"You surely don't seek your companions
  Among those so wretchedly low?

You, wife of my son, and the mother
  Of my son's son! Let us go
To your home at once. Alice! Alice!
  Don't touch that vile drunken man,
The loathsome being has fallen
  As low as humanity can.
His very breath is pollution;
  Redemption for such, there is none.
He!—O my God! it is Archie!
  It is Archie, my son! my son!"

HOW THE ORGAN WAS PAID FOR.

KATE A. BRADLEY.

Loud the organ tones came swelling all the crowded aisles
    along;
Gladdest praise their music thrilling in a burst of wordless song.
Oft the chink of falling money sounded soft the notes between,
But the plate seemed slow in filling—little silver could be seen.

Hands in pockets lingered sadly, faces looked unwilling, cold;
Gifts from slow, unwilling fingers o'er the plate's rich velvet
    rolled.
"It's Thanksgiving, dear," a mother whispered to her question-
    ing son;
"We must give to the new organ, all our pennies, every one.

"Then it will be ours, all paid for, and will sweeter music send
In thanksgiving up to heaven, with the angels' praise to blend."
Slowly passed the plate of off'rings, while a child-voice whispered
    low:
"I put in my every penny; mamma, will the organ know

"That I gave the yellow penny Uncle Charlie sent to me?"
"Yes, dear," whispered soft the mother, "God your gift will
    surely see."
"Give, oh, give!" the music pleaded. "Give, that loud I may
    rejoice!"
Then thro' all the waiting stillness, piped a shrill, indignant
    voice:

" Mamma, do you think the organ saw that rich old Deacon Cox
Only gave one little penny when they passed the music-box?"
Quick the little voice was quiet, but a flush of honest shame
From awakened hearts uprising, over many faces came.

And the deacon, slowly rising, as the organ died away,
Said, " I humbly here acknowledge to a wicked heart to-day,
Friends and brothers; but my sinning I will alter as I live,
And the half of what is lacking here to-day, I freely give;

" That our glorious new organ may give praise to God on high,
With no debt of earth upon it that our gold can satisfy."
Then arose another brother, and another still, and more,
Giving with a lavish spending as they never gave before.

Till the plate was overflowing and the organ debt secure;
Then they took a contribution for Thanksgiving and the poor.
And as outward with the music a glad stream of people flows,
Soft a childish voice cries, " Mamma, I am sure the organ
      knows!"

OLD ACE.

FRED EMERSON BROOKS.

Can any pleasure in life compare
With a charming drive in the balmy air?
A buggy light with shimmering wheel;
Springs whose resistance you barely feel;
A spirited horse of royal breed,
With just a little more style and speed
Than any you meet, and it matters not
If his gait be pace or a swinging trot.

The tassel sways on the graceful whip;
You grasp the reins with a tighter grip;
Your horse is off for a splendid dash
And needs no touch of the urging lash.
You feel the puff of the startled air;
It floats his mane and it lifts your hair!
The hoof marks time in its measured beat,
For the swelling nostril that scorns defeat!

One glorious day in the balmy spring
John Dorr was out with his new horse King.
Though both were rich, it was his design
To buy him a faster horse than mine.
By his side the sweetest girl in the town,
Of handsome features and eyes so brown,
That gazing in where the lashes curled
Was like a view of another world
Where the angel lives and the angel sings;
And she was one that had dropped her wings
And come to earth just to let men see
How sweet the angels in heaven may be!
I envied the breeze its constant bliss
Of passing her cheek to steal a kiss!

I loved the girl when we both were young,
But getting older I'd lost my tongue.
I learned in college Latin and Greek,
But Cupid's language I could not speak.
While Jack was perfect in Cupid's art,
The only language he knew by heart.
I envied John in his ride that day,
And jogged old Spot in a leisure way,
That two-mile drive to the sulphur spring,
To test the speed of his new horse King.

John took the lead and it touched his pride;
For the fastest horse and the fairest bride
Had been his boast!   Did I pass him by?
My heart, I reckon, could answer why—
I'm almost certain I lost the race
By lagging behind to look at Grace!

Jack seemed more proud of his horse that day
Than he was of Grace, which made me say:
" Be sure of your game before you boast;
From dead defeat there may rise a ghost!
I'll race you back to the town," said I,
" For Gracie's glove!"   But he made reply:
" What use to you is the senseless glove
From the soft white hand of the girl I love?

Suppose you win," he laughed in my face,
"You get the mitten and I get Grace!"
Said I: "No trophy I would so prize—"
And I caught a look from her soft brown eyes
That drove the rest of it out of my head—
I don't remember just what I said!

John laughed away till his eyes were wet;
"Increase the wager; I'll take the bet!"
"My glove," said Grace, "and the hand within,
Shall be the prize of the one to win!"
I looked at John, but he didn't chaff,
He didn't smile and he didn't laugh!
"Must I, then, race you for such a bride,"
Said John, "and carry the load beside?"

"I'll carry," said I, "the precious load!"
Her bright eye flashed and her fair cheek glowed!
She took her seat with little ado;
I tucked the robe and my heart in too!
Said I: "Old Spot!" as I stroked his neck,
And rubbed his nose and loosened his check,
"She's Bob's own Grace, if you do your best!"
He pricked his ears just as if he guessed
The time had come when his master's need
Had staked all happiness on his speed.

When all was ready Grace shouted "Go!"
A word both horses seemed to know.
You heard the hoof with its measured sway
Pacing along the great highway.
You saw the swell of the panting side,
The pink that glows in the nostril wide.
I knew old Spot, if he kept that pace,
Would win my choice of the human race.
No word was spoken between us two;
The tongue is silent when hope is new.
A mile, a mile and a half we sped,
And still old Spot was a neck ahead.

Jack touched his horse with the tasseled whip;
Then Gracie, pursing her rosy lip,

Uttered a sound like a lover's kiss—pss—ss! pss—ss!
The world is ruled by a sound like this!
To urge a horse a capital plan,
And often used to encourage man;
But she never dreamed she had let me in
To her heart's fond wish that I should win.

The only time in the race she spoke
Was when, over-urged, Jack's trotter broke.
"He's running his horse, and that's not fair!"
And blushing up to her auburn hair,
She grabbed the whip from my willing hand—
A move that John seemed to understand—
For she raised it high as much as to say,
Well, running's a game that two can play!
So he brought him down to an honest trot,
But couldn't keep up with dear old Spot,
Who forged ahead when he saw the whip
And passed the stake with never a skip.

On through the village he kept his speed,
For I was too happy to mind the steed;
He would not stop when the race was done,
But started home with the prize he'd won!
Nor stopped till he reached the farm-house gate,
Where good old mother was sure to wait.

I know the horse is a trifle old,
But you can't buy him with all your gold!
My Gracie loves him and pats his neck,
And says he's the best card in the deck!
And rubs his nose till he kisses her face;
She has changed his name to dear old Ace,
And smiling says: "It's the proper thing,
For it takes the Ace to beat the King!"
As she purses her lips for the well-known smack,
"I'm glad the Queen didn't take the Jack!"

KNITTING.

J. S. CUTTER.

Grandma sits in her easy chair,
  Knitting a stocking for baby May;
Slipping the stitches with loving care,
  Knitting and dreaming the time away;
Thinking of other little feet,
  Cold and silent, at rest so long;
And, as she dreams of the old times sweet,
  Her heart runs over in simple song:
    Narrow, and widen, and slip, and bind!
      Swift and silent the needles run;
      Hands are willing and heart is kind;
      Honest workers are hard to find;
      Baby's stocking begun!

Grandma dreams of a glad spring day,
  Years and years and years ago,
When her hair was gold, now so thin and gray,
  And her faded cheeks wore a rosy glow;
And Robin comes to the farm-yard gate,
  And tells his love in his bashful way:
And grandma sings, while the hour grows late,
  The song she sung on her wedding-day:
    Narrow, and widen, and slip, and bind!
      Click the needles and sing the song!
      Swift and silent the skeins unwind;
      Hands are willing and heart is kind;
      Baby's stocking grows long!

Grandma thinks of the children three—
  Bob, and Charlie, and little Bess—
Lisping prayers at her mother-knee,
  Making music her life to bless.
O'er her face comes a shade of pain,
  Brought by thoughts of the long ago;
Trembling voice breaks forth again,
  The song runs on while the tear-drops flow:

Narrow, and widen, and slip, and bind!
　Work and trust while the moments run;
Eyes with tears are often blind;
Hands are willing and heart is kind;
　Baby's stocking half done!

Grandma's hands have tired grown;
　Poor old hands, that have worked so long!
Daylight swift from the earth has flown;
　Almost silent has grown the song;
Still she knits, as she sits and dreams,
　Hurrying onward to reach the toe;
Deftly turning the even seams,
　While she murmurs in accents low:
　　Narrow, and widen, and slip, and bind!
　　　Hands grow tired at set of sun;
　　Hands are willing and heart is kind;
　　Life grows short while the skeins unwind;
　　　Baby's stocking most done!

Grandma stops, and her knitting falls
　Idly down on the sanded floor;
Shining needles and half-wound balls;
　Grandma's knitting, alas! is o'er.
So we found her at close of day,
　White head resting upon her breast;
Knitting finished and laid away;
　Loving fingers for aye at rest.
　　Narrow, and widen, and slip, and bind!
　　　Skein at last to the end has run;
　　Heart stops beating that once was kind;
　　Hands are folded that ne'er repined;
　　　Baby's stocking is done!

THE ROAD TO HEAVEN.

GEORGE R. SIMS.

How is the boy this morning? Why do you shake your head?
Ah! I can see what's happened—there's a screen drawn round
　the bed.

So! poor little Mike is sleeping the last long sleep of all;
I'm sorry—but who could wonder, after that dreadful fall?

Let me look at him, doctor—poor little storm-tossed waif!
His frail bark's out of the tempest, and lies in God's harbor safe;
Didn't you know his story?   Ah, you weren't here, I believe,
When they brought the poor little fellow to the hospital Christ-
    mas eve!

'Twas a raw cold air that evening—a biting Christmassy frost—
I was looking about for a collie—a favorite dog I'd lost.
Some ragged boys, so they told me, had been seen with one that
    night
In one of the bridge recesses, so I hunted left and right.

I fancied the place was empty, but, as I passed along,
Out of the darkness floated the words of a Christmas song,
Sung in a childish treble—'twas a boy's voice, hoarse with cold,
Quavering out the anthem of angels and harps of gold.

I stood where the shadows hid me, and peered out until
I could see two ragged urchins, blue with the icy chill,
Cuddling close together, crouched on a big stone seat—
Two little homeless arabs, waifs of the heartless street.

One was singing the carol, when the other, with big, round eyes—
It was Mike—looked up in wonder, and said: "Jack, when we dies
Is that the place as we goes to—that place where ye'r dressed
    in white?
And has golden harps to play on, and it's warm and jolly and
    bright?

"Is that what they mean by heaven, as the misshun folks talks
    about,
Where the children's always happy and nobody kicks 'em out?"
Jack nodded his head, assenting, and then I listened and heard
The talk of the little arabs—listened to every word.

Jack was a Sunday scholar, so I gathered from what he said,
And sang in the road for a living—his father and mother were
    dead;
And he had a drunken granny, who turned him into the street;
She drank what he earned, and often he hadn't a crust to eat.

Mike'd a drunken father and mother, who sent him out to beg,
Though he'd just got over a fever, and was lame with a withered
      leg;
He told how he daren't crawl homeward, because he had begged
      in vain,
And his parents' brutal fury haunted his baby brain.

"I wish I could go to heaven," he cried, as he shook with fright;
"If I thought as they'd only take me, why I'd go this very night.
Which is the way to heaven? How d'ye they get there, Jack?"
Jack climbed on the bridge's coping and looked at the water
      black.

"That there's *one* road to heaven," he said, as he pointed down
To where the cold, dark waters surged muddy and thick and
      brown.
"If we was to fall in there, Mike, we'd be dead; and right
      through there
Is the place where it's always sunshine, and the angels has
      crowns to wear."

Mike rose and looked at the water; he peered in the big, broad
      stream
Perhaps with the childish notion he might catch the golden
      gleam
Of the far-off land of glory. He leaned right over and cried—
"If them are the gates of heaven, how I'd like to be inside!"

He'd stood but a moment looking, how it happened I cannot tell,
When he seemed to lose his balance, gave a short, shrill cry and
      fell—
Fell over the narrow coping, and I heard his poor head strike
With a thud on the stonework under; then splash in the waves
      went Mike.

We brought him here that evening. For help I had managed
      to shout—
A boat put from off the landing, and they dragged his body out;
His forehead was cut and bleeding, but a vestige of life we
      found;
When they brought him here he was senseless, but slowly the
      child came round.

I came here on Christmas morning—the ward was all bright
　　and gay
With mistletoe, green, and holly, in honor of Christmas day;
And the patients had clean, white garments, and a few in the
　　room out there
Had joined in a Christmas service—they were singing a Christ-
　　mas air.

They were singing a Christmas carol when Mike from his stupor
　　woke,
And dim on his wandering senses the strange surroundings broke.
Half-dreamily he remembered the tale he had heard from Jack—
The song, and the white-robed angels, the warm, bright heaven
　　came back.

"I'm in heaven," he whispered faintly. "Yes, Jack must have
　　told me true!"
And as he looked about him, came the kind old surgeon through.
Mike gazed at his face a moment, put his hand to his fevered
　　head,
Then to the kind old doctor, "Please, are you God?" he said.

Poor little Mike! 'Twas heaven, this hospital ward, to him—
A haven of warmth and comfort, till the flickering lamp grew
　　dim;
And he lay like a tired baby in a dreamless, gentle rest,

And now he is safe forever where such as he are best.
This is the day of scoffers; but who shall say that night,
When Mike asked the road to heaven, that Jack didn't tell him
　　right?
'Twas the children's Jesus pointed the way to the kingdom come
For the poor little tired arab, the waif of the city slum.

CHANGING COLOR.

HATTIE G. CANFIELD.

Oh, every one was sorry for Ned!
"It's a perfect shame," so the people said;
"And who was Ned?" Why, don't you know?
Ned was the deacon's daughter's beau,—

Honest and manly, hard to beat,
Five foot ten in his stocking feet.

Bess was the sweetest girl in the place,
With a soul as fair as her winsome face;
The deacon's daughter, kind and gay,
And used to having her own sweet way.
Now, *two* good people *may* agree,—
The deacon, Bess, and Ned make *three*.

Old Deacon Green was a "moneyed man;"
His motto was: "Get and keep if you can."
Honest in all his dealings?"   Yes,
Honest as you, or Ned, or Bess;
But charity had left his creed,
And he was stingy in thought and deed.

"I tell you no man borrows from me;
If he wants any help, let him find it," said he;
"And Bess, my girl, hear what I say,
You send that shiftless Ned away!
I have no use for the lazy dunce,
I heard that he borrowed a dollar once.

"Now when *I* borrow—you hear me, Bess?—
Then you may purchase your wedding-dress.
Until that time Ned Brown, you see,
Must be a minus quantity."
And Bessie murmured soft and low:
"That's something Ned would like to know."

That night the moon and the silent stars
Saw two young heads near the meadow bars,
And heard Bess say: "I think to-morrow
Some one will really have to borrow!"
Two hearts were happier, I know,
Because the new moon told me so.

Next morn, Bess seized her shopping-bag,
Harnessed the deacon's corpulent nag,
And drove to town; I wonder why
She chose that early hour to buy!

A small boy with a freckled face
Was standing near the market-place;
He waved his cap when he saw sweet Bess,
As fair as a flower, in her muslin dress.
"Good-morning, Cousin Bob," said she;
"You're just the boy I want to see!

"I'll give all you ask, and more,
If you will ride to father's door,
And say to him, 'Bess is in town,
Going to marry that Ned Brown.'
After you tell him, drive away,
No matter what he has to say."

Imagine the deacon, if you can!
Poor Bob ne'er saw an uglier man
Than Deacon Green, that summer day
He watched his old nag trot away;
The words he used are hard to spell,
And really wouldn't do to tell.

"There is Bess in Blickingham town,
Ready to marry that scamp, Brown;
I can reach her as best I may—
Even my old nag's gone to-day!
The parson would lend me—I must borrow,
For Bess may not be there to-morrow."

The parson lent him his dapple gray,
And he made for the town without delay.
There stood Bess in the market-place,
And near her the determined face
Of our friend Brown was plainly seen—
A sight to madden Deacon Green.

The young folks entered the old town-hall,
The scene of many a county ball,
And Bessie's father walked in, too;
I wonder what he meant to do?
This much I know—the words then said
Came chiefly from the lips of Ned.

"Deacon Green, did you borrow the gray
  That brought you to Blickingham town to-day?
  You did? Then Bess shall be my wife,
  And here's an end to all our strife!"
  Said Bess: "I knew dear father meant
  To give his full and free consent."

"But," gasped the deacon, "I never said
  My daughter could marry you, Ned!"
"I heard you say," cried blue-eyed Bess,
"That I might purchase my wedding-dress
  When you borrowed from any one.
  And now, you see, the deed is done!

"It can't be helped; and, father dear,
  Forgive us, won't you, now and here?"
  The deacon frowned, but chuckled too:
"That's all you've left for me to do!
  You're full of business, and I guess
  Your head is pretty level, Bess;
  You took your father's nag away,
  And made him toe the mark to-day;
  And though I'm *Green*, ere we leave town,
  My only daughter shall be *Brown!*"

IN THE NIGHT.

ELLA WHEELER WILCOX.

Sometimes in the night when I sit and write,
  I hear the strangest things,
As my brain grows hot with a burning thought
  That struggles for form and wings.
I can hear the beat of my swift blood's feet
  As it speeds with a rush and whir,
From heart to brain and back again,
  Like a race-horse under the spur.

With my soul's fine ear I listen and hear
  The tender silence speak,

As it leans on the breast of night to rest,
  And presses his dusky cheek.
And the darkness turns in its sleep and yearns
  For something that is kin—
And I hear the hiss of a scorching kiss,
  As it folds and fondles sin.

In its hurrying race thro' leagues of space
  I can hear the earth catch breath,
As it heaves and moans, and shudders and groans,
  And longs for the rest of death.
And high and far from a distant star,
  Whose name is unknown to me,
I hear a voice that says, "Rejoice!
  For I keep ward o'er thee."

Oh, sweet and strange are the sounds that range
  Thro' the chambers of the night;
And the watcher who waits by the dim, dark gates,
  May hear, if he lists aright.

THE OLD OAKEN BUCKET.

SAMUEL WOODWORTH.

How dear to this heart are the scenes of my childhood,
  When fond recollection presents them to view!
The orchard, the meadow, the deep-tangled wildwood,
  And every loved spot which my infancy knew;—
The wide-spreading pond, and the mill that stood by it,
  The bridge, and the rock where the cataract fell;

The cot of my father, the dairy-house nigh it,
    And e'en the rude bucket which hung in the well.
The old oaken bucket, the iron-bound bucket,
The moss-covered bucket which hung in the well.

That moss-covered vessel I hail as a treasure;
    For often, at noon, when returned from the field,
I found it a source of an exquisite pleasure,
    The purest and sweetest that nature can yield,
How ardent I seized it, with hands that were glowing!
    And quick to the white-pebbled bottom it fell;
Then soon, with the emblem of truth overflowing,
    And dripping with coolness, it rose from the well;
The old oaken bucket, the iron-bound bucket,
The moss-covered bucket, arose from the well.

How sweet from the green, mossy brim to receive it,
    As, poised on the curb, it inclined to my lips!
Not a full blushing goblet could tempt me to leave it,
    Though filled with the nectar that Jupiter sips.
And now, far removed from the loved situation,
    The tear of regret will intrusively swell,
As fancy reverts to my father's plantation,
    And sighs for the bucket which hangs in the well '
The old oaken bucket, the iron-bound bucket,
The moss-covered bucket which hangs in the well.

THE FUNERAL.

WILL CARLETON.

I WAS walking in Savannah, past a church decayed and dim,
When there slowly through the window came a plaintive funeral
    hymn;
And a sympathy awakened, and a wonder quickly grew,
Till I found myself environed in a little negro pew.

Out at front a colored couple sat in sorrow, nearly wild;
On the altar was a coffin, in the coffin was a child.

I could picture him when living—curly hair, protruding lip—
And had seen, perhaps, a thousand, in my hurried Southern trip.

But no baby ever rested in the soothing arms of Death
That had fanned more flames of sorrow with his little fluttering
      breath;
And no funeral ever glistened with more sympathy profound
Than was in the chain of tear-drops that enclasped those mourners
      round.

Rose a sad old colored preacher at the little wooden desk—
With a manner grandly awkward, with a countenance grotesque;
With simplicity and shrewdness on his Ethiopian face;
With the ignorance and wisdom of a crushed undying race.

And he said: "Now don' be weepin' for dis pretty bit o' clay—
For de little boy who lived dere, he done gone an' run away!
He was doin' very finely, an' he 'preciate your love;
But his sure 'nuff Father want him in de large house up above.

"Now he didn't give you dat baby, by a hundred thousan' mile!
He just think you need some sunshine, an' he lend it for awhile!
An' he let you keep an' love it till your hearts was bigger grown,
An' dese silver tears your sheddin's jes de interest on de loan.

"Here's yer oder pretty chilrun!—don' be makin' it appear
Dat your love got sort o' 'nop'lized by dis little fellow here;
Don' pile up too much your sorrow on deir little mental shelves,
So's to kind o' set 'em wonderin' if dey're no account demselves.

"Just you think, you poor deah mournahs, creepin' long o'er Sor-
      row's way,
What a blessed little picnic dis yere baby's got to-day!
Your good faders and good moders crowd de little fellow round
In de angel-tented garden of de **Big Plantation Ground.**

"An' dey ask him, 'Was your feet sore?' an' take off his little shoes,
An' dey wash him, an' dey kiss him, an' dey say, 'Now, what's de
      news?'
An' de Lawd done cut his tongue loose; den de little fellow say,
'All our folks down in de valley tries to keep de hebbenly way.'

"An' his eyes dey brightly sparkle at de pretty tings he view;
Den a tear come, an' he whisper, 'But I want my pa'yents, to!'
But de Angel Chief Musician teach dat boy a little song;
Says, 'If only dey be fait'ful dey will soon be comin' long.'

"An' he'll get an education dat will proberbly be worth
Seberal times as much as any you could buy for him on earth;
He'll be in de Lawd's big school house, widout no contempt or fear:
While dere's no end to de bad tings might have happened to him
    here.

"So, my pooah dejected mounahs, let your hearts wid Jesus rest,
An' don' go ter criticisin' dat ar One w'at knows de best!
He have sent us many comforts—He have right to take away—
To de Lawd be praise an' glory, now and ever!—Let us pray."

THE LIFE FOR WHICH I LONG.

JOHN G. WHITTIER.

WHEN on my day of light the night is falling,
    And in the winds from unsunned spaces blown,
I hear far voices out of darkness calling
    My feet to paths unknown.

Thou who hast made my home of life so pleasant,
    Leave not its tenant when its walls decay;
O love divine, O Helper ever present,
    Be Thou my help and stay!

Be near me when all else is from me drifting,
    Earth, sky, home's picture, days of shade and shine,
And kindly faces to my own uplifting
    The love which answers mine.

I have but Thee, O Father! Let Thy spirit
    Be with me, then, to comfort and uphold;
No gate of pearl, no branch of palm I merit,
    Nor street of shining gold.

Suffice it if, my good and ill unreckoned,
  And both forgiven through Thy 'bounding grace,
I find myself by hands familiar beckoned
  Unto my fitting place—

Some humble door among Thy many mansions,
  Some sheltering shade where sin and striving cease,
And flows forever through heaven's green expansions
  The river of Thy peace.

There, from the music round about me stealing,
  I fain would learn the new and holy song,
And find at last, beneath Thy trees of healing,
  The life for which I long.

THE RAIN UPON THE ROOF.

COATES KINNEY.

When the humid shadows hover
  Over all the starry spheres,
And the melancholy darkness
  Gently weeps in rainy tears,
What a joy to press the pillow
  Of a cottage chamber bed,
And to listen to the patter
  Of the soft rain overhead.

Every tinkle on the shingles
  Wakes an echo in the heart,
And a thousand dreamy fancies
  Into busy being start;
And a thousand recollections
  Weave their bright hues into woof,
As I listen to the patter
  Of the rain upon the roof.

Now in fancy comes my mother,
  As she used, long years agone,

To regard her darling dreamers
　　Ere she left them till the dawn.
Oh! I see her bending o'er me,
　　As I list to the refrain,
Which is played upon the shingles
　　By the patter of the rain.

Then my little seraph sister,
　　With her wings and wavy hair,
And my bright-eyed cherub brother—
　　A serene, angelic pair—
Glide around my wakeful pillow,
　　With their smile, or mild reproof,
As I listen to the murmurs
　　Of the rain upon the roof.

And another comes to thrill me
　　With her eyes delicious blue;
I forget while gazing on her
　　That her heart was all untrue.
I remember but to love her,
　　With a rapture kin to pain,
While my heart's quick pulses vibrate
　　To the patter of the rain.

There is naught in art's bravuras
　　That can work with such a spell
In the spirit's pure, deep fountains
　　Whence the holy passions well,
As that melody of Nature,
　　That subdued, subduing strain
Which is played upon the shingles
　　By the patter of the rain.

Spurgeon in his pulpit.

FORTY YEARS AGO.

I've wandered to the village, Tom; I've sat beneath the tree,
Upon the school-house playground, which sheltered you and me;
But none were there to greet me, Tom, and few were left to know,
That played with us upon the green, some forty years ago.

The grass was just as green, Tom, barefooted boys at play,
Were sporting just as we did then, with spirits just as gay,
But Master sleeps upon the hill, which, coated o'er with snow,
Afforded us a sliding place, just forty years ago.

The school-house has altered some—the benches are replaced
By new ones, very like the same our pen-knives had defaced;
But the same old bricks are in the wall—the bell swings to and fro,
Its music just the same, dear Tom, 'twas forty years ago.

The boys were playing some old game, beneath the same old tree,
I do forget the name just now—you've played the same with me—
On that same spot, 'twas played with knives, by throwing so and so,
The leader had a task to do—there forty years ago.

The river's running just as still, the willows on its side
Are larger than they were, Tom, the stream appears less wide;
But the grape-vine swing is ruined now, where once we played the
		beau,
And swung our sweethearts, pretty girls, just forty years ago.

The spring that bubbled 'neath the hill, close by the spreading
		beech,
Is very low—'twas once so high, that we could almost reach;
And kneeling down to get a drink, dear Tom, I startled so,
To see how much I've changed, since forty years ago.

Near by the spring, upon an elm, you know I cut your name,
Your sweetheart's just beneath it, Tom, and you did mine the same;
Some heartless wretch has peeled the bark, 'twas dying sure but
		slow,
Just as that one, whose name you cut, died forty years ago.

My lids have long been dry, Tom, but tears came in my eyes,
I thought of her I loved so well, those early broken ties;
I visited the old church-yard, and took some flowers to strew
Upon the graves of those we loved, some forty years ago.

Some are in the church-yard laid—some sleep beneath the sea,
But few are left of our old class, excepting you and me;
And when our time shall come, Tom, and we are called to go,
I hope they'll lay us where we played, just forty years ago.

THE AGED STRANGER.

BRET HARTE.

"I was with Grant"—the stranger said;
  Said the farmer, "Say no more,
But rest thee here at my cottage porch,
  For thy feet are weary and sore."

"I was with Grant"—the stranger said;
  Said the farmer, "Nay, no more,—
I prithee sit at my frugal board,
  And eat of my humble store.

"How fares my boy,—my soldier boy,
  Of the old Ninth Army Corps?
I warrant he bore him gallantly
  In the smoke and the battle's roar!"

"I know him not," said the aged man,
  "And, as I remarked before,
I was with Grant"—"Nay, nay, I know,"
  Said the farmer, "say no more;

"He fell in battle,—I see, alas!
  Thou'dst smooth these tidings o'er—
Nay, speak the truth, whatever it be,
  Though it rend my bosom's core.

"How fell he,—with his face to the foe,
    Upholding the flag he bore?
O say not that my boy disgraced
    The uniform that he wore!"

"I cannot tell," said the aged man,
    "And should have remarked before,
That I was with Grant—in Illinois—
    Some three years before the war."

Then the farmer spake him never a word,
    But beat with his fist full sore
That aged man who had worked for Grant
    Some three years before the war.

OUR PATTERN.

PHEBE CARY.

A WEAVER sat one day at his loom
    Among the colors bright,
With the pattern for his copying
    Hung fair and plain in sight.

But the weaver's thoughts were wandering
    Away on the distant track,
As he threw the shuttle in his hand
    Wearily forward and back.

And he turned his dim eyes to the ground
    And tears fell on the woof,
For his thoughts, alas! were not with his home
    Nor the wife beneath its roof.

When her voice recalled him suddenly
    To himself, as she sadly said;
"Ah, woe is me! for your work is spoiled,
    And what will we do for bread?"

And then the weaver looked and saw
  His work must be undone;
For the threads were wrong, and the colors dimmed
  Where the bitter tears had run.

"Alack! alack!" said the weaver,
  "And this had all been right
If I had not looked at my work, but kept
  The pattern in my sight."

Ah, sad it was for the weaver,
  And sad for his luckless wife;
And sad it will be for us if we say,
  At the end of our task of life:

"The colors that we had to weave
  Were bright in our early years;
But we wove the tissues wrong and stained
  The woof with bitter tears.

"We wove a web of doubt and fear—
  Not faith, and hope and love—
Because we looked at our work, and not
  Our pattern above."

AN ORDER FOR A PICTURE.

O good painter, tell me true,
  Has your hand the cunning to draw
  Shapes of things that you never saw?
Ay? Well, here is an order for you.
Woods and cornfields, a little brown,—
  The picture must not be over-bright,
  Yet all in the golden and gracious light
Of a cloud, when the summer sun is down.

  Alway and alway, night and morn,
  Woods upon woods, with fields of corn

Lying between them, not quite sere,
And not in the full, thick, leafy bloom,
When the wind can hardly find breathing room
   Under their tassels,—cattle near,
Biting shorter the short, green grass,
And a hedge of sumach and sassafras,
With bluebirds twittering all around,—
(Ah, good painter, you can't paint sound!)
   These, and the house where I was born,
Low and little, and black and old,
With children, many as it can hold,
All at the windows, open wide,—
Heads and shoulders clear outside,
And fair young faces all ablush:
   Perhaps you may have seen, some day,
   Roses crowding the self-same way,
Out of a wilding, wayside bush.

Listen closer.   When you have done
   With woods and cornfields and grazing herds,
   A lady, the loveliest ever the sun
Looked down upon, you must paint for me;
Oh, if I only could make you see
   The clear blue eyes, the tender smile,
The sovereign sweetness, the gentle grace,
The woman's soul, and the angel's face
   That are beaming on me all the while,
   I need not speak these foolish words:
   Yet one word tells you all I would say,—
She is my mother: you will agree
   That all the rest may be thrown away.

Two little urchins at her knee
You must paint, sir; one like me,
   The other with a clearer brow,
   And the light of his adventurous eyes
   Flashing with boldest enterprise:
At ten years old he went to sea,—
   God knoweth if he be living now;

He sailed in the good ship "Commodore,"—
Nobody ever crossed her track
To bring us news, and she never came back.
    Ah, 'tis twenty long years and more
Since that old ship went out of the bay
    With my great-hearted brother on her deck:
    I watched him till he shrank to a speck,
And his face was toward me all the way.
Bright his hair was, a golden brown,
    The time we stood at our mother's knee:
That beauteous head, if it did go down,
    Carried sunshine into the sea!

Out in the fields one summer night,
    We were together, half afraid
Of the corn-leaves' rustling, and the shade
    Of the high hills, stretching so still and far,—
Loitering till after the low little light
    Of the candle shone through the open door,
And over the haystack's pointed top,
All of a tremble and ready to drop,
    The first half hour, the great yellow star,
    That we with staring, ignorant eyes,
Had often and often watched to see,
    Propped and held in its place in the skies
By the fork of a tall red mulberry tree,
    Which close in the edge of our flax-field grew,—
Dead at the top,—just one branch full
Of leaves, notched round, and lined with wool,
    From which it tenderly shook the dew
Over our heads, when we came to play
In its handbreadth of shadow day after day.
    Afraid to go home, sir; for one of us bore
A nest full of speckled and thin-shelled eggs;
The other, a bird, held fast by the legs,
Not so big as a straw of wheat:
The berries we gave her she wouldn't eat,
But cried and cried, till we held her bill,
So slim and shining, to keep her still.

At last we stood at our mother's knee.
    Do you think, sir, if you try,
    You can paint the look of a lie?
    If you can, pray have the grace ·
    To put it solely in the face
Of the urchin that is likest me.

    I think 'twas solely mine, indeed:
But that's no matter—paint it so;
    The eyes of our mother—(take good heed)—
Looking not on the nestful of eggs,
Nor the fluttering bird, held so fast by the legs,
But straight through our faces down to our lies,
And oh, with such injured, reproachful surprise!
  I felt my heart bleed where that glance went, as though
    A sharp blade struck through it.
                You, sir, know
That you on the canvas are to repeat
Things that are fairest, things most sweet,—
Woods and cornfields and mulberry tree,—
The mother,—the lads, with their bird, at her knee:
    But, oh, that look of reproachful woe!
High as the heavens your name I'll shout,
If you paint me the picture, and leave that out.

DANIEL GRAY.

In all of the late Dr. Holland's writings we know of nothing which equals in pathos and tenderness the following beautiful poem, and its value is enhanced when it is known that the author described his own father in "Old Daniel Gray":

    IF I shall ever win the home in heaven,
      For whose sweet rest I humbly pray,
    In the great company of the forgiven,
      I shall be sure to find old Daniel Gray.

    Old Daniel Gray was not a man who lifted
      On ready words his weight of gratitude,

And was not called among the gifted,
  In the prayer-meeting of his neighborhood.

He had a few old-fashioned words and phrases,
  Linked in with sacred texts and Sunday rhymes,
And I suppose that in his prayers and graces
  I've heard them at least a thousand times.

I see him now—his form, his face, his motions,
  His homespun habit and his silver hair,
And hear the language of his trite devotions,
  Rising behind the straight-backed kitchen chair.

I can remember how the sentence sounded—
  "Help us, O Lord, to pray and not to faint!"
And how the "conquering and to conquer" rounded
  The loftier inspirations of the saint.

He had some notions that did not improve him:
  He never kissed his children—so they say,
And finest scenes and fairest flowers would move him
  Less than a horse-shoe picked up on his way.

He had a hearty hatred of oppression,
  And righteous word for sin of any kind:
Alas, that the transgressor and transgression
  Were linked together in his honest mind.

He could see naught but vanity in beauty,
  And naught but weakness in a fond caress,
And pitied men whose views of Christian duty
  Allowed indulgence in such foolishness.

Yet there were love and tenderness within him,
  And I am told that when his Charley died,
Nor nature's needs nor gentle words could win him
  From his fond vigils at the sleeper's side.

And when they came to bury little Charley,
  They found fresh dew-drops sprinkled in his hair;
And on his breast a rose-bud gathered early,
  And guessed, but did not know, who put it there.

Honest and faithful, consistent in his calling,
    Strictly attendant on the means of grace,
Instant in prayer, and fearful most of failing,
    Old Daniel Gray was always in his place.

A practical old man and yet a dreamer,
    He thought in some strange, unlooked-for way,
His mighty Friend in Heaven, the great Redeemer,
    Would honor him with wealth some golden day.

This dream he carried in a hopeful spirit,
    Until in death his patient eye grew dim,
And his Redeemer called him to inherit
    The heaven of wealth long gathered up for him.

So if I ever win the home in heaven,
    For whose sweet rest I humbly hope and pray,
In the great company of the forgiven,
    I shall be sure to find old Daniel Gray.

THE OLD MAN GOES TO TOWN.

WELL, wife, I've been to 'Frisco, an' I called to see the boys;
I'm tired, an' more'n half deafened with the travel and the noise;
So I'll sit down by the chimbley, and rest my weary bones,
And tell how I was treated by our 'ristocratic sons.

As soon's I reached the city, I hunted up our Dan—
Ye know he's now a celebrated wholesale business man.
I walked down from the depo'—but Dan keeps a country seat—
An' I thought to go home with him, an' rest my weary feet.

All the way I kep' a-thinkin' how famous it 'ud be
To go 'round the town together—my grown-up boy an' me,
An' remember the old times, when my little "curly head"
Used to cry out "Good-night, papa!" from his little trundle-bed.

I never thought a minute that he wouldn't want to see
His gray an' worn old father, or would be ashamed of me;

So when I seen his office, with a sign writ out in gold,
I walked in 'thout knockin'—but the old man was too bold.

Dan was settin' by a table, an' a-writin' in a book;
He knowed me in a second; but he gave me such a look!
He never said a word o' you, but axed about the grain,
An' ef I thought the valley didn't need a little rain.

I didn't stay a great while, but inquired after Rob;
Dan said he lived upon the hill—I think they call it Nob;
An' when I left, Dan, in a tone that almost broke me down,
Said, "Call an' see me, won't ye, whenever you're in town?"

It was rather late that evenin' when I found our Robert's house;
There was music, lights, and dancin', and a mighty big carouse.
At the door a nigger met me, an' he grinned from ear to ear,
Sayin' "Keerds ob invitation, or you nebber git in here."

I said I was Bob's father; an' with another grin
The nigger left me standin' and disappeared within.
Bob came out on the porch—he didn't order me away;
But he said he hoped to see me at his office the next day.

Then I started fur a tavern, fur I knowed there, anyway,
They wouldn't turn me out so long's I'd money fur to pay.
An' Rob an' Dan had left me about the streets to roam,
An' neither of them axed me if I'd money to git home.

It may be the way o' rich folks—I don't say 'at it is not—
But we remember some things Dan and Rob have quite forgot.
We didn't quite expect this, wife, when, twenty years ago,
We mortgaged the old homestead to give Rob and Dan a show.

I didn't look fur Charley, but I happened just to meet
Him with a lot o' friends o' his'n a-comin' down the street.
I thought I'd pass on by him, for fear our youngest son
Would show he was ashamed o' me, as Rob and Dan had done.

But as soon as Charley seen me, he, right afore 'em all,
Said: "God bless me, there's my father!" as loud as he could bawl.
Then he introduced me to his frien's, an' sent 'em all away,
Tellin' 'em he'd see 'em later, but was busy for that day.

Then he took me out to dinner, an' he axed about the house,
About you, an' Sally's baby, an' the chickens, pigs an' cows;
He axed about his brothers, addin' that 'twas ruther queer,
But he hadn't seen one uv 'em fur mighty nigh a year.

Then he took me to his lodgin', in an attic four stairs high—
He said he liked it better 'cause 'twas nearer to the sky.
An' he said: "I've only one room, but my bed is pretty wide,"
An' so we slept together, me an' Charley, side by side.

Next day we went together to the great Mechanics' Fair,
An' some o' Charley's picters was on exhibition there.
He said if he could sell 'em, which he hoped to pretty soon,
He'd make us all a visit, an' be richer than Muldoon.

An' so two days an' nights we passed, an' when I come away,
Poor Charley said the time was short, an' begged fur me to stay.
Then he took me in a buggy, an' druv me to the train,
An' said in just a little while he'd see us all again.

You know we never thought our Charley would ever come to much;
He was always readin' novels an' poetry and such.
There was nothing on the farm he ever seemed to want to do,
An' when he took to paintin' he disgusted me clear through!

So we gave to Rob and Dan all we had to call our own,
An' left poor Charley penniless to make his way alone;
He's only a poor painter; Rob and Dan are rich as sin;
But Charley's worth a pair of 'em with all their gold thrown in.

Those two grand men, dear wife, were once our prattling babes—
        an' yet
It seems as if a mighty gulf 'twixt them an' us is set;
An' they'll never know the old folks till life's troubled journey's
        past,
And rich and poor are equal underneath the sod at last.

An' maybe when we all meet on the resurrection morn,
With our earthly glories fallen, like the husks from the ripe corn,—
When the righteous Son of Man the awful sentence shall have said,
The brightest crown that's shining there may be on Charley's head.

WHY HE WOULDN'T SELL THE FARM.

A. ALPHONSE DAYTON.

HERE, John! you drive the cows up, while your mar brings out
    the pails;
But don't ye let me ketch yer hangin' onter them cows' tails,
An' chasin' them acrost that lot at sich a tarin' rate;
An', John, when you cum out, be sure and shet the pastur' gate.

It's strange that boy will never larn to notice what I say;
I'm 'fraid he'll git to rulin' me, if things goes on this way;
But boys is boys, an' will be boys, till ther grown up to men,
An' John's 'bout as good a lad as the average of 'em.

I'll tell ye, stranger, how it is; I feel a heap o' pride
In thet boy—he's our only one sence little Neddy died;
Don't mind me, sir, I'm growin' old, my eye-sight 's gittin' dim;
But 't seems sumhow a kind o' mist cums long o' thoughts of him.

Jes' set down on the door step, Squar, an' make yerself to hum;
While Johnny's bringin' up the cows, I'll tell ye how it cum
Thet all our boys has left us, 'ceptin' Johnny there,
And I reckon, stranger, countin' all, we've had about our share.

Thar was our first boy, Benjamin, the oldest of them all,
He was the smartest little chap, so chipper, pert, an' small,
He cum to us one sun-bright morn, as merry as a lark,
It would ha' done your soul good, Squar, to seen the little spark.

An' thar was Tom, "a han'sum boy," his mother allus said,
He took to books, and l'arned so spry, we put the sprig ahead—
His skoolin' cleaned the little pile we'd laid by in the chest,
But I's bound to give the boy a chance to do his "level best."

Our third one's name was Samuel; he grow'd up here to hum,
An' worked with me upon the farm till he was twenty-one;
Fur Benjamin had l'arned a trade—he didn't take to work;
Tom, mixin' up in politics, got 'lected County Clerk.

We kin all remember, stranger, the year of sixty-one,
When the spark thet tetched the powder off in that Confed'ret gun
Flashed like a streak o' lightnin' up acrost from East to West,
An' left a spot thet burned like fire in every patriot's breast.

An' I tell ye what it was, Squar, my boys cum up to the scratch,
They all had a share o' the old man's grit, with enough of their
     own to match—
They show'd ther colors, an' set ther flint, ther names went down
     on the roll,
An' Benjamin, Thomas, an' Sam was pledged to preserve the old
     flag whole.

They all cum hum together at the last, rigged up in soldier's
     clothes;
It made my old heart thump with pride, an' ther mother's spirits rose,
Fur she'd been "down in the mouth" sumwhat, sence she'd heard
     what the boys had done,
Fur it took all three, an' it's hard enough fur a mother to give up
     one.

But ther warn't a drop of coward's blood in her veins, I ken tell
     you first,
Fur she'd send the boys, an' the old man, too, if worst had come
     to worst;
I shall never forgit the last night, when we all kneeled down to
     pray,
How she give 'em, one by one, to God, in the hush of the twilight
     gray.

An' then, when morning broke so clear—not a cloud was in the
     sky—
The boys cum in with sober looks to bid us their last good-bye;
I didn't 'spect she would stand it all with her face so firm and
     calm,
But she didn't break nor give in a peg till she cum to kissin' Sam.

An' then it all cum out at onst, like a storm from a thunder-cloud—
She jest sot down on the kitchen-floor, broke out with a sob so
     loud

Thet Sam give up, an' the boys cum back, and they all got down
    by her there,
An' I'm thinkin' 't would make an angel cry to hev seen thet
    partin', Squar!

I think she had a forewarnin', fur when they brought back poor
    Sam,
She sot down by his coffin there, with her face so white an' calm,
An' the neighbors thet cum a-pourin' in to see our soldier dead,
Went out with a hush on their tremblin' lips, an' the words in ther
    hearts unsaid.

Stranger, perhaps you heerd of Sam, how he broke thro' thet
    Secesh line,
An' planted the old flag high an' dry, where its dear old stars could
    shine;
An' after our soldiers won the day, an' a-gatherin' up the dead,
They found our boy with his brave heart still, and the flag above
    his head.

An' Tom was shot at Gettysburg, in the hottest of the fray—
They said thet he led his gallant boys like a hero thro' thet day;
But they brought him back with his clear voice hushed in the
    silent sleep of death,
An' another grave grew grassy green 'neath the kiss of the Sum-
    mer's breath.

An' Benjamin, he cum hum at last, but it made my old eyes ache
To see him lay with thet patient look, when it seemed thet his
    heart would break
With his pain an' wounds; but he lingered on till the flowers died
    away,
An' then we laid him down to rest, in the calm of the Autumn day.

Will I sell the old farm, stranger, the house where my boys were
    born?
Jes' look down thro' the orchard, Squar, beyond that field o' corn—
Ken ye see them four white marble stuns gleam out thro' the
    orchard glade?
Wall, all thet is left of our boys on arth rests under them old trees'
    shade.

But there cums John with the cows, ye see, an' it's 'bout my milkin'-
    time;
If ye happen along this way agin, jes' stop in at eny time.
Oh, ye axed if I'd eny notion the old farm would ever be sold:
Wall! may be, Squar, but I'll tell ye plain, 'twill be when the old
    man's cold.

MY EARLY HOME.

ALEXANDER CLARK.

LOVE, Peace, and Repose! the tenderest trio
    Of musical words ever blended in one—
That one word is *Home*—'mid the hills of Ohio—
    Dear home of my childhood in years that are gone.

There, father and mother, two sisters, one brother,
    With hopes, like their hearts, united, abide,
Their treasures in this world are few; in another,
    A heritage holy and glory beside.

In fancy I wander, this sweet summer morning,
    Away to the wheat-field, just over the hill;
'Tis harvest-time now, and the reapers are coming
    To gather the waiting grain, golden and still.

Many harvests have passed, many summers have ended,
    Since here I oft toiled, with glad reapers, before,
And felt the great bounty of Heaven extended,
    Giving joy to the worker, and bread to the poor.

Long ago, I remember, when thirsty and tiring,
    The harvesters came to the old maple shade,
How they quaffed the pure water, so cool and inspiring,
    That gushed from the fountain that Nature had made.

And I think of the orchard, and the apples that yellowed,
    Half hidden by leaves in the " big early tree: "
Ah, the apples, how luscious, when ripened and mellowed,
    Then dropped in the clover for sisters and me!

Old home of my youth, so humble, so cherished,
　Thy hallowèd memory cheers me to-day;
When all other thoughts of the past shall have perished,
　Remembrance of thee shall illumine my way.

Sweet home in Ohio, now farewell for ever!
　I've wandered afar from thy dear cottage door;
I'll visit thee, love thee; but never, oh, never,
　Will thy charms, or my childhood, return any more.

MY MOTHER.

The feast was o'er. Now brimming wine,
In lordly cup, was seen to shine
　Before each eager guest;
And silence filled the crowded hall
As deep as when the herald's call
　Thrills in the loyal breast.

Then up arose the noble host,
And, smiling, cried: "A toast! a toast!
　To all our ladies fair;
Here, before all, I pledge the name
Of Stanton's proud and beauteous dame,
　The Lady Gundamere."

Quick to his feet each gallant sprang,
And joyous was the shout that rang,
　As Stanley gave the word;
And every cup was raised on high,
Nor ceased the loud and gladsome cry
　Till Stanley's voice was heard.

"Enough, enough," he, smiling, said,
And lowly bent his haughty head;
　"That all may have their due,
Now each in turn must play his part
And pledge the lady of his heart,
　Like a gallant knight and true."

Then, one by one, each guest sprang up,
And drained in turn the brimming cup,
  And named the loved one's name;
And each, as hand on high he raised,
His lady's grace and beauty praised,
  Her constancy and fame.

'Tis now St. Leon's turn to rise;
On him are fixed these countless eyes;
  A gallant knight is he;
Envied by some, admired by all,
Far famed in lady's bower and hall,
  The flower of chivalry.

St. Leon raised his kindling eye,
And held the sparkling cup on high:
  " I drink to one," he said,
" Whose image never may depart,
Deep graven on this grateful heart,
  Till memory be dead;

" To one whose love for me shall last
When lighter passions long have past,
  So deep it is, and pure;
Whose love hath longer dwelt, I ween,
Than any yet that pledged hath been
  By these brave knights before."

Each guest upstarted at the word
And laid a hand upon his sword
  With fury-flashing eye;
And Stanley said: " We crave the name,
Proud knight, of this most peerless dame,
  Whose love you count so high."

St. Leon paused, as if he would
Not breathe her name in careless mood
  Thus lightly to another;
Then bent his noble head, as though
To give that word the reverence due,
  And gently said, " My mother."

REVERIES OF THE OLD KITCHEN.

Far back in my musings my thoughts have been cast
To the cot where the hours of my childhood were passed;
I loved all its rooms to the pantry and hall,
But that blessed old kitchen was dearer than all.
Its chairs and its table none brighter could be,
And all its surroundings were sacred to me—
To the nail in the ceiling, the latch on the door,
And I love every crack on the old kitchen floor.

I remember the fire-place with mouth high and wide,
The old-fashioned oven that stood by its side,
Out of which, each Thanksgiving, came puddings and pies,
That fairly bewildered and dazzled my eyes.
And then, too, St. Nicholas, slyly and still,
Came down every Christmas our stockings to fill;
But the dearest of memories I've laid up in store,
Is the mother that trod on the old kitchen floor.

Day in and day out, from morning till night,
Her footsteps were busy, her heart always light,
For it seemed to me then, that she knew not a care,
The smile was so gentle her face used to wear;
I remember with pleasure what joy filled our eyes,
When she told us the stories that children so prize;
They were new every night, though we'd heard them before
From her lips, at the wheel, on the old kitchen floor.

I remember the window, where mornings I'd run
As soon as the daybreak, to watch for the sun;
And thought, when my head scarcely reached to the sill,
That it slept through the night in the trees on the hill,
And the small tract of ground that my eyes there could view
Was all of the world that my infancy knew;
Indeed, I cared not to know of it more,
For a world of itself was that old kitchen floor.

To-night those old visions come back at their will,
But the wheel and its music forever are still;
The band is moth-eaten, the wheel laid away,
And the fingers that turned it lie mould'ring in clay;
The hearthstone, so sacred, is just as 'twas then,
And the voices of children ring out there again;
The sun through the window looks in as of yore,
But it sees strange feet on the old kitchen floor.

I ask not for honor, but this I would crave,
That when the lips speaking are closed in the grave,
My children would gather theirs round by their side,
And tell of the mother who long ago died:
'Twould be more enduring, far dearer to me,
Than inscription on granite or marble could be,
To have them tell often, as I did of yore,
Of the mother who trod on the old kitchen floor.

IT SNOWS.

"It snows!" cries the School-boy, "Hurrah!" and his shout
  Is ringing through parlor and hall,
While swift as the wing of a swallow, he's out,
  And his playmates have answered his call;
It makes the heart leap but to witness their joy;
  Proud wealth has no pleasure, I trow,
Like the rapture that throbs in the pulse of the boy,
  As he gathers his treasures of snow;
Then lay not the trappings of gold on thine heirs,
While health, and the riches of nature, are theirs.

"It snows!" sighs the Imbecile, "Ah!" and his breath
  Comes heavy, as clogged with a weight:
While, from the pale aspect of nature in death
  He turns to the blaze of his grate;

And nearer and nearer his soft-cushioned chair
    Is wheeled toward the life-giving flame;
He dreads a chill puff of the snow-burdened air,
    Lest it wither his delicate frame;
Oh! small is the pleasure existence can give,
When the fear we shall die only proves that we live!

"It snows!" cries the Traveller, "Ho!" and the word
    Has quickened his steed's lagging pace;
The wind rushes by, but its howl is unheard,
    Unfelt the sharp drift in his face;
For bright through the tempest his own home appeared,
    Ay, through leagues intervened he can see;
There's the clear, glowing hearth, and the table prepared,
    And his wife with her babes at her knee;
Blest thought! how it lightens the grief-laden hour,
That those we love dearest are safe from its power!

"It snows!" cries the Belle, "Dear, how lucky!" and turns
    From her mirror to watch the flakes fall;
Like the first rose of summer, her dimpled cheek burns,
    While musing on sleigh-ride and ball:
There are visions of conquests, of splendor, and mirth,
    Floating over each drear winter's day;
But the tintings of Hope, on this storm-beaten earth,
    Will melt like the snow-flakes away;
Turn, turn thee to Heaven, fair maiden, for bliss;
That world has a pure fount ne'er opened in this.

"It snows!" cries the Widow, "Oh God!" and her sighs
    Have stifled the voice of her prayer:
Its burden you'll read in her tear-swollen eyes,
    On her cheek sunk with fasting and care.
'Tis night, and her fatherless ask her for bread,
    But "He gives the young ravens their food,"
And she trusts, till her dark hearth adds horror to dread,
    And she lays on her last chip of wood.
Poor sufferer! that sorrow thy God only knows;
'Tis a most bitter lot to be poor, when it snows!

THE INQUIRY.

Tell me, ye winged winds that round my pathway soar
Do ye not know some spot where mortals weep no more?
Some lone and pleasant dell, some valley in the west
Where, free from toil and pain, the weary soul may rest?
The loud wind dwindled to a whisper low
And sighed for pity as it answered—"No."

Tell me, thou mighty deep, whose billows round me play,
Knowest thou some favorite spot, some island far away,
Were weary one may find the bliss for which she sighs—
Where sorrow never lives, and friendship never dies?
The loud waves rolling in perpetual flow
Stopped for a while and sighed to answer—"No."

And thou, serenest moon, that with such lovely face
Dost look upon the earth asleep in night's embrace,
Tell me in all thy round hast thou not seen some spot
Where miserable man may find a happier lot?
Behind a cloud the moon withdrew in woe,
And a voice sweet but sad responded—"No."

Tell me, my secret soul, Oh! tell me, Hope and Faith,
Is there no resting place from sorrow, sin and death?
Is there no happy spot where mortals may be blessed,
Where grief may find a balm, and weariness a rest?
Faith, Hope, and Love, best subjects to mortals given,
Waved their bright wings and whispered—"Yes, in Heaven!"

THE MAN WITH THE MUSKET.

THEY are building as Babel was built, to the sky,
    With clash and confusion of speech;
They are piling up monuments massive and high
    To lift a few names out of reach.

And the passionate green-laurelled god of the great,
  In a whimsical riddle of stone,
Has chosen a few from the field and the state,
  To sit on the steps of his throne.

But I—I will pass from this rage of renown,
  This ant-hill commotion and strife;
Pass by where the marbles and bronzes look down,
  With their fast frozen gestures of life,
On, out of the nameless who lie 'neath the gloom
  Of the pitying cypress and pine;
Your man is the man of the sword and the plume,
  But the man with the musket is mine.

I knew him, I tell you! And also I knew
  When he fell on the battle-swept ridge,
That the poor battered body that lay there in blue
  Was only a plank in the bridge,
Over which some should pass to a fame
  That shall shine while the high stars shall shine!
Your hero is known by an echoing name,
  But the man of the musket is mine.

I knew him! All through him the good and the bad
  Ran together and equally free;
But I judge, as I trust Christ has judged the poor lad,
  For death made him noble to me!
In the cyclone of war, in the battle's eclipse,
  Life shook out its lingering sands,
And he died with the names that he loved on his lips,
  His musket still grasped in his hands!
Up close to the flag, my soldier went down;
  In the salient front of the line;
You may take for your heroes the men of renown,
  But the man of the musket is mine!

There is peace in the May-laden grace of the hours
  That come when the day's work is done,
And peace with the nameless, who under the flowers
  Lie asleep in the slant of the sun.

Beat the taps!   Put out lights! and silence all sound;
  There is rifle-pit strength in the grave!
They sleep well who sleep, be they crowned or uncrowned,
  And death will be kind to the brave.

IN THE MINING TOWN.

"'Tis the last time, darling," he gently said,
As he kissed her lips like the cherries red,
While a fond look shone in his eyes of brown,
"My own is the prettiest girl in town:
To-morrow the bell from the tower will ring
A joyful peal.   Was there ever a king
So truly blest, on his royal throne,
As I shall be when I claim my own?"

'Twas a fond farewell; 'twas a sweet good-bye,
But she watched him go with a troubled sigh.
So, into the basket that swayed and swung
O'er the yawning abyss he lightly sprung,
And the joy of her heart seemed turned to woe
As they lowered him into the depths below,
Her sweet young face, with its tresses brown,
Was the fairest face in the mining town.

Lo! the morning came; but the marriage-bell,
High up in the tower, rang a mournful knell
For the true heart buried 'neath earth and stone,
Far down in the heart of the mine—alone.
A sorrowful peal on their wedding-day,
For the breaking heart and the heart of clay,
And the face that looked from her tresses brown
Was the saddest face in the mining town.

Thus time rolled on its weary way
Until fifty years, with their shadows gray,

Had darkened the light of her sweet eyes' glow,
And had turned the brown of her hair to snow.
Oh! never a kiss from a husband's lips,
Or the clasp of a child's sweet finger-tips,
Had lifted one moment the shadows brown
From the saddest heart in the mining town.

Far down in the depths of the mine one day,
In the loosened earth they were digging away,
They discovered a face, so young, so fair,
From the smiling lip to the bright brown hair,
Untouched by the finger of Time's decay.
When they drew him up to the light of day
The wondering people gathered 'round
To gaze at the man thus strangely found.

Then a woman came from among the crowd,
With her long white hair, and her slight form bowed,
She silently knelt by the form of clay,
And kissed the lips that were cold and gray.
Then the sad old face with its snowy hair
On his youthful bosom lay pillowed there,
He had found her at last, his waiting bride,
And the people buried them side by side.

MY MOTHER-IN-LAW.

She is coming, she is coming; unhappy is my fate:
Time, tide, and my wife's mother were never known to wait.
She is coming like a martinet; domestic peace must fly,
With all the tender graces that are absent when she's nigh.
She will wash and scold the children and boss the servant girl,
Rip-saw my lamb-like temper and set my nerves awhirl;
Talk volumes on economy, but all the time declare
My wife's allowance is not half as much as I should spare.
A perfect fiend at bargaining, she'll sally out to buy
A host of things I can't afford, all purchased on the sly.

I'll have to give up smoking to get the children frocks,
And my corns will soon be aching from the patches on my socks.
She'll need a peck of buttons to sew on here and there,
And spools of twist and cotton for every rip and tear;
And, to cap the awful climax, she so well knows how to bake,
And as a cook is unsurpassed from oyster stew to steak.
That while I hate to have her come. my hatred's tinged with woe.
When she departs, I must confess, I hate to see her go!

JACK'S WAY.

Yes, Jack could do most anything, and do it mighty well;
What he knew would fill ten volumes; what he didn't—who could
      tell?
His temper was angelic and his tongue was always kind,
As a fresh and jolly joker his match was hard to find;
He buzzed and hustled round and round, and yet 'twas very funny!
He never did and never would go in for makin' money.

Now when it came to farming, he knew exactly why
The crops were light, the prices low, the seasons wet or dry;
He often told the village merchant how to run a store,
And showed the parson just the way to make the devil sore;
'Twas fine to hear the shrewd advice he was forever givin',
And yet—to save his life—the man could never make a livin'.

The year diphthery, scarlet fever, and the measles came,
He never tired of showin' where the doctors were to blame:
And when he talked on teachin', hotel-keepin', and the law,
You know'd 'twas all compressed within the compass of his jaw;
Of all the men you ever seed he seemed the most disarvin',
Though—while he seldom paid a debt—his family was starvin'.

He'd lend the clothes from off his back, then turn around and borry,
But before you got your own returned you'd be both mad and sorry.
'Twas thus he buzzed his way through life. a puzzle and a care,
Without a foe, he made his friends and relatives despair:
And then outlived them all and died in peace at seventy-seven,
He made no money here below, he'll do without in heaven.

THE REASON WHY.

It isn't that I've got a thing agin' you, Parson Peak,
Nor agin' the many "tried and true" I've met there every week;
It's not for this I've stayed away so many Sabba' days
From the cherished little meetin'-house where oft I've joined in
       praise.
But listen—if you care to know—and I will tell you all.
I think 'twas about two year ago—or was it three, last fall?
The wealthy members voted that they'd have the seats made free,
And most of us was willin' with the notion to agree.

Perhaps the meanin' of the word I didn't quite understand;
For the Sunday after, walkin' 'long with Elsie hand in hand
(You know the little blue-eyed girl—her mother now is dead,
And I am Elsie's grandpa; but let me go ahead).
Well, thinkin' o' the Master and how homelike it would be
To take a seat just anywhere, now that the seats was free,
I walked in at the open door, and up the centre aisle,
And sat down tired, but happy in the light of Elsie's smile.

I listened to your preachin' with an "amen" in my heart,
And when the hymns was given out, I tried to do my part;
And my love seemed newly kindled for the one great power above,
And something seemed to answer back: "For love I give thee love."
But when the benediction came, and we was passin' out,
A whispered sentence, with my name, caused me to turn about.
'Twas not exactly words like this, but words that meant it all:
"It's strange that paupers never know their place is by the wall."

It wasn't 'bout myself I cared for what the speaker said,
But the little blossom at my side, with pretty upturned head;
And lookin' down at Elsie, there, I thought of Elsie's mother,
And thoughts my better nature scorned, I tried in vain to smother.
I've been to meetin' twice since then, and set down by the wall,
But kept a-thinkin'—thinkin'—till my thoughts was turned to gall;
And when the old familiar hymns was given out to sing,
One look at Elsie's shinin' curls would choke my utterin'.

And so I thought it best awhile to stay at home and praise,
Or take a walk in field or wood, and there trace out His ways.
"It's better so," my old heart said, "than gather with the throng,
And let your feelin's rankle with a real or fancied wrong."
But I'm prayin', parson, all the time (and wish you'd help me pray),
When one and all are gathered home in the great comin' day;
When men are weighed by honest deeds and love to fellow-men,
I won't be thought a pauper in the light I'm seen in then.

A FRIENDLY HAND.

WHEN a man an't got a cent, and he's feelin' kind o' blue,
An' the clouds hang dark an' heavy, an' won't let the sunshine
      through,
It's a great thing, oh, my brethren, for a feller just to lay
His hand upon your shoulder in a friendly sort o' way!

It makes a man feel curious; it makes the tear-drops start,
And you sort o' feel a flutter in the region of the heart.
You can't look up an' meet his eyes; you don't know what to say,
When his hand is on your shoulder in a friendly sort o' way!

Oh, the world's a curious compound, with its honey and its gall,
With its cares and bitter crosses; but a good world after all.
And a good God must have made it—leastways, that's what I say
When a hand rests on my shoulder in a friendly sort o' way!

THE JOLLY OLD PEDAGOGUE.

'TWAS a jolly old pedagogue, long ago,
   Tall and slender, and sallow and dry;
His form was bent and his gait was slow,
His long, thin hair was as white as snow,
   But a wonderful twinkle shone in his eye;

And he sang every night as he went to bed,
  "Let us be happy down here below,
The living should live, though the dead be dead,"
  Said the jolly old pedagogue, long ago.

He taught his scholars the rule of three,
  Writing and reading, and history, too;
He took the little ones upon his knee,
For a kind old heart in his breast had he,
  And the wants of the little child he knew;
"Learn while you're young," he often said,
  "There's so much to enjoy down here below,
Life for the living and rest for the dead!"
  Said the jolly old pedagogue, long ago.

With the stupidest boy he was kind and cool,
  Speaking only in gentlest tones;
The rod was hardly known in the school—
Whipping to him was a barbarous rule,
  And too hard work for the poor old bones;
Besides it was painful, he sometimes said,
  "We should make life pleasant down here below,
Life for the living, and rest for the dead,"
  Said the jolly old pedagogue, long ago.

He lived in the house by the hawthorne lane,
  With roses and woodbine over the door;
His rooms were quiet, and neat and plain,
But a spirit of comfort there held reign,
  And made him forget he was old and poor;
"I need so little," he often said,
  "And my friends and relatives here below;
Won't litigate over me when I am dead,"
  Said the jolly old pedagogue, long ago.

He sat at the door one midsummer night,
  After the sun had sunk in the west,
And the lingering beams of golden light
Made his kindly old face look warm and bright;

> While the odorous night wind whispered low
> Gently, gently he bowed his head—
>   There were angels waiting for him, I know,
> He was sure of happiness, living or dead,
>   This jolly old pedagogue, long ago!

PHILIP BARTON—ENGINEER.

DIED DECEMBER 18, 1882.

PHILIP BARTON, of Denver—have you ever heard the name?—
Sleeps to-night in his icy tomb, wrapped in the martyr's fame.
Philip Barton, of Denver, slender and fair and young,
Never such deeds of daring has spirit or mortal sung;
Only the great white mountains watch where the hero lies,
Only the stars of heaven look down from the darkened skies;
Yet to-night 'mid storm and darkness, to-night 'mid wind and rain,
I read of his act of daring, I read of his death and pain.
You do well, oh, Western mountains, to guard his resting-place—
Silent his merry laughter, and white his boyish face—
Surely, yon wind-swept cedars bent in their rocks and sighed,
That night of storm and darkness, that night when Barton died.

* * * * * * *

Who was he? Simply an engineer, and the youngest on the line;
But many a year he held his place in the cab of "49."
Many a trip had he looked ahead, over that icy track,
Stretching about the mountains and across the "Foster Back;"
Many the time had he made the curve—never again he will—
Around the edge of Miller's bend, just as it mounts the hill—
An ugly bit of mountain road, whenever the upper snow
Chances to slide from its rocky nest, on to the rails below.
Sixty miles from Denver, and the rock, in solid wall,
Rising to the very stars—hung as if to fall
Down to where the swift Arkansas, in sullen flow,
Sweeps against its stony banks, a thousand feet below.
And that night down the cañon—running at "forty," no less—
Plunged the two great engines, dragging the night express;

On over the bridge at the river and into a forest of pines,
With Barton's face at the window, watching for danger signs;
Behind was the second engine, ahead was the wall of snow,
Which the prong of the great plow lifted and hurled to the rocks
    below.
Black was the midnight darkness over the curve ahead,
Save for the little gleam of light which the rushing engine shed,
Firm was the hand of the engineer, clear and cool his brain,
As leaning out of the swaying cab he peered before the train,
On into the awful silence and darkness like a wall,
As if the mantle of the Dead lay stretching over all,
Straight ahead the rushing engines, swinging, swaying on the track,
Gallant riders in the saddle, flying chambers at their back.
Sudden a shout of horror, wild as a cry of death,
Came, while the train swept forward—swift as hurried breath—
Sharp rang a warning whistle, from "49," ahead,
"Danger—down brakes!" the signal that quick whistle said.
Danger—for that moment from the summit of the hill,
Barton, watching out ahead, saw with sudden thrill,
A mighty shadow deepen, and heard a muffled roar,
Like the deep-toned beating of surf upon the shore.
An instant, and he understood—some broken cars of freight
Were rushing down that incline, hurled by their heavy weight.
Along the slippery track! a dozen, more or less,
Black in the Drummond light, full at the night express.
Never one moment for halting, scarcely a moment for fear,
Firmer the grasp on the lever, calmer the engineer.
He heard the rasping of the brakes, the slowing of the train,
But only pulled his throttle in to pull it out again.
"Jump!" he cried to his fireman, "jump for the landing, Phin!
I'm going to stop the runaway, and break my coupling-pin!"
Out goes the trembling throttle—crack, and with a will,
Old "49" and her engineer went charging for the hill;
Up to meet the coming of those deadly dealing cars,
Just as a gallant hunter spurs ere he leaps the bars,
Just as a charging trooper, with white but earnest face,
Clings to his horse's saddle, as Barton kept his place;
Swift as the equinox, wild as a whirlwind's breath,
"49" and her rider swept up to that awful death.

The grandest charge of cavalry the world has ever known,
The solitary Roman made who faced such odds alone,
But now without an order, without one word or cheer,
With half a prayer upon his lips, swept on that engineer,
Up to the terrible crash, there 'mid the mountain snow,
That hurled the cab, like an arrow, on the icy rocks below,
Crushing the gallant body, till the wreck burst into flame,
As martyrs' spirits rise to God beyond man's praise or blame,
Till the stars sent waving back their white signal ray,
To tell that engineer below he had the right of way.

   *   *   *   *   *   *   *

Such is the story I read to-night, read in wind and rain,
Till Philip Barton's face looked in from each wet window pane,
Until the wind seemed bearing, where'er its fury blows,
The virtue of his hero deed from off the mountain snows;
Where wrapped his icy mantle, but bright with martyr's flame,
They guard with vigilance their dead—he of the Barton name.

WHEN SAM'WEL LED THE SINGIN'.

Of course I love the House o' God,
    But I don't feel to hum there
The way I useter to, afore
    New-fangled ways had come there.
Though things are finer now a heap,
    My heart it keeps a-clingin'
To our big, bare old meetin'-house,
    Where Sam'wel led the singin'.

I 'low it's sorter solemn-like
    To hear the organ pealin';
It kinder makes yer blood run cold,
    An' fills ye full o' feelin',
But, somehow, it don't tech the spot—
    Now, mind ye, I ain't slingin'
No slurs—ez that bass viol did
    When Sam'wel led the singin'.

I tell ye what, when he struck up
  The tune, an' sister Hanner
Put in her purty treble—eh?
  That's what you'd call sopranner—
Why, all the choir, with might an' main,
  Set to, an' seemed a-flingin'
Their hull souls out with ev'ry note,
  When Sam'wel led the singin'.

An', land alive, the way they'd race
  Thro' grand old "Coronation"!
Each voice a-chasin' t'other round,
  It jes' beat all creation!
I allus thought it must a' set
  The bells o' Heaven a-ringin',
To hear us "Crown Him Lord of All,"
  When Sam'wel led the singin'.

Folks didn't sing for money then;
  They sung because 'twas in 'em,
An' must come out, I useter feel—
  If Parson couldn't win 'em
With preachin' an' with prayin' an'
  His everlastin' dingin'—
That choir'd fetch sinners to the fold,
  When Sam'wel led the singin'.

HE WORRIED ABOUT IT.

"The sun's heat will give out in ten million years more,"
  And he worried about it;
"It will sure give out then, if it doesn't before,"
  And he worried about it.
It would surely give out, so the scientists said
In all scientific books that he read,
And the whole mighty universe then would be dead,
  And he worried about it.

"And some day the earth will fall into the sun,"
     And he worried about it;
"Just as sure and as straight as if shot from a gun,"
     And he worried about it.
"When strong gravitation unbuckles her straps,
Just picture," he said, "what a fearful collapse!
It will come in a few million ages, perhaps,"
     And he worried about it.

"The earth will become much too small for the race,"
     And he worried about it,
"When we'll pay $30 an inch for pure space,"
     And he worried about it;
"The earth will be crowded so much, without doubt,
That there'll be no room for one's tongue to stick out,
And no room for one's thoughts to wander about,"
     And he worried about it.

"The Gulf Stream will curve and New England grow torrider,"
     And he worried about it,
"Than was ever the climate of southernmost Florida,"
     And he worried about it.
"The ice crop will be knocked into small smithereens,
And crocodiles block up our mowing machines,
And we'll lose our fine crops of potatoes and beans,"
     And he worried about it.

"And in less than ten thousand years, there's no doubt,"
     And he worried about it,
"Our supply of lumber and coal will give out,"
     And he worried about it.
"Just then the ice age will return cold and raw,
Frozen men will stand stiff with arms outstretched in awe,
As if vainly beseeching a general thaw,"
     And he worried about it.

His wife took in washing (a dollar a day)—
     He didn't worry about it;
His daughter sewed shirts, the rude grocer to pay—
     He didn't worry about it;

While his wife beat her tireless rub-a-dub-dub
On the washboard drum in her old wooden tub,
He sat by the stove and he just let her rub—
    He didn't worry about it.

SPELLING DOWN.

WELL, Jane, I stayed in town last night,
    (I know I hadn't oughter),
And went to see the spellin' match,
    With cousin Philip's daughter.
I told her I was most too old;
    She said I wasn't nuther—
A likely gal is Susan Jane;
    The image of her mother.

I begged and plead with might and main,
    And tried my best to shake her,
But blame the gal, she stuck and hung,
    Until I had to take her.
I ain't much used to city ways,
    Or city men and women,
And what I see, and what I heard,
    Just sot my head a-swimmin'.

The hall was filled with stylish folks,
    In broadcloth, silks, and laces,
Who, when the time had come to spell,
    Stood up and took their places;
And Mayor Jones, in thunder tones,
    And waistcoat bright and yeller,
Gave out the words to one and all,
    From a new-fangled speller.

The people looked so bright and smart,
  Thinks I, it's no use foolin',
They've got the spellin'-book by heart,
  With all their city schoolin';
Till Orvil Kent, the Circuit Judge,
  Got stuck on Pennsylvania,
And Simon Swift, the merchant clerk,
  Went down on kleptomania.

Then Caleb Dunn, the broker's son,
  He put two n's in money,
And Susan Jane, she smirked and smiled,
  And left one out in funny.
And Leonard Rand, the Harvard chap,
  With features like a lady,
Spelled lots o' French and Latin words,
  And caved on rutabaga.

And as I sot there quiet like,
  A-winkin' and a-blinkin',
The gaslight glarin' in my eyes,
  I couldn't help a-thinkin'
How things were changed since you and I,
  In other winter weather,
Drove o'er the snow-bound Eaton pikes
  To spellin' school together.

Again the bleak New England hills
  Re-echoed to the singin'
Of Yankee girls, with hair in curls,
  Who set the welkin ringin';
They wan't afraid to sing when asked,
  And never would refuse to;
Somehow the singin' now-days, Jane,
  Don't sound much as it used to.

Twelve couple, then, a sleigh-load made,
  Packed close to keep from freezin';
Lor' bless the black-eyed rosy girls,
  They didn't mind the squeezin';

Your sweetheart never would complain
  Because you chanced to crowd her,
They'd more of flesh and blood them days,
  And less of paint and powder.

Down past the Quaker meetin'-house,
  And through the tamarack holler,
'Mid mirth and song we sped along,
  With other loads to foller,
Until (the gaslight dimmer grew—
  I surely wa'n't a dreamin')—
Upon the distant hill I see
  The school-house lights a-gleamin'.

The pedagogue gave out the words,
  His steel-bowed specs adjustin',
To linsey girls, with hair in curls,
  And boys in jeans and fustian;
The letters rang out sharp and clear,
  Each syllable pronouncin',
For he who broke the master's rule
  Was certain of a trouncin'.

Brave hearts went down amid the strife;
  The words came thicker, faster,
Like body-guard of veterans scarred,
  The boys closed round the master—
All down but two! Fair Lucy's locks
  Swept over Rufus' shoulder,
The room is still, the air grows chill,
  The winds blow fiercer, colder.

"P-h-t-h-y-s-i-c,"
  Lisped Lucy, in a flurry;
"P-h-t-h-*i*-s-i-c,"
  Cried Rufus, in a hurry.
No laurel wreath adorned his brow
  Twined by a blood-stained Nero;
Yet in his homespun suit of blue,
  Young Rufus stood a hero.

The master sleeps beneath the hill,
  The voice of Rufus Bennet,
Who snapped the word from Lucy Bird,
  Was heard within the Senate.
And countless millions bless the name
  Of him who set in motion
The tidal wave which freed the slave
  From ocean unto ocean.

The girls who charmed us with their songs
  'Mid heavenly choirs are singin';
Their feet have pressed the shining street,
  Where golden harps are ringin'.
We've both grown old and feeble, Jane,
  Our views may not be true ones;
Yet somehow all the old ways seem
  Much better than the new ones.

LITTLE MEG AND I.

You asked me, mates, to spin a yarn, before we go below;
Well, as the night is calm and fair, and no chance for a blow,
I'll give you one,—a story true as ever yet was told—
For, mates, I wouldn't lie about the dead; no, not for gold.
The story's of a maid and lad, who loved in days gone by:
The maiden was Meg Anderson, the lad, messmates, was I.

A neater, trimmer craft than Meg was very hard to find;
Why, she could climb a hill and make five knots agin the wind;
And as for larnin', hulks and spars! I've often heard it said
That she could give the scholars points and then come out ahead.
The old school-master used to say, and, mates, it made me cry,
That the smartest there was little Meg; the greatest dunce was I.

But what cared I for larnin' then, while she was by my side;
For, though a lad, I loved her, mates, and for her would have died;
And she loved me, the little lass, and often have I smiled
When she said, " I'll be your little wife," 'twas the prattle of a child.

For there lay a gulf between us, mates, with the waters running
    high;
On one side stood Meg Anderson, on the other side stood I.

Meg's fortune was twelve ships at sea and houses on the land;
While mine—why, mates, you might have held my fortune in your
    hand.
Her father owned a vast domain for miles along the shore;
My father owned a fishing-smack, a hut, and nothing more;
I knew that Meg I ne'er could win, no matter how I'd try,
For on a couch of down lay she, on a bed of straw lay I.

I never thought of leaving Meg, or Meg of leaving me,
For we were young, and never dreamed that I should go to sea,
Till one bright morning father said: "There's a whale-ship in the
    bay:
I want you, Bill, to make a cruise—you go aboard to-day."
Well, mates, in two weeks from that time I bade them all good-bye,
While on the dock stood little Meg, and on the deck stood I.

I saw her oft before we sailed, whene'er I came on shore,
And she would say: "Bill, when you're gone, I'll love you more
    and more;
And I promise to be true to you through all the coming years."
But while she spoke her bright blue eyes were filled with pearly
    tears.
Then, as I whispered words of hope and kissed her eyelids dry,
Her last words were: "God speed you, Bill!" so parted Meg and I.

Well, mates, we cruised for four long years, till at last, one sum-
    mer's day,
Our good ship, the Minerva, cast anchor in the bay
Oh, how my heart beat high with hope, as I saw her home once
    more,
And on the pier stood hundreds, to welcome us ashore;
But my heart sank down within me as I gazed with anxious eye—
No little Meg stood on the dock, as on the deck stood I.

Why, mates, it nearly broke my heart when I went ashore that day,
For they told me little Meg had wed, while I was far away.

They told me, too, they forced her to't—and wrecked her fair young
    life—
Just think, messmates, a child in years, to be an old man's wife.
But her father said it must be so, and what could she reply?
For she was only just sixteen—just twenty-one was I.

Well, mates, a few short years from then—perhaps it might be
    four—
One blustering night Jack Glinn and I were rowing to the shore,
When right ahead we saw a sight that made us hold our breath—
There floating in the pale moonlight was a woman cold in death.
I raised her up: oh, God, messmates, that I had passed her by!
For in the bay lay little Meg, and over her stood I.

JOHN MAYNARD.

'TWAS on Lake Erie's broad expanse,
    One bright midsummer day,
The gallant steamer Ocean Queen
    Swept proudly on her way.
Bright faces clustered on the deck,
    Or leaning o'er the side,
Watched carelessly the feathery foam,
    That flecked the rippling tide.

Ah, who beneath that cloudless sky,
    That smiling bends serene,
Could dream that danger, awful, vast,
    Impended o'er the scene—
Could dream that ere an hour had sped,
    That frame of sturdy oak
Would sink beneath the lake's blue waves,
    Blackened with fire and smoke,

A seaman sought the captain's side,
    A moment whispered low;
The captain's swarthy face grew pale,
    He hurried down below.

Alas, too late!   Though quick and sharp
  And clear his orders came,
No human efforts could avail
  To quench th' insidious flame.

The bad news quickly reached the deck,
  It sped from lip to lip,
And ghastly faces everywhere
  Looked from the doomèd ship.
"Is there no hope—no chance of life?"
  A hundred lips implore;
"But one," the captain made reply,
  "To run the ship on shore."

A sailor, whose heroic soul
  That hour should yet reveal,—
By name John Maynard, Eastern born,—
  Stood calmly at the wheel.
"Head her south-east!" the captain shouts,
  Above the smothered roar,
"Head her south-east without delay!
  Make for the nearest shore!"

No terror pales the helmsman's cheek,
  Or clouds his dauntless eye,
As in a sailor's measured tone
  His voice responds, "Ay, Ay!"
Three hundred souls,—the steamer's freight,--
  Crowd forward, wild with fear,
While at the stern the dreadful flames
  Above the deck appear.

John Maynard watched the nearing flames,
  But still, with steady hand
He grasped the wheel, and steadfastly
  He steered the ship to land.
"John Maynard," with an anxious voice,
  The captain cries once more,
"Stand by the wheel five minutes yet,
  And we will reach the shore."

Through flames and smoke that dauntless heart
  Responded firmly, still
Unawed, though face to face with death,
  "With God's good help I will!"

The flames approach with giant strides,
  They scorch his hands and brow;
One arm disabled seeks his side,
  Ah, he is conquered now!
But no, his teeth are firmly set,
  He crushes down the pain,—
His knee upon the stanchion pressed,
  He guides the ship again.

One moment yet! one moment yet!
  Brave heart, thy task is o'er!
The pebbles grate beneath the keel,
  The steamer touches shore.
Three hundred grateful voices rise
  In praise to God, that He
Hath saved them from the fearful fire,
  And from th' ingulfing sea.

But where is he, that helmsman bold?
  The captain saw him reel—
His nerveless hands released their task,
  He sunk beside the wheel.
The wave received his lifeless corpse,
  Blackened with smoke and fire.
God rest him! Hero never had
  A nobler funeral pyre!

KATIE LEE AND WILLIE GRAY.

Two brown heads with tossing curls,
Red lips shutting over pearls,
Bare feet, white and wet with dew,
Two eyes black and two eyes blue—
Little boy and girl were they,
Katie Lee and Willie Gray.

They were standing where a brook,
Bending like a shepherd's crook,
Flashed its silver, and thick ranks
Of willow fringed its mossy banks—
Half in thought and half in play,
Katie Lee and Willie Gray.

They had cheeks like cherry red,
He was taller, 'most a head;
She with arms like wreaths of snow,
Swung a basket to and fro,
As they loitered, half in play,
Katie Lee and Willie Gray.

"Pretty Katie," Willie said,
And there came a dash of red
Through the brownness of the cheek,
"Boys are strong and girls are weak,
And I'll carry, so I will,
Katie's basket up the hill."

Katie answered with a laugh,
"You shall only carry half;"
Then said, tossing back her curls,
"Boys are weak as well as girls."
Do you think that Katie guessed
Half the wisdom she expressed?

Men are only boys grown tall;
Hearts don't change much, after all;

And when, long years from that day,
Katie Lee and Willie Gray
Stood again beside the brook,
Bending like a shepherd's crook—

Is it strange that Willie said,
While again a dash of red
Crowned the brownness of his cheek,
"I am strong and you are weak;
Life is but a slippery steep,
Hung with shadows cold and deep.

"Will you trust me, Katie dear?
Walk beside me without fear?
May I carry, if I will,
All your burdens up the hill?"
And she answered, with a laugh,
"No, but you may carry half."

Close beside the little brook,
Bending like a shepherd's crook,
Working with its silver hands
Late and early at the sands,
Stands a cottage, where, to-day,
Katie lives with Willie Gray.

In the porch she sits, and lo!
Swinging a basket to and fro,
Vastly different from the one
That she swung in years agone;
This is long, and deep, and wide,
And has rockers at the side.

A STRANGE LOVE.

I CLASPED her struggling to my heart,
  I whispered love unknown;
One kiss on her red lips I pressed,
  And she was all my own.

I loved her with a love profound,
　　E'en death could not destroy,
And yet, I must confess, I found
　　My bliss had some alloy.

For once I saw her unaware
　　Upon a fellow's lap;
He claiming kisses ripe and rare—
　　I did not like the chap.

She had some faults (so have we all),
　　But one I hope to throttle;
She had, alas, what I may call
　　A weakness for the bottle.

One morn I caught her ere was made
　　Her toilet, and beneath
An old straw hat her laugh betrayed,
　　My darling had no teeth.

Unconscious of my presence she,
　　With artful antics rare,
Tossed off the hat, and—Gracious me!
　　Her head was minus hair.

But love is founded on a rock,
　　And mighty in its might;
For I could learn without a shock,
　　She could not read or write.

She could not dance nor sing a tone,
　　And scarcely could converse;
But what cared I, she was my own,
　　For better or for worse.

And yet I loved her and confessed
　　Devotion, and, it may be,
You'd do the same if you possessed
　　Another such a baby.

HALF-WAY DOIN'S.

BELUBBED fellow-trabelers: In holdin' forth to-day,
I doesn't quote no special verse for what I has to say.
De sermon will be berry short, an' dis here am de tex'—
Dat half-way doin's ain't no 'count for dis worl' or de nex'.

Dis worl' dat we's a-libbin' in is like a cotton-row,
Whar ebery cullud gentleman has got his line to hoe;
And every time a lazy nigger stops to take a nap,
De grass keeps on a-growin' for to smudder up his crap.

When Moses led de Jews acrost de waters ob de sea,
Dey had to keep a-goin' jes' as fas' as fas' could be:
Do you suppose dat dey could eber hab succeeded in deir wish,
And reached de Promised Land at last—if dey had stopped to fish?

My frien's, dar was a garden once, where Adam libbed wid Eve,
Wid no one round to bodder dem, no neighbors for to thieve,
And ebery day was Christmas, and dey got deir rations free,
And eberything belonged to dem; except an apple tree.

You all know 'bout de story—how de snake come snoopin' round—
A slump-tail, rusty moccasin, a-crawlin' on de groun'—
How Eve and Adam eat de fruit, and went and hid deir face,
Till de angel oberseer come and drove 'em off de place.

Now 'spose dat man and 'oman hadn't 'tempted for to shirk,
But had gone about deir gardenin' and 'tended to deir work,
Dey wouldn't hab been loafin' whar dey had no business to,
And de debbel neber'd had a chance to tell 'em what to do.

No half-way doin's, bredren! It'll neber do, I say!
Go at your task and finish it, and den's de time to play—
For eben if de crap is good, de rain'll spile de bolls,
Unless you keeps a-pickin' in de garden ob your souls.

Keep a-plowin' and a-hoein' and a-scrapin' ob de rows,
And when de ginnin's ober you can pay up what you owes;

But if you quits a-workin' ebery time de sun is hot,
De sheriff's gwine ter lebby on eberyting you's got.

Whateber 'tis you're dribin' at, be shore and dribe it through,
And don't let nuffin stop you, but do what you's gwine ter do;
For when you sees a nigger foolin', den, as shore's you're born,
You's gwine to see him comin' out de small end ob de horn.

I thanks you for de 'tention you has gib dis afternoon—
Sister Williams will oblidge us by a-raisin' ob a tune—
I see dat Brudder Johnson's 'bout to pass aroun' de hat,
And don't let's hab no half-way doin's when it comes to dat!

YOU PUT NO FLOWERS ON MY PAPA'S GRAVE.

With sable-draped banners, and slow measured tread,
The flower-laden ranks pass the gates of the dead;
And seeking each mound where a comrade's form rests,
Leave tear-bedewed garlands to bloom on his breast.
Ended at last is the labor of love;
Once more through the gateway the saddened lines move—
A wailing of anguish, a sobbing of grief,
Falls low on the ear of the battle-scarred chief;
Close crouched by the portals, a sunny-haired child
Besought him in accents which grief rendered wild:

"Oh! sir, he was good, and they say he died brave—
Why! why! did you pass by my dear papa's grave?
I know he was poor, but as kind and as true
As ever marched into the battle with you—
His grave is so humble, no stone marks the spot,
You may not have seen it.   Oh, say you did not!
For my poor heart would break if you knew he was there,
And thought him too lowly your offerings to share.
He didn't die lowly—he poured his heart's blood,
In rich crimson streams, from the top-crowning sod
Of the breastworks which stood in front of the fight—
And died shouting, 'Onward! for God and the right!'

O'er all his dead comrades your bright garlands wave,
But you haven't put *one* on *my* papa's grave.
If mamma were here—but she lies by his side,
Her wearied heart broke when our dear papa died."

"Battalion! file left! countermarch!" cried the chief,
"This young orphaned maid hath full cause for her grief."
Then up in his arms from the hot, dusty street,
He lifted the maiden, while in through the gate
The long line repasses, and many an eye
Pays fresh tribute of tears to the lone orphan's sigh.

"This way, it is—here, sir—right under this tree;
They lie close together, with just room for me."

"Halt!   Cover with roses each lowly green mound—
A love pure as this makes these graves hallowed ground."

"Oh! thank you, kind sir! I ne'er can repay
The kindness you've shown little Daisy to-day;
But I'll pray for you here, each day while I live,
'Tis all that a poor soldier's orphan can give.
I shall see papa soon, and dear mamma too—
I dreamed so last night, and I know 'twill come true;
And they will both bless you, I know, when I say
How you folded your arms round their dear one to-day—
How you cheered her sad heart, and soothed it to rest,
And hushed its wild throbs on your strong, noble breast;
And when the kind angels shall call *you* to come,
We'll welcome you there to our beautiful home,
Where death never comes, his black banners to wave,
And the beautiful flowers ne'er weep o'er a grave."

MEASURING THE BABY.

WE measured the riotous baby
    Against the cottage wall—
A lily grew on the threshold,
    And the boy was just as tall;

A royal tiger-lily,
  With spots of purple and gold,
And a heart like a jewelled chalice,
  The fragrant dew to hold.

Without, the blue-birds whistled
  High up in the old roof-trees,
And to and fro at the window
  The red rose rocked her bees;
And the wee pink fists of the baby
  Were never a moment still,
Snatching at shine and shadow
  That danced on the lattice-sill.

His eyes were wide as blue-bells—
  His mouth like a flower unblown—
Two little bare feet like funny white mice,
  Peeped out from his snowy white gown;
And we thought, with a thrill of rapture,
  That yet had a touch of pain,
When June rolls around with her roses,
  We'll measure the boy again.

Ah me! in a darkened chamber,
  With the sunshine shut away,
Through tears that fell like a bitter rain,
  We measured the boy to-day;
And the little bare feet, that were dimpled
  And sweet as a budding rose,
Lay side by side together,
  In a hush of a long repose!

Up from the dainty pillow,
  White as the risen dawn,
The fair little face lay smiling,
  With the light of heaven thereon;
And the dear little hands, like rose leaves
  Dropped from a rose, lay still,
Never to snatch at the sunshine
  That crept to the shrouded sill.

We measured the sleeping baby
  With ribbons white as snow,
For the shining rosewood casket
  That waited him below;
And out of the darkened chamber
  We went with a childless moan—
To the height of the sinless angels
  Our little one had grown.

THE ISLE OF LONG AGO.

OH, a wonderful stream is the river of Time,
  As it runs through the realm of tears,
With a faultless rhythm and a musical rhyme,
And a boundless sweep and a surge sublime,
  As it blends with the Ocean of Years.-

How the winters are drifting, like flakes of snow,
  And the summers, like buds between;
And the year in the sheaf—so they come and they go
On the river's breast, with its ebb and flow,
  As it glides in the shadow and sheen.

There's a magical isle up the river of Time,
  Where the softest of airs are playing;
There's a cloudless sky and a tropical clime,
And a song as sweet as a vesper chime,
  And the Junes with the roses are staying.

And the name of that Isle is the Long Ago,
  And we bury our treasures there;
There are brows of beauty and bosoms of snow—
There are heaps of dust—but we love them so!—
  There are trinkets and tresses of hair;

There are fragments of song that nobody sings,
  And a part of an infant's prayer,

There's a lute unswept, and a harp without strings;
There are broken vows and pieces of rings,
   And the garments that she used to wear.

There are hands that are waved, when the fairy shore
   By the mirage is lifted in air;
And we sometimes hear, through the turbulent roar,
Sweet voices we heard in the days gone before,
   When the wind down the river is fair.

Oh, remembered for aye, be the blessed Isle,
   All the day of our life till night—
When the evening comes with its beautiful smile,
And our eyes are closing to slumber awhile,
   May that "Greenwood" of Soul be in sight!

THE CANE-BOTTOMED CHAIR.

In tattered old slippers that toast at the bars,
And ragged old jacket, perfumed with cigars,
Away from the world and its toils and its cares,
I've a snug little kingdom, up four pairs of stairs.

To mount to this realm is a toil, to be sure,
But the fire there is bright, and the air rather pure;
And the view I behold on a sunshiny day
Is grand, through the chimney-pots over the way.

This snug little chamber is crammed in all nooks
With worthless old nicknacks and silly old books,
And foolish old odds, and foolish old ends,
Cheap bargains from brokers, cheap keepsakes from friends

Old armor, prints, pictures, pipes, china (all cracked),
Old rickety tables, and chairs broken-backed,—
A two-penny treasury, wondrous to see,
What matter?   'Tis pleasant to you, friend, and me.

No better divan need the Sultan require
Than the creaking old sofa that basks by the fire;
And 'tis wonderful, surely, what music you get
From the rickety, ramshackle, wheezy spinnet.

That praying-rug came from a Turcoman's camp;
By Tiber once twinkled that old brazen lamp;
A Mameluke fierce yonder dagger has drawn;
'Tis a murderous knife to toast muffins upon!

Long, long through the hours and the night and the chimes,
Here we talk of old books and old friends and old times;
And we sit in a fog made of rich Latakie;
This chamber is pleasant to you, friend, and me.

But of all the cheap treasures that garnish my nest,
There's one that I love and cherish the best;
For the finest of couches that's padded with hair,
I never would change thee, my cane-bottomed chair!

'Tis a bandy-legged, high-shouldered, worm-eaten seat,
With a creaking old back, and twisted old feet;
But since the fair morning when Fanny sat there,
I bless thee and love thee, old cane-bottomed chair!

If chairs have but feeling, in holding such charms,
A thrill must have passed through your withering old arms.
I looked and I longed, I wished in despair—
I wished myself turned to a cane-bottomed chair.

It was but a moment she sat in this place;
She'd a scarf on her neck and a smile on her face,—
A smile on her face, and a rose in her hair,
As she sat there and bloomed in my cane-bottomed chair.

And so I have valued my chair ever since,
Like the shrine of a saint or the throne of a prince.
Saint Fanny, my patroness sweet, I declare
The queen of my heart and my cane-bottomed chair.

When the candles burn low, and the company's gone,
In the silence of night, I sit here alone—

I sit here alone; but we yet are a pair—
My Fanny I see in my cane-bottomed chair.

She comes from the past, and revisits my room;
She looks, as she then did, all beauty and bloom;
So smiling and tender, so fresh and so fair;
And yonder she sits in my cane-bottomed chair!

THE LAST HYMN.

THE Sabbath day was ended in a village by the sea,
The uttered benediction touched the people tenderly,
And they rose to face the sunset in the glowing, lighted west,
And then hastened to their dwellings for God's blessed boon of rest.

And they looked across the waters, and a storm was raging there,
A fierce spirit moved above them—a wild spirit of the air;
And it lashed and shook and tore them, till they thundered, groaned
    and boomed,
And alas! for any vessel in their yawning gulfs intombed.

Very anxious were the people on the rocky coast of Wales,
Lest the dawn of coming morrows should be telling awful tales,
When the sea had spent its passion and should cast upon the shore
Bits of wreck and swollen victims, as it had done heretofore.

With the rough winds blowing round her, a brave woman strained
    her eyes,
And she saw along the billows a large vessel fall and rise.
Oh, it did not need a prophet to tell what the end must be!
For no ship could ride in safety near the shore on such a sea.

Then pitying people hurried from their homes and thronged the
    beach.
Oh, for power to cross the water and the perishing to reach!
Helpless hands were wrung with sorrow, tender hearts grew cold
    with dread;
And the ship, urged by the tempest, to the fatal rock-shore sped.

"She has parted in the middle!   Oh, the half of her goes down!
God have mercy!   Is heaven far to seek for those who drown?"
Lo! when next the white, shocked faces looked with terror on the
    sea,
Only one last clinging figure on the spar was seen to be.

Near the trembling watchers came the wreck tossed by the wave,
And the man still clung and floated, though no power on earth
    could save.
"Could we send him a short message? here's a trumpet.   Shout
    away!"
'Twas the preacher's hand that took it, and he wondered what to
    say.

Any memory of his sermon—firstly—secondly!   Ah, no!
There was but one thing to utter in that awful hour of woe;
So he shouted through the trumphet, "Look to Jesus.   Can you
    hear?"
And "Ay, ay, sir!" rang the answer o'er the water loud and clear

Then they listened.   He is singing, "Jesus, lover of my soul!"
And the winds brought back the echo, "While the nearer waters
    roll;"
Strange, indeed, it was to hear him, "Till the storm of life is passed,"
Singing bravely from the waters, "Oh, receive my soul at last!"

He could have no other refuge.   "Hangs my helpless soul on Thee;
Leave, ah, leave me not"—the singer dropped at last into the sea,
And then the watchers, looking homeward, through their eyes with
    tears made dim,
Said, "He passed to be with Jesus in the singing of that hymn."

LEAVING THE HOMESTEAD.

You're going to leave the homestead, John;
    You're twenty-one to-day,
And the old man will be sorry, John,
    To see you go away.

You've labored late and early, John,
  And done the best you could;
I ain't a-going to stop you, John—
  I wouldn't if I could.

The years they come and go, my boy,
  The years they come and go;
And raven locks and tresses brown
  Grow white as driven snow.
My life has known its sorrows, John,
  Its trials and troubles sore;
Yet God withal has blessed me, John,
  "In basket and in store."

But one thing let me tell you, John,
  Before you make your start,
There's more in being honest, John,
  Twice o'er than being smart.
Though rogues may seem to flourish, John,
  And sterling worth to fail,
O, keep in view the good and true;
  'Twill in the end prevail.

Don't think too much of money, John,
  And dig and delve and plan,
And rake and scrape in every shape,
  To hoard up all you can.
Though fools may count their riches, John,
  In dollars, pounds, or pence,
The best of wealth is youth and health,
  And good, sound common sense.

There's shorter cuts to fortune, John—
  We see them every day—
But those who love their self-respect,
  Climb up the good old way.
"All is not gold that glitters," John,
  And makes the vulgar stare;
And those we deem the richest, John,
  Have oft the least to spare.

Be good, be pure, be noble, John,
  Be honest, brave, and true,
And do to others as ye would
  That they should do to you;
And place your trust in God, my boy,
  " Though fiery darts be hurled,"
Then you can smile at Satan's rage,
  And face a frowning world.

Good-bye! May Heaven guard and bless
  Your footsteps day by day!
The old house will be lonesome, John,
  When you are gone away.
The cricket's song upon the hearth
  Will have a sadder tone;
The old familiar spots will be
  So lonely when you're gone.

SOMEBODY'S MOTHER.

THE woman was old and ragged and gray,
And bent with the chill of the winter's day.

The street was wet with the recent snow,
And the woman's feet were aged and slow.

She stood at the crossing and waited long,
Alone, uncared for, amid the throng

Of human beings who passed her by,
Nor heeded the glance of her anxious eye.

Down the street with laughter and shout,
Glad in the freedom of " school let out,"

Came the boys like a flock of sheep,
Hailing the snow piled white and deep.

Past the woman so old and gray
Hastened the children on their way,

Nor offered a helping hand to her,
So meek, so timid, afraid to stir,

Lest the carriage wheels or the horses' feet
Should crowd her down in the slippery street.

At last came one of the merry troop—
The gayest laddie of all the group;

He paused beside her and whispered low,
" I'll help you across if you wish to go."

Her aged hand on his strong young arm
She placed, and so without hurt or harm,

He guides her trembling feet along,
Proud that his own were firm and strong.

Then back again to his friends he went,
His young heart happy and well content.

" She's somebody's mother, boys, you know,
For all she's aged and poor and slow;

And I hope some fellow will lend a hand
To help my mother, you understand,

If ever she's poor and old and gray,
When her own dear boy is far away."

And " somebody's mother" bowed low her head
In her home that night, and the prayer she said

Was, " God be kind to the noble boy,
Who is somebody's son and pride and joy ! "

OLD GRANDPA'S SOLILOQUY.

IT wasn't so when I was young—
  We used plain language then;
We didn't speak of "them galoots,"
  Meanin' boys or men.

When speaking of the nice hand-write
  Of Joe, or Tom, or Bill,
We did it plain—we didn't say,
  "He slings a nasty quill."

An' when we saw a girl we liked,
  Who never failed to please,
We called her pretty, neat, and good,
  But not "about the cheese."

Well, when we met a good old friend
  We hadn't lately seen,
We greeted him, but didn't say,
  "Hello, you old sardine!"

The boys sometimes got mad an' fit;
  We spoke of kicks and blows;
But now they "whack him on the snoot,"
  Or "paste him on the nose."

Once when a youth was turned away
  By her he held most dear,
He walked upon his feet—but now
  He "walks off on his ear."

We used to dance when I was young,
  And used to call it so;
But now they don't—they only "sling
  The light fantastic toe."

Of death we spoke in language plain
  That no one did perplex;
But in these days one doesn't die—
  He "passes in his checks."

We praised the man of common sense;
  "His judgment's good," we said
But now they say: "Well, that old plum
  Has got a level head."

It's rather sad the children now
  Are learnin' all such talk;
They've learned to "chin" instead of chat,
  An' "waltz" instead of walk.

To little Harry yesterday—
  My grandchild, aged two—
I said, "You love grandpa?" said he,
  "You bet your boots I do."

The children bowed to a stranger once;
  It is no longer so—
The little girl, as well as boys,
  Now greets you with "Helloa!"

Oh, give me back the good old days,
  When both the old and young
Conversed in plain, old-fashioned words,
  And slang was never "slung."

THE GALLANT BRAKEMAN.

Dust-grimed features, weather-beaten,
  Hands that show the scars of toil,
Do you envy him his station,
  Patient tiller of the soil?
In the storms or in the sunshine
  He must mount the speeding train,
Ride outside at post of duty,
  Heeding not the drenching rain.

In the pleasant summer weather,
  Standing on the car-top high,
He can view the changing landscapes
  As he rushes swiftly by;

While notes this beauteous picture
  Which the lonely landscape makes;
Suddenly across his dreaming
  Comes the quick shrill cry for brakes.

But when winter's icy fingers
  Cover earth with snowy shroud,
And the north wind, like a mad-man,
  Pushing on with shrieking loud;
Then behold the gallant brakeman
  Spring to heed the engine's call,
Running over the icy car-top—
  God protect him if he fall.

Do not scorn to greet him kindly,
  He will give you smile for smile,
Tho' he's nothing but a brakeman,
  Do not deem him surely vile;
Speak to him in kindly language,
  Tho' his clothes are coarse and plain,
In his fearless bosom, beats a
  Heart that feels both joy and pain.

He may have a widowed mother,
  He may be her only joy,
Mayhap in her home she's praying
  For the safety of her boy;
How he loves that dear old mother,
  Toiling for her day by day,
Always bringing her some present
  Every time he draws his pay.

Daily facing death and danger,
  One misstep or slip of hand
Sends the poor unlucky brakeman
  To the dreaded unknown land;
When we scan our ev'ning paper,
  Note what its filled columns say,
One brief line attracts our notice,
  One more brakeman killed to-day.

In her little lonely cottage,
   Waiting in the waning light,
Sits the luckless brakeman's mother,
   She expects her boy to-night;
Some one brings the fatal message,
   God have mercy! hear her pray,
As she reads the fearful story—
   Killed while coupling cars to-day.

RETROSPECT.

It has been said, and sadly oft repeated,
   That pleasure's parting draught is always pain;
Yet, who has drunk, and finding he was cheated,
   Has never once returned to drink again?

Who has not, looking backward, broken-hearted,
   When all life's joys have bitter grown as gall,
Sighed for blissful dreams long since departed,
   Or wept because he'd ever dreamed at all?

And who, when dim years, like towering mountains,
   Have hidden quite forever from his view
The effervescent gleams of pleasure's fountains,
   Would not their fleeting shadows still pursue?

PLANTATION PROVERBS.

Spec' dars poor-off colored darkies up in heben white as snow,
Spec' dars lots of likely niggas buckin' cordwood down below.

Nebber steer a midnight journey by de screamin' ob de loon—
Neber spec' ter prove yer beauty by a tussel wid de moon.

Ef yo' coat is las' year's pattern, plod erlong an' nebber min',
Dar's a pile ob healthy growin' in de humbly punkin vine.

Allus sabe de dryes' field corn fur de grindin' at de mill;
Allus sabe yo' stronges' breathin' fur de journey up de hill.

Nebber harness up de sto' clerk ter pull frough de fiel' han's part;
When yo' spec' ter tote de firewood use de common punkin cart.

A VOICE FROM THE POORHOUSE.

"My dear friends," the doctor said, "I favor license for selling
    rum,
These fanatics tell us with horror of the mischief liquor has done.
I say, as a man an' physician, the system's requirements is such.
That unless we at times assist nature the body and mind suffer
    much.
'Tis a blessing when worn out and weary, a moderate drink now
    and then."
From the minister in the pulpit came an audible murmur "Amen."
"'Tis true that many have fallen, became filthy drunkards and
    worse,
Harmed others? No, I don't uphold them. They made their
    blessing a curse.
Must I be denied for their sinning? Must the weak ones govern
    the race?
Why, every good thing God has given is only a curse out of place.
It's only excess that destroys us. A little is good now and then."
From the white-haired, pious old deacon came a fervent loud
    spoken "Amen!"
Then a murmur arose up from the people from amidst that listen-
    ing throng,
They had come from their homes with a purpose to crush out and
    trample out wrong.
But their time-honored, worthy physician, grown portly in person
    and purse,
Had shown in the demon of darkness a blessing instead of a curse;
And now they were eager, impatient, to vote when the moment
    should come;
They felt it their right and their duty to license the selling of rum.

Then up from a seat in the corner, from among the listening
    throng,
From amidst the people there gathered to crush out and trample
    out wrong,
Rose a woman, her thin hands uplifted, while from her frost-cov-
    ered hair
Gazed a face of such agonized whiteness, a face of such utter de-
    spair,
The vast throng grew hushed in a moment, grew silent with terror
    and dread,
They gazed on the face of that woman as we gaze on the face of
    the dead.
Then the hush and the silence was broken, a voice so shrill and so
    clear
Rang out thro' the room: "Look upon me; ye wonder what
    chance brought me here.
Ye know me, an' now ye shall hear me; I speak to you, lovers of
    wine;
For once I was young, rich and happy, home, husband and chil-
    dren were mine.
Where are they? I ask you. Where are they?
My beautiful home went to pay the deacon who sold them the
    poison that dragged them down lower each day.
I plead, I besought, I entreated, I showed them the path they were
    in,
But the deacon said, they believed him, that only excess was a sin.
An' where are my boys? God forgive you! They heeded your
    counsel, not mine.
You, doctor, beloved an' respected, you could see no danger in
    wine.
Me boys so proud an' so manly, me husband so noble an' brave,
They lie in the church-yard side by side, each filling a drunkard's
    grave.
I have come from the poorhouse to tell me story, an' now it is done,
Go on if ye will, in yer madness, and license the selling of rum;
Before the great judgment eternal, when the last dread moment
    has come,
Shall I stand there to witness against you, my dear friends, the
    victims of rum?"

A PARODY.

THE boy stood on the back-yard fence, whence all but him had fled,
The flames that lit his father's barn shone just above the shed.
One bunch of crackers in his hand, two others in his hat,
With piteous accents loud he cried, "I never thought of that!"
A bunch of crackers to the tail of one small dog he'd tied;
The dog in anguish sought the barn, and 'mid its ruins died.
The sparks flew wide, and red and hot, they lit upon that brat;
They fired the crackers in his hand, and e'en those in his hat.

Then came a burst of rattling sound—the boy! Where was he
      gone?
Ask of the winds that far around strewed bits of meat and bone:
And scraps of clothes, and balls, and tops, and nails, and hooks,
      and yarn—
The relics of that dreadful boy that burnt his father's barn.

ROOM AT THE TOP.

'MID the hurry and strife in the pathway of life,
   Those who press with the jostling crowd
Must tread in the footsteps where others have trod,
   Stand only where others have stood.

But he who would stray from the old beaten way
   Must oft go unblest and alone:—
Must seek for himself a path all untrod,
   Though he bridge it, or hew it of stone!

There are thousands to go in a way prescribed so,
   To one, who successful, would lead,
Or dare to dissent from the time-honored rule,
   Nor the taunts of the multitude heed.

Thus, the higher we scale up the mount from the vale,
  One by one from the rocks will out drop,—
Those who toiled by our side, till for valiant and strong,
  There is always found room at the top.

'Tis noble to dare, and the rough way prepare
  For a loftier purpose in life!
A higher endeavor ne'er failed of its meed,
  Though it grasp not the bays in the strife.

And 'tis only to him who strives that shall win;
  The victor will never find place
With idlers that loitered along by the way,
  Or started not out in the race.

Up the ladder of fame there are few that will climb
  To its loftiest height with brave hope;
Though its base may e'er rest with the clamoring throng,
  There will always be room at the top!

Strive on, though with fears!   As the far summit nears,
  Look not downward. but ever up;
However so crowded the heights that are gained,
  There will always be room at the top.

THE FOURTH OF JULY.

Patrick an' Bridget, just shtep still the door,
Faith! seed ye ever the loike soight before?
Flags all a-flyin' from windy an' roof,
Horses decked wid 'em from forelock to hoof.
All the small childer a-poppin' off cracks—
Troth, but they sound loike shillelahs' bould whacks!
Shpake up, swate Biddy, an' answer me, Pat;
Seed yez in Kerry the loike of all that?
"Phat is the row?" to a shpalpeen, sez I,
"Dade, thin," sez he, "it's the Foorth uv July!"

Thin I drawed in from the windy me head,
Not wan word wiser for all that he said;
Long kem a leddy, so shmoilin' an' gay,
Troth, I spyakes oop till hersilf wid me say:
"Plaze, mem," I axed her, "what manes the parade?
Whoy is the racket an' blatherin' made?
Who's been a-foightin', an' what was the row?
Shtop a bit, leddy, an' tell me thrue, now."
Faith she looks oop, wid the shmoile in her eye,
"*They're sillybratin' the Foorth uv July!*"

What a gossoon wuz this Foorth uv July!
Who was the cratur', an' whin did he die?
Whist! Biddy, darlint, an' hear the band play!
See the lads steppin' so frisky an' gay!
Bould sojer laddies in all their galore,
Troth, but there's music an' dhrums to the fore!
Flags all a-flyin' an' powdher ablaze—
Thrue for yez, Biddy, these folk have quare ways.
Sure, thin, St. Pathrick was betther, sez I,
A *dale* betther mon, nor the Foorth uv July.

ASLEEP AT THE SWITCH.

THE first thing I remember was Carlo tugging away,
With the sleeve of my coat fast in his teeth, pulling, as much as to
    say:
"Come, master, awake, attend to the switch, lives now depend
    upon you.
Think of the souls in the coming train, and the graves you are
    sending them to.
Think of the mother and the babe at her breast, think of the
    father and son,
Think of the lover and loved ones, too; think of them doomed
    every one

To fall, as it were, from your very hand into you fathomless ditch,
Murdered by one who should guard them from harm, who now lies
    asleep at the switch."
I sprang up amazed, scarce knew where I stood, sleep had o'er-
    mastered me so.
I could hear the wind hollowly howling, and the deep river dash-
    ing below;
I could hear the forest leaves rustling, as the trees by the tempest
    were fanned,
But what was that noise in the distance, that I could not quite un-
    derstand?
I heard it at first indistinctly, like the rolling of some muffled
    drum;
Then nearer and nearer it came to me, till it made my very ears
    hum—
What is this light that surrounds me, and seems to set fire to my
    brain?
What whistle's that yelling so shrill?   Oh! I know, it's the train.
We often stand facing some danger, and seem to take root to the
    place,
So I stood with this demon before me, its heated breath scorching
    my face.
Its headlight made daylight of darkness, and glared like the eyes
    of some witch.
The train was almost upon me before I remembered the switch.
I sprang to it, seizing it wildly, the train dashing fast down the
    track.
The switch resisted my efforts, some demon seemed holding it back.
On, on, came the fiery-eyed monster, and shot by my face like a
    flash,
I swooned to the earth the next moment, and knew nothing of the
    great crash.
How long I remained there unconscious, 'tis impossible for me to
    tell;
But my stupor was almost a heaven, and my waking almost a hell.
For then I heard the piteous moaning and shrieking of husbands
    and wives,
And I thought of the day we all shrink from, when I must account
    for their lives.

Mothers rushed by me like maniacs, their eyes glaring madly and
    wild;
Fathers, losing their courage, gave way to their grief like a child;
Children, searching for parents, I noticed as by me they sped—
And lips that could form naught but mamma, were calling for one
    perhaps dead.
My mind was made up in a moment—the river should hide me
    away,
When under the still burning rafters I suddenly noticed there lay
A little white hand. She who owned it was doubtless an object
    of love
To him whom her loss would drive frantic, though she guarded him
    now from above.
I tenderly lifted the rafters, and quietly laid them one side—
Oh! how little she thought of the journey when she left for this
    dark fatal ride.
I lifted the last log from off her. While searching for some spark
    of life,
Turned her little face up in the starlight, and recognized Maggie!
    my wife!
O Lord! Thy scourge is a hard one. At a blow Thou has shat-
    tered my pride,
My life will be one endless nightmare, with Maggie away from my
    side.
I fancied I stood on trial—the jury and judge I could see—
And every eye in the court-room was steadily fixed upon me,
And fingers were pointing in scorn, till I felt my face blushing
    blood red,
And the next thing I heard were the words: "Hanged, sir!
    Hanged by the neck until dead!"
Then I felt myself pulled once again, and my hand caught tight
    hold of a dress,
And I heard: "What's the matter, dear Jim? You've had a bad
    nightmare, I guess."
And there stood Maggie, my wife, with never a scar from the ditch.
I'd been taking a nap on my couch, and had not been asleep at
    the switch.

THE VILLAGE CHOIR.

HALF a bar, half a bar,
  Half a bar onward!
    Into an awful ditch,
    Choir and precentor hitch,
    Into a mess of pitch,
  They led the Old Hundred.
Trebles to right of them,
Tenors to left of them,
Basses in front of them,
  Bellowed and thundered.
Oh, that precentor's look,
When the sopranos took
Their own time and hook
  From the Old Hundred.

Screeched all the trebles here,
Boggled the tenors there,
Raising the parson's hair.
  While his mind wandered;
Theirs not to reason why
This psalm was pitched too high;
Theirs but to gasp and cry
  Out the Old Hundred.
Trebles to right of them,
Tenors to left of them,
Basses in front of them,
  Bellowed and thundered.
Stormed they with shout and yell,
Not wise they rang, nor well,
Drowning the sexton's bell,
  While all the church wondered.

Dire the precentor's glare,
Flashed his pitchfork in air,
Sounding the fresh keys to bear
  Out the Old Hundred.

Swiftly he turned his back,
Reached he his hat from rack,
Then from the screaming pack,
   Himself he sundered.
Tenors to right of him,
Trebles to left of him,
Discords behind him
   Bellowed and thundered.
Oh, the wild howls they wrought:
Right to the end they fought!
Some tune they sang, but not,
Not the Old Hundred.

NOTHING.

"Blessed be nothing!" an old woman said,
As she scrubbed away for her daily bread;
"I'm better off than my neighbor, the squire;
He's afraid of robbers, afraid of fire,
Afraid of flood to wreck his mill,
Afraid of something to cross his will.
I've nothing to burn, and nothing to steal
But a bit of pork and a barrel of meal.
A house that only keeps off the rain
Is easy burnt up and built again!
I sing at my washing, and sleep all night.
Blessed be nothing!   My heart is light."

"Blessed be nothing!" the young man cried,
As he turned with a smile to his smiling bride.
"Banks are breaking, and stocks are down;
There's dread and bitterness all over town;
There are brokers groaning and bankers sad,
And men whose losses have made them mad;
There's silk and satin, but want of bread,
And many a woman would fain be dead,

Whose little children sob and cling
For the daily joy she cannot bring.
Blessed be nothing, for you and me!
We have no riches on wings to flee."

Blessed be nothing! if man might choose,
For he who hath it hath nought to lose;
Nothing to fear from flood or fire,
All things to hope for and desire;
The dream that is better than waking days;
The future that feeds the longing gaze.
Better, far better, than aught we hold,
As far as mining exceedeth gold,
Or hope fruition in earth below,
Or peace that is in us outward show.

Almost, when worn by weary years,
Tired with a pathway of thorns and tears,
When kindred fail us, and love has fled,
And we know the living less than the dead,
We think that the best of mortal good
Is a painless, friendless solitude.
For the pangs are more than the peace they give
Who make our lives so sad to live.
Blessed be nothing! it knows no loss,
Nor the sharpest nail of the Master's cross;
No friend to deny us, of none bereft,
And though we have no one, yet God is left.

Yet, having nothing, the whole is ours,
No thorns can pierce us who have no flowers;
And sure is the promise of His word,
Thy poor are blessed in spirit, Lord!
Whatever we lose of wealth or care,
Still there is left us the breath of prayer—
That heavenly breath of a world so high,
Sorrow and sinning come not nigh;
The sure and certain mercy of Him
Who sitteth between the cherubim,

Yet cares for the lonely sparrow's fall,
And is ready and eager to help us all.
Rich is His bounty to all beneath;
To the poorest and saddest He giveth death.

THE MOTHER'S REPROOF.

MRS. E. P. REQUA.

A LIGHT footfall on the sounding floor,
And a tiny face peeps in at the door,
"Ah, mamma, I've found you out at last;
Why did you shut you in so fast?
Mamma, dolly has lost her shoe,
I can't find it anywhere; come and look too."
I laid down my pen with numerous sighs,
And started on this new enterprise;
Search and research were all in vain,
Till a bright thought was born in my brain.
I opened the oven door, and lo!
There lay the shoe as black as a sloe!
Laid in a patty-pan, baked for a pie,
"You've ruined your dolly's shoe," cried I;
She simply arched her eyebrows, when
She answered, "Make her another, then."
Vainly I seek some quiet nook,
In which to hide with my pen or book;
Vainly, for each new-found retreat
Is still invaded by pattering feet;
Pattering feet, and demands like these—
"Mamma, a pencil and ink, if you please;
See, I am coming to sit down by you;
Mamma is writing, I want to write, too."
Till a spirit that nature had never endowed
With marvellous patience, made murmur loud:
"At such a lot I may well repine,
Ne'er was more absolute thralldom than mine."

This, in the day of my pride and strength;
The coveted freedom came at length,
Came, and it lay on my spirit sore,
No pattering feet on the silent floor!
Quiet and leisure, could that suffice,
Quiet and leisure at such a price!
My favorite authors in vain invite;
"No little face will intrude to-night;"
I turned to my needle, the arrowy grief
That pierced me, on viewing the half-formed leaf,
On a little garment that ne'er will be worn;
Well I remember the sorrowful morn,
When two little arms were over it placed,
And I threw it aside in petulant haste.
Mothers, weighed down with a mother's care,
Thinking your burdens too great to bear,
Tempted your hearts at their lot to repine,
Could ye but fathom the sorrow of mine!
Mothers, whose little ones round you throng,
Cherish them, sing to them all the day long.

Ye may rejoice, but never I,
Whose hopes entombed with my darling lie.
O joyless mother!   O garish sun!
O coveted wealth that the grave has won!
In this empty world I find no part—
Where shall I go with my breaking heart?
Why sinks not my frame beneath the stroke?
With anguish no words can depict I *woke!*
She lay there beside me in slumber mild,
My lost, and recovered, and *living* child!
Nor yet had the light of morning broke,
But her eyes to the touch of my lips awoke.
She marvelled to see the smiles and tears
That greeted her waking: "Dearest of dears,
Mother and you will be merry to-day;
You shall help me write, and I'll help you play;
Dolly shall have two pairs of new shoes,
And anything else that my darling may choose."

The little arms around me were thrown,
The little breast heaved against my own;
Ye only, who thus have suffered, may guess
The hallowed rapture of that caress!

THE ROUND OF LIFE.

ALEXANDER LAMONT.

Two children down by the shining strand,
  With eyes as blue as the summer sea,
While the sinking sun fills all the land
  With the glow of a golden mystery:
Laughing aloud at the sea-mew's cry,
  Gazing with joy on its snowy breast,
Till the first star looks from the evening sky,
  And the amber bars stretch over the west.

A soft green dell by the breezy shore,.
  A sailor lad and a maiden fair;
Hand clasped in hand, while the tale of yore
  Is borne again on the listening air,
For love is young, though love be old,
  And love alone the heart can fill;
And the dear old tale, that has been told
  In the days gone by, is spoken still.

A trim-built home on a sheltered bay;
  A wife looking out on the listening sea;
A prayer for the loved one far away,
  And prattling imps 'neath the old roof-tree;
A lifted latch and a radiant face
  By the open door in the falling night;
A welcome home and a warm embrace
  From the love of his youth and his children bright.

An aged man in an old arm-chair;
  A golden light from the western sky;

His wife by his side, with her silvered hair,
  And the open book of God close by,
Sweet on the bay the gloaming falls,
  And bright is the glow of the evening star;
But dearer to them are the jasper walls
  And the golden streets of the Land afar.

An old church-yard on a green hillside,
  Two lying still in their peaceful rest;
The fishermen's boats going out with the tide
  In the fiery glow of the amber west.
Children's laughter and old men's sighs,
  The night that follows the morning clear,
A rainbow bridging our darkened skies,
  Are the round of our lives from year to year.

PARTING.

THE truest friends must part, they say,
  The fondest hearts must sever,
But friendship's bonds may last for aye,
  And mem'ry live forever.

And you will go, and I shall miss
  Each word, each look, each smile,
Each vanish'd pressure of your kiss,
  And long for you the while.

Each thing that we have seen and lov'd,
  Each flow'r, each bird, each tree,
Each place where we've together rov'd
  Will hold a charm for me.

Then fare you well—this parting's pain
  To those whom Fate must sever,
I only say good-bye again—
  And trust 'tis not forever!

OUR CHRISTMAS.

JULIA WALCOTT.

WE didn't have much of a Christmas,
   My papa and Rosie and me,
For mamma'd gone out to the prison
   To trim up the poor pris'ner's tree;
And Ethel, my big grown-up sister,
   Was down at the 'sylum all day,
To help at the great turkey dinner,
   And teach games for the orphans to play.
She belongs to a club of young ladies,
   With a "*beautiful objick*," they say,
'Tis to go among poor lonesome children
   And make all their sad hearts more gay.

And Auntie, you don't know my Auntie?
   She's my own papa's half-sister Kate;
She was 'bliged to be round at the chapel
   Till 'twas.—Oh, sometimes *dreadfully* late,
For she pities the poor worn-out curate:
   His burdens, she says, are so great,
So she 'ranges the flowers and the music,
   And he goes home around by our gate.
I should think this way *must* be the longest,
   But then, I suppose he knows best,
Aunt Kate says he intones most splendid;
   And his name is Vane Algernon West.

My papa had bought a big turkey,
   And had it sent home Christmas Eve;
But there wasn't a soul here to cook it,
   You see Bridget had threatened to leave
If she couldn't go off with her cousin,
   (He doesn't look like her one bit),
She says she belongs to a "union,"
   And the union won't let her submit

So we ate bread and milk for our dinner,
  And some raisins and candy, and then
Rose and me went down-stairs to the pantry
  To look at the turkey again.

Papa said he would take us out riding—
  Then he thought that he didn't quite dare,
For Rosie'd got cold and kept coughing;
  There was dampness and chills in the air.
Oh, the day was *so* long and so lonesome!
  And our papa was lonesome as we;
And the parlor was dreary—no sunshine,
  And all the sweet roses,—the tea,
And the red ones, and ferns and carnations,
  That have made our bay-window so bright,
Mamma'd picked for the men at the prison;
  To make their bad hearts pure and white.

And we all sat up close to the window,
  Rose and me on our papa's two knees,
And we counted the dear little birdies
  That were hopping about on the trees.
Rosie wanted to be a brown sparrow;
  But I thought I would rather, by far,
Be a robin that flies away winters
  Where the sunshine and gay blossoms are.
And papa wished he was a jail-bird,
  'Cause he thought that they fared the best;
But we all were real glad we weren't turkeys,
  For then we'd been killed with the rest.

That night I put into my prayers,—
  "Dear God, we've been lonesome to-day,
For Mamma, Aunt, Ethel, and Bridget,
  Every one of them all went away.—
Won't you please make a club, or society,
  'Fore it's time for next Christmas to be,
To take care of philanterpists' fam'lies,
  Like papa and Rosie and me?"—

And I think that my papa's grown pious,
 For he listened, as still as a mouse,
Till I got to Amen;—then *he* said it
 So it sounded all over the house.

WRITE THEM A LETTER TO-NIGHT.

OLYETTE ELLIS.

DON'T go to the theatre, grange or ball,
 But stay in your room to-night;
Deny yourself of the friends that call,
 And a good long letter write—
Write to the sad old folks at home,
 Who sit when the day is done,
With folded hands and downcast eyes,
 And think of the absent one.

Don't selfishly scribble "excuse my haste,
 I've scarcely the time to write,"
Lest their brooding thoughts go wandering back
 To many a by-gone night,
When they lost their needed sleep and rest,
 And every breath was a prayer—
That God would leave their delicate babe
 To their tender love and care.

Don't let them feel that you've no more need
 Of their love or counsel wise;
For the heart grows strongly sensitive
 When age has dimmed the eyes—
It might be well to let them believe
 You never forgot them, quite;
That you deem it a pleasure, when far away,
 Long letters home to write.

Don't think that the young and giddy friends,
    Who make your pastime gay,
Have half the anxious thought for you
    That the old folks have to-day.
The duty of writing do not put off;
    Let sleep or pleasure wait,
Lest the letter for which they looked and longed
    Be a day or an hour *too late.*

For the sad old folks at home,
    With locks fast turning white,
Are longing to hear from the absent one—
    Write them a letter to-night.

THE RIDE OF GREAT-GRANDMOTHER LEE.

[A STORY OF REVOLUTIONARY TIMES.]

EBEN E. REXFORD.

This is the tale of Great-grandmother Lee,
Just as my grandmother told it to me;
A tale of the old Colonial time,
And a woman's bravery, set to rhyme.

Great-grandmother Lee was a maiden then,
But her hand was promised a lover when
The war for freedom was fought and won,
And the world applauded a grand deed done
By those who in action and brave words spoke
The anger they felt 'neath a tyrant's yoke.
"We will be free of it." Thus said they.
"Down with King George's galling sway!"

There was fighting near and fighting far;
The air seemed charged with the stress of war.
Never a day went by that brought
No rumor of battle somewhere fought,

And those at home almost held their breath
As the days went by with their tales of death.

Backward and forward, on every side,
Swept the ever-changing battle-tide;
Often it brought near home the men
Who had gone to the war, then turned again
And bore them farther and farther away,
And no tidings would come for many a day
From those whose lot was to come and go
As the winds of conflict might chance to blow.

One day a postman brought news that stirred
With eager hope all the hearts that heard;
"Lieutenant Lee had been sent," he said,
"With twoscore men to Marblehead
In charge of some prisoners. It might be
They would come that way." At the name of Lee,
How the eyes of Great-grandmother Ruth grew bright,
And the heart that was heavy with hope grew light!

But next day the news went about the town
That a band of Britishers, marching down
From Boston or Concord, had been seen
That town and the Marblehead hills between.
"They will lie in wait for Lieutenant Lee,
And, dreaming not of his danger, he
Will keep straight on till it is too late
To escape the foes that in ambush wait."

Great-grandmother Ruth heard the news they brought,
And up to her brain leaped a sudden thought—
Some one must go, and at once, to warn
Lieutenant Lee. Ere another morn
He might fall, perhaps, an easy prey
To the British men who in ambush lay.
But who should go? All the men in town
Were old, or crippled, or broken down
With wounds or sickness. "Not one," cried she,
"To carry the news to Lieutenant Lee!

I will go myself." And her blue eyes shone
With a courage born not of love alone,
But the spirit that nerved the arm and heart
Of those who in war bore a soldier's part.
"A woman can't fight very well," she said;
"But there's many a thing she can do instead
That's as good as fighting. My British men,
I'll take a hand in your game." And then
She saddled her horse, and as night came down,
They saw her galloping out of the town.
"She goes to warn her lover," they said,
"Of a danger that lurks in the way ahead.
Brave is the girl's heart and strong her steed,"
And every one cheered her and said "God speed!"

Twoscore miles to make ere the first cock crowed—
Great-grandmother Ruth planned her route as she rode.
"Lieutenant Lee and his men will take
The old post-road by Hingham's Lake;
There I must meet them, and they can turn
To the north on the highway that runs by Kern;
And thus they can slip past the ambushed foe
Who hides on the new road, miles below.
Ah, ha! my Britishers, watch and wait;
You'll find out the truth when it is too late!"

The dusk closed round her; the stars grew bright,
And the moon made day of the brief June night.
"Five miles are behind us," she cried, as she passed
The ford in the valley, and still more fast
She urged her steed down the road that runs
Through Sudbury town and the smaller ones
That lie to the south. Often those in bed
Were roused by the sound of a horse's tread,
And said to each other, "Some one rides fast,"
And e'en as they said it the place was passed
By the midnight rider. "The stars say One,"
She cried to her horse, "and our ride's half done."

Two—"We do well." Three—"The miles are few.
Doll, do you know what depends on you?"

Four—and upon her keen eyes break
The sight she has longed for of Hingham's Lake.
"Our ride is ended," and she draws rein
In the shade of the pine trees on Hingham's plain,
To wait for the coming of those who are nigh,
With a smile on her lip and a laughing eye.

"Hark! they are coming. Good steed of mine,
We will bid them stand and give countersign,"
She says, as the tramp of men's feet sounds near.
"He, my lover, is almost here,"
And her face grows bright like a damask rose
When all of a sudden its leaves unclose
At a warm wind's kiss, and break all apart,
To reveal the glow at the blossom's heart.

"Halt!" The soldiers, startled, heard
A woman's voice speak the well-known word;
Then out of the shadow of pines rode she.
"Ruth, my Ruth!" cried Lieutenant Lee,
"Is this your ghost, or are you a dream?"
Then his arms were round her, and it would seem
That the touch of her lips was proof enough
That the vision was hardly of ghostly stuff.

"There's no time for love-making now," laughed she;
"There's something more urgent, Lieutenant Lee."
Then she told them what she had come to tell.
"Ruth, my heroine, you've done well,"
Cried Lieutenant Lee, and his face was bright.
"Such help as this nerves our hearts for fight.
Men, what say you? This girl should be
Made colonel, at least, for her bravery.
Cheers for brave Colonel Ruth, my men!"
And the morning rang and rang again
With hearty cheers for the girl whose deed
Had brought them warning in time of need.

There is little need for me to make
The story longer. At Hingham's Lake

They turned to the north, and by this detour
The British were left in the lurch. Quite sure
Am I that no happier girl than she
Who rode by the side of Lieutenant Lee
Could be found in all the land that day.
Ere night in Marblehead safe were they.
The story of Ruth and her long night ride
Spread through the village and country side,
And they came in crowds, it is said, to pay
Respect to her, and "Well done" to say.
"I don't care so much for their praise," said she,
As she smiled in the face of Lieutenant Lee,
"As I do to know that I helped you play
A trick on the British, and won the day."

PATRICK DOLIN'S LOVE-LETTER.

It's Patrick Dolin meself and no other,
That's after informin' you without any bother,
That your own darling self put me heart in a blaze,
And made me your sweetheart the rest of my days,
So now I sits down to write ye this letter,
To tell how I loves ye, as none can love better.
Mony's the day sure since first I got smitten
With your own purty face that's as bright as a kitten's,
And yer illigant figger, that's just the right size.
Faith, I'm all over in love wid ye, clear up to the eyes,
And if these feelin's you'll only reciprocate,
I gives ye my hand and heart, everything but me hate.
Och, now while I write, me heart's in a flutter,
For I can't help feelin' every word that I utter;
You'll think me deceivin', or tellin' a lie,
If I tell who's in love wid me, just ready to die;
There's Bridget McCregan, full of coketish tricks,
Keeps flatterin' me pride to get me heart in a fix;
And Bridget, ye know, has great expectations,
From the father that's dead, and lots of relations;

Then there's Biddy O'Farrel, the cunningest elf,
Sings "Patrick me darling," and that manes meself;
I might marry them both if I felt so inclined,
But there's no use talking of the likes of their kind:
I trates them alike without any imparshality,
And maintain meself on the ground of neutrality,
For the same I've got meself in a quonderum,
For they keep tazing and tazing, to make me fond of them;
But the more they taze me, the greater the dislike,
And it's sick that I am with their blathering sight.
If there's any truth in dreams, we'd been one long ago,
For I keep dreaming every night, I am lovin' ye so.
By the holy St. Patrick, I loves ye and no other,
And for the likes of ye forsake father and mother.
On me knees, Helen darling, I ask yer consent,
For better or worse, without a rid cent;
If ye refuse me, bedad, I'm like to go crazy,
And cut me throat with a razor to make me soul aisy.
I'm a Catholic, ye know, but for the sake of relation,
Wouldn't mind to change creed and sign a recantation.
I'd do anything in the world, anything ye would say,
If ye'd be Mistress Dolin instead of Miss Day,
I'd save all me money, and buy a new coat,
And go to New Orleans by the steam packet-boat;
I'd buy a half acre and build a nice house,
Where nothing would taze us, so much as a mouse;
And you'll hear nothing else, from year out to year in,
But sweet words of kindness from yer Patrick Dolin.
As to the matter of property, Helen me honey,
I've great expectations, but not a ha'p'orth of money;
Me father's a merchant who keeps a great store,
"WARM MEALS FOR A QUARTHER" is the sign on the
    door;
And there he sells lickers, and all sorts of trash
That beats all the stores for bringing in cash;
But better than all is me kind-hearted ould aunty
That lives in the patch in her nate little shanty,
For oft have I dreamed me ould aunty had died
And left me her shanty, with a trifle beside.

'Tis meself that would say, predicting no wrong,
That aunty must die some time before very long,
And every morning I'm waking, 'tis expecting to find
That the spirit has left aunty and shanty behind;
Then there on the patch would we live, Helen darlin',
With never a hard word, bickering or quarrellin';
But if ye should die—forgive me the thought,
I'd behave meself as a dacent man ought;
I'd spend all me days in wailing and crying,
And wish for nothing better than just to be dying.
You'd see on marble slabs, reared up side by side,
"Here lies Patrick Dolin."   "Here lies Helen his bride."
Yer indulgence in conclusion on my letter I ask,
For to write a love-letter is no aisy task;
I've an impediment of speech, as me letter all shows,
And a cold in me head that makes me write through me nose.
Please write me a letter, to me great-uncle's care,
With the prescription upon it, " Patrick Dolin, Esquire,
In haste," write in big letters on the outside of the cover,
And believe me, forever, yer distractionate lover.
  Written with me own hand.

         his
      PATRICK × DOLIN.
       mark.

HANNAH JANE.

D. R. LOCKE (PETROLEUM V. NASBY.)

SHE isn't half so handsome as when, twenty years agone,
At her old home in Piketon, Parson Avery made us one;
The great house crowded full of guests of every degree,
The girls all envying Hannah Jane, the boys all envying me.

Her fingers then were taper, and her skin as white as milk,
Her brown hair, what a mass it was! and soft and fine as silk;
No wind-moved willow by a brook had ever such a grace,
Her form of Aphrodite, with a pure Madonna face.

She had but meagre schooling; her little notes to me
Were full of little pot-hooks, and the worst orthography;
Her "dear" she spelled with double e, and "kiss" with but one s;
But when one's crazed with passion what's a letter more or less?

She blundered in her writing, and she blundered when she spoke,
And every rule of syntax, that old Murray made, she broke;
But she was beautiful and fresh, and I—well, I was young;
Her form and face o'erbalanced all the blunders of her tongue.

I was but little better. True, I'd longer been at school;
My tongue and pen were run, perhaps, a little more by rule;
But that was all, the neighbors round who both of us well knew,
Said, which I believed—she was the better of the two.

All's changed; the light of seventeen's no longer in her eyes;
Her wavy hair is gone—that loss the coiffeur's art supplies;
Her form is thin and angular, she slightly forward bends;
Her fingers, once so shapely, now are stumpy at the ends.

She knows but very little, and in little are we one;
The beauty rare, that more than hid that great defect, is gone.
My *parvenu* relations now deride my homely wife,
And pity me that I am tied to such a clod for life.

I know there is a difference; at reception and levee
The brightest, wittiest, and most famed of women smile on me;
And everywhere I hold my place among the greatest men;
And sometimes sigh, with Whittier's judge, "Alas! it might have
      been."

When they all crowd around me, stately dames and brilliant belles,
And yield to me the homage that all great success compels,
Discussing art and statecraft, and literature as well,
From Homer down to Thackeray, and Swedenborg on "hell,"

I can't forget that from these streams my wife has never quaffed,
Has never with Ophelia wept, nor with Jack Falstaff laughed;
Of authors, actors, artists—why, she hardly knows the names,
She slept while I was speaking on the *Alabama* claims.

I can't forget—just at this point another form appears—
The wife I wedded as she was before my prosperous years;

I travel o'er the dreary road we travelled side by side,
And wonder what my share would be if Justice should divide!

She had four hundred dollars left her from the old estate;
On that we married, and, thus poorly armored, faced our fate.
I wrestled with my books; her task was harder far than mine,—
'Twas how to make two hundred dollars do the work of nine.

At last I was admitted, then I had my legal lore,
An office with a stove and desk, of books perhaps a score;
She had her beauty and her youth, and some housewifely skill;
And love for me and faith in me, and back of that a will.

I had no friends behind me—no influence to aid;
I worked and fought for every little inch of ground I made.
And how she fought beside me! never woman lived on less;
In two long years she never spent a single cent for dress.

Ah! how she cried for joy when my first legal fight was won,
When our eclipse passed partly by and we stood in the sun;
The fee was fifty dollars—'twas the work of half a year—
First captive, lean and scraggy, of my legal bow and spear.

I well remember when my coat (the only one I had),
Was seedy grown and threadbare, and in fact, most "shocking bad,"
The tailor's stern remark when I a modest order made:
"Cash is the basis, sir, on which we tailors do our trade!"

Her winter cloak was in his shop by noon that very day;
She wrought on hickory shirts at night that tailor's skill to pay;
I got a coat, and wore it; but alas, poor Hannah Jane
Ne'er went to church or lecture till warm weather came again.

Our second season she refused a cloak of any sort,
That I might have a decent suit in which t' appear in court;
She made her last year's bonnet do, that I might have a hat;
Talk of the old-time flame-enveloped martyrs after that!

No negro ever worked so hard, a servant's pay to save,
She made herself most willingly a household drudge and slave.
What wonder that she never read a magazine or book,
Combining as she did in one, nurse, housemaid, seamstress, cook!

What wonder that the beauty fled that I once so adored!
Her beautiful complexion my fierce kitchen fire devoured;
Her plump, fair, soft, rounded arm was once too fair to be con-
    cealed;
Hard work for me that softness into sinewy strength congealed.

I was her altar, and her love the sacrificial flame:
Oh! with what pure devotion she to that altar came,
And tearful flung thereon—alas! I did not know it then—
All that she was, and more than that, all that she might have been.

At last I won success. Ah! then our lives were wider parted;
I was far up the rising road; she, poor girl! where we started.
I had tried my speed and mettle, and gained strength in every race;
I was far up the heights of life—she drudging at the base.

She made me take each Fall the stump; she said 'twas my career;
The wild applause of list'ning crowds was music to my ear.
What stimulus had she to cheer her dreary solitude?
For me she lived, and gladly, in unnatural widowhood.

She coudn't read my speech, but when the papers all agreed
'Twas the best one of the session, those comments she could read;
And with a gush of pride thereat, which I had never felt,
She sent them to me in a note, with half the words misspelt.

I to the legislature went, and said that she should go
To see the world with me, and what the world was doing, know.
With tearful smile she answered "No! four dollars is the pay;
The Bates House rates for board *for one* is just that sum per day."

At twenty-eight the State House, on the bench at thirty-three;
At forty every gate in life is opened wide to me.
I nursed my powers, and grew, and made my point in life; but she—
Bearing such pack-horse weary loads, what could a woman be?

What could she be? O shame! I blush to think what she has
    been—
The most unselfish of all wives to the selfishest of men.
Yes, plain and homely now she is; she's ignorant, tis 'true;
For me she rubbed herself quite out; I represent the two.

Well, I suppose that I might do as other men have done—
First break her heart with cold neglect, then shove her out alone.
The world would say 'twas well, and more, would give great praise
        to me
For having borne with "such a wife" so uncomplainingly.

And shall I? No! The contract 'twixt Hannah, God, and me,
Was not for one or twenty years, but for eternity.
No matter what the world may think; I know down in my heart,
That if either, I'm delinquent. She has bravely done her part.

There's another world beyond this, and on the final day,
Will intellect and learning 'gainst such devotion weigh?
When the great one, made of us two, is torn apart again,
I'll fare the worst, for God is just, and He knows Hannah Jane.

THOUGHTS FOR A DISCOURAGED FARMER.

JAMES WHITCOMB RILEY

THE summer winds is sniffin' round the bloomin' locus' trees,
And the clover in the pastur' is a big day for the bees,
And they been a-swiggin' honey, above-board and on the sly,
Till they stutter in their buzzin' and stagger as they fly.

They's been a heap o' rain, but the sun's out to-day,
And the clouds of the wet spell is all cleared away,
And the woods is all the greener, and the grass is greener still;
It may rain again to-morrow, but I don't think it will.

Some say the crops is ruined, and the corn's drownded out,
And propha-sy the wheat will be a failure, without doubt;
But the kind Providence that has never failed us yet,
Will be on hand onc't more at the 'leventh hour, I bet!

Does the medder-lark complain, as he swims high and dry,
Through the waves of the wind and the blue of the sky?
Does the quail set up and whistle in a disappointed way,
Er hang his head in silence and sorrow all the day?

Is the chipmuck's health a failure?   Does he walk or does he run?
Don't the buzzards ooze around up there, just like they've allus
    done?
Is there anything the matter with the rooster's lungs or voice?
Ort a mortal be complainin' when dumb animals rejoice?

Then let us, one and all, be contented with our lot:
The June is here this morning and the sun is shining hot.
Oh, let us fill our hearts with the glory of the day,
And banish ev'ry doubt and care and sorrow far away!

Whatever be our station, with Providence for guide,
Such fine circumstances ort to make us satisfied;
For the world is full of roses, and the roses full of dew,
And the dew is full of heavenly love that drips for me and you.

THE KISS IN THE TUNNEL.

THEY were sitting five seats back, but I plainly heard the smack,
  As we dashed into the tunnel near the town,
And the currents of my veins ran like gushing April rains,
  Though I'm grave and gray and wear a doctor's gown.

Once—alas! so long ago—on the rails I journeyed so,
  With a maiden in a jaunty jersey sack,
And I kissed her with my eyes, as the timid stars the skies,
  But I longed, oh, how I longed! for one real smack!

Did she know it?   I dare say!   (She'd a sweet clairvoyant way
  In the glancing of her eyes so bright and blue.)
Ne'er a bee such honey sips as the nectar on her lips;
  But I longed, and longed in vain, as on we flew.

Just as yearning reached its height, lo! there came a sudden night,
  And like steel to magnet clove my mouth to hers!
I shall never more forget how like drops of rain they met,
  In the bosom of a rose that lightly stirs!

When we came again to light, both our faces had turned white—
  White as clouds that float in summer from the South.
Missed I glances, missed I smiles! but on air I rode for miles,
  With the sweetness of love's dew upon my mouth.

So the kiss that some one stole, in the rayless Stygian hole,
  While with loud imprisoned clangor on we rushed.
Caused the sluggish streams of age, with young madness leap and
      rage—
  And my wife restored to daylight, laughed and blushed.

MAKE THE BEST OF IT.

BE gay! What is the use of repining?
  Merry mirth can keep tears at bay;
All sorrows have a joy for their lining,
  Heaven's hope can chase fear away

Be gay! You are to blame if life's dreary;
  See how Nature smiles thro' her tears;
Heavy hearts make the footsteps grow weary,
  But happiness lengthens the years.

Be gay! Earth wasn't made for you solely,
  It'll last after you go away.
It's the soul, not the body, that's holy;
  Why grieve for a poor lump of clay?

THE COMING MILLIONS

S. W. FOSS.

JIM CROKER lived far in the woods, a solitary place,
Where the bushes grew, like whiskers, on his unrazored face;
And the black bear was his brother and the catamount his chum,
And Jim he lived and waited for the millions yet to come.

Jim Croker made a clearing and he sowed it down to wheat,
And he filled his lawn with cabbage and he planted it with beet,
And it blossomed with potatoes, and with peach and pear and
    plum,
And Jim he lived and waited for the millions yet to come.

Then Jim he took his ancient axe and cleared a forest street,
While he lived on bear and succotash and young opossum meat,
And his rhythmic axe strokes sounded and the woods no more
    were dumb,
While he cleared a crooked highway for the millions yet to come.

Then they came like aimless stragglers, they came from far and
    near,
A little log house settlement grew round the pioneer;
And the sound of saw and broadaxe made a glad industrial hum.
Jim said, "The coming millions, they have just begun to come."

And a little crooked railway wound round mountain, hill, and lake,
Crawling toward the forest village like an undulating snake;
And one morn the locomotive puffed into the wilderness,
And Jim said, "The coming millions, they are coming by express"

And the village grew and prospered, but Jim Croker's hair was
    grayer;
When they got a city charter, and old Jim was chosen Mayor;
But Jim declined the honor, and moved his household goods
Far away into the forest, to the old primeval woods.

Far and far into the forest moved the grizzled pioneer,
There he reared his hut and murmured, "I will build a city here."
And he hears the woodfox barking, and he hears the partridge
    drum,
And the old man sits and listens for the millions yet to come.

THE LIGHTNING-ROD DISPENSER.

If the weary world is willing, I've a little word to say
Of a lightning-rod dispenser that dropped down on me one day,
With a poem in his motions, with a sermon in his mien,
With hands as white as lilies, and a face uncommon clean.
No wrinkle had his vestments, and his linen glistened white,
And his new-constructed necktie was an interesting sight;
Which I almost wished his razor had made red that white-skinned
    throat,
And the new-constructed necktie had composed a hangman's knot,
Ere he brought his sleek-trimmed carcass for my woman folks to
    see,
And his rip-saw tongue a-buzzin' for to gouge a gash in me.

But I couldn't help but like him—as I always think I must,
The gold of my own doctrines in a fellow-heap of dust;
When I fired my own opinions at this person, round by round,
They drew an answering volley, of a very similar sound
I touched him on religion, and the hopes my heart had known;
He said he'd had experiences quite similar of his own.
I told him of the doubtin's that made dark my early years;
He had laid awake till morning with that same old breed of
    fears.
I told him of the rough path I hoped to heaven to go;
He was on that very ladder, only just a round below.
I told him of my visions of the sinfulness of gain;
He had seen the self-same picters, though not quite so clear and
    plain.
Our politics was different, and at first he galled and winced;
But I arg'ed him so able he was very soon convinced.

And 'twas getting toward the middle of a hungry summer day;
There was dinner on the table, and I asked him would he stay?
And he sat down among us, everlasting trim and neat,
And asked a short, crisp blessing, almost good enough to eat;

Then he fired up on the mercies of our Great Eternal Friend,
And gave the Lord Almighty a good, first-class recommend;
And for full an hour we listened to the sugar-coated scamp,
Talking like a blessed angel—eating like a—blasted tramp.

My wife, she liked the stranger, smiling on him warm and sweet
(It always flatters women when their guests are on the eat),
And he hinted that some ladies never lose their early charms,
And kissed her latest baby, and received it in his arms.
My sons and daughters liked him, for he had progessive views,
And chewed the quid of fancy, and gave down the latest news;
And couldn't help but like him, as I fear I always must,
The gold of my own doctrines in a fellow-heap of dust.

He was spreading desolation through a piece of apple pie,
When he paused, and looked upon us with a tear in his off-eye,
And said, "O, happy family! your blessings make me sad;
You call to mind the dear ones that in happier days I had:
A wife as sweet as this one; a babe as bright and fair;
A little girl with ringlets, like that one over there.
I worshipped them too blindly!—my eyes with love were dim!
God took them to his own heart, and now I worship Him.
But had I not neglected the means within my way,
Then they might still be living, and loving me to-day.

"One night there came a tempest, the thunder-peals were dire;
The clouds that tramped above us were shooting bolts of fire;
In my own house, I, lying, was thinking, to my blame,
How little I had guarded against those shafts of flame,
When, crash!—through roof and ceiling the deadly lightning cleft,
And killed my wife and children, and only I was left.

"Since that dread time I've wandered, and naught for life have
        cared,
Save to save others' loved ones, whose lives have yet been spared;
Since then it is my mission, where'er by sorrow tossed,
To sell to virtuous people good lightning-rods—at cost.
With sure and strong protection I'll clothe your buildings o'er,
'Twill cost you fifty dollars (perhaps a trifle more);
What little else it comes to at lowest price I'll put
(You signing this agreement to pay so much per foot)."

I signed it, while my family all approving stood about,
And dropped a tear upon it—(but it didn't blot it out)!
That very day with wagons came some men, both great and small,
They climed upon my buildings just as if they owned 'em all;
They hacked 'em, and they hewed 'em, much against my loud de-
    sires;
They trimmed 'em up with gewgaws, and they bound 'em down
    with wires;
They trimmed 'em and they wired 'em, and they trimmed an' wired
    'em still,
And every precious minute kept a-running up the bill.

My soft-spoke guest a-seeking, did I rave and rush and run;
He was supping with a neighbor, just a three-mile further on.
"Do you think," I fiercely shouted, "that I want a mile of wire
To save each separate hay-cock out o' heaven's consumin' fire?
Do you think to keep my buildin's safe from some uncertain harm,
I'm goin' to deed you over all the balance of my farm?"

He looked up quite astonished, with a face devoid of guile,
And he pointed to the contract with a reassuring smile:
It was the first occasion that he disagreed with me;
But he held me to that paper with a firmness sad to see;
And for that thunder story, ere the rascal finally went,
I paid two hundred dollars, if I paid a single cent.
And if any lightnin'-rodder wants a dinner-dialogue
With the restaurant department of an enterprising dog,
Let him set his mill a-runnin' just inside my outside gate,
And I'll bet two hundred dollars that he won't have long to wait.

THE LITTLE PEDDLER.

I WAS busily sewing one bright summer day,
And thought little Chatterbox busy at play,
When a sunshiny head peeped into my room,
And a merry voice called, "Buy a broom? Buy a broom?"

"No, not any to-day, sir," I soberly said,
But soon the door opened: "Pins, needles, and thread,
Combs, brushes? My basket is piled up so high!
If you only will look, ma'am, I'm sure you will buy."

Again I refused him, but soon he came back,
This time bending o'er with an odd-looking pack;
"Ribbons, collars, and handkerchiefs? Cheap as can be;
They came in my big ship over the sea."

"Hard times, sir," I answered; "no money to spare;
To sell your fine things you must travel elsewhere."
His roguish eyes twinkled, as closing the door
He departed, but came in a minute or more—

Right under my window, the sly little fox!
Crying, "Strawberries! Strawberries! ten cents a box!"
I resolved to reward such persistence as this,
So I bought all he had, and for pay gave a kiss.

THE MODEL CHURCH.

WELL, wife, I've found the model church! I worshipped there to-
    day;
It made me think of good old times, before my hairs were gray.
The meetin'-house was finer built than they were years ago;
But then I found, when I went in, it wasn't built for show.

The sexton didn't seat me 'way back by the door;
He knew that I was old and deaf, as well as old and poor.
He must have been a Christian, for he led me boldly through
The long aisle of that pleasant church to find a pleasant pew.

I wish you'd heard the singin'—it had the old-time ring—
The preacher said with trumpet-voice, "Let all the people sing:"
The tune was "Coronation," and the music upwards rolled
Till I thought I heard the angels striking all their harps of gold.

My deafness seemed to melt away, my spirit caught the fire,
I joined my feeble, trembling voice with that melodious choir,
And sang, as in my youthful days, "Let angels prostrate fall,
Bring forth the royal diadem and crown him Lord of all."

I tell you, wife, it did me good to sing that hymn once more,
I felt like some wrecked mariner who gets a glimpse of shore;
I almost want to lay aside this weather-beaten form
And anchor in the blessed port forever from the storm.

The preachin'! well, I can't just tell all that the preacher said;
I know it wasn't written, I know it wasn't read;
He hadn't time to read, for the lightnin' of his eye
Went passing 'long from pew to pew, nor passed a sinner by.

The sermon wasn't flowery, 'twas simple Gospel truth,
It fitted poor old men like me, it fitted hopeful youth.
'Twas full of consolation for weary hearts that bleed,
'Twas full of invitations to Christ—and not to creed.

The preacher made sin hideous in Gentiles and in Jews;
He shot the golden sentences straight at the finest pews.
And, though I can't see very well, I saw the falling tear
That told me hell was some way off, and heaven very near.

How swift the golden moments fled within that holy place!
How brightly beamed the light of heaven from every happy face!
Again I longed for that sweet time when friend shall meet with
     friend,
When congregations ne'er break up and Sabbaths have no end.

I hope to meet that minister, the congregation, too,
In the dear home beyond the skies, that shines from heaven's blue,
I doubt not I'll remember, beyond life's evening gray,
The face of God's dear servant who preached His Word to-day.

Dear wife, the fight will soon be fought, the victory be won,
The shining goal is just ahead, the race is nearly run.
O'er the river we are nearin', they are thronging to the shore,
To shout our safe arrival where the weary weep no more.

A HANDFUL OF EARTH.

CELIA THAXTER.

HERE is a problem, a wonder for all to see:
  Look at this marvellous thing I hold in my hand!
This is a magic surprising, a mystery,
  Strange as a miracle, harder to understand.

What is it? only a handful of earth; to your touch
  A dry rough powder you trample beneath your feet;
Dark and lifeless; but think for a moment how much
  It hides and holds that is beautiful, bitter or sweet.

Think of the glory of color!   The red of the rose,
  Green of the myriad leaves and the fields of grass;
Yellow, as bright as the sun, where the daffodil blows,
  Purple where violets nod as the breezes pass.

Think of the manifold power of the oak and the vine;
  Nut and fruit and cluster; and ears of corn;
Of the anchored water-lily, a thing divine!
  Unfolding its dazzling snow to the kiss of morn.

Strange that this lifeless thing gives vine, flower, tree,
  Color and shape and character, fragrance, too;
That the timber which builds the house, the ship for the sea,
  Out of this powder its strength and its toughness drew.

That the cocoa among the palms should suck its milk
  From this dry dust, while dates from the self-same soil
Summer their sweet, rich fruits; that our shining silk
  The mulberry-leaves should yield to the worm's slow toil.

Who shall compass or fathom God's thought profound?
  We can but praise, for we may not understand;
But there's no more beautiful riddle, the whole world round,
  Than is hid in this heap of dust I hold in my hand.

IT MIGHT HAVE BEEN.

It might have been!   When life is young,
And hopes are bright, and hearts are strong
To battle with the heartless throng,
When youth and age are far between,
Who heeds the words so sadly sung?—
    It might have been!

It might have been!   When life is fair,
Youth stands beside the boundless sea
That ebbs and flows unceasingly,
And dreams of name and golden fame;
And who shall limit the To-be
    That's dawning there?

It might have been!   When life is bright,
And love is in its golden prime,
Youth recks not of the coming night,
Nor dreams that there may be a time
When love will fail, or change, or die
    Eternally!

It might have been!   When Time grows gray,
And spring-tide's hopes have passed away,
Old age looks back on by-gone years—
Their many wants, and doubts, and fears—
And through the mist a way is seen:
    The Might-have-been!

It might have been!   When age is sad,
Weary of waiting for the fame
That after all is but a name,
When life has lost the charm it had,
True knowledge makes regret more keen—
    It might have been!

It might have been!   When youth is dead,
And love that was so false has fled,

When all the mockeries of the past
Have lost their tinsel rays at last,
The one true love is clearly seen,
    That might have been!

It might have been!   Ah, me! ah, me!
And who shall tell the misery
Of knowing all that life has lost?
By thinking of the countless cost,
Poor comfort can the sad heart glean!
    It might have been!

It might have been!—nay, rather rest,
Believing what has been was best!
The life whose sun has not yet set
Can find no room for vain regret,
And only folly crowns as queen
    Its Might-have-been!

A SONG WITHOUT WORDS.

MARY ELIZABETH BLAKE.

"PLAY us a tune," cried the children,
  "Something merry and sweet,
Like birds that sing in the summer,
  Or nodding o' the wheat,
Dancing across the meadows
  While the warm sun burns and glows,
Till we fancy we smell in winter
  The breath of a sweet June rose."

"Play us a tune," said the mother,
  "Something tender and low,
Like a thought that comes in the autumn,
  When the leaves are ready to go.

When the fire on the hearth is lighted,
  And we know not which is best,
The long, bright evenings coming,
  Or the long, bright days at rest."

And the dear little artist bending
  Over the swaying bow,
Drew tones so merry and gladsome,
  And tones so soft and low,
That we scarce could tell who listened,
  Which song had the sweetest words,
The one that sang of the fireside
  Or the one that sang of the birds.

TOMMY'S PRAYER.

In a dark and dismal alley where the sunshine never came,
Dwelt a little lad named Tommy, sickly, delicate, and lame;
He had never yet been healthy, but had lain since he was born,
Dragging out his weak existence well-nigh hopeless and forlorn.

He was six, was little Tommy, 'twas just five years ago
Since his drunken mother dropped him, and the babe was crippled
    so.
He had never known the comfort of a mother's tender care,
But her cruel blows and curses made his pain still worse to bear.

There he lay within the cellar from the morning till the night,
Starved, neglected, cursed, ill-treated, naught to make his dull life
    bright;
Not a single friend to love him, not a living thing to love—
For he knew not of a Saviour, or a heaven up above.

'Twas a quiet, summer evening; and the alley, too, was still;
Tommy's little heart was sinking, and he felt so lonely, till,
Floating up the quiet alley, wafted inward from the street,
Came the sound of some one singing, sounding, oh! so clear and
    sweet.

Eagerly did Tommy listen as the singing nearer came—
Oh! that he could see the singer!   How he wished he wasn't lame.
Then he called and shouted loudly, till the singer heard the sound,
And on noting whence it issued, soon the little cripple found.

'Twas a maiden rough and rugged, hair unkempt, and naked feet,
All her garments torn and ragged, her appearance far from neat;
" So yer called me," said the maiden, " wonder wot yer wants o' me ;
Most folks call me Singing Jessie ; wot may your name chance to
        be ? "

" My name's Tommy ; I'm a cripple, and I want to hear you sing,
For it makes me feel so happy—sing me something, anything."
Jessie laughed, and answered, smiling, " I can't stay here very long,
But I'll sing a hymn to please you, wot I calls the ' Glory song.' "

Then she sang to him of heaven, pearly gates, and streets of gold,
Where the happy angel children are not starved or nipped with
        cold ;
But where happiness and gladness never can decrease or end,
And where kind and loving Jesus is their Sovereign and their
        Friend.

Oh! how Tommy's eyes did glisten as he drank in every word
As it fell from " Singing Jessie "—was it true, what he had heard ?
And so anxiously he asked her : " Is there really such a place ? "
And a tear began to trickle down his pallid little face.

" Tommy, you're a little heathen ; why, it's up beyond the sky,
And if yer will love the Saviour, yer shall go there when yer die."
" Then," said Tommy, " tell me, Jessie, how can I the Saviour love,
'When I'm down in this 'ere cellar, and he's up in heaven above ? "

So the little ragged maiden, who had heard at Sunday-school
All about the way to heaven, and the Christian's golden rule,
Taught the little cripple Tommy how to love, and how to pray,
Then she sang a " Song of Jesus," kissed his cheek and went away

Tommy lay within the cellar which had grown so dark and cold,
Thinking all about the children in the streets of shining gold;
And he heeded not the darkness of that damp and chilly room,
For the joy in Tommy's bosom could disperse the deepest gloom.

"Oh! if I could only see it," thought the cripple, as he lay.
"Jessie said that Jesus listens, and I think I'll try and pray;"
So he put his hands together, and he closed his little eyes,
And in accents weak, yet earnest, sent this message to the skies:

"Gentle Jesus, please forgive me, as I didn't know afore
That yer cared for little cripples who is weak and very poor,
And I never heard of heaven till that Jessie came to-day
And told me all about it, so I wants to try and pray.

"You can see me, can't yer, Jesus? Jessie told me that yer could,
And I somehow must believe it, for it seems so prime and good;
And she told me if I loved you, I should see yer when I die,
In the bright and happy heaven that is up beyond the sky.

"Lord, I'm only just a cripple, and I'm no use here below,
For I heard my mother whisper she'd be glad if I could go;
And I'm cold and hungry sometimes; and I feel so lonely, too,
Can't yer take me, gentle Jesus, up to heaven along o' you?

"Oh! I'd be so good and patient, and I'd never cry or fret;
And your kindness to me, Jesus, I would surely not forget;
I would love you all I know of, and would never make a noise—
Can't you find me just a corner, where I'll watch the other boys?

"Oh! I think yer'll do it, Jesus, something seems to tell me so,
For I feel so glad and happy, and I do so want to go;
How I long to see yer, Jesus, and the children all so bright!
Come and fetch me, won't yer, Jesus? Come and fetch me home
        to-night!"

Tommy ceased his supplication, he had told his soul's desire,
And he waited for the answer till his head began to tire;
Then he turned towards his corner, and lay huddled in a heap,
Closed his little eyes so gently, and was quickly fast asleep.

Oh, I wish that every scoffer could have seen his little face
As he lay there in the corner, in that damp and noisome place:
For his countenance was shining like an angel's, fair and bright,
And it seemed to fill the cellar with a holy, heavenly light.

He had only heard of Jesus from a ragged singing girl,
He might well have wondered, pondered, till his brain began to
    whirl;
But he took it as she told it, and believed it then and there,
Simply trusting in the Saviour, and His kind and tender care.

In the morning, when the mother came to wake her crippled boy,
She discovered that his features wore a look of sweetest joy,
And she shook him somewhat roughly, but the cripple's face was
    cold—
He had gone to join the children in the streets of shining gold.

Tommy's prayer had soon been answered, and the Angel Death
    had come
To remove him from his cellar, to his bright and heavenly home,
Where sweet comfort, joy, and gladness never can decrease or end,
And where Jesus reigns eternally, his Sovereign and his Friend.

ONE OF THE LITTLE ONES.

'TWAS a crowded street, and a cry of joy
Came from a ragged, barefoot boy—
A cry of eager and glad surprise,
And he opened wide his great black eyes,
As he held before him a coin of gold
He had found in a heap of rubbish old
By the curbstone there.

       The passers-by
Paused at hearing that joyous cry,
As if 'twere a heavenly chime that rung,
Or a note from some angel-song had been sung.
There, in the midst of the hurry and din
That raged the city's heart within,
And they wondered to hear that song of grace
Sung in such strange, unusual place.

As ofttimes into a dungeon deep
Some ray of sunlight perchance will creep,
So did that innocent childish cry
Break on the musings of passers-by,
Bidding them all at once forget
Stocks, quotations, and tare and tret,
And the thousand cares with which are rife
The daily rounds of a business life.

"How it sparkles!" the youngster cried,
As the golden piece he eagerly eyed;
"Oh, see it shine!" and he laughed aloud;
Little heeding the curious crowd
That gathered around, "Hurrah!" said he,
"How glad my poor old mother will be!
I'll buy her a brand-new Sunday hat,
And a pair of shoes for Nell, at that,
And baby sister shall have a dress—
There'll be enough for all, I guess;
And then I'll——"

   "Here," said a surly voice,
"That money's mine. You can take your choice
Of giving it up or going to jail."
The youngster trembled, and then turned pale
As he looked and saw before him stand
A burly drayman with outstretched hand;

Rough and uncouth was the fellow's face,
And without a single line or trace
Of the goodness that makes the world akin.
"Come, be quick! or I'll take you in,"
Said he.

   "For shame!" said the listening crowd.
The ruffian seemed for a moment cowed.
"The money's mine," he blustered out;
"I lost it yesterday hereabout.
I don't want nothin' but what's my own,
And I am going to have it."

The lad alone

Was silent.   A tear stood in his eye,
And he brushed it away; he would not cry.
"Here, mister," he answered, "take it, then;
If it's yours, it's yours; if it hadn't been——"
A sob told all he would have said,
Of the hope so suddenly raised, now dead;

And then with a sigh, which volumes told,
He dropped the glittering piece of gold
Into the other's hand.   Once more
He sighed—and his dream of wealth was o'er.
But no!   Humanity hath a heart
Always ready to take the part
Of childish sorrow, whenever found.

"Let's make up a purse"—the word went round
Through the kindly crowd, and the hat was passed,
And the coins came falling thick and fast.

"Here, sonny, take this," said they.   Behold,
Full twice as much as the piece of gold
He had given up was in the hand
Of the urchin.   He could not understand
It all.   The tears came thick and fast,
And his grateful heart found voice at last.

But, lo! when he spoke, the crowd had gone—
Left him, in gratitude, there alone.
Who'll say there is not some sweet good-will
And kindness left in this cold world still?

THE CHRISTMAS BABY.

Hoot! ye little rascal! ye come it on me this way,
Crowdin' yerself amongst us this blusterin' winter's day,
Knowin' that we already have three of ye, an' seven,
An' tryin' to-make yerself out a Christmas present o' Heaven!

Ten of ye have we now, sir, for this world to abuse;
An' Bobbie he have no waistcoat, an' Nellie she have no shoes,
An' Sammie he have no shirt, sir (I tell it to his shame),
An' the one that was just before ye we ain't had time to name!

An' all o' the banks be smashin', an' on us poor folk fall;
An' Boss he whittles the wages when work's to be had at all;
An' Tom he have cut his foot off, an' lies in a woful plight,
An' all of us wonders at mornin' as what we shall eat at night;

An' but for your father an' Saudy a-findin' somewhat to do,
An' but for the preacher's woman, who often helps us through,
An' but for your poor dear mother a-doin' twice her part,
Ye'd a-seen us all in heaven afore *ye* was ready to start!

An' now *ye* have come, ye rascal! so healthy an' fat an' sound,
A-weighin', I'll wager a dollar, the full of a dozen pound!
With yer mother's eyes a-flashin', yer father's flesh an' build,
An' a good big mouth an' stomach all ready for to be filled!

No, no! don't cry, my baby! hush up, my pretty one!
Don't get my chaff in yer eye, boy—I only was just in fun.
Ye'll like us when ye know us, although we're cur'us folks;
But we don't get much victual, an' half our livin' is jokes!

Why, boy, did ye take me in earnest? come sit upon my knee;
I'll tell ye a secret, youngster, I'll name ye after me;
Ye shall have all yer brothers an' sisters with ye to play,
An' ye shall have yer carriage, an' ride out every day!

Why, boy, do ye think ye'll suffer?   I'm gettin' a trifle old,
But it'll be many years yet before I lose my hold;
An' if I should fall on the road, boy, still, them's yer brothers,
        there,
An' not a rogue of 'em ever would see ye harmed a hair!

Say! when ye come from heaven, my little namesake dear,
Did ye see, 'mongst the little girls there, a face like this one here?
That was yer little sister—she died a year ago,
An' all of us cried like babies when they laid her under the snow!

Hang it! if all the rich men I ever see or knew
Come here with all their traps, boy, an' offered 'em for you,
I'd show 'em to the door, sir, so quick they'd think it odd,
Before I'd sell to another my Christmas gift from God!

REPENTANCE.

If the Lord were to send down blessings from heaven as thick and
    as fast as the fall
Of the drops of rain or the flakes of snow, I'd love Him and thank
    Him for all;
But the gift that I'd crave, and the gift that I'd keep, if I'd only
    one to choose,
Is the gift of a broken and contrite heart,—and that He will not
    refuse.

For what is my wish and what is my hope, when I've toiled and
    prayed and striven,
All the days that I live upon earth? It is this—to be forgiven.
And what is my wish and what is my hope, but to end where I
    begin,
With an eye that looks to my Saviour, and a heart that mourns
    for its sin!

Well, perhaps you think I am going to say I'm the chief of sinners;
    and then
You'll tell me, as far as you can see, I'm no worse than other men.
I've little to do with better or worse—I haven't to judge the rest;
If other men are no better than I, they are bad enough at the best.

I've nothing to do with other folks; it isn't for me to say
What sort of men the Scribes might be, or the Pharisees in their
    day;
But we know that it wasn't for such as they that the kingdom of
    heaven was meant;
And we're told we shall likewise perish unless we do repent.

And what have I done, perhaps you'll say, that I should fret and
    grieve?
I didn't wrangle, nor curse, nor swear; I didn't lie nor thieve;
I'm clear of cheating and drinking and debt.—Well, perhaps, but
    I cannot say;
For some of these I hadn't a mind, and some didn't come in my
    way.

For there's many a thing I could wish undone, though the law
    might not be broken;
And there's many a word, now I come to think, that I could wish
    unspoken.
I did what I thought to be the best, and I said just what came to
    my mind;
I wasn't so honest that I could boast, and I'm sure that I wasn't
    kind.

Well, come to things that I might have done, and then there'll be
    more to say;
We'll ask for the broken hearts I healed, and the tears that I wiped
    away.
I thought for myself and I wrought for myself—for myself, and
    none beside:
Just as if Jesus had never lived, as if He had never died.

But since my Lord has looked on me, and since He has bid me look
Once on my heart and once on my life and once on His blessed
    Book,
And once on the cross where He died for me, He has taught me
    that I must mend,
If I'd have Him to be my Saviour, and keep Him to be my Friend.

Since He's taken this long account of mine and has crossed it
    through and through,
Though He's left me nothing at all to pay, He has given me
    enough to do;
He has taught me things that I never knew, with all my worry
    and care,—
Things that have brought me down to my knees, and things that
    will keep me there.

He has shown me the law that works in Him and the law that
    works in me,—
Life unto life and death unto death—and has asked how these agree;
He has made me weary of self and of pelf; yes, my Saviour has
    bid me grieve
For the days and years when I didn't pray, when I didn't love nor
    believe.

Since He's taken this cold, dark **heart of** mine, and has pierced it
    through and through,
He has made me mourn both for **things I** did and for things that
    I didn't do;
And what is my wish and what is my thought, but to end where I
    begin,
With an eye that looks to my Saviour, and a heart that mourns
    for its sin!

THE FIREMAN'S STORY.

"A FRIGHTFUL face?" Wal, yes, yer correct;
    That man on the enjine thar,
Don't pack the handsomest countenance—
    Every inch of it sportin' a scar;
But I tell you, pard, thar ain't money enough
    Piled up in the national banks
To buy that face—nor a single scar—
    (No, I never indulges.   Thanks.)

Yes, Jim is an old-time engineer,
    An' a better one never war knowed!
Bin a-runnin' yar since the fust machine
    War put on the Quincy Road;
An' thar ain't a galoot that pulls a plug
    From Maine to the jumpin'-off place
That knows more about the big iron hoss
    Than him with the battered-up face.

"Git hurt in a mash-up?" No, 'twar done
    In sort o' legitimate way;
He got it a-tryin' to save a gal
    Up yer on the road last May.
I heven't much time fur to spin you the yarn,
    For we pull out at two twenty-five—
Jist wait till I climb up an' toss in some coal
    So's to keep old "90" alive—

Jim war pullin' the Burlin'ton passenger then,
    Left Quincy a half an hour late,
An' war skinnin' along purty lively, so's not
    To lay out No. 21 freight.
The "90" war more than a-'hoopin' 'em up,
    An' a-quiverin' in every nerve!
When all to once Jim yelled "Merciful God!"
    As she shoved her sharp nose 'round a curve.

I jumped to his side o' the cab, an' ahead,
    'Bout two hundred paces or so,
Stood a gal on the track, her hands raised aloft,
    An' her face jist as white as the snow.
It seems she war too paralyzed with the fright
    That she couldn't move for'ard or back,
An' when Jim pulled the whistle she fainted an' fell
    Right down in a heap on the track!

I'll never forgit till the day o' my death
    The look that cum over Jim's face;
He throw'd the old lever cla'r back like a shot
    So's to slaken the "90's" wild pace.
Then let on the air-brakes as quick as a flash,
    An' out through the window he fled,
An' skinned 'long the runnin' board cla'r in front,
    An' lay on the pilot ahead.

Then jist as we reached whar the poor creetur' lay,
    He grabbed a tight hold of her arm,
An' raised her right up so's to throw her one side,
    Out o' reach of danger an' harm.

But somehow he slipped an' fell with his head
  On the rail as he throw'd the young lass,
An' the pilot, in strikin' him, ground up his face
  In a frightful and horrible mass!

As soon as we stopped I backed up the train
  To that spot where the poor fellow lay,
An' thar sot the gal with his head in her lap,
  An' wipin' the warm blood away.
The tears rolled in torrents right down from her eyes,
  While she sobbed like her heart war all broke—
I tell you, my friend, such a sight as that ar'
  Would move the tough heart of an oak!

We put Jim aboard an' run back to town,
  Whar for week arter week the boy lay,
A-hoverin' right in the shadder o' death,
  An' that gal by his bed every day.
But nursin' an' doctorin' brought him around—
  Kinder snatched him right outen the grave—
His face ain't so han'som' as 'twar, but his heart
  Remains just as noble an' brave.

   *   *   *   *   *

Of course thar's a sequel—as story-books say—
  He fell dead in love, did this Jim;
But he hadn't the heart to ax her to have
  Sich a batter'd-up rooster as him.
She know'd how he felt, an' last New Year's Day
  War the fust o' leap-year, you know,
So she jist cornered Jim an' proposed on the spot,
  An' you bet he didn't say no.

He's buildin' a house up thar on the hill,
  An' has laid up a snug pile o' cash;
The weddin's to be on the first o' next May,
  Jist a year from the day o' the mash—
The gal says he risked his dear life to save hers,
  An' she'll jist turn the tables about,
An' give him the life that he saved—thar's the bell.
  Good-day, sir, we're goin' to pull out.

THE LOST BABIES.

Come, my wife, put down the Bible,
  Lay your glasses on the book,
Both of us are bent and aged—
  Backward, mother, let us look.
This is still the same old homestead
  Where I brought you long ago,
When the hair was bright with sunshine
  That is now like winter's snow.
Let us talk about the babies,
  As we sit here all alone,
Such a merry troop of youngsters;
  How we lost them one by one.

Jack, the first of all the party,
  Came to us one winter's night;
Jack, you said, should be a parson,
  Long before he saw the light.
Do you see the great cathedral,
  Filled the transept and the nave,
Hear the organ grandly pealing,
  Watch the silken hangings wave;
See the priest in robes of office,
  With the altar at his back—
Would you think that gifted preacher
  Could be your own little Jack?

Then a girl with curly tresses
  Used to climb upon my knee,
Like a little fairy princess
  Ruling at the age of three.
With the years there came a wedding—
  How your fond heart swelled with pride
When the lord of all the country
  Chose your baby for his bride!

Watch that stately carriage coming,
   And the form reclining there—
Would you think that brilliant lady
   Could be your own little Clare?

Then the last, a blue-eyed youngster—
   I can hear him prattling now—
Such a strong and sturdy fellow,
   With his broad and honest brow.
How he used to love his mother!
   Ah! I see your trembling lip!
He is far off on the water,
   Captain of a royal ship.
See the bronze upon his forehead,
   Hear the voice of stern command—
'Tis the boy who clung so fondly
   To his mother's gentle hand?

Ah! my wife, we've lost the babies,
   Ours so long and ours alone;
What are we to these great people,
   Stately men and women grown?
Seldom do we ever see them:
   Yes, a bitter tear-drop starts,
As we sit here in the fire-light,
   Lonely hearth and lonely hearts.
All their lives are full without us;
   They'll stop long enough one day
Just to lay us in the church-yard,
   Then they'll each go on their way.

THE STAGE-DRIVER'S STORY.

I KNOW it's presumin' for one sich as me
   For to talk to a lady so grand;
It's jist like an imp from Satan's domains
   Chinnin' one from the heavenly land!

But you've axed for my story, ma'am, neat and perlite,
   And I'll tell it the best thet I kin;
Leavin' out all thet's rough or of vulgar degree,
   Skippin' over all teches of sin.

I cum to these mountains in '50, and hyar
   I've remained, as yer see, ever sence;
I drove on the Overland Line 'til the keers
   Slung the coaches 'way over the fence.
An' then I tried minin', an' went through my pile
   In a manner most decidedly flat;
Then I chopped on that lay, an' got in fur to herd
   Texas cattle up thar on the Platte.

"From the States?" do you ask? Yes, I fust saw the light
   In Ohio, an' right thar I stayed
Till I tired o' the civilized racket, ye see;
   Couldn't coon to legitimate trade.
Then I packed up my duds an' bid—some one—good-bye,
   An' headed my hoss for the West,
An' cum to these mountains to buck agin luck—
   To swallow my dose with the rest!

"Got a wife?" Lookee hyar, ma'am—I'd rather not talk
   On sich subjects as that, fur ye see,
It moutn't be flatterin' to let out the truth;
   It perhaps 'd reflect upon me.
"Got an object in axin," ye say? Wal, I swar!
   I can't see how I'd interest you;
An' I guess—eh? "you must know?" Wal, then, ma'am, I had
   A wife thet was noble an' true.

Ye see, 'twar like this: When I lived in the States
   Somehow I war all outen luck,
An' I stood in with nothin' but cussed hard times,
   No matter what racket I struck;
Till at last I gin up an' concluded to leave—
   An' Mary approved o' the plan,
An' sed, "Go along, Tom, an' when ye git rich
   Ye'll find yer companion on han'."

But the same cussed luck follered right in my trail,
   So I jist quit a-writin' back home—
Fur I wanted the folks thar to think White war dead,
   An' continued as usual to roam.
I strayed hyar an' thar—with no settled place—
   Fur to camp—with no object in view;
No ambition to rastle fur more than enough
   To grub me—indeed, ma'am, it's true!

"Do I love Mary yit?" Why, ma'am—(darn it all,
   Thet smoke keeps a-smartin' my eyes,
Makes 'm water as though I war drappin' sum weep—
   When the wind's south thet smoke allers flies)."
"Want an answer?" Wal, ma'am, I mus' say (darn thet
     smoke)—
   I mus' say thet in all these long years
She's bin right in my thoughts, an' many's the night
   I lay thinkin' of Mary—in tears.

Her picter I carry right hyar in my heart—
   Jist a thought of her fills me with bliss,
An' the day grows as dark as the bottomless pit
   When I think p'raps she's dead afore this.
I've treated her shaddy, but, ma'am, 'twar hard luck
   Thet made me shake home in thet style,
An' I'm hopin' till yit the keerds 'll soon change
   An' begin to run right arter a while!

An' if ever I git jist a small stake ahead,
   I'm a-goin' to toddle back thar,
An' I'll ax Mary's pardon an' settle right down,
   An' be decent—I will, ma'am, I'll swar!
What's that? lookee hyar, ma'am; great heavens! jist turn
   Yer face more around ter this light!
Hist yer veil—great Lord of all marcy above!
   Why, Mary Elizabeth White!

BACK WHERE THEY USED TO BE.

Pap's got his patent right, and rich as all creation;
　But where's the peace and comfort that we all had before?
Let's go a-visitin' back to Griggsby Station—
　Back where we used to be so happy and so pore!

The likes of us a livin' here!　It's just a mortal pity
　To see us in this great, big house, with cyarpets on the stairs,
And the pump right in the kitchen; and the city! city! city!—
　And nothing but the city all around us everywheres!

Climb clean above the roof and look from the steeple,
　And never see a robin, nor a beech or ellum tree!
And right here, in earshot of at least a thousan' people,
　And none that neighbors with us or we want to go and see!

Let's go a-visitin' back to Griggsby Station—
　Back where the latch-string's a-hangin' from the door,
And every neighbor 'round the place is dear as a relation—
　Back where we used to be so happy and so pore!

I want to see the Wiggenses—the whole kit and billin',
　A-driven' up from Shallow Ford, to stay the Sunday through,
And I want to see 'em hitchen' at their son-in-law's and pilin'
　Out there at Lizy Ellen's like they used to do!

I want to see the piece-quilts that Jones girl is makin',
　And I want to pester Laury 'bout their freckled hired hand,
And joke about the widower she come purt' nigh a-takin',
　Till her pap got his pension 'lowed in time to save his land.

Let's go a-visitin' back to Griggsby Station—
　Back where's nothin' aggervatin' any more,
She's away safe in the wood around the old location—
　Back where we used to be so happy and so pore!

I want to see Merindy and help her with her sewin',
　And hear her talk so lovin' of her man that's dead and gone,

And stand up with Emanuel, to show me how he's growin',
　And smile as I have saw her 'fore she put her mournin' on.

And I want to see the Samples, on the old lower Eighty,
　Where John, our oldest boy, he was took and buried—for
His own sake and Katy's—and I want to cry with Katy,
　As she reads all his letters over, writ from the war.

What's in all this grand life and high situation,
　And nary pink for hollyhawk bloomin' at the door?
Let's go a-visitin' back to Griggsby Station—
　Back where we used to be so happy and so pore.

JOHN BURNS, OF GETTYSBURG.

HAVE you heard the story that gossips tell
Of Burns of Gettysburg?—No? Ah, well:
Brief is the glory that hero earns,
Briefer the story of poor John Burns:
He was the fellow who won renown,—
The only man who didn't back down
When the rebels rode through his native town:
But held his own in the fight next day,
When all his townsfolk ran away.
That was in July, sixty-three,
The very day that General Lee,
Flower of Southern chivalry,
Baffled and beaten, backward reeled
From a stubborn Meade and a barren field.
I might tell how, but the day before,
John Burns stood at his cottage door,
Looking down the village street,
Where, in the shade of his peaceful vine,
He heard the low of his gathered kine,
And felt their breath with incense sweet;
Or I might say when the sunset burned
The old farm gable, he thought it turned

The milk that fell, in a babbling flood
Into the milk-pail, red as blood!
Or how he fancied the hum of bees
Were bullets buzzing among the trees.
But all such fanciful thoughts as these
Were strange to a practical man like Burns,
Who minded only his own concerns,
Troubled no more by fancies fine
Than one of his calm-eyed, long-tailed kine.
Quite old-fashioned and matter-of-fact,
Slow to argue, but quick to act.
That was the reason, as some folks say,
He fought so well on that terrible day.
And it was terrible.   On the right
Raged for hours the heavy fight,
Thundered the battery's double bass,—
Difficult music for men to face;
While on the left—where now the graves
Undulate like the living waves
That all that day unceasing swept
Up to the pits the rebels kept—
Round-shot ploughed the upland glades,
Sown with bullets, reaped with blades;
Shattered fences here and there
Tossed their splinters in the air;
The very trees were stripped and bare;
The barns that once held yellow grain
Were heaped with harvests of the slain;
The cattle bellowed on the plain,
The turkeys screamed with might and main,
And brooding barn-fowl left their rest,
With strange shells bursting in each nest.

Just where the tide of battle turns,
Erect and lonely stood old John Burns.
How do you think the man was dressed?
He wore an ancient long buff vest,
Yellow as saffron,—but his best;
And, buttoned over his manly breast,

Was a bright blue coat, with rolling collar,
And large gilt buttons,—size of a dollar,—
With tails that the country-folk called "swaller."
He wore a broad-brimmed, bell-crowned hat,
White as the locks on which it sat.
Never had such a sight been seen
For forty years on the village green,
Since old John Burns was a country beau
And went to the "quiltings" long ago.

Close at his elbows all that day,
Veterans of the Peninsula,
Sunburnt and bearded, charged away;
And striplings, downy of lip and chin,—
Clerks that the Home Guard mustered in,—
Glanced, as they passed, at the hat he wore,
Then at the rifle his right hand bore;
And hailed him, from out their youthful lore,
With scraps of a slangy *repertoire:*
"How are you. White Hat?"   "Put her through."
"Your head's level," and "Bully for you!"
Called him "Daddy,"—begged he'd disclose
The name of the tailor who made his clothes,
And what was the value he set on those;
While Burns, unmindful of jeer and scoff,
Stood there picking the rebels off,—
With his long brown rifle, and bell-crown hat,
And the swallow-tails they were laughing at.

'Twas but a moment, for that respect
Which clothes all courage their voices checked,
And something the wildest could understand
Spake in the old man's strong white hand;
And his corded throat, and the lurking frown
Of his eyebrows under his old bell-crown;
Until, as they gazed, there crept an awe
Through the ranks in whispers, and some men saw
In the antique vestments and long white hair,
The Past of the Nation in battle there;
And some of the soldiers since declare

That the gleam of his old white hat afar,
Like the crested plume of the brave Navarre,
That day was their oriflamme of war.

So raged the battle.   You know the rest:
How the rebels, beaten and backward pressed,
Broke at the final charge and ran.
At which John Burns—a practical man—
Shouldered his rifle, unbent his brows,
And then went back to his bees and cows.

That is the story of old John Burns:
This is the moral the reader learns:
In fighting the battle, the question's whether
You'll show a hat that's white, or a feather!

GOOD-NIGHT.

CHARLES M. DICKINSON.

WHEN the lessons and the tasks are all ended,
    And the school for the day is dismiss'd,
The little ones gather around me,
    To bid me good-night and be kiss'd:
Oh, the little white arms that encircle
    My neck in their tender embrace!
Oh, the smiles that are halos of heaven,
    Shedding sunshine of love on my face!

And when they are gone I sit dreaming
    Of my childhood, too lovely to last:
Of joy that my heart will remember
    While it wakes to the pulse of the past,
Ere the world and its wickedness made me
    A partner of sorrow and sin;
When the glory of God was about me,
    And the glory of gladness within.

All my heart grows as weak as a woman's,
  And the fountains of feeling will flow,
When I think of the paths steep and stony,
  Where the feet of the dear ones must go;
Of the mountains of sin hanging o'er them,
  Of the tempest of Fate blowing wild;
Oh, there's nothing on earth half so holy
  As the innocent heart of a child!

They are idols of hearts and of households;
  They are angels of God in disguise;
His sunlight still sleeps in their tresses,
  His glory still gleams in their eyes;
Those truants from home and from heaven,
  They have made me more manly and mild,
And I know now how Jesus could liken
  The kingdom of God to a child.

I ask not a life for the dear ones,
  All radiant, as others have done,
But that life may have just enough shadow
  To temper the glare of the sun:
I would pray God to guard them from evil,
  But my prayer would bound back to myself;
Ah! a seraph may pray for a sinner,
  But a sinner must pray for himself.

The twig is so easily bended,
  I have banished the rule and the rod;
I have taught them the goodness of knowledge,
  They have taught me the goodness of God;
My heart is the dungeon of darkness,
  Where I shut them for breaking a rule;
My frown is sufficient correction;
  My love is the law of the school.

I shall leave the old house in the autumn,
  To traverse its threshold no more;
Ah! how I shall sigh for the dear ones
  That meet me each morn at the door!

I shall miss the "good-nights" and the kisses,
    And the gush of their innocent glee,
The group on the green, and the flowers
    That are brought every morning to me.

I shall miss them at morn and at even,
    Their song in the school and the street;
I shall miss the low hum of their voices,
    And the tread of their delicate feet.
When the lessons of life are all ended,
    And Death says, "The school is dismiss'd!"
May the little ones gather around me,
    To bid me good-night, and be kiss'd!

OUR FAVORITES.

ROCK ME TO SLEEP.

MRS. ELIZABETH AKERS.

BACKWARD, turn backward, O Time! in your flight,
Make me a child again, just for to-night!
Mother, come back from the echoless shore,
Take me again to your heart, as of yore;
Kiss from my forehead the furrows of care,
Smooth the few silver threads out of my hair;
Over my slumbers your loving watch keep—
Rock me to sleep, mother, rock me to sleep!

Backward, flow backward, O swift tide of years!
I am weary of toil, I am weary of tears;
Toil without recompense, tears all in vain,
Take them, and give me my childhood again!
I have grown weary of dust and decay,
Weary of flinging my soul-wealth away,
Weary of sowing for others to reap;
Rock me to sleep, mother, rock me to sleep!

Tired of the hollow, the base, the untrue,
Mother, O mother! my heart calls for you!
Many a summer the grass has grown green,
Blossomed and faded, our faces between;
Yet with strong yearning and passionate pain,
Long I to-night for your presence again;
Come from the silence so long and so deep—
Rock me to sleep, mother, rock me to sleep!

Over my heart, in the days that are flown,
No love like mother-love ever has shone.
No other worship abides and endures
Faithful, unselfish, and patient, like yours;
None like a mother can charm away pain
From the sorrowing soul and the world-weary brain;
Slumber's soft calm o'er my heavy lids creep;
Rock me to sleep, mother, rock me to sleep!

Come, let your brown hair, just lighted with gold,
Fall on your shoulders again as of old;
Let it fall over my forehead to-night,
Shielding my eyes from the flickering light;
For oh! with its sunny-edged shadows once more,
Haply will throng the sweet visions of yore;
Lovingly, softly its bright billows sweep—
Rock me to sleep, mother, rock me to sleep!

Mother, dear mother! the years have been long
Since last I was hushed by your lullaby song;
Sing then again,—to my soul it shall seem
Womanhood's years have been only a dream;
Clasp to your arms in a loving embrace,
With your soft, light lashes just sweeping my face,
Never hereafter to wake or to weep;
Rock me to sleep, mother, rock me to sleep!

NO TIME LIKE THE OLD TIME.

OLIVER WENDELL HOLMES.

There is no time like the old time, when you and I were
young,
When the buds of April blossomed and the birds of springtime
sung!
The garden's brightest glories by summer suns are nursed,
But O, the sweet, sweet violets, the flowers that opened first!

There is no place like the old place, where you and I were born,
Where we lifted first our eyelids on the splendors of the morn
From the milk-white breast that warmed us, from the clinging
    arms that bore,
Where the dear eyes glistened o'er us that will look on us no more!

There is no friend like the old friend, who has shared our morning
    days,
No greeting like his welcome, no homage like his praise;
Fame is the scentless sunflower, with gaudy crown of gold;
But Friendship is the breathing rose, with sweets in every fold.

There is no love like the old love, that we courted in our pride;
Though our leaves are falling, falling, and we're fading side by
    side;
There are blossoms all around us, with the colors of our dawn,
And we live in borrowed sunshine when our day-star is withdrawn.

There are no times like the old times—they shall never be forgot!
There is no place like the old place—keep green the dear old spot!
There are no friends like our old friends—may Heaven prolong
    their lives!
There are no loves like our old loves—God bless our loving wives!

TOLD BY THE HOSPITAL NURSE.

O. B. McBEATH.

"OFTEN have strange cases?"   Yes, sir; frequently a case lies here
With a story interesting, oft pathetic, sometimes queer—
Novel-like, were not the heroes flesh and blood, as I and you.
Such a one I well remember—patient Number Fifty-two.
In the road a toddling child, a mother's agonizing scream—
And thundering down the roadway speeds a carter's frightened
    team.
All unnerved stares each bystander, seems there's nothing can be
    done;
A sudden rush, a hasty clutch, and the child from death is won.

But a horrid sight lies in the road for the gathering crowd to view—
A brave man crushed by the cruel wheels—he filled bed Fifty-two.
Through that night he suffered greatly, bravely bore it, Fifty-two;
But the morning, breaking gently, saw his hours on earth were few,
So I sat me down beside him, hinting with a bated breath
Life to all was so uncertain; had he ever thought of death?
Would he hear the Bible woman tell the tale of heavenly love,
Of the calm and peaceful haven far beyond the stars above?
Where the wicked cease from troubling and the weary are at rest.
Might I bring her to his bedside just to tell the story blest?
" Yes," he whispered, " bring her to me; let me hear the good old
        Book."
Quickly came the Bible woman, by his bed her seat she took.
Noble little woman was she, gentle mannered in her ways;
Rumor said her life was blighted, crossed in love in bygone days,
And her life from thence devoted to the needs of sick and poor,
Soothing with her sweet attentions stricken souls at death's dark
        door.
Quietly I stole away then, leaving her by Fifty-two,
Gently telling in her own way story old yet ever new.
But ere long the Bible woman beckoned me to come again,
Fifty-two was fast succumbing, death's cold creeping numbed his
        pain.
This I saw and whispered softly, "Ask him if we cannot send
Anywhere that he might mention, anywhere he has a friend."
Then the little Bible woman, in a voice as sweet as low,
Put the question gently to him, to receive his answer, " No."
Once again did she address him, with her soft hand on his brow,
Smoothed the burning, throbbing temples, " Fifty-two, you'll 'tell
        me now.
Let me take a cherished message, let me tell your conduct brave,
How you dashed into the roadway, risked your life a child's to
        save."
" P'raps it's best," then came his answer; " let them know the news
        at home.
No need now to struggle further, for I feel my time has come.
Years ago, when but a youngster, nothing but a country lad,
Life to me seemed bright and joyous, just a round of promise
        glad,

For I loved the squire's daughter, and she loved me as I loved.
With amaze her father heard this, hot with anger her reproved
For such waywardness in stooping after hands by him employed.
Said 'twas but a pack of nonsense; if again she him annoyed
By such folly he would stop it. For her sake I had to go,
Quit the old folk and my sweetheart—hard to do, as lovers know.
Yet I felt a kind of lightsome—country lads they hear so much
Of the fortunes in the big towns—God knows there are few of
    such;
For I've labored, hoped and struggled, while the old folk home they
    died.
Long I worked on with a stout heart, picturing with honest pride
That one day when I might venture to redeem the vow I'd made
To my cherished one that evening when we met in twilight shade.
Ere we parted, I remember, being seized by lover's whim,
Pleading for some trifling token her own Jack could take with him
'Midst the mighty city's throbbing while he strove in Fortune's
    race—
Something he could dearly treasure, something he would ne'er dis-
    grace.
Years rolled on, I wore her token with a sacredness of heart;
As a knight of old I'd promised 'Death her charm and me should
    part.'
And it's coming, creeping on me—God, how true the words are
    now!
'Death her charm and me should part,'" gasped he, "but I've kept
    my vow."
Sinking fast, he feebly whispered, "Tell her I've been loyal, true;
Nurse, you'll say a good word, won't you, for your patient, Fifty-
    two?
Give her this," and then he laid bare with a trembling, nervous
    hand,
Round his neck a slender coil of dark brown hair in plaited band.
"Tell my Maggie I have worn it since she placed it there that
    night."
Here the Bible woman trembled, while her face turned ghastly
    white.
"Take it off, nurse, let me kiss it; say in heaven I wait for her."
But ere I could raise a finger, with excitement all astir

Sank the little Bible woman on her knees beside his bed,
"Jack, my own Jack! here's your Maggie!"   Sir, I had to turn my
    head.
Painter ne'er could paint the picture round the bed of Fifty-two,
And it's useless my attempting to describe the scene to you.
How he feebly murmured "Maggie!"   How she sobbed in an-
    guished joy,
While the old love leapt within her as she kissed her country boy.
"Strange if true, sir?"   'Tis indeed a story true as it is queer,
And the little Bible woman since his death still visits here.
This in strictest confidence, sir.   That's the little lady there
By the table tending flowers.   "What about the plait of hair?"
"Nurse," said she, "like him, I'll wear it, sacred now to me is this,
Consecrated by the ritual of my brave Jack's dying kiss."

HEAVEN.

BY ELLA WHEELER.

I DOUBT not but to every mind of mortal,
    That Heaven in a different form appears,
And every one who hopes to pass the portal,
    Where God shall wipe away all bitter tears,
Seeth the mansion in a separate guise,
And there are many heavens to many eyes.

To me, it seems a world where all the sweetness
    That I have in my wildest dreams conceived;
The subtle beauty and the rare completeness
    That I have missed in life, and, missing, grieved;
The things that I have sought for all my life,
And if I found, found mixed with pain and strife.

That rest, that mortal mind can never measure;
    That peace, that we can never understand;
The keen delights that fill the soul with pleasure;
    These, *these* I deem are what that blessed land
Lying beyond the pearly gates doth hold,—
Where the broad street is paved with shining gold.

A total putting off of care and sorrow,
  As we put by old garments.   Rest so deep
That 'tis not marred by thoughts of the to-morrow,
  Or pained by tears, for never any weep.
The love, unchangeable, unselfish, strong,—
That I have craved, with heart and soul, so long.

All these I hope, in that vast Forever,
  Of which we dream, nor mortal eye hath seen,
When death's pale craft shall bear me o'er the river,
  To find in waiting on the shores of green.
And in that haven, how my soul shall raise
Unceasing songs of gratitude and praise.

THE DAPPLE MARE.

J. G. SAXE.

"Once on a time," as ancient tales declare,
  There lived a farmer in a quiet dell
In Massachusetts, but exactly where,
  Or when, is really more than I can tell—
Except that, quite above the public bounty,
He lived within his means, and Bristol county.

By patient labor and unceasing care,
  He earned, and so enjoyed, his daily bread;
Contented always with his frugal fare,
  Ambition to be rich ne'er vexed his head;
And thus unknown to envy, want, or wealth,
He flourished long in comfort, peace, and health.

The gentle partner of his humble lot,
  The joy and jewel of his wedded life,
Discharged the duties of his peaceful cot
  Like a true woman and a faithful wife;
Her mind improved by thought and useful reading,
Kind words and gentle manners showed her breeding.

Grown old at last, the farmer called his son,
  The youngest, (and the favorite, I suppose,)
And said—"I long have thought, my darling John,
  'Tis time to bring my labors to a close;
So now to toil I mean to bid adieu,
And deed, my son, the homestead farm to you."

The boy embraced the boon with vast delight,
  And promised, while their precious lives remained,
He'd till and tend the farm from morn till night,
  And see his parents handsomely maintained;
God help him, he would never fail to love, nor
Do aught to grieve his generous old gov'nor!

The farmer said—"Well, let us now proceed,
  (You know there's always danger in delays,)
And get 'Squire Robinson to write the deed;
  Come—where's my staff? we'll soon be on the way."
But John replied with tender, filial care,
"You're old and weak—I'll catch the Dapple Mare."

The mare was saddled, and the old man got on,
  The boy on foot trudged cheerfully along,
The while, to cheer his sire, the duteous son
  Beguiled the weary way with talk and song.
Arrived at length, they found the 'Squire at home,
And quickly told him wherefore they had come.

The deed was writ in proper form of law,
  With many a "foresaid," "therefore," "and the same,"
And made throughout without mistake or flaw,
  To show that John had now a legal claim
To all his father's land—conveyed, given, sold,
Quit-claimed, *et cetera*—to have and hold.

Their business done, they left the lawyer's door,
  Happier, perhaps, than when they entered there;
And started off as they had done before—
  The son on foot, the father on the mare.
But ere the twain a single mile had gone
A brilliant thought occurred to Master John.

Alas for truth!—alas for filial duty!
  Alas! that Satan in the shape of pride,
(His most bewitching form save that of beauty,)
  Whispered the lad: "My boy, you ought to ride!"
"Get off!" exclaimed the jounker, "'tisn't fair
That you should always ride the Dapple Mare."

The son was lusty, and the sire was old,
  And so, with many an oath and many a frown,
The hapless farmer did as he was told,—
  The man got off the steed, the boy got on,
And rode away as fast as she could trot,
And left his sire to trudge it home on foot!

That night, while seated round the kitchen fire,
  The household sat, cheerful as if no word
Or deed provoked the injured father's ire,
  Or aught to make him sad had e'er occurred—
Thus spoke he to his son: "We quite forgot,
I think, t' include the little turnip lot!

"I'm very sure, my son, it wouldn't hurt it,"
  Calmly observed the meditative sire,
"To take the deed, my lad, and just insert it."
  Here the old man inserts it—in the fire!
Then cries aloud with most triumphant air:
"Who now, my son, shall ride the Dapple Mare!"

THE OLD OAKEN BUCKET.

SAMUEL WOODWORTH.

How dear to this heart are the scenes of my childhood,
  When fond recollection presents them to view!
The orchard, the meadow, the deep-tangled wildwood,
  And every loved spot which my infancy knew;—
The wide-spreading pond, and the mill that stood by it,
  The bridge, and the rock where the cataract fell;

ESEK'S BABY.

Esek wuz a n'atheist—
　　Least he useter say so, cuz
Somehow he could never see
　　What the plan o' nater wuz.
Useter say he'd prayed an' prayed;
　　Things went cross wise jest the same!
Never hed no sorter show—
　　Thet's before the baby came.

Useter say aour heaven's here.
　　Land o' love, I'd hope it ain't!
Also thet aour hell's on airth—
　　'Twuz enough ter try a saint.
But ther's nuthin' wuz too good
　　Fer thet baby, an' I faound
Jest by accident, ez 'twere,
　　Esek sorter shiftin' raound.

Made a diffunce, don't ye see?
　　Sorter needed God ter pray to.
S'pose ther's hell!　Thet ain't no place
　　Fer a babe ter go away to!
Got so thet we useter find him
　　Tellin' baby Bible stories.
Lookin' sort o' guilty though;
　　Said he spoke in allegories.

By an' bye, when she got big,
　　He jined the church fer an example;
Got ter be a pillar, too;
　　Useter kote him fer a sample!
Sorter habit, I p'sume,
　　But he sorter grew ter love it.
Call him atheist naow!　Wal, sir,
　　Guess you'd hev ter fight ter prove it!

KEEPING HIS WORD.

"Only a penny a box," he said,
  But the gentleman turned away his head,
  As if he shrank from the squalid sight
  Of the boy who stood in the fading light.
"Oh, sir!" he stammered, "you cannot know,"
  And he brushed from his matches the flakes of snow,
  That the sudden tear might have chance to fall—
"Or I think—I think you would take them all.
  Hungry and cold at our garret pane,
  Ruby will watch till I come again,
  Bringing the loaf. The sun has set,
  And he hasn't a crumb of breakfast yet.
  One penny, and then I can buy the bread!"
  The gentleman stopped: "And you?" he said;
"I? I can put up with them,—hunger and cold,
  But Ruby is only five years old.
  I promised our mother before she went,—
  She knew I would do it, and died content,—
  I promised her, sir, through best, through worst,
  I always would think of Ruby first."
  The gentleman paused at his open door,
  Such tales he had often heard before;
  But he fumbled his purse in the twilight drear,
"I have nothing less than a shilling here."
"Oh, sir, if you'll only take the pack,
  I'll bring you the change in a moment back,
  Indeed you may trust me!" "Trust you?—no—
  But here is the shilling—take it, and go."
  The gentleman lolled in his easy-chair,
  And watched his cigar wreath melt in air,
  And smiled on his children, and rose to see
  The baby asleep on its mother's knee.
"And now it is nine by the clock," he said,
"Time that my darlings were all abed;
  Kiss me good-night, and each be sure,
  When you're saying your prayers, remember the poor."

Just then came a message, "A boy at the door,"
But ere it was uttered he stood on the floor,
Half-breathless, bewildered, and ragged and strange;
"I am Ruby, Mike's brother; I've brought you the change.
Mike's hurt, sir; 'twas dark, and the snow made him blind,
And he didn't take notice the train was behind,
Till he slipped on the track; and then it whizzed by;
He's home in the garret, I think he will die.
Yet nothing would do him, sir, nothing would do,
But out through the storm, I must hurry to you.
Of his hurt he was certain you wouldn't have heard,
And so you might think he had broken his word."
When the garret they hastily entered and saw
Two arms, mangled, helpless, outstretched from the straw;
"You did it,—dear Ruby!—God bless you!" he said,
And the boy, gladly smiling, sank back, and was—dead.

THE CONVICT'S CHRISTMAS EVE.

WILL CARLETON.

The term was done; my penalty was past;
I saw the outside of the walls at last.
When I left that stone punishment of sin,
'Twas 'most as hard as when I first went in.
It seemed at once as though the swift-voiced air
Told slanderous tales about me everywhere;
As if the ground itself was shrinking back
For fear 'twould get the Cain's mark of my track.

Men looked me over with close, careless gaze,
And understood my downcast, jail-bred ways.
My hands were so grime-hardened and defiled,
I really wouldn't have dared to pet a child;
If I had spoken to a dog that day,
He would have tipped his nose and walked away;
The world itself seemed to me every bit
As hard a prison as the one I'd quit.

So I trudged round appropriately slow
For one with no particular place to go.

The houses scowled and stared as if to say:
"You jail-bird, we are honest; walk away!"
The factory seemed to scream when I came near,
"Stand back! unsentenced men are working here!"
And virtue had th' appearance all the time
Of trying hard to push me back to crime.

It struck me strange, that stormy, snow-bleached day,
To watch the different people on the way.
All carrying bundles, of all sorts of sizes,
As carefully as gold and silver prizes.
Well-dressed or poor, I could not understand
Why each one hugged a bundle in his hand.
I asked an old policeman what it meant.
He looked me over with eyes shrewdly bent,
While muttering in a voice that fairly froze:
"It's 'cause to-morrow's Christmas, I suppose."
And then the fact came crashing over me,
How horribly alone a man can be!

I don't pretend what tortures yet may wait
For souls that have not run their reckonings straight;
It isn't for mortal ignorance to say
What kind of night may follow any day;
There may be pain for sin some time found out
That sin on earth knows nothing yet about;
But I don't think there's any harbor known
Worse for a wrecked soul than to be alone.

So evening saw me straggling up and down
Within the gayly-lighted, desolate town,
A hungry, sad-hearted hermit all the while,
My rough face begging for a friendly smile.
Folks talked with folks in new-made warmth and glee,
But no one had a word or look for me;
Love flowed like water, but it could not make
The world forgive me for my one mistake.

An open church some look of welcome wore;
I crept in soft, and sat down near the door.
I'd never seen, 'mongst my unhappy race
So many happy children in one place;

I never knew how much a hymn could bring
From heaven, until I heard those children sing;
I never saw such sweet-breathed gales of glee
As swept around that fruitful Christmas-tree.

You who have tripped through childhood's merry days
With passionate love protecting all your ways,
Who did not see a Christmas-time go by
Without some present for your sparkling eye,
Thank God, whose goodness gave such joy its birth,
And scattered heaven-seeds in the dust of earth!
In stone-paved ground my thorny field was set;
I never had a Christmas present yet.

Just then a cry of " Fire!" amongst us came;
The pretty Christmas-tree was all aflame;
And one sweet child there in our startled gaze
Was screaming, with her white clothes all ablaze.
The crowd seemed crazy-like, both old and young,
And very swift of speech, though slow of tongue.
But one knew what to do, and not to say,
And he a convict, just let loose that day!

I fought like one who deals in deadly strife;
I wrapped my life around that child's sweet life;
I choked the flames that choked her, with rich cloaks,
Stol'n from some good but very frightened folks;
I gave the dear girl to her parents' sight,
Unharmed by anything excepting fright;
I tore the blazing branches from the tree;
And all was safe, and no one hurt but me.

That night, of which I asked for sleep in vain—
That night, that tossed me round on prongs of pain,
That stabbed me with fierce tortures through and through,
Was still the happiest that I ever knew.
I felt that I at last had earned a place
Among my race, by suffering for my race:
I felt the glorious facts wouldn't let me miss
A mother's thanks—perhaps a child's sweet kiss;
That man's warm gratitude would find a plan
To lift me up, and help me be a man.

Next day they brought a letter to my bed.
I opened it with tingling nerves and read:
" You have upon my kindness certain claims
For rescuing my young child from the flames;
Such deeds deserve a hand unstained by crime;
I trust you will reform while yet there's time.
The blackest sinner may find mercy still.
(Inclosed please find a thousand dollar bill.)
Our paths of course on different roads must lie;
Don't follow me for any more.   Good-bye."

I scorched the dirty rag till it was black;
Inclosed it in a rag and sent it back.
That very night I cracked a tradesman's door,
Stole with my blistered hands ten thousand more,
Which next day I took special pains to send
To my good, distant, wealthy, high-toned friend,
And wrote upon it in a steady hand,
In words I hoped he wouldn't misunderstand:
" Money is cheap, as I have shown you here,
But gratitude and sympathy are dear.
These rags are stolen—have been—may often be;
I trust the one wasn't that you sent to me.
Hoping your pride and you are reconciled—
From the black, sinful rescuer of your child."

I crept to court—a crushed, triumphant worm—
Confessed the theft, and took another term.
My life closed, and began; and I am back
Among the rogues that walk the broad-gauged track.
I toil 'mid every sort of sin that's known;
I walk rough roads—but do not walk *alone!*

CONCERNING KISSES.

There's a jolly Saxon proverb that is pretty much like this,
That a man is half in heaven if he has a woman's kiss.
There is danger in delaying, for the sweetness may forsake it;
So I tell you, bashful lover, if you want a kiss, why, take it.

Never let another fellow steal a march on you in this;
Never let a laughing maiden see you spoiling for a kiss.
There's a royal way to kissing, and the jolly ones who make it
Have a motto that is winning—if you want a kiss, why, take it.

Any fool may face a cannon, anybody wear a crown,
But a man must win a woman if he'd have her for his own;
Would you have the golden apple, you must find the tree and
    shake it;
If the thing is worth the having, and you want a kiss, why, take it.

Who would burn upon the desert with the forest smiling by?
Who would change his sunny summer for a bleak and wintry
    sky?
Oh, I tell you there is magic, and you cannot, cannot break it;
For the sweetest part of loving is to *want* a kiss and *take* it!

A TRUE STORY.

The moments were stealing and slipping by,
    With laughter, and fun, and glee;
The children were merry, and so was I—
    A happy circle of three.

"Oh, look!" cried Mab, as a sudden turn
    Brought the fading fire to view,
"Let's watch the coals as they slowly burn,
    And tell us a story true!"

We knelt on the rug before the blaze
    That flickered, and rose, and fell.
"Long years ago, in the old, old days,"
    I answer, "I've heard them tell

Of a maid who was courted by lovers twain.
    The first he was rich and old;
But his vows and pleadings were all in vain;
    She hated his yellow gold.

"The other was noble, and brave, and young,
    And loved her with passion true.
'You'll rue, if you heark to his flattering tongue!'
    Cried friends, when the truth they knew.

But she loved him well, though his purse was light,
    And married him firm and fast!"
I pause a moment, for out in the night,
    A step that I knew came past.

"And oh, did she ever repent or rue
    Her choice till the day she died?"
In the open door stood a form we knew.
    "Ask papa!" I gayly cried.
They shouted and laughed and guessed the truth,
    And learned a lesson as well,
That love is the holiest crown of youth—
    A blessing no tongue can tell!

"INASMUCH."

You say that you want a meetin'-house for the boys in the gulch up
    there,
And a Sunday-school with pictur'-books?   Well, put me down for
    a share.
I believe in little children; it's as nice to hear 'em read
As to wander round the ranch at noon and see the cattle feed.
And I believe in preachin', too—by men for preachin' born,
Who let alone the husks of creed, and measure out the corn.
The pulpit's but a manger where the pews are gospel-fed;
And they say 'twas to a manger the star of glory led.
So I'll subscribe a dollar toward the manger and the stalls:
I always give the best I've got whenever my partner calls.
And, stranger, let me tell you: I'm beginning to suspect
That all the world are partners, whatever their creed or sect;
That life is a sort of pilgrimage, a sort of Jericho road,
And kindness to one's fellows the sweetest law in the code.
No matter about the 'nitials; from a farmer, you understand,
Who's generally had to play it alone from rather an or'nary
    hand.
I've never struck it rich; for farming, you see, is slow,
And whenever the crops are fairly good, the prices are always low.
A dollar isn't much, but it helps to count the same:
The lowest trump supports the ace, and sometimes wins the game.

It assists a fellow's praying when he's down upon his knees—
" Inasmuch as you have done it to one of the least of these."
I know the verses, stranger, so you needn't stop to quote:
It's a different thing to know them or to say them off by rote.
I'll tell you where I learned them, if you'll step in from the rain.
'Twas down in 'Frisco, years ago; had been there hauling grain.
It was near the city limits, on the Sacramento pike,
Where stores and sheds are rather mixed, and shanties scatterin'
	like.
Not the likeliest place to be in, I remember, the saloon,
With grocery, market, baker-shop, and bar-room all in one.
And this made up the pictur'—my hair was not then gray,
But everything seems still as real as if 'twere yesterday.
A little girl with haggard face stood at the counter there,
Not more than ten or twelve at most, but worn with grief and care;
And her voice was kind of raspy, like a sort of chronic cold,—
Just the tone you find in children who are prematurely old.
She said: "Two bits for bread and tea, ma has n't much to eat;
She hopes next week to work again, and buy us all some meat.
We've been half starved all winter, but spring will soon be here,
And she tells us, 'Keep up courage, for God is always near.'"
Just then a dozen men came in—the boy was called away
To shake the spotted cubes for drinks, as Forty-niners say.
I never heard from human lips such oaths and curses loud
As rose above the glasses of that crazed and reckless crowd.
But the poor tired girl sat waiting, lost at last to revels deep,
On a keg beside a barrel in the corner, fast asleep.
Well, I stood there, sort of waiting, until some one at the bar
Said, "Hullo!   I say, stranger, what have you over thar?"
The boy then told her story, and that crew, so fierce and wild,
Grew intent, and seemed to listen to the breathing of the child.
The glasses were all lowered; said the leader: "Boys, see here;
All day we've been pouring whiskey, drinking deep our Christmas
	cheer.
Here's two dollars—I've got feelings which are not entirely dead—
For this little girl and mother suffering for the want of bread."
" Here's a dollar," "Here's another," and they all chipped in their
	share,
And they planked the ringing metal down upon the counter there.

Then the spokesman took a golden double-eagle from his belt,
Softly stepped from bar to counter, and beside the sleeper knelt;
Took the two bits from her fingers; changed her silver piece for
    gold.
"See there, boys; the girl is dreaming." Down her cheeks the
    tear-drops rolled.
On by one the swarthy miners passed in silence to the street.
Gently he awoke the sleeper, but she started to her feet
With a dazed and strange expression, saying: "Oh, I thought
    'twas true!
Ma was well, and we were happy; round our door-stone roses
    grew.
We had everything we wanted, food enough and clothes to wear;
And my hand burns where an angel touched it soft with fingers
    fair."
As she looked, and saw the money in her fingers glistening bright,
"Well, now, ma has long been praying, but she won't believe me
    quite,
How you've sent 'way up to heaven, where the golden treasures
    are,
And have also got an angel clerking at your grocery bar."
That's a Christmas story, stranger, which I thought you'd like to
    hear;
True to fact and human nature, pointing out one's duty clear.
Hence to matters of subscription, you will see that I'm alive;
Just mark off that dollar, stranger; I think I'll make it five.

THE LITTLE QUAKER SINNER.

A little Quaker maiden, with dimpled cheek and chin,
Before an ancient mirror stood, and viewed her form within.
She wore a gown of sober gray, a cape demure and prim,
With only simple fold and hem, yet dainty, neat, and trim.
Her bonnet, too, was gray and stiff; its only line of grace
Was in the lace, so soft and white, shirred round her rosy face.

Quoth she: "Oh, how I hate this hat! I hate this gown and
    cape!
I do wish all my clothes were not of such outlandish shape!

The children passing by to school have ribbons in their hair;
The little girl next door wears blue.   Oh, dear, if I could dare,
I know what I should like to do!"   (The words were whispered low,
Lest such tremendous heresy should reach her aunts below.)

Calmly reading in the parlor sat the good aunts, Faith and Peace,
Little dreaming how rebellious throbbed the heart of their young
        niece.
All their prudent, humble teaching willfully she cast aside,
And, her mind now fully conquered by vanity and pride,
She, with trembling heart and fingers, on a hassock sat her down,
And this little Quaker sinner *sewed a tuck into her gown!*

"Little Patience, art thou ready?   Fifth-day meeting-time has
        come,
Mercy Jones and Goodman Elder with his wife have left their
        home."
'Twas Aunt Faith's sweet voice that called her, and the naughty
        little maid,
Gliding down the dark old stair-way, hoped their notice to evade;
Keeping shyly in their shadow as they went out of the door,
Ah, never little Quakeress a guiltier conscience bore!

Dear Aunt Faith walked looking upward; all her thoughts were
        pure and holy;
And Aunt Peace walked gazing downward, with an humble mind
        and lowly.
But "tuck-tuck!" chirped the sparrows, at the little maiden's side;
And, in passing Farmer Watson's, where the barn-door opened wide,
Every sound that issued from it, every grunt and every cluck,
Seemed to her affrighted fancy like "a tuck!" "a tuck!" "a tuck!"
In meeting, Goodman Elder spoke of pride and vanity,
While all the Friends seemed looking round that dreadful tuck to
        see.
How it swelled in its proportions, till it seemed to fill the air,
And the heart of little Patience grew heavier with her care.
Oh, the glad relief to her, when, prayers and exhortations ended,
Behind her two good aunties her homeward way she wended.

The pomps and vanities of life she'd seized with eager arms,
And deeply she had tasted of the world's alluring charms,—

Yea, to the dregs had drained them, and only this to find:
All was vanity of spirit and vexation of the mind.
So, repentant, saddened, humbled, on a hassock she sat down,
And this little Quaker sinner *ripped the tuck out of her gown!*

THE NEW BONNET.

A foolish little maiden bought a foolish little bonnet,
With a ribbon, and a feather, and a bit of lace upon it;
And, that the other maidens of the little town might know it,
She thought she'd go to meeting the next Sunday just to show it.

But though the little bonnet was scarce larger than a dime,
The getting of it settled proved to be a work of time;
So when 'twas fairly tied, and the bells had stopped their ringing,
And when she came to meeting, sure enough, the folks were
    singing.

So this foolish little maiden stood and waited at the door;
And she shook her ruffles out behind and smoothed them down
    before.
"Hallelujah! Hallelujah!" sang the choir above her head.
"Hardly knew you! Hardly knew you!" were the words she
    thought they said.

This made the little maiden feel so very, very cross,
That she gave her little mouth a twist, her little head a toss;
For she thought the very hymn they sang was all about her bon-
    net,
With the ribbon, and the feather, and the bit of lace upon it.

And she would not wait to listen to the sermon or the prayer,
But pattered down the silent street, and hurried down the stair,
Till she reached her little bureau, and in a band-box on it,
Had hidden, safe from critic's eye, her foolish little bonnet.

Which proves, my little maidens, that each of you will find
In every Sabbath service but an echo of your mind;
And the silly little head, that's filled with silly little airs,
Will never get a blessing from sermon or from prayers.

LITTLE JIM.

The cottage was a thatched one, the outside old and mean,
But all within that little cot was wondrous neat and clean;
The night was dark and stormy, the wind was howling wild,
As a patient mother sat beside the death-bed of her child:
A little worn-out creature, his once bright eyes grown dim:
It was a collier's wife and child, they called him little Jim.

And oh! to see the briny tears fast hurrying down her cheek,
As she offered up the prayer, in thought, she was afraid to speak,
Lest she might waken one she loved far better than her life;
For she had all a mother's heart, had that poor collier's wife.
With hands uplifted, see, she kneels beside the sufferer's bed,
And prays that He would spare her boy, and take herself instead.

She gets her answer from the child: soft fall the words from him,
" Mother, the angels do so smile, and beckon little Jim;
I have no pain, dear mother, now, but, Oh! I am so dry,
Just moisten poor Jim's lips again, and, mother, don't you cry."
With gentle, trembling haste she held the liquid to his lips;
He smiled to thank her, as he took each little, tiny sip.

" Tell father, when he comes from work, I said good-night to him,
And, mother, now I'll go to sleep." Alas! poor little Jim!
She knew that he was dying; that the child she loved so dear
Had uttered the last words that she might ever hope to hear.
The cottage door is opened, the collier's step is heard,
The father and the mother meet, yet neither speak a word.

He felt that all was over, he knew his child was dead,
He took the candle in his hand, and walked toward the bed;
His quivering lips gave token of the grief he'd fain conceal,
And see, his wife has joined him—the stricken couple kneel;
With hearts bowed down by sadness, they humbly ask of Him
In heaven once more to meet again their own poor little Jim.

OUR LITTLE SPEAKER.

SELECTIONS

FOR THE

BOYS AND GIRLS.

THE GRUMBLER.

HIS YOUTH.

His cap was too thick, and his coat was too thin;
He couldn't be quiet, he hated a din;
He hated to write, and he hated to read;'
He was certainly very much injured indeed!
He must study and toil over work he detested;
His parents were strict, and he never was rested;
He knew he was wretched as wretched could be,
There was no one so wretchedly wretched as he.

HIS MANHOOD.

His farm was too small, his taxes too big;
He was selfish and lazy, and cross as a pig;
His wife was too silly, his children too rude,
And just because he was uncommonly good!
He hadn't got money enough to spare;
He had nothing at all fit to eat or to wear;
He knew he was wretched as wretched could be,
There was no one so wretchedly wretched as he.

HIS OLD AGE.

He finds he has sorrows more deep than his fears;
He grumbles to think he has grumbled for years;
He grumbles to think he has grumbled away
His home and his children, his life's little day;
But alas! 'tis too late! it is no use to say
That his eyes are too dim and his hair is too gray;
He knows he is wretched as wretched can be,
There is no one so wretchedly wretched as he.

WHAT A BOY CAN DO.

These are some of the things that a boy can do:
He can whistle so loud the air turns blue;
He can make all the sounds of beast and bird,
And a thousand noises never heard.

He can crow or cackle, or he can cluck
As well as a rooster, hen, or duck;
He can bark like a dog, he can low like a cow,
And a cat itself can't beat his "me-ow."

He has sounds that are ruffled, striped, and plain;
He can thunder by as a railway train,
Stop at the stations a breath, and then
Apply the steam and be off again.

He has all his powers in such command
He can turn right into a full brass band,
With all of the instruments ever played,
As he makes of himself a street parade.

You can tell that a boy is very ill
If he's wide awake and keeping still.
But earth would be—God bless their noise!—
A dull old place if there were no boys.

THE BOY WHO HELPS HIS MOTHER.

As I went down the street to-day
    I saw a little lad
Whose face was just the kind of face
    To make a person glad.
It was so plump and rosy-cheeked,
    So cheerful and so bright,
It made me think of apple-time,
    And filled me with delight.

I saw him busily at work,
    While blithe as blackbird's song
His merry, mellow whistle rang
    The pleasant street along.
"Oh, that's the kind of lad I like!"
    I thought, as I passed by;
"These busy, cheery, whistling boys
    Make grand men by-and-bye."

Just then a playmate came along
    And leaned across the gate—

A plan that promised lots of fun
   And frolic to relate.
"The boys are waiting for us now,
   So hurry up!" he cried;
My little whistler shook his head,
   And, "Can't come," he replied.

"Can't come? Why not, I'd like to know?
   What hinders?" asked the other.
"Why, don't you see?" came the reply.
   "I'm busy helping mother.
She's lots to do, and so I like
   To help her all I can;
So I've no time for fun just now,"
   Said this dear little man.

"I like to hear you talk like that,"
   I told the little lad;
"Help mother all you can, and make
   Her kind heart light and glad."
It does me good to think of him
   And know that there are others
Who, like this manly little boy,
   Take hold and help their mothers.

TOO MUCH THANKSGIVING PIE.

A small boy sat on the top of the fence,
   And thought he was quite a bright fellow,
For he counted the days till Thanksgiving time,
   And he counted the pumpkins yellow.

And he said, as he sat in royal state
   On top of the fence so high,
"A pumpkin pie most highly I rate,"
   And he mused on the pleasures of by-and-bye.

And now near at hand was Thanksgiving Day,
   And the kitchen was all in a whirl,
And his mother was busy as busy could be,
   Likewise his aunt and the servant girl.

To take a pie this small boy intended,
   For what was one pie more or less?
No doubt his mother would be offended,
   But who the culprit, she'd never guess.

His chance soon came, for a neighbor came in
To ask for the loan of the rolling-pin;
And when none were looking or standing by,
This dreadful boy ran off with a pie.

The pie was hot and burned him so,
And running so fast he stubbed his toe,
That over he fell, hot pie and all,
And loudly did for his mother call.

She sadly looked at her pride and joy,
And separated pie from boy.
He cried very hard at having done wrong,
But he knew he'd cry more before very long.

Next day at dinner all wondered why
This small boy was debarred from pie;
But his mother and he alone knew the reason,
And he thought their remarks quite out of season.

THE DYING CONFESSION OF PADDY McCABE.

SAMUEL LOVER.

Paddy McCabe was dying one day,
   And Father Molloy he came to confess him;
Paddy prayed hard he would make no delay,
   But forgive him his sins and make haste for to bless him.
"First tell me your sins," says Father Molloy,
"For I'm thinking you've not been a very good boy."

"Oh," says Paddy, "so late in the evenin' I fear
'Twould trouble you such a long story to hear,
For you've ten long miles o'er the mountain to go,
While the road *I've* to travel's much longer, you know:
So give us your blessin' and get in the saddle;
To tell all my sins my poor brain would addle;

And the docthor gave orthers to keep me so quiet—
'Twould disturb me to tell all my sins, if I'd thry it—
And your Reverence has towld us unless we tell *all*
'Tis worse than not makin' confession at all:
So I'll say, in a word, I'm no very good boy,
And therefore your blessin', sweet Father Molloy."

"Well, I'll read from a book," says Father Molloy,
  " The manifold sins that humanity's heir to;
And when you hear those that your conscience annoy,
  You'll just squeeze my hand, as acknowledging thereto."
Then the Father began the dark roll of iniquity,
And Paddy, thereat, felt his conscience grow rickety,
And he gave such a squeeze that the priest gave a roar.
"Oh, murther," says Paddy, "don't read any more;
For if you keep readin', by all that is thrue,
Your Reverence's fist will be soon black and blue;
Besides, to be troubled my conscience begins,
That your Reverence should have any hand in *my* sins.
So you'd better suppose I committed them all—
For whether they're great ones, or whether they're small,
Or if they're a dozen, or if they're fourscore,
'Tis your Reverence knows how to absolve them, asthore.
So I'll say, in a word, I'm no very good boy,
And therefore your blessin', sweet Father Molloy."

"Well," says Father Molloy, "your sins I forgive,
  So you must forgive all your enemies truly,
And promise me also that, if you should live,
  You'll leave off your old tricks, and begin to live newly."
"I forgive ev'rybody," says Pat, with a groan,
"Except that big vagabone, Micky Malone;
And him I will murdher if ever I can—"
"Tut, tut!" says the priest, "you're a very bad man;
For without your forgiveness, and also repentance,
You'll ne'er go to heaven, and that is my sentence."
"Pooh!" says Paddy McCabe, "that's a very hard case,
With your Reverence in heaven I'm content to make pace;
But with heaven and your Reverence I wonder—*och hone,*
You would think of comparin' that blackguard Malone.

But since I'm hard pressed, and that I *must* forgive,
I forgive—if I die; but as sure as I live
That ugly blackguard I will surely desthroy !—
So *now* for your blessin', sweet Father Molloy !"

A FAITHFUL ENGINEER.

Life is like a crooked railroad,
    And the engineer is brave
Who can make a trip successful
    From the cradle to the grave.
There are stations all along it
    Where, at almost any breath,
You'll be "flagged" to stop your engine
    By the passenger of death.
You may run the grades of trouble
    Many days and years with ease,
But time may have you " side-tracked"
    By the switchman of disease.
You may cross the bridge of manhood,
    Run the tunnel long of strife,
Having God for your conductor
    On the "lightning train" of life.
Always mindful of instructions,
    Watchful duty never lack ;
Keep your hand upon the throttle
    And your eye upon the track.

Name your engine " True Religion";
    When you're running, day or night,
Use the coal of " Faith" for fuel,
    And she'll always run you right.
You need never fear of " sticking"
    On the up grades 'long the road ;
If you've got " Hope" for a fireman,
    You can always pull the load.
You will often find obstruction,
    By the cunning devil lain,
On a fill, a curve, or some place,
    When he'll try to " ditch your train."

But you needn't fear disaster.
　"Jerk her open!"　"Let her go!"
For the King who ruleth all things,
　All his plans will overthrow.
Put your trust in God, the Saviour;
　Keep a-going; don't look back;
Keep your hand upon the throttle
　And your eye upon the track.

When you've made the trip successful,
　And you're at your journey's end,
You will find the angels waiting
　To receive you as a friend.
You'll approach the Superintendent,
　Who is waiting for you now
With a blessed smile of welcome
　And a crown to deck your brow.
Never falter in your duty,
　Put your faith and hope in Him,
And you'll always find your engine
　In the best of running trim.
Ring your bell and blow your whistle,
　Never let your courage slack;
Keep your hand upon the throttle
　And your eye upon the track.

WHEN FATHER CARVES THE DUCK.

E. V. WRIGHT.

We all look on with anxious eyes
　When father carves the duck,
And mother almost always sighs
　When father carves the duck;
Then all of us prepare to rise,
And hold our bibs before our eyes,
And be prepared for some surprise,
　When father carves the duck.

He braces up and grabs a fork
　Whene'er he carves a duck,

And won't allow a soul to talk,
  Until he's carved the duck.
The fork is jabbed into the sides,
Across the breast the knife he slides,
While every careful person hides
  From flying chips of duck.

The platter's always sure to slip
  When father carves a duck,
And how it makes the dishes skip!
  Potatoes fly amuck!
The squash and cabbage leap in space,
We get some gravy in our face,
And father mutters Hindoo grace
  Whene'er he carves a duck.

We then have learned to walk around
  The dining-room and pluck
From off the window-sills and walls
  Our share of father's duck.
While father growls and blows and jaws,
And swears the knife was full of flaws,
And mother laughs at him because
  He couldn't carve a duck.

WHAT DOES IT MATTER?

It matters little where I was born,
  Or if my parents were rich or poor;
Whether they shrank at the cold world's scorn,
  Or walked in the pride of wealth secure;
But whether I live an honest man,
  And hold my integrity firm in my clutch,
I tell you, my brother, plain as I can,
  It matters much!

It matters little where be my grave,
  If on the land or in the sea,
By purling brook, or 'neath stormy wave,
  It matters little or naught to me;

But whether the angel of death comes down
 And marks my brow with a loving touch,
As the one who shall wear the victor's crown,
 It matters much!

YOUNG AMERICA.

"Come hither, you madcap darling!"
 I said to my four-year-old.
"Pray what shall be done to the bad, bad girl
 Who will not do as she's told?
Too well you love your own wee way,
 While little you love to mind;
But mamma knows what is best for you,
 And isn't she always kind?"

So I told her of "Casabianca,"
 And the fearful burning ship.
"Do you think," said I, "such a child as that
 His mother would have to whip?"
And my heart went out with the story sad
 Of this boy so nobly brave,
Who would not *dare* to disobey,
 Even his life to save.

Then her eyes grew bright as the morning,
 And they seemed to look me through.
Ah—ah, thought I, you understand
 The lesson I have in view.
"Now what do you think of this lad, my love?
 Tell all that is in your heart."
"I fink," she said, "he was drefful good,
 But he wasn't the least bit smart."

DID NOT PASS.

(First verse can be recited by teacher or omitted.)

"So, John, I hear you did not pass;
 You were the lowest in your class,
  Got not a prize of merit.
But grumbling now is no avail;

Just tell me how you came to fail,
  With all your sense and spirit?"

"Well, sir, I missed, 'mong other things,
  The list of Egypt's shepherd kings
    (I wonder who does know it).
  An error of three years I made
  In dating England's first crusade;
    And, as I am no poet,

"I got Euripides all wrong,
  And could not write a Latin song;
    And as for Roman history,
  With Hun and Vandal, Goth and Gaul,
  And Gibbon's weary 'Rise and Fall,'
    'Twas all a hopeless mystery.

"But, father, do not fear or sigh
  If Cram' does proudly pass me by,
    And pedagogues ignore me;
  I've common sense, I've will and health,
  I'll win my way to honest wealth;
    The world is all before me.

"And though I'll never be a Grecian,
  Know Roman laws or art Phœnician,
    Or sing of love and beauty,
  I'll plow, or build, or sail, or trade,
  And you need never be afraid
    But that I'll do my duty."

SELECTIONS FOR A MISSIONARY EXERCISE.

SENDING THE WORD OF GOD.

We would ask no higher service,
  Lord, that we might do for thee,
Than thy blessed Word to carry
  To the lands beyond the sea.

There could be no gladder moment
  In our lives, whate'er betide,

Than the moment we might show them
  Love of Him who for them died.

Oh, to see the hopeless faces
  Brighten at the glad good news
Of a light beyond earth's shadows—
  Happiness if they but choose!

Oh, to let the peace of heaven
  On those souls benighted shine!
With its rays effulgent beaming
  From the source of light divine.

It is ours to send the message
  To the lands beyond the sea,
Ours to send the balm of healing
  To the souls in misery.

Let us labor, let us hasten,
  While the day doth lend its light,
Ere the evening shadows gather—
  None can work when cometh night.

CHINA.

SUITABLE FOR A YOUNG LADY.

Land beyond the western ocean,
  Kissed by sunset's dying ray,
Land where nature's gifts are scattered
  In profusion, rich and gay—
Ancient China—proud and haughty,
  Rich in much, yet lacking all,
While her doors were barred and bolted
  'Gainst the Gospel's gentle call.
But at last she heard a murmur,
  'Twas a breeze from heaven blown,
Gently whispering life eternal,
  Peace and rest through God's dear Son.
Now the doors of proud old China
  Open stand, inviting all,

And she waits to hear the message.
  Are we ready for that call?
Shall we linger? Shall we waver?
  Saying: "God their souls will save—
Little is required, if little
  Doth the soul benighted have"?
Down the ages, sweetly flowing,
  Comes the loving Lord's command:
"Into all the world now go ye—
  I am with you to the end."
Shall we coldly doubt and linger,
  Choosing selfish ease and gain,
When the mandate of the Master
  Comes in words so clear and plain?
It is ours to do our duty
  Without doubt or questioning word,
Ours to do the task assigned us,
  Leaving all the rest with God.

INDIA.

(Should be spoken slowly.)

Dear, kind friends, I'm here to tell you
  Of a land, far, far away.
Where the nation sits in darkness,
  Waiting for the dawn of day.

Gross that darkness, for they know not
  Of a light beyond the cloud;
Depths of ignorance engulf them,
  And their sorrows cry aloud.

Little children bear great burdens
  In that sorrow-stricken land;
Who is there to lift those burdens?
  Who to lend a helping hand?

Who will break the iron fetters
  Caste has welded, sure and fast?
Who will lead them out and upward,
  From that Egypt, dark and vast?

Do not say, "We cannot enter"—
  God has opened up a way—
Lo! the field is white for harvest,
  Why so long do ye delay?

India—fairest of the jewels
  Sparkling in earth's diadem—
Must be treasured for the Master,
  Must be won, at last, for Him.

THE MISSIONARY HEN.

I know a funny little lad—
  We call him careful Ben—
Who has among his many pets
  A *missionary hen.*

"A missionary hen!" you say;
  "What sort of fowl is that?"
Just listen, and you'll all agree
  That she is called just right.

Now Benny went to Sunday-school,
  And there he heard them tell
About the children far away
  Who hear no Sabbath bell;

Who never heard of Jesus' name
  Nor how He came to earth,
And gave His life upon the cross
  To save their souls from death.

He knew they had no pleasant homes,
  No teachers kind and true
To tell them of a Saviour's love,
  Or what they ought to do.

Ben's pocket-book was very lean,
  The pennies there were few;
But Bennie's mother helped him out—
  She gave him work to do.

He climbed the mow to hunt the eggs,
  He crawled beneath the barn;
And his reward was one old hen
  That he might call his own.

Dear me! the way that old hen laid
  Was wonderful to view!
She seemed to know her business well,
  And sought to mind it too.

She was a missionary hen,
  For all her eggs he sold
For pennies for the mission-box—
  They were as good as gold.

Ben's pennies now were never scarce,
  He did not have to beg;
He thought his hen would beat the goose
  That laid the golden egg.

Financial ruin never more
  Can ever threaten Ben,
For revenue he leans upon
  That old trustworthy hen.

She raised a brood of ten fine chicks,
  Ben soon will draft them in,
And make them share the burdens of
  His missionary hen.

LITTLE CHILDREN.

We're very little children,
  That you can plainly see,—
But don't you all remember
  When you were such as we?

We'll make good men and women,
  Like you are, by-and-bye;
We try each day to be *so* good,
  And never, never cry.

We bring our nice bright pennies—
  They're very small we know,
But put them all together,
  To dollars they will grow.

Now if there were no children,
  No big folks would you see,
So, if there were no pennies,
  No dollars would there be.

THE CHILDREN'S DAY.

Dear friends and teachers, kind and true,
  You're welcome,—one and all;
We think it very kind that you
  Have heard the children's call.

Some little songs we have to sing,
  Some little words to say—
We pray you listen patiently,
  For this is *Children's Day.*

Great things have we to tell to you,
  Of children far away,
Who have no parents, good like ours—
  No happy homes have they.

They never heard of God's dear Son,
  Who left His home above,
And suffered on the cruel cross,
  That all might know His love.

We want to bear the news to them,
  But we are weak and small;
Unless encouragement we have
  Naught can we do at all.

And so, dear friends, we welcome you,
  Your presence, courage brings;
We hope to prove, before you leave,
  The strength in *little* things.

A ROGUE.

Grandma was nodding, I rather think;
Harry was sly and quick as a wink;
He climbed in the back of her great arm-chair,
And nestled himself very snugly there;
Grandma's dark locks were mingled with white,
And quick this fact came to his sight;
A sharp twinge soon she felt at her hair,
And woke with a start, to find Harry there.
"Why, what are you doing, my child?" she said.
He answered, "I'se pulling a basting fread!"

GRANDPAPA'S SPECTACLES.

Grandpapa's spectacles cannot be found;
He has searched all the rooms, high and low, 'round and
    'round;
Now he calls to the young ones, and what does he say?
"Ten cents for the child who will find them to-day."

Then Henry and Nelly and Edward all ran,
And a most thorough hunt for the glasses began,
And dear little Nell, in her generous way,
Said: "I'll look for them, grandpa, without any pay."

All through the big Bible she searches with care
That lies on the table by grandpapa's chair;
They feel in his pockets, they peep in his hat,
They pull out the sofa, they shake out the mat.

Then down on all fours, like two good-natured bears,
Go Harry and Ned under tables and chairs,
Till, quite out of breath, Ned is heard to declare,
He believes that those glasses are *not anywhere.*

But Nelly, who, leaning on grandpapa's knee,
Was thinking most earnestly where they *could* be,
Looked suddenly up in the kind, faded eyes,
And her own shining brown ones grew big with surprise.

She slapped both her hands—all her dimples came out—
She turned to the boys with a bright, roguish shout :
" You may leave off your looking, both Harry and Ned,
For there are the glasses on grandpapa's head ! "

SUPPOSE.

PHŒBE CARY.

Suppose, my little lady,
    Your doll should break her head,
Could you make it whole by crying
    Till your eyes and nose were red?
And wouldn't it be pleasanter
    To treat it as a joke;
And say you're glad 'twas dolly's
    And not your head that broke?

Suppose you're dressed for walking,
    And the rain comes pouring down,
Will it clear off any sooner
    Because you scold and frown?
And wouldn't it be nicer
    For you to smile than pout,
And so make sunshine in the house
    When there is none without?

Suppose your task, my little man,
    Is very hard to get,
Will it make it any easier,
    For you to sit and fret?
And wouldn't it be wiser,
    Than waiting like a dunce,
To get to work in earnest,
    And learn the thing at once?

Suppose that some boys have a horse,
    And some a coach and pair,
Will it tire you less while walking
    To say, " It isn't fair"?

And wouldn't it be nobler
  To keep your temper sweet,
And in your heart be thankful
  You can walk upon your feet?

Suppose the world don't please you,
  Nor the way some people do,
Do you think the whole creation
  Will be altered just for you?
And isn't it, my boy or girl,
  The wisest, bravest plan,
Whatsoever comes, or doesn't come,
  To do the best you can?

JOHNNY'S OPINION OF GRANDMOTHERS.

Grandmothers are very nice folks;
  They beat all the aunts in creation;
They let a chap do as he likes
  And don't worry about education.

I'm sure I can't see it at all,
  What a poor fellow ever could do
For apples and pennies and cakes,
  Without a grandmother or two.

Grandmothers speak softly to " ma's "
  To let a boy have a good time;
Sometimes they will whisper, 'tis true,
  T'other way when a boy wants to climb.

Grandmothers have muffins for tea,
  And pies, a whole row, in the cellar,
And they're apt (if they know it in time)
  To make chicken-pies for a feller.

And if he is bad now and then,
  And makes a great racketing noise,
They only look over their specs
  And say, " Ah, these boys will be boys!

" Life is only so short at the best;
  Let the children be happy to-day."

Then they look for a while at the sky,
  And the hills that are far, far away.

Quite often, as twilight comes on,
  Grandmothers sing hymns very low
To themselves, as they rock by the fire,
  About heaven, and when they shall go.

And then a boy, stopping to think,
  Will find a hot tear in his eye,
To know what must come at the last,
  For grandmothers all have to die.

I wish they could stay here and pray,
  For a boy needs their prayers every night.
Some boys more than others, I s'pose;
  Such fellers as me need a sight.

WHICH LOVED BEST?

"I love you, mother," said little Ben,
Then forgetting his work, his cap went on.
And he was on to the garden swing,
And left her the water and wood to bring.

"I love you, mother," said rosy Nell—
"I love you better than tongue can tell;"
Then she teased and pouted full half the day,
Till her mother rejoiced when she went to play.

"I love you, mother," said little Fan,
"To-day I'll help you all I can;
How glad I am school doesn't keep;"
So she rocked the babe till it fell asleep.

Then, stepping softly, she fetched the broom,
And swept the floor and tidied the room;
Busy and happy all day was she,
Helpful and happy as child could be.

"I love you, mother," again they said,
Three little children going to bed;
How do you think that mother guessed
Which of them really loved her best?

ONLY A BOY.

Only a boy with his noise and fun,
The veriest mystery under the sun;
As brimful of mischief and wit and glee,
As ever a human frame can be,
And as hard to manage—what! ah me!
    'Tis hard to tell,
    Yet we love him well.

Only a boy with his fearful tread,
Who cannot be driven, must be led!
Who troubles the neighbors' dogs and cats,
And tears more clothes and spoils more hats,
Loses more kites and tops and bats
    Than would stock a store
    For a week or more.

Only a boy with his wild, strange ways,
With his idle hours or his busy days,
With his queer remarks and his odd replies,
Sometimes foolish and sometimes wise,
Often brilliant for one of his size,
    As a meteor hurled
    From the planet world.

Only a boy, who may be a man
If nature goes on with her first great plan—
If intemperance or some fatal snare
Conspires not to rob us of this our heir,
Our blessing, our trouble, our rest, our care,
    Our torment, our joy!
    "Only a boy!"

THE LOVERS.

PHŒBE CARY.

Sally Salter, she was a young teacher who taught,
And her friend, Charley Church, was a preacher who praught,
Though his enemies called him a screecher who scraught.

His heart, when he saw her, kept sinking and sunk,
And his eye, meeting hers, began winking and wunk;
While she, in her turn, kept thinking and thunk.

He hastened to woo her, and sweetly he wooed,
For his love grew until to a mountain it grewed,
And what he was longing to do then he doed.

In secret he wanted to speak, and he spoke,
To seek with his lips what his heart long had soke;
So he managed to let the truth leak, and it loke.

He asked her to ride to the church, and they rode;
They so sweetly did glide that they both thought they glode,
And they came to the place to be tied, and were toed.

"Then homeward," he said, "let us drive," and they drove,
And as soon as they wished to arrive, they arrove,
For whatever he couldn't contrive, she controve.

The kiss he was dying to steal then he stole;
At the feet where he wanted to kneel, then he knole;
And he said, "I feel better than ever I fole."

So they to each other kept clinging, and clung,
While Time his swift circuit was winging and wung;
And this was the thing he was bringing and brung:

The man Sally wanted to catch, and had caught;
That she wanted from others to snatch, and had snaught;
Was the one that she now liked to scratch, and she scraught.

And Charley's warm love began freezing and froze,
While he took to teazing, and cruelly toze
The girl he had wished to be squeezing and squoze.

"Wretch!" he cried, when she threatened to leave him, and left,
"How could you deceive me, as you have deceft?"
And she answered, "I promised to cleave, and I've cleft."

A TWILIGHT STORY.

MARY J. PORTER.

"Auntie, will you tell a story?" said my little niece of three,
As the early winter twilight fell around us silently.
So I answered to her pleading: "Once, when I was very small,
With my papa and my mamma I went out to make a call;

And a lady, pleased to see us, gave me quite a large bouquet,
Which I carried homeward proudly, smiling all along the way.

"Soon I met two other children, clad in rags and sad of face,
Who grew strangely, wildly joyous as I neared their standing-
place.
'Twas so good to see the flowers! 'Give us one—oh, one!' they
cried.
But I passed them without speaking, left them with their wish
denied.
Yet the mem'ry of their asking haunted me by night and day,
'Give us one!' I heard them saying, even in my mirthful play.

"Still I mourn, because in childhood I refused to give a flower:
Did not make those others happy when I had it in my power."
Suddenly I ceased my story. Tears were in my niece's eyes—
Tears of tenderness and pity—while she planned a sweet surprise;
"I will send a flower to-morrow to those little children dear."
Could I tell her that their childhood had been gone this many a
year?

BOYS WANTED.

"Wanted, a boy." How often we
These very common words may see,
Wanted—a boy to errands run,
Wanted for everything under the sun.
All that the men to-day can do
To-morrow the boys will be doing too,
For the time is ever coming when
The boys must stand in place of men.

Wanted—the world wants boys to-day,
And she offers them all she has for pay.
Honor, wealth, position, fame.
A useful life and a deathless name.
Boys to shape the paths for men,
Boys to guide the plow and pen,
Boys to forward the tasks begun.

The world is anxious to employ
Not just one, but every boy

Whose heart and brain will e'er be true
To work his hands shall find to do.
Honest, faithful, earnest, kind;
To good awake, to evil blind;
Heart of gold without alloy.
Wanted: The world wants such a boy.

PRESENTATION SPEECH.

DEAR TEACHER: I am commissioned by my schoolmates to ask your acceptance of this little token of their respect and affection. We wished in some way to show our appreciation of your ability as a preceptor, and of your patience and kindness in dealing with the faults to which that variety of the human species called the Boy is proverbially prone, and, after some debate as to the method of doing so, concluded that the most befitting exponent of our feelings would be a memento to which we could all contribute, and which, however insignificant its value might be when measured by the magnitude of our obligations, would agreeably remind you that we are not ungrateful. With our little gift, receive, dear sir, our warmest wishes for your health and prosperity. We hope to do credit to your tutelage. If we do not, it is our own fault, for you have done your part faithfully and zealously. You have taught us to look up to you not only as a wise instructor, but as a guardian and friend, and when we go into the world to turn the lessons you have taught to profitable account, we shall not forget to whom we owe our requirements, but shall remember you ever with almost filial regard.

PRESENTATION SPEECH.

DEAR TEACHER: I have been requested by the young ladies of this school (or institution) to offer you a slight token of our affection and regard. I cannot tell you how delighted I am to be the means of conveying to you the expression of our united love. What we offer you is but a poor symbol of our feelings, but we know you will receive it kindly, as a simple indication of the attachment which each one of us cherishes for you in her heart of hearts. You have made our lessons pleasant to us—so pleasant that it would be ungrateful to call them tasks. We know that we have often tried your temper and forbearance, but you have dealt gently with us in our waywardness, teaching us, by example as well as precept, the advantages of magnanimity and self-control. We will never forget you. We shall look back to this school (or institution) in after-life, not as a place of penance, but as a scene of mental enjoyment, where the paths of learning were strewn with flowers; and whenever memory recalls our school-days, our hearts will warm toward you as they do to-day. I have been requested by my schoolmates not to address you formally, but as a beloved and respected friend. In that light, dear teacher, we all regard you. Please accept, with our little present, our earnest good wishes. May you always be as happy as you have endeavored to make your pupils, and may they—nothing better could be wished for them—be always as faithful to their duties to others as you have been in your duties to them.

AN OPENING ADDRESS.

I am a very little boy (or girl), and I suppose that is why the teacher puts me first to-day. But I am big enough to tell you that we are very glad to see you.

I hope you will like our school very much. We will sing our best songs, and say our prettiest verses, and be just as good as we can all the time you stay, for we want you to come again.

WELCOME.

Kind friends, we welcome you to-day
   With songs of merry glee;
Your loving smiles we strive to win,
   Each face we love to see.

Sweet welcomes then to one and all,
   And may your smiles approve;
And may we never miss the light
   Of faces that we love.

TOTAL ANNIHILATION.

Oh, he was a Bowery bootblack bold,
   And his years they numbered nine;

Rough and unpolished was he, albeit
　　He constantly aimed to shine.

As proud as a king, on his box he sat,
　　Munching an apple red;
While the boys of his set looked wistfully on,
　　And "Give us a bite!" they said.

But the bootblack smiled a lordly smile;
　　"No free bites here!" he cried.
Then the boys they sadly walked away,
　　Save *one* who stood at his side.

"Bill, give us the core?" he whispered low.
　　That bootblack smiled once more,
And a mischievous dimple grew in his cheek:
　　"There *ain't goin' to be no core!*"

THAT'S BABY.

One little row of ten little toes,
To go along with a brand-new nose,
Eight new fingers and two new thumbs,
That are just as good as sugar-plums—
　　　　　　　　That's baby.

One little pair of round new eyes,
Like a little owl's, so old and wise,
One little place they call a mouth,
Without one tooth from north to south—
　　　　　　　　That's baby.

Two little cheeks to kiss all day,
Two little hands, so in his way,
A brand-new head, not very big,
That seems to need a brand-new wig—
　　　　　　　　That's baby.

Dear little row of ten little toes,
How much we love them nobody knows;
Ten little kisses on mouth and chin,
What a shame he wasn't a twin!—
　　　　　　　　That's baby.

WORDS OF WELCOME.

Kind friends and dear parents, we welcome you here
To our nice pleasant school-room, and teacher so dear;
We wish but to show how much we have learned,
And how to our lessons our hearts have been turned.

But hope you'll remember we all are quite young.
And when we have spoken, recited, and sung,
You will pardon our blunders, which, as all are aware,
May even extend to the President's chair.

Our life is a school-time, and till that shall end,
With our Father in heaven for teacher and friend,
Oh, let us perform well each task that is given,
Till our time of probation is ended in heaven.

THE FIRST PAIR OF BREECHES.

I've got a pair of breeches now,
 And I'll have to be a man;
I know I can if just I try,
 My mamma says I can!

I'm going to school now very soon,
 And learn my A, B, C;
My mamma says I'm too young yet,
 But I am 'way past three.

And I've got pockets in my pants,
 To put my pencil in;
For mamma says that I must write
 In school when I begin.

I'll soon be tall as papa—now
 I'll grow as fast as I can,
And don't you think that very soon
 I'll be a full-grown man?

WHEN MAMMA WAS A LITTLE GIRL.

When mamma was a little girl
 (Or so they say to me)
She never used to romp and run,
Nor shout and scream with noisy fun,
 Nor climb an apple tree.
She always kept her hair in curl,—
When mamma was a little girl.

When mamma was a little girl
 (It seems to her, you see)
She never used to tumble down,
Nor break her doll, nor tear her gown,
 Nor drink her papa's tea.
She learned to knit, "plain," "seam," and "purl,"—
When mamma was a little girl.

But grandma says—it must be true—
 "How fast the seasons o'er us whirl!
Your mamma, dear, was just like you,
 When she was grandma's little girl."

THE WATERMILLION.

There were a watermillion
 Growing on a vine,
And there were a pickaninny
 A-watching it all the time.

And when that watermillion
 Were a-ripening in the sun,
And the stripes along its jacket
 Were coming one by one,

That pickaninny hooked it,
 And toting it away,
He ate that entire million
 Within a single day.

He ate the rind and pieces,
 And finished it with vim,
And then that watermillion
 Just up and finished him.

THE CHICKENS.

Said the first little chicken, with a queer little squirm,
"I wish I could find a fat little worm."
Said the next little chicken, with an odd little shrug,
"I wish I could find a fat little slug."
Said the third little chicken, with a sharp little squeal,
"I wish I could find some nice yellow meal."
Said the fourth little chicken, with a small sigh of grief,
"I wish I could find a little green leaf."
Said the fifth little chicken, with a faint little moan,
"I wish I could find a wee gravel stone."
"Now, see here," said the mother, from the green garden patch,
"If you want any breakfast, just come here and scratch."

FUNNY, ISN'T IT?

The pipers are not made of pipes,
 And cowards are not made of cows;
And lyres are not made of lies,
 While bowers are not made of bows.
The wickets are not made of wicks,
 And candles are not made of cans;
And tickets are not made of ticks,
 While panels are not made of pans.
The cattle are not made of cats,
 While willows are not made of wills;
And battles are not made of bats,
 And pilgrims not made of grim pills.
The cornets are not made of corns,
 A hotel is not made of a hoe;
And hornets are not made of horns,
 While all poets cannot be Poe.

AMONG THE ANIMALS.

One rainy morning, just for a lark,
I jumped and stamped on my new Noah's ark:
I crushed an elephant, smashed a gnu,
And snapped a camel clean in two;

I finished the wolf without half tryin',
The wild hyena and roaring lion;
I knocked down Ham, and Japheth, too,
And cracked the legs of the kangaroo.

I finished, besides, two pigs and a donkey,
A polar bear, opossum, and monkey;
Also the lions, tigers, and cats,
And dromedaries and tiny rats.

There wasn't a thing that didn't feel,
Sooner or later, the weight o' my heel;
I felt as grand, as grand could be,
But oh, the whipping my mammy gave me!

A LITTLE BOY'S LECTURE.

LADIES AND GENTLEMEN: Nearly four hundred years ago the mighty mind of Columbus, traversing unknown seas, clasped this new continent in its embrace.

A few centuries later arose one here who now lives in all our hearts as the Father of his Country. An able warrior, a sagacious statesman, a noble gentleman. Yes, Christopher Columbus was *great*. George Washington was *great*. But here, my friends, in this glorious nineteenth century is—a *grater!* (Exhibiting a large, bright tin grater. The large kind used for horse-radish could be most easily distinguished by the audience.)

BABY HAS GONE TO SCHOOL.

The baby has gone to school; ah, me!
What will the mother do?
With never a call to button or pin,
Or tie a little shoe?

How can she keep herself busy all day
With the little "hindering thing" away?

Another basket to fill with lunch,
   Another "good-bye" to say,
And the mother stands at the door to see
  Her baby march away;
And turns with a sigh that is half relief
And half a something akin to grief.

She thinks of a possible future morn,
   When the children, one by one,
Will go from their home out into the world
   To battle with life alone,
And not even the baby be left to cheer
The desolate home of that future year.

She picks up garments here and there,
   Thrown down in careless haste,
And tries to think how it would seem
   If nothing were misplaced;
If the house were always as still as this,
How could she bear the loneliness?

PLAYING FOR KEEPS.

NETTIE H. PELHAM.

Through my open window, summer breezes straying,
Bring the shouts of school-boys with their marbles playing.
Watch that little fellow; hear him gayly jest;
He is very lucky, winning from the rest.

I hear a girl's voice saying: "Tom, you must not play
And keep the marbles that you win. What will mamma say?"
"Oh," replies young Tommy, with a happy smile,
As he adds more marbles to his growing pile,
"Nobody's a-cheatin', we're all a-playin' fair,
And I'm almost certain mamma wouldn't care."

Tommy's luck is changing, and the happy smile
Leaves his face as quickly as the marbles leave his pile.

Now the game is ended, and he counts the cost:
Crockeries, mibs, and agates, all, oh! all are lost!
"Give me back my marbles!" Tommy wildly weeps;
"Mamma says it's wicked when you play for keeps!"

THE REASON WHY.

"When I was at the party,"
 Said Betty (aged just four),
"A little girl fell off her chair,
 Right down upon the floor;
And all the other little girls
 Began to laugh but me—
I didn't laugh a single bit,"
 Said Betty, seriously.

"Why not?" her mother asked her,
 Full of delight to find
That Betty—bless her little heart!—
 Had been so sweetly kind.
"Why didn't you laugh, darling?
 Or don't you like to tell?"
"I didn't laugh," said Betty,
 "'Cause it was me that fell!"

SPEECH FOR A BOY.

Nobody knows the nerve it takes
 To rise up in a crowd,
And speak out so that all can hear,
 With voice both clear and loud,
For often men of sense have failed,
 When *first* they'd try to speak,
And ere they could pronounce a word,
 Begin to feel quite weak.

So you, therefore, must not expect
 Great things from one so small;
I'd rather make a little speech
 Than to say none at all.

No man can ever get to be
  Renown'd, or great, or wise,
Unless, when he is small and young,
  He bravely strives to rise.

I've done my very best, kind friends,
  This to my credit score;
For you will readily agree,
  "Angels can do no more!"

SPEECH FOR A LITTLE GIRL.

I never made a speech before;
  But that's no reason why,
Because I never spoke before,
  I ought not now to try.

There are some silly little girls,
  Who are afraid to speak,
For fear some one will laugh at them;
  I think this very weak.

I hope I'll always have the sense
  To do as I am told;
Then people will not laugh at me,
  Or think I am too bold.

A LITTLE BOY'S SPEECH.

I am a little boy, you see,
  Not higher much than pappy's knee;
Some of the big boys said that I
  To make a speech ought not to try.
This raised my spunk, and I am here,
  Small as to you I may appear.
And though my voice, I know, is weak,
  I'll show these boys that I *can* speak.

WHEN SCHOOL IS OUT.

Did you ever hear a rush and a roar,
Such as you have never heard before?

If you haven't, I pray you pass the door
Of the public school when school is o'er.

A cataract cleft with a thunder-cloud,
A demon dancing about in a shroud,
A thousand wild animals bellowing aloud,
Could make no more noise than this rollicking crowd.

Gay little rebels sparkling with fun,
Half resenting that school has begun;
Away they start on a race and a run,
And laughing gayly every one!

And we who pass by the school-house door,
And hear the rush and maddening roar,
Sigh that our own school-days are o'er,
And long to run and shout once more!

So run, boys, run, and enjoy the fun,
The happiest days have just begun.
Dance and frolic, shout and run,
Each and all and every one.

AN ADDRESS TO A TEACHER.

Dear Teacher: The pleasant duty has been assigned me by my schoolmates of presenting you this token as an evidence of our lasting esteem, friendship, and love. We could not consent to part with you without leaving in your hands some memorial, however trifling, of deep and abiding gratitude for your unceasing efforts to benefit us. When in future days you look upon this memento, let it be a pleasant token of the deepest love and reverence of our young hearts.

VALEDICTORY.

It now, kind friends, devolves on me
To speak our Val-e-dic-to-ry;
You've seen our exhibition through,
We've tried to please each one of you—
And if we've failed in any part,
Lay it to *head*, and not to *heart;*

For we have striven, night and day,
To study well both speech and play.
We hope, within another year,
Again before you to appear.
But ere we part—before you go—
We wish you, one and all, to know
We thank you for your presence here—
Such kindness does our bosoms cheer,
And causes every boy to feel
He ought to study with more zeal;
While all the girls it will inspire
With an ambition to rise higher.
We feel much more than words can tell—
Accept our heart-felt thanks—farewell!

VALEDICTORY.

Our exercises for the day
Will close without much more delay.
We thank you for the interest
Your kind attention has expressed.
We know we are but young and weak,
To stand before a crowd to speak;
But mighty *oaks* from *acorns* grow,
And some of us, for aught you know,
May climb the noble hill of fame,
And make a great and lasting name;
While none of us, we hope, may live
To loving hearts one pain to give.
Again we tender thanks to you;
Till next we meet, kind friends, adieu!

CLOSING ADDRESS.

Kind friends who have listened to our efforts to-day, I thank
you in the name of the whole school for your presence and your
attention. We hope we have not disappointed you. With many
of us it has been our first attempt at public speaking. Long ago,

a boy declaimed—before much such an audience, I dare say, as this —who said: "Tall oaks from little acorns grow"; and it is just as true to-day as then. We are fitting ourselves, little by little, to fill the places of the men and women of to-day. Years hence, you may hear from us mingling with the great world, helping forward, in one way and another, life's good work.

Teacher, we thank you for all your kind endeavors to do us good. May your good wishes for us be all fulfilled in years to come.

Schoolmates, we part companionship to-day to go to our several homes, our various amusements, and our separate work. We part friends, and carry with us pleasant memories of the happy faces here. May our future lives be as useful as our term has been pleasant. And may the world, the great school in which we are all scholars, find us faithful in all the good lessons we have to learn;—in short, may we make our lives a grand success, and be admitted to a higher school in the life to come.

And now, friends all, with thanks for the past, and good wishes for the future, it is mine to say good-bye.

Before Christmas.

OH! What shall I do with Papa?
 I've talked till enough has been said.
I've talked and I've preached to the man;
 And, really, it's tired my head.

He looks into all open drawers,
 And rummages ev'ry high shelf.
I scold him, but what is the use?
 He isn't ashamed of himself.

There's never a day but he asks:
 "Pet, what are you making for me?"
There isn't a thing in the house
 That he isn't anxious to see.

Mamma says he does it in sport;
 It must be his nature to tease.
My pardon I think he should beg;
 But I can't get him down on his knees.

For six weeks, and more, I have tried
To finish a beautiful pair
Of slippers I'm making for him;
But they are a trouble and care.

And I'm making the loveliest rack,
To keep all his newspapers in;
But when I am all settled down,
And my work I fairly begin,

I hear his voice somewhere, down-stairs.
He asks: "What's become of the child?"
And if I don't turn my door key
He comes in and sets me so wild!

He goes to the bank ev'ry day;
But is home at a little past three.
Of course, for the rest of the day,
From all kinds of work he is free.

And then he goes staring around,
To that he was always inclined;
And Mamma, to tell the plain truth,
Don't know how to teach him to mind.

She speaks in the sweetest of tones;
   And bids him to be quiet and read.
She says: "Now don't bother the child,"
   But he laughs and says: "Oh! indeed!"

Sometimes ne pretends that he reads;
   But over his paper he peeps.
I think he is always awake;
   For no one can tell when he sleeps

Well, a man will never give heed
   To a woman's wholesome advice.
If I were the owner of one,
   I never would speak to him twice.

And I'm very sure I would cure
   All his prying, bothering ways;
Or he'd go to the bank and stay
   Until after the holidays.

For my mother I'm making a scarf—
   An elegant, cardinal red.
I work at it all my spare time;
   But never a word has she said.

To show that she even suspects
　　I am making something for her.
She glides in and out of the room;
　　I sit where I am; I don't stir.

Why should I when she's so polite?
　　She never is looking at me,
Or troubling herself to find out
　　How much of my work she can see.

O, Papa! do shut up your eyes!
　　But, then, I don't know as you can;
And Mamma declares, with a smile,
　　That you are a wide-awake man.

But you are so kind and so good;
　　And I have been talking for fun.
Why, you're the best man I have seen,
　　The very best under the sun.

The things I am making for you!
　　You'll have them at Christmas; you'll see
I haven't the faintest idea
　　What you will be giving to me.

And I am not going to ask;

    I know they'll be lovely and new.

And oh! they'll be precious to me,

    For they'll be exactly like you.

A Lesson in A Dream.

IN years gone by I had a child,

    I thought her very fair,

With rosy cheeks and dimpled chin,

    Brown eyes and golden hair.

She was a wayward, laughing child,

    So full of careless glee,

I often mourned to think how sad

    Her future lot might be.

But grandma said, "Though faulty, she

    No penalty incurs;

You'll never find a woman's head

    On shoulders young as hers."

One night I had a fearful dream;
  The memory haunts me yet;
A dream so fraught with agony
  I never can forget.

Methought in answer to my call,
  She came with measured tread;
When, lo, upon her shoulders fair
  Was poised a woman's head?

I saw the scanty grizzled locks,
  The features stern and bold,
Instead of brown eyes, dimpled chin,
  And floating locks of gold.

A harsh voice from the thin lips said,
  "You were displeased with me,
So I've exchanged my giddy head
  For a steady one, you see."

"O woe is me! What have I done?"
  I cried in my despair;
"Lost are my darling's childish ways,
  Brown eyes and golden hair!"

"Wake, mamma, wake!" a sweet voice called,
　"Oh, tell me, mamma, why
You toss and moan so in your sleep?
　It makes me want to cry."

I opened wide my wondering eyes
　With rapture to behold
Again the brown eyes, dimpled chin
　And floating curls of gold.

I caught my darling to my heart,
　I kissed her o'er and o'er;
Restored to me as from the dead,
　I could not ask for more.

Be patient, mothers, every day,
　Although with mischief rife
Are the fair-haired, bright-eyed little ones,
　So full of love and life."

Remember, Boys.

LITTLE friends, when you are at play on the street,
　　Half frantic with frolic, laughter and noise,
Don't ever forget to bow when you meet—
　　When you meet an old man with gray hairs, my
　　　　boys.

Is the aged man feeble, decrepit and lame?
　　Does he lean on his staff with unsteady poise?
Never mock at his sorrow, but stop in your game
　　And bow to the man with gray hairs, my boys.

If he sometimes halts in his tottering pace
　　To witness the flow of your innocent joys,
Don't jostle the old man out of his place,
　　But greet his gray locks with a bow. my boys.

Remember, the years are only a few
　　Since he, on the street with his games and toys,
Was healthy and happy and active like you;
　　And bright as the sun were his curls, my boys.

But age has furrowed the cheek that was fair;
  While sorrows have broken his once mellow
    voice;
And now there is many a silvery hair
  On the head where the curls were so bright, my
    boys.

The Spring-day of youth is a gem; it is gold.
  But Time all its glorious luster destroys;
And, gay little friends, if you live to be old,
  Your steps will be slow, your locks gray, my
    boys.

So, when you are blithely at play on the street,
  Half frantic with frolic and laughter and noise,
Remember to pleasantly bow when you meet—
  When you meet an old man with gray hairs,
    my boys.

WE live in deeds, not years; in thoughts, not breaths,
In feelings, not in figures on a dial.
We should count time by heart-throbs. He most lives
Who thinks most, feels the noblest, acts the best.

Two Boys.

TWO boys came into the world one day;
    And each gave joy to a mother's heart.
The one was sad, and the other gay,
    And both were fitted to play their part.
One was sober, quiet, and sad;
But quick and bright was the other lad.

One went out with his flag unfurled
    To meet the breeze; and was swiftly borne
To the Friendly Isles, and there gayly whirled
    Over the breakers from night till morn;
Young and careless and full of joy,
All hearts made room for the lovely boy.

His handsome face and his merry glance,
    His ready wit and good-natured wiles,
Made even the distant ones advance
    To bask in the light of his sunny smiles.
Ah, he was flattered and much caressed,
And many a glass to his lips was pressed.

Many a glass of a poisoned sweet,
    Fearing nought, did he drain, in truth,
That in slippery places drew the feet
    Of the friendly and unsuspecting youth;
And down and down he began to go,
Caught in the treacherous undertow.

The other boy, of a quiet turn,
    Of awkward manners and solemn looks
And surly speech, cared little to learn
    The lessons of life not found in books;
Cross, ill-natured, severe and grim,
Little joy could be had with him.

His friends were few; but 'twas all the same,
    What did he care for a smile or a frown?
He'd his way to make—a decided aim;
    And no one living could put him down;
Lord of himself, stubborn and proud,
He kept his place 'mid the jostling crowd.

No heed to those who would lead astray,
    No heed to the siren spell he gave;
But went right on in an earnest way
    Till he rode at ease on the topmost wave;

And those who thought him a churl began
To respect and honor the self-made man.

'Tis thus that the children play their part;
    And the boys we love for their liveliness,
Who hold our hearts from the very start,
    Seldom if ever attain success.
Easily tempted they are, and so
Caught in life's treacherous undertow.

Thanksgiving.

I'LL tell you about it, my darling, for grandma's
    explained it all,
So that I understand why Thanksgiving always
    comes late in the fall,
When the nuts and the apples are gathered, and
    the work in the field is done,
And the fields, all reaped and silent, are asleep in
    the autumn sun.

It is then that we praise Our Father who sends
    the rain and the dew,
Whose wonderful loving kindness is every morning
    new;

Unless we'd be heathen, Dolly, or worse, we must
    sing and pray,
And think about good things, Dolly, when we
    keep Thanksgiving Day.

But I like it very much better when from church
    we all go home,
And the married brothers and sisters, and the
    troups of cousins come,
And we're ever so long at the table, and dance and
    shout and play,
In the merry evening, Dolly, that ends Thanksgiv-
    ing Day.

Temperance Address.

[FOR A VERY YOUNG LECTURER.]

I THINK that every mother's son,
    And every father's daughter,
Should drink—at least till twenty-one
    Just nothing but cold water.

And after that they might drink tea
    But nothing any stronger.
If all folks would agree with me
    They'd live a great deal longer.

The Leaves and the Wind.

"COME, little leaves," said the wind one day—
"Come o'er the meadows with me and play;
Put on your dresses of red and gold—
Summer is gone and the days grow cold."

Soon as the leaves heard the wind's loud call,
Down they came fluttering, one and all:
Over the brown fields they danced and flew,
Singing the soft little songs that they knew:

"Cricket, good-by, we've been friends so long!
Little brook, sing us your parting song—
Say you are sorry to see us go;
Ah, you will miss us, right well we know.

"Dear little lambs, in your fleecy fold,
Mother will keep you from harm and cold;
Fondly we've watched you in vale and glade:
Say, will you dream of our loving shade?"

Dancing and whirling the little leaves went;
Winter had called them, and they were content.
Soon fast asleep in their earthy beds,
The snow laid a coverlet over their heads.

Time Enough.

TWO little squirrels, out in the sun—
One gathered nuts, the other had none;
"Time enough yet," his constant refrain,
"Summer is still just on the wane."

Listen, my child, while I tell you his fate;
He roused him at last, but he roused him too late.
Down fell the snow from a pitiless cloud,
And gave little squirrel a spotless white shroud.

Two little boys in a school-room were placed;
One always perfect, the other disgraced;
"Time enough yet for learning," he said,
"I will climb, by and by, from the foot to the head."

Listen, my friends; their locks are turned gray;
One, as a governor, sitteth to-day;
The other, a pauper, looks out at the door
Of the almshouse, and idles his days as of yore.

Two kinds of people we meet every day;
One is at work, the other at play.
Living uncared for, dying unknown,
The busiest hive hath ever a drone.

The Blue and the Gray.

THEY sat together, side by side,
   In the shade of an orange tree;
One had followed the flag of Grant,
   The other had fought with Lee.

The boy in blue had an empty sleeve,
   A crutch had the boy in gray;
They talked of the long and weary march.
   They talked of the bloody fray.

"My chief is dead," the Johnny said,
   " A leader brave was he;
And sheathed fore'er at Lexington,
   Doth hang the sword of Lee."

"My leader lives,"—the boy in blue
   Spoke low and with a sigh—
"But all the country waits in fear
   That he to-day may die."

"God bless our Grant!" the vet'ran said,
   And dropped a tear, and then
In heartfelt tones the answer came,
   For the rebel said—"*Amen.*"

Which Loved Best.

"I LOVE you, mother," said little John,
Then, forgetting his work, his cap went on,
And he was off to the garden swing,
And left her the water and wood to bring.

"I love you, mother," said rosy Nell,—
"I love you better than tongue can tell;"
Then she teased and pouted full half the day,
Till her mother rejoiced when she went to play.

"I love you, mother," said little Fan;
"To day I'll help you all I can:
How glad I am school doesn't keep!"
So she rocked the babe till it fell asleep;

Then stepping softly she fetched the broom,
And swept the floor, and tidied the room:
Busy and happy all day was she,—
Helpful and happy as a child could be.

"I love you, mother," again they said,
Three little children going to bed:
How do you think that mother guessed
Which of them really loved her best?

Don't Fret.

DON'T fret if your neighbor earns more than you do
    Don't frown if he gets the most trade;
Don't envy your friend if he rides in his coach,
    Don't mind if you're left in the shade.

Don't rail at the schoolboy who fails in his task,
    Nor envy the one who succeeds;
Don't laugh at the man who is Poverty's slave,
    Nor think the rich never have needs.

It's not wisdom to covet our neighbor's good gifts;
    We would seldom change places, I ween,
If we knew all our neighbor's affairs as our own,
    For things are not what they seem.

You see the rich merchant enjoying his ride,
    And think he exults over you;
You do not imagine that he feels the same,
    And thinks you more blest of the two.

You see people pass in and out of a store,
    But you must not judge business thereby;
You must look at the books, at the way they "foot up,"
    Ere you venture your judgment to try.

You don't know what you say when you envy a man
  Either fortune, or friends, or a home;
His fortune and friends may be only in name,
  And his home far less blest than your own.

You may know the old adage, which teaches the fact,
  That a skeleton must be somewhere;
If not found in library, kitchen, or hall,
  It is hid in the closet with care.

So don't envy the blest, nor despise the outcast,
  Don't judge by the things which you see;
Make the burdens of men as light as you can,
  And the lighter your burden will be.

Bad Thoughts.

BAD Thought's a thief! He acts his part;
  Creeps through the window of the heart;
  And, if he once his way can win,
  He lets a hundred robbers in.

Answered Prayers.

PRAYED for riches and achieved success.
  All that I touched turned into gold. Alas!
My cares were greater and my peace was less
  When that wish came to pass.

I prayed for glory; and I heard my name
  Sung by sweet children and by hoary men.
But ah! the hurts, the hurts that come with fame
  I was not happy then.

I prayed for love, and had my soul's desire;
  Through quivering heart and body and through brain
There swept the flame of its devouring fire;
  And there the scars remain.

I prayed for a contented mind. At length
  Great light upon my darkened spirit burst.
Great peace fell on me, also, and great strength.
  Oh! had that prayer been first!

Wanted----A Minister's Wife.

At length we have settled a Pastor,—
    I am sure I cannot tell why
The people should grow so restless,
    Or candidates grow so shy.
But after two years' searching
    For the "smartest" man in the land,
In a fit of desperation
    We took the nearest at hand.

And really he answers nicely
    To "fill up the gap," you know;
To "run the machine" and "bring up arrears,"
    And make things generally go.
He has a few little failings;
    His sermons are commonplace quite;
But his manner is very charming,
    And his teeth are perfectly white.

And so of all the "dear people,"
    Not one in a hundred complains,

For beauty and grace of manner
    Are so much better than *brains.*
But the parish have all concluded
    He needs a partner for life.
To shine a gem in the parlor:
    "Wanted—a Minister's Wife!"

Wanted—a perfect lady,
    Delicate, gentle, refined,
With every beauty of person,
    And every endowment of mind.
Fitted by early culture
    To move in a fashionable life—
Please notice our advertisement:
    "Wanted—a Minister's Wife!"

Wanted—a thorough-bred worker,
    Who well to her household looks,
(Shall we see our money wasted,
    By extravagent Irish cooks?)
Who cut the daily expenses
    With economy sharp as a knife,
And washes and scrubs in the kitchen:
    "Wanted—a Minister's Wife!"

A "very domestic person,"
  To "callers" she must not be "out;"
It has such a bad appearance
  For her to be gadding about,—
Only to visit the parish
  Every year of her life,
And attend the funerals and weddings:
  "Wanted—a Minister's Wife!"

To conduct the "ladies' meetings,"
  The "sewing circle" attend,
And when we have "work for the soldiers,"
  Her ready assistance to lend;
To clothe the destitute children,
  Where sorrow and want are rife,
To hunt up Sunday School scholars:
  "Wanted—a Minister's Wife!"

Careful to entertain strangers,
  Travelling agents and "such;"
Of this kind of "angel visits"
  The deacons had so much,
As to prove a perfect nuisance,
  And "hopes these plagues of their life

Can soon be sent to their parsons:
"Wanted—a Minister's Wife!"

A perfect pattern of prudence
　To all others, spending less,
But never disgracing the parish
　By looking shabby in dress.
Playing the organ on Sunday
　Would aid our laudable strife
To save the society's money:
　"Wanted—a Minister's Wife!"

And when we have found the person,
　We hope, by working the two,
To lift our debt, and build a new church—
　Then we shall know what to do:
For they will be worn and weary,
　Needing a change of life,
And we'll advertise—"Wanted—
　A Minister and his Wife!"

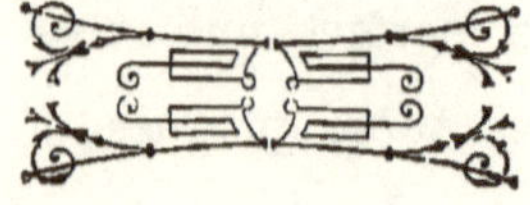

A Child's Conclusion.

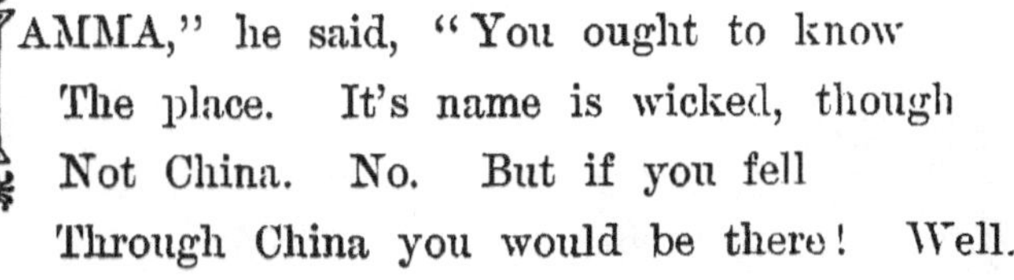

AMMA," he said, "You ought to know
The place. It's name is wicked, though
Not China. No. But if you fell
Through China you would be there! Well.

"Fred said something very bad,
Named Satan, stayed down there and had
Oh, such a fire to burn things! You
Just never mind. It can't be true.

"Because I've digged and digged to see
Where all that fire could ever be,
And looked and looked down through the dark,
And never saw a single spark.

"But Heaven is sure; because if I
Look up, I always see the sky—
Sometimes the gold-gates shine clear through—
And when you see a thing, it's true!"

A THING of beauty is a joy forever:
Its loveliness increases; It will never
Pass into nothingness.

Young Ladies of the Present Day.

THE fair young girls of the present day
　　Are warper's dolls indeed;
They cannot stand the sun's warm rays,
　　Or knead a loaf of bread.

They cannot scrub the kitchen floor,
　　Or make a chamber bed,
Or take a step beyond the door
　　For they are almost dead.

But if there's a party or a ball
　　Within some miles around,
They'll dress in all their finery,
　　And go off with a bound.

They'll lie in bed the whole next day,
　　Or stupidly sit down
To read the last new novel which
　　Has found its way to town.

The Water Drinkers.

PASSED a garden where roses bright
  Were clustering close to the lillies white;
  The noonday sun was ablaze o'erhead:
"We're very thirsty," the flowers said.

"Thou lovely lily, so fair to see,
  Oh, wherefore shouldst thou thirsty be?
  For gladly into thy cup I'll pour
  The sparkling wine from my choicest store!"

  The lily folded her pure white cup
  And closed each ivory petal up!
  The rosebud shook in the breeze her head;
"We drink the rain and the dew," she said.

  I took my wine to the birds that flew
  Around the bank where the flowers grew.
  They would not come of my glass to taste;
  The lark flew up to the sky in haste.

  The thrush sang "No" from her leafy spray,
  The robin hopped with a chirp away;

The blackbird raised from the stem his head;
"Our drink is that of the flowers," he said.

I saw a child on that summer's day
Amid the flowers and birds at play;
I brought him wine, but he answered, "No,"
With rosy lips as he bade me go.

"I do not care for the ruby wine
While water fresh from the stream is mine!"
He smiled and merrily shook his head;
"My drink is that of the birds," he said.

Misplaced Confidence.

I SAT me down upon my nest;
I covered with my soft, warm breast
Eleven eggs, so fair and white,
And knew, or thought I knew, that when
A certain time had passed, that then
Eleven chicks would greet my sight.

Three weeks in this most dignified
Retirement did I sit and bide
    My time. I did not even take
The necessary exercise.
From dawn to dark, sunset or rise,
    I sat there, for dear duty's sake.

I hardly dared to eat or sleep,
Lest I should miss the first faint peep.
    If ever living hen did try
To do her very level best
By eleven eggs in a nest,
    Her utmost duty, then did I.

I heard them peck against the shell;
I was more glad than I can tell,
    So glad was I when first they peeped.
And now the end is come, and now,
' pray you, let me tell you how,
    And what the sad reward I've reaped.

When first they left the nest, my eyes
Were stricken with a great surprise;
    With dire dismay my heart was struck.

They waddled! waddled! Do you hear?
As sure as 1 am standing here,
　　My every chicken was a duck!

Imagine, if you can, in part,
The sadness that weighed down my heart
　　When first this broke upon my view;
A sense of confidence abused,
A sense of being most ill-used
　　Made me a sad hen through and through.

I'd had my dreams; how I would bring
Each little, feathery, fluffy thing
　　Up unto henhood, fair and sweet.
And now what chance have I? It fills
My heart with grief to see their bills
　　And their ridiculous webbed feet.

Hens have some rights! I do not know
That there is aught that I can do;
　　But I'm resolved, for one, that, when
I'm so imposed upon, I'll dare
To tell the story everywhere.
　　I will, indeed, though but a hen.